*No man could say no
to Francesca Bonnard . . .
or her scandalous ways.*

# Your Scandalous Ways

Francesca had put up her guard again and distanced herself from him. He could feel it as palpably as if she'd thrust him away with her hand.

He was not sure what had happened, what had made her withdraw. All he knew was that he felt her mistrust humming in the air between them.

This was going to be a good deal trickier than he'd imagined. She had a brain and something more, though he wasn't sure yet what the *more* was.

He had no doubt now, though, that Francesca Bonnard was going to be a considerable challenge. He hadn't had a true challenge in a long time.

His heart went a little faster.

Perhaps this would be fun, after all.

### By Loretta Chase

# LORETTA CHASE

# Your Scandalous Ways

**AVON**

*An Imprint of HarperCollinsPublishers*

AVON BOOKS
*An Imprint of* HarperCollins*Publishers*
10 East 53rd Street
New York, New York 10022-5299

# Acknowledgments

Thanks to:

Anna Baldi for helping me put the correct Italian words in my characters' mouths.

Owen Halpern, Sherrie Holmes, Margaret Evans Porter, and Katherine Shaw for their invaluable help with matters Venetian.

My family and friends, with special thanks to Walter, Cynthia, Mary Jo, Nancy, and Twin Girl.

# Author's Note

Lord Byron's spelling, like that of many people of the time, including Jane Austen, is more haphazard than ours. His punctuation is distinctively his own. So no, those are not typos in the poem excerpts. Those are . . . Byron.

# Prologue

I want a hero . . .
Lord Byron

*Don Juan, Canto the First*

*Rome*
*July 1820*

She led the way up the stairs to her bedroom, discarding articles of clothing as she went.

Marta Fazi was agile, certainly. Her dark gaze locked with James's, she climbed backward without a misstep. Her teeth gleamed white against her olive skin as she laughingly flung away the mask, the veil, the cloak that concealed a frail excuse for a gown: a flimsy article, little more than an elaborate shift, held together with a few easily untied ribbons and strings.

She left the emeralds on: the heavy necklace with its great pendant stone dangling between her breasts, the matching earrings, the bracelet.

James paused to ease out of his coat, taking his

time. He slung it over his shoulder as he climbed after her, maintaining the pose of mild curiosity he'd used to bait the hook.

Accustomed to getting what she wanted, Marta couldn't resist a challenge, and James hadn't to do much acting to become one. Given a choice, he wouldn't have touched her with a barge pole. Since he hadn't a choice, he'd simply let his reluctance show. That, as he'd expected, had piqued her vanity.

She was handsome, admittedly. He'd heard that Lord Byron had written a poem about her, not for publication. She was of the type the poet admired: Dark and passionate, she was what he would call "a magnificent animal."

James was not nearly so enthusiastic about the type. He was thirty-one years old, and Marta was not his first passionate, uninhibited, and sexually talented foreign adventuress. If he survived this encounter, though, she'd be the last. If he didn't survive it—which was equally likely—she'd be the last.

*Either way I win*, he thought.

If he failed this mission, he'd die a slow and painful death. He would not be mourned as a hero. No one would know that he'd died trying to save the world. They probably wouldn't even find his body—or what was left of it.

*For bloody damned king and bloody damned country*, he told himself as the door closed behind him, *one last time*.

He took off his waistcoat and dropped that and his coat over a chair near the door as he continued to advance and she continued to retreat, unerringly, toward the bed.

Clearly, she knew the way backward and in the dark, though the room wasn't altogether dark. Servants must have readied it shortly before, because the candles were lit. They must have expected her to have company because they'd lit only two.

These offered light enough to show him her gleaming white teeth as her lips parted. It was light enough to make green fire of the emeralds and rainbow sparks of the small diamonds circling them. Even without light, he'd know where she was. Her perfume filled the room with a too-sweet aroma, like decaying roses.

She ran her hands over her full, firm breasts and down over her hips. She was magnificently formed, and knew it.

"You see, I keep nothing from you," she said. "I give myself completely."

Her speech told him she'd spent most of her life in southern Italy and had had a little—a very little—education. He detected, too, a foreign note: her native Cyprus, no doubt. Though his antecedents, like hers, were mixed, the Italian he spoke, his mother's language, was flawless. Since he'd inherited his mother's black, curling hair and his maternal grandfather's Roman profile, Marta had no inkling that he was not only the son of an English nobleman but an agent of His Majesty's government.

In short, James Cordier was an even greater fraud than this alluring panther. The trick was to make sure she didn't find out.

"Not quite completely," he said as he unfastened his trousers. "The stones are pretty, but your beauty needs no adornment, you know."

Not to mention that heavy jewelry was a damned nuisance during a plogging. *Yer could put yer eye out with one a them things*, he might have told her, in the accents he'd learned in his eventful youth.

She laughed. "Ah, flattery at last. I thought I should never hear it from you."

He stepped out of his trousers. "The sight before me stimulates my tongue," he said.

"Good." Her gaze lowered. "And the little man is stimulated, too, I see."

Of course it was. James might have had his fill of her sort but he was a man, after all, and she was exciting. They usually were, the deadly ones.

She unhooked the earrings and laid them on the table by the bed. She unclasped the bracelet, and dropped it next to the earrings.

He pulled his shirt over his head.

She was fumbling with the clasp of the necklace.

"Allow me," he said.

It was an old clasp, very probably the original, and wanted both care and a sharp eye. The parure had not been intended for ordinary evening wear but for state occasions: It had been created for a queen more than two centuries ago. Its current owners, ejected by Napoleon, had had to secret their treasures and themselves to a safe refuge. The treasures had been on their way home in the care of a trusted retainer when she and two confederates, garbed as nuns, had stolen it.

The age and history of the emeralds did not

signify to her. Marta Fazi had grown up on the streets; she was literate—though just barely—amoral, and ruthless. She had a weakness for good-looking men and a passion for emeralds.

This was what James knew of her and all he needed to know to do the job he'd been sent to do.

Get the gems, get out, get them to their rightful owner, and let the diplomats sort out the details.

The jewels now lying in a careless tangle on the bed stand, James proceeded to business. "To battle" was probably nearer the mark.

He was a soldier, after all, though the army he belonged to was unacknowledged. Nobody pinned any medals on men like him, or mentioned him in dispatches.

And if he got caught, no one would rescue him.

*So, Jemmy, my boy, whatever you do, he advised himself, don't get caught.*

Then he gave the girl what she wanted, and did it thoroughly. Whatever he felt about his work, he was at least still capable of enjoying a handsome, passionate female more or less as any other man would.

When at last she seemed reasonably sated—for the moment, at any rate—he whispered, "I'm famished. What about you?"

"Ah, yes," she murmured. "Wine, something to eat . . . and then we regain our strength. The bell for the servant is beside you."

"Let's let the servants sleep," he said. "I'd rather forage."

She laughed drowsily. "So you would. I marked you for a hunter when first I saw you."

*You got that part right.*

He rose from the bed. His trousers were near at hand, as he'd taken care they should be. He pulled them on, then found his shirt. His back to her, he pulled it over his head, then slid the jewels from the table, the billowing cloth concealing the movement.

The rest was absurdly easy. The bed curtains hid from her view the door and the chair where he'd left his waistcoat and coat. He collected the garments and slipped through the door.

Another man would have postponed his exit until she fell asleep. James, however, was of Lady Macbeth's mind: "If it were done when 'tis done, then 'twere well/It were done quickly."

It would be well to move quickly in this case. Marta would soon notice the stones were gone, and she took betrayal very ill, indeed. The last man who'd annoyed her had lost his privates first. He'd lost them slowly, in bits.

James might have minutes to get away. He might have mere seconds.

He hurried down the stairs.

One second. Two. Three. Four. Five. Six. Seven—

"Stop him!" she screamed. "Get him! Break his knees!"

As he left the landing, a burly ruffian barreled up the stairs. James flung his arm out sideways, stiff as a tollbooth bar. The servant saw it too late. He ran straight into it, the muscled arm catching him across the throat. He fell backward, down the stairs, landing head first.

At the top of the stairs she was howling in Greek

for her men, telling them to keep him alive: She had plans for him.

A knife whizzed past his head.

In piercing shrieks she described what she'd do to him, which parts she'd cut off first.

James sidestepped the servant's inert body and ran into the hall, toward the entrance.

A door burst open and another of her henchmen exploded toward him. James stiff-armed this one, too, but this time with a forward thrust, catching the brute in the chest. The man's knees folded and he fell straight down onto his back.

James heard him yowl in pain. Kneecap broken, most likely.

His screams were nothing to Marta's.

James kept moving.

In the next instant he slipped through the door.

And in the blink of an eye, he'd melted into the night.

# Chapter 1

Didst ever see a Gondola? For fear
    You should not, I'll describe it to you exactly:
'Tis a long cover'd boat that's common here,
    Carved at the prow, built lightly,
        but compactly;
Row'd by two rowers, each call'd 'Gondolier,'
    It glides along the water looking blackly,
Just like a coffin clapt in a canoe,
Where none can make out what you say or do.

                        Lord Byron, *Beppo*

*Venice*
*Tuesday, 19 September 1820*

*P*enises. Everywhere.

    Francesca Bonnard thoughtfully regarded the ceiling.

A century or two ago, the Neroni family had gone mad for ornamental plasterwork. The walls and ceilings of the palazzo she rented were a riot of plaster draperies, fruits, and flowers. Most fas-

cinating to her were these winged children called
*putti*. They crawled about the ceilings, lifting
plaster draperies or creeping among the folds,
looking for who knew what. They clung to the
frames of the ceiling paintings and to the gold
medallions over the doors. They vastly outnum-
bered the four bare-breasted women lolling in the
corners and the four muscled adult males sup-
porting the walls.

They were all boys, all naked. Thus the view
overhead was of many little penises—forty at last
count, though there seemed to be more today. Were
they reproducing spontaneously or were the buxom
females and virile adult males getting up to mischief when the house was asleep?

In her three years in Venice, Francesca had entered a number of ostentatious houses. Hers won
the prize for decorative insanity—not to mention
quantity of immature male reproductive organs.

"I shouldn't mind them so much," she said, "but
they are so distracting. The first time visitors call,
they spend the better part of the visit dumbstruck,
gaping at the walls and ceiling. After giving the
matter serious thought, I've decided that Dante got
his idea for the *Inferno* from a visit to the Palazzo
Neroni."

"Let them gape," said her friend Giulietta. She
rested her elbow on the arm of her chair and, chin
in hand, regarded the deranged ceiling. "While
your guests stare at the *putti*, you might stare at
them as rudely as you like."

They made a complementary pair: Francesca tall
and exotic, Giulietta smaller, and sweet-looking.

Her heart-shaped face and innocent brown eyes made her seem a mere girl. At six and twenty, however, she was only a year younger than Francesca. In experience, Giulietta was eons older.

No one would ever call Francesca Bonnard sweet-looking, she knew. She'd inherited her mother's facial features, most notably her distinctive eyes with their unusual green color and almond shape. Her thick chestnut hair was her French paternal grandmother's. The rest came from Sir Michael Saunders, her scoundrel father, and his predecessors. The Saunderses tended to be tall, and she was—compared, at least, to most women. The few extra inches had caused the caricaturists to dub her "the Giantess" and "the Amazon" in the scurrilous prints they produced during the divorce proceedings.

Her divorce from John Bonnard—recently awarded a barony and now titled Lord Elphick—was five years behind her, however, as was all the nonsense she'd believed then about love and men. Now she carried her tall frame proudly and dressed to emphasize every curve of her lush figure.

Men had betrayed and abandoned and hurt her once upon a time.

Not anymore.

Now they begged for her notice.

Several were coming today for precisely that purpose. This was why Francesca did not entertain her friend in the smaller, less oppressive room, the one adjoining her boudoir, in another, more private part of the house. That comfortable, almost *putti*-free parlor was reserved for intimates, and she had yet to decide which if any of her soon-to-arrive guests would win that status.

She wasn't looking forward to deciding.

She left the sofa on which she'd been lounging—a position that would have horrified her governess—and sauntered to the window.

The canal it overlooked wasn't *the* canal, the Grand Canal, but one of the larger of the maze of secondary waterways or *rii* intersecting the city. Though not far from the Grand Canal, hers was one of the quieter parts of Venice.

This afternoon was not so quiet, for rain beat down on the balcony outside and occasionally, when the wind shifted, against the glass. She looked—and blinked. "Good grief, I think I see signs of life across the way."

"The Ca' Munetti? Really?"

Giulietta rose and joined her at the window.

Through the sheeting rain, they watched a gondola pause at the water gates of the house on the other side of the narrow canal.

*Ca'*, Francesca knew, was Venetian shorthand for *casa* or house. Once upon a time, only the Ducal Palace bore the title *palazzo*, and every other house was simply a *casa*. Nowadays, any house of any size, great and small, might call itself a *palazzo*. The one opposite might have done so, certainly. Outwardly, from the canal side, it was similar to hers, with a water gate leading to the ground floor hall or *andron*; balconied windows on the *piano nobile*, the first floor; then a more modest second floor; and above that, attics for the servants.

No one had lived in the Ca' Munetti, however, for nearly a year.

"A single gondolier," Francesca said. "And two passengers, it appears. That's all I can make out in this wretched downpour."

"I see no baggage," Giulietta said.

"It might have been sent ahead."

"But the house is dark."

"They haven't yet hired servants, then." The Munetti family had taken their servants with them when they moved. Though they were not as hard up as some of the Venetian nobility, they'd either found Venice too expensive or the Austrians who ruled it too tedious. Like the owners of the Palazzo Neroni, they preferred to let their house to foreigners.

"A strange time of year to come to Venice," said Giulietta.

"Perhaps we've made it fashionable," said Francesca. "Or, more likely, since they're bound to be foreigners, they don't know any better."

Everyone who could afford to do so abandoned Venice during the steaming summers. They moved to their villas on the mainland in July and tended not to return from *villeggiatura*—summer holiday—until St. Martin, the eleventh of November and the official start of winter.

Francesca had left the Count de Magny's villa in Mira early, following a quarrel about a visitor from England, Lord Quentin. Here in her own house, she answered to no one. Here, too, she wasn't the locals' prime entertainment. She'd never cared much for rusticating, in any event. She preferred town life. On rare occasions, she even missed London, though not nearly so much as she'd done at first—not that she ever admitted to missing anything about England at all.

A manservant entered to set the table for tea.

"Arnaldo, have you heard anything about the Ca' Munetti?" Francesca asked him.

"The baggage came first, late yesterday," said Arnaldo. "Not very much. They have hired the gondolier, Zeggio, who is a cousin of the wife of the cousin of our cook. He says the new master is connected to the Albani family. He desires to study with the Armenian monks, as your friend Lord Byron did."

Eyebrows raised, Giulietta met Francesca's gaze. Then they laughed.

"Byron studied with the Armenian monks," said Giulietta. "But he was *not* a monk."

"Still, only two servants . . ." Francesca watched the water gates open.

"Perhaps the new tenant is a Venetian, after all," Giulietta said. "They are too poor to keep a proper staff. Only foreigners and whores can afford a houseful of servants."

Arnaldo went out, and the conversation reverted to English.

"My new neighbor might be a miserly foreigner," Francesca said. "Or a hermit."

"In any of these cases, he is not for us."

"Good heavens, no." Francesca let out a peal of laughter.

Her laughter was as famous as her unusual looks, perhaps more so.

After the divorce set her adrift from respectable Society, she'd had to learn how to manage men. She'd learned quickly. Fanchon Noirot, her Parisian mentor, had told her she had the gift.

The most important lesson Francesca learned was how to talk to men—or, more important, how to listen to them.

But when Francesca Bonnard laughed, men listened, with all their being.

"When you laugh," Lord Byron had told her, "men catch their breath."

"They'd do better to catch hold of their purses," she'd answered.

Then he'd laughed, albeit ruefully, because it was true.

Francesca Bonnard was a courtesan, so expensive that very few men could afford her. Lord Byron wasn't one of them.


*Meanwhile, across the canal*

Of all the cities in all the world, she had to come to this one.

It was deuced inconvenient.

Not to mention wet.

James's gondola had set out from the mainland in a drizzle and traveled the Grand Canal in a torrent so fierce that they'd closed the casements of the *felze*, the vessel's black passenger cabin. Only a blur of houses and stone piers was visible through the blinds. No sound came to him but the rain drumming on the cabin and deck of the boat.

One might almost believe this was the underworld his Roman ancestors had believed in. He might be floating upon the River Styx, among the shades of the dead.

That flight of imagination thudded to earth—or water, rather—when he heard the echo of oars under a bridge and their gondolier's announcement, "*Ponte di Rialto.*"

The gondolier's name was Zeggio. At first glance, the Venetian appeared too young to guide anybody anywhere, too pretty to be performing manual labor, and too innocent to be taken seriously. This appearance explained why James's associates deemed Zeggio the most suitable guide in Venice. He was, in fact, thirty-two years old, far from innocent, and they'd employed him before.

He was a highly regarded local agent. Nonetheless, he aspired to become the Venetian version of James Cordier.

Poor sod.

After turning off the Grand Canal into a narrower waterway, then another, they came at last to the Ca' Munetti.

"Ah, Venice," James said as he took in the view—such as it was—in front of and behind him. The buildings and gondolas were merely darker shapes in the grey haze. "A fine place, indeed, but for the damp."

His servant Sedgewick said something under his breath. He was a small fellow, so thoroughly nondescript that people tended to take no notice of him whatsoever. That would be their first mistake, possibly their last.

"What was that, Sedgewick?" James said.

"Wish I was in England," his former batman muttered.

"Who doesn't?" said the master. England would be colder, and certainly no sunnier, but it was England, after all, not yet another damned country filled with foreigners.

Not that James was a foreigner here, precisely. His mother was related to at least half the great families of Italy, her ancestry as distinguished as that of his father, Lord Westwood.

Venice, however, wasn't Italy.

Venice was . . . Venice.

The gondola paused at the water gate and James glanced up at the house opposite, where *she* lived.

*She* being Francesca Bonnard, daughter of the infamous swindler, the late Sir Michael Saunders; former wife of the so-called pillar of rectitude Lord Elphick; and at present the most expensive whore in Venice.

Some would say that winning the last title was not the achievement it might have been, say, three centuries earlier. Venice had come down in the world, most obviously in recent decades. La Bonnard, however, was reputed to be the most expensive of her ilk in all of the Veneto and very possibly all of Italy and, some said, the Continent.

Why the queen of courtesans should come to Venice at all was the pertinent question. The fabled city was poor, a large number of its noble families had departed, and its floods of visitors had thinned to a trickle.

Why hadn't she remained in Paris, where she'd

first achieved fame three or four years ago and where she might choose among multitudes of wealthy victims? Or why not Vienna? Or, at the very least, Rome or Florence?

He'd probably find out why, sooner or later, if he needed to. It had better be sooner. He had plans, and she'd interrupted them.

He'd recovered the emeralds from Marta Fazi and delivered them to their owner. In exchange for the British government's doing him this little favor, the owner had signed an important treaty. He'd rewarded James as well, quite handsomely.

That was supposed to be James's last mission. He was supposed to be on his way home, to a well-earned retirement.

But no.

He was wishing Lord Elphick's discarded wife in Hades as the water gates opened and the gondola came to a stop.

He stepped out of the boat onto the stone and marble squares that paved the *andron*. Dark boarding covered the walls. The space was cold, and the musty odor of damp filled his nostrils.

They followed Zeggio up a staircase to the *piano nobile*, and found themselves in a vast central hall. This *portego*, as the Venetians called it, ran from one end of the house to the other.

It was clearly designed for show. The line of magnificent chandeliers down the center of the ceiling and rows of immense candelabra standing on tables along the wall—all dripping the famously magnificent glass work of Murano—would, when fully lit, have made a dazzling display of the gilt, the plaster ornamenting the walls, the sculpture, the paintings.

"All this, on top of water," Sedgewick said, shaking his head as he looked about him. "What sort of people is it, I wonder, goes and builds a city on stilts on a swampy lot of islands?"

"Italians," said James. "There's a reason they once ruled the world, and a reason Venice once ruled the seas. You must at least give credit for a marvel of engineering."

"I'll give them credit for an easy route to malaria," said Sedgewick. "And another easy one to typhus."

"Oh, but there is no disease now," Zeggio assured them. "The malaria she comes in the summer and the typhus he comes in the spring. Now is a most healthy time."

"There's always your pneumonia," Sedgewick said. "Your putrid sore throat. Your consumption. Your affection of the lungs."

"That's my Sedgewick," James said. "Likes to look on the bright side."

Zeggio led them down the great hall into one of the side rooms at the canal end. "You will see," he said. "In the autumn and the winter, Venice is more agreeable than the mainland. This is why everyone returns on the day of San Martino."

Everyone except her.

She had been staying in Mira at the summer villa of the comte de Magny, a friend from her Paris days and possibly a former lover, possibly a current one: Rumor had it both ways. The trouble was, late in August, following a series of conversations with James's superior, Lord Quentin, she'd abandoned

Magny to the local beauties and returned to Venice with all her baggage. Quentin having failed to persuade the lady to turn over to him certain letters in her possession, and other agents having failed to locate them by more underhand methods, his lordship had summoned James back to work before his traveling trunks could be loaded onto the ship headed for England . . . away from the conspiracies, assassins, and bloodthirsty whores, this time for good.

When was the last time he'd spoken to normal, respectable people with their mundane secrets? When was the last time he'd been among men and women who didn't lurk in the darkest corners of human life? When was the last time he'd gazed into the eyes of an innocent young woman who wasn't his sister? He couldn't remember.

He turned his attention to his surroundings.

Though silk, velvet, and gilt were plentiful here, too, the side room was several degrees more domestic than the *portego*. It was warmer as well, on this unseasonably cold day, for a fire had been lit before they arrived.

Still, the place had a weary air overall.

"Old-fashioned and shopworn," Sedgewick said, looking about him with a critical eye.

"Venice she is like the beautiful *cortigiana*—the courtesan—who has"—Zeggio frowned, searching for the phrase he wanted—"dropped on the hours of trouble."

"Fallen on hard times," James said.

"Fallen on hard times," Zeggio repeated. He murmured the phrase to himself a few times. "I see. The same but not the same."

James crossed to a window and looked out across the narrow canal. A feminine silhouette passed the lighted window opposite. After a moment, the figure returned and paused there. Even though the rain obscured everything, even though it was second nature to stand out of the light, and even though the window's tracery partially screened him from view, he stepped back further into the shadows.

"The signora is at home today," said Zeggio. He went to the window. "Her friend will be there as well. Yes, that is Signorina Sabbadin's gondola, as I thought. They drink tea together almost every day. They are like this." He held up his hand, index and middle finger pressed together. "Like sisters. All of her friends follow Madame to *Venezia*, because it is too dull where she is not. But here we are never dull. Even now, we have the opera, the ballet, the plays. And soon, after Christmas, begins the Carnival."

James gazed out at the rain. "Sedgewick, if Carnival begins and we're still in Venice," he said, "please shoot me."

"Yes, sir," said Sedgewick. "You'll want to start right away, then."

James nodded. "Zeggio, find out where she's going tonight. I'll want to dress appropriately."

"La Fenice, I have no doubt," said Zeggio.

"Ah, yes," James said. "Venice's most splendid theater. Where better to display herself?"

"It is because they perform the Rossini work," Zeggio said. "*La Gazza Ladra*."

"*The Thieving Magpie*," James translated for Sedgewick, whose many talents did not extend to foreign languages.

"Again and again she goes to this opera," Zeggio said. "But I will ask, to make certain. Then I arrange for someone who will bring you to her box to introduce you, yes?"

"I don't want to be introduced until I understand her better," James said. "I'll want a day or two for reconnaissance."

"Got to understand the target first," Sedgewick explained to Zeggio. "But the master never has no trouble understanding women. We'll make quick work of her, I don't doubt."

"We'd better," James said. A large, two-oared gondola approached the Palazzo Neroni. "Who's that?"

Zeggio studied it for a moment. "Oh, that one. He comes to Venice soon after she returns. He is the Crown Prince of Gilenia. Very beautiful, with golden hair in little curls. He is a little stupid, but they say she favors him."

Gilenia was a barely invisible speck on the map of Europe, but it was part of James's job to know all the specks. "Prince Lurenze," he said. "What is he, a boy of one and twenty?"

"With respect, sir, you was six years younger than that when you was recruited," Sedgewick said.

"So true," said Zeggio. "Signor Cordier is a legend. Almost I think him a myth until I see for myself."

"There's a considerable difference," said James, "between the troublesome younger son of an English nobleman and the heir to one of Europe's oldest monarchies. Royals are a good deal more sheltered. And the Gilenian royals are kept in cotton wool. I'm amazed his parents let him out of their sight."

"They send with him a great retinue," said Zeggio. "All the diplomats court him. This is one of his difficulties with the ladies: He is never alone."

"That must make for interesting experiences in the boudoir," said James. "If he's had any, which is not at all certain."

"You think the lad's a virgin?" said Sedgewick.

"I shouldn't lay a wager on it," said James. "But his experience will be extremely limited." He made a dismissive gesture. "He'll be no problem at all. And if Magny keeps to his villa like other sensible folk, I foresee no difficulty with him."

"And the lady?" said Veggio.

"Oh, the women's never no problem for the master," said Sedgewick. "No problem at all."

*Meanwhile, in London*

John Bonnard, Baron Elphick, stood behind the desk of his study. Though he'd passed his fortieth birthday, his dark gold hair was still thick, his hazel eyes were unclouded, and most of his teeth remained in his head. All in all, despite a shortish stature and slight physique, he was deemed one of the most attractive men in England.

Had observers been able to see the inner man, they might have had a different opinion.

At the moment he bore a nearer resemblance to

his inner self, because he was scowling at the letter that lay before him. The letter was creased, as though it had been crumpled repeatedly and flattened out.

Most of the letters his former wife sent him ended up in this condition. Oddly enough, none of them ended up in the fire.

The petite, dark-haired woman standing across the desk from him looked down at the letter and up into his face. Johanna Ide wore the expression of one who has watched the same scene unfold time and again. She did not roll her beautiful eyes, though. Elphick's mistress of more than twenty years—and co-conspirator in all things—was well aware that in this one case, matters had not proceeded as she and he had so confidently expected.

He'd had another letter from his wife. It had put him in a temper, as usual.

"The bitch," he said.

"I know, my dear, but she won't trouble you for much longer."

He looked up. "No, she won't. Everything is in hand. I had a message this morning. Marta Fazi's been released from prison. It took long enough, and cost enough. But it's done, and she ought to be on her way to Verona, if she isn't there already."

It was Johanna's turn to frown. She knew Marta Fazi was one of many women Elphick had used over the years. Each one believed she was the only one he truly loved. Johanna, who knew better, encouraged these liaisons. It was business, and their business was achieving power. If this hadn't been the case, she and Elphick would have done the impractical thing and wed each other years ago. But being ambitious—soulmates in every way—they'd married other people. She was widowed now and he divorced, yet they hesitated to wed each other until everything was settled at last: until he became prime minister and his former wife was rendered hors de combat . . . until, in short, Johanna could be absolutely certain no one would find out what sort of man he was inside, and she wouldn't suffer the consequences with him.

"I know what you're thinking," he said. "You'd prefer I employ someone else to recover the letters."

"Fazi is barely literate," said Johanna.

"She'll recognize my handwriting," he said. "I've sent her love notes enough. She'll be told what names to look for. That's all she needs to know."

"She's slightly unhinged as well," Johanna said.

"She may do what she likes to Francesca, so long as she gets the letters first," he said.

"I feel quite the same, dear, I assure you. But I should like to be certain Marta has the letters before your former wife has a fatal accident."

"Marta doesn't usually kill women," he said. His gaze drifted down to the letter. "She's more likely to spoil Francesca's pretty face. That will send the slut's highborn lovers packing."

The highborn lovers were the real problem.

Five years ago, Francesca Bonnard had stolen from this very desk letters that, read by anyone with an understanding of the kinds of missives that passed between foreign agents, could prove incriminating, fatally so.

Fortunately, at the time she'd stolen them, she was

the most hated and despised woman in Great Britain. Had she tried to expose her husband's decades of clandestine dealings with the French, no one would have believed her. Everyone would have believed the letters were forgeries, a despicable effort to drag her grossly abused spouse down into the cesspit with her. He might have even been able to bring charges against her of slander and sedition.

She'd known better than to attempt to expose him, though. She'd simply gone abroad and become a whore while John Bonnard had continued to climb the ranks of his party and eventually get himself a barony.

But he'd made a few enemies along the way, and these people were now looking for ways to undermine him. One of his more worrisome foes, Lord Quentin, was in Italy. Not a good sign.

Meanwhile, instead of quickly sinking into the gutter and dying, impoverished, diseased, and mad, as Johanna and Elphick had confidently expected, Francesca Bonnard had climbed in the world, too. Now she consorted with men of influence.

Now she was a problem, a very dangerous one.


*Meanwhile, in Verona*


"Do you not understand?" Marta Fazi raged at the gentleman who'd brought the message to the little cottage. "I've lost my best men, thanks to that Roman pig, whoever he is. Three of them crippled—useless. Another half dozen the soldiers took away. They are still in prison."

"We got you out," said the messenger. "It cost a bloody fortune in bribes."

"I am worth it," she said, chin aloft. "My Lord Elphick knows. But what can I do when my best men are useless?"

"Use your second-best men," said the messenger.

She scowled at something across the room. She stalked past him to a shelf and turned a little statue of the madonna to face the wall. "Why does she look at me like this?" she said. "She knows what I have suffered. That cruel man. May he burn in hell."

"Never mind the cruel man," the messenger said.

She swung round, her black eyes glittering with rage. "Never mind? Do you know what he did?"

"I know he made you lose your temper and go on a rampage, which is how you ended up in prison and cost us—"

"My emeralds!" she cried. "My beautiful emeralds! He took them!"

"This is rather more important than—"

"Queens wore those emeralds!" she raged on. "They were *mine!*" She pressed her first to her bosom. "Do you know what I had to do to get them, those beautiful stones?" Her dark eyes filled. She, who mutilated for sport and killed with a smile on her face, wept over green minerals. "I loved them like children. My own little babies. Where will I find jewels to match those again? When I find that black-hearted pig who took them—"

"You can look for him later. Right now—"

"Who did this to me? Who is he?"

"We don't know. We don't have time to find out. Forget him. Forget the emeralds. You'll never get them back. They've gone back to the royal coffers they came out of."

"No!" She snatched the little madonna from the shelf and threw it across the room. It hit the back of a chair and shattered into fragments. "Forget? Marta Fazi never forgets! Not even a ring does he leave me. Not one ring! Nothing. Gone! All gone!"

"*She* has jewelry," the messenger said. "She's famous for it."

The storm abruptly abated.

"Mrs. Bonnard has sapphires, pearls, rubies, diamonds," the messenger said into the intense quiet. "And emeralds."

"Emeralds?" Marta smiled like a child offered sweetmeats.

"Very fine emeralds that once belonged to the Empress Josephine," the messenger said. "Get the letters and no one will mind if you take a few baubles as well. Deliver those letters safely to his lordship and he'll give you the Crown Jewels."

*Venice, that night, at the opera*

Though the season had not officially started, the boxes and pit of La Fenice were very nearly filled. This, James was aware, was partly because Rossini's popular *La Gazza Ladra* was being performed and partly because Francesca Bonnard and her friends occupied one of the most expensive of the theater's four tiers of boxes. As many people were looking up at her box as were looking at the stage.

And, this being Italy, many other people were doing neither.

As he well knew, Italian theaters were a different species from those in England. In Italy, theaters were social centers. To accommodate sociable theatergoers, the stairs and refreshment rooms were enormous. The vast foyers had been used until very recently for gambling. Now, with gambling forbidden, theatergoers were reduced to playing backgammon.

During the season, the educated classes attended the theater four or five times a week. Since this was a home away from home, the boxes were large as well, many of them furnished like drawing rooms and used in much the same way. From some, one could barely see the stage.

During the performance, people ate, drank, and talked. They played at cards, flirtation, and seduction. Servants went in and out. The opera or play provided background color and music, for the most part.

But at certain important times in the performance—the start of a favorite aria, for instance—the audience became hushed, and attended with all its might.

Such a hush was not in progress as James entered the box where Francesca Bonnard held court. Several parties on stage were screeching and bellowing something or other to which no one was paying the slightest heed.

No one paid James any heed, either. He appeared to be merely one of the several wigged and liveried servants going in and out with this or that: food, wine, a shawl. Playing a servant was easy. Those they served took little notice of them. He might stab the crown prince of Gilenia in the neck in front of a dozen witnesses, and later, not one of those witnesses would be able to identify James as the killer. No one would remember what kind of wig or livery he wore.

He was certain of this, having done away with two pieces of human slime under similar conditions.

Lurenze, however, was merely in the way. Since, given the lady's reputation, one must expect a male—or several—to be in the way, James preferred the obstacle to be young and not overly intelligent. The French count Magny, with the advantages of age and experience—which included not losing his head, literally, during the Terror or thereafter—might have proved a more serious obstacle.

James's attention shifted from the golden-haired boy to the harlot beside him. They sat at the front of the box, Lurenze in the seat of honor at her right. He'd turned in his seat to gaze worshipfully at her. She, facing the stage, pretended not to notice the adoration.

From where he stood, James had only the rear view, of a smoothly curving neck and shoulders. Her hair, piled with artful carelessness, was a deep chestnut with fiery glints where the light caught it. A few loose tendrils made her seem the slightest degree tousled. The effect created was not of one who'd recently risen from bed but one who had a moment ago slipped out of a lover's embrace.

Subtle.

And most effective. Even James, jaded as he was, was aware of a stirring-up below the belly, a narrowing of focus, and a softening of brain.

But then, she ought to be good at stirring up men, he thought, considering her price.

His gaze drifted lower.

A sapphire and diamond necklace adorned her long, velvety neck. Matching drops hung at her shell-like ears. While Lurenze murmured something in her ear, she let her shawl slip down.

James's jaw dropped.

The dress had almost no back at all! She must have had her corset specially made to accommodate it.

Her shoulder blades were plainly visible. An oddly shaped birthmark marked the right one.

He pulled his eyes back into his head and his tongue back into his mouth.

Well, then, she was a fine piece, as well as a bold one, no question about that. Someone thought she was worth those sapphires, certainly, and that was saying something. James wasn't sure he'd ever seen their like, and he'd seen—and stolen—heaps of fine jewelry. They surpassed the emeralds he'd reclaimed from Marta Fazi not many months ago.

Bottle in hand, he advanced to fill their glasses.

Lurenze, who'd leaned in so close that his yellow curls were in danger of becoming entangled with her earrings, paused, leaned back a little, and frowned. Then he took out his quizzing glass and studied her half-naked back. "But this is a serpent," he said.

*It is?*

James, surprised, leaned toward her, too. The prince was right. It wasn't a birthmark but a *tattoo*.

"You, how dare you to stare so obscene at the lady?" Lurenze said. "Impudent person! Put your eyes back in your face. And watch before you spill—"

"Oops," James said under his breath as he let the bottle in his hand tilt downward, splashing wine on the front of his highness's trousers.

Lurenze gazed down in dismay at the dark stain spreading over his crotch.

"*Perdono, perdono,*" James said, all false contrition. "*Sono mortificato, eccellenza.*" He took the towel from his arm and dabbed awkwardly and not gently at the wet spot.

Bonnard's attention remained upon the stage, but her shoulders shook slightly. James heard a suppressed giggle to his left, from the only other female in the box. He didn't look that way but went on vigorously dabbing with the towel.

The red-faced prince pushed his hand away. "Stop! Enough! Go away! Ottar! Where is my servant? *Ottar!*"

Simultaneously, a few hundred heads swiveled their way and a few hundred voices said, in angry unison, "*Shh!*"

Ninetta's aria was about to begin.

"*Perdonatemi, perdonatemi,*" James whispered.

"*Mi dispiace, mi dispiace.*" Continuing to apologize, he backed away, the picture of servile shame and fear.

La Bonnard turned round then, and looked James full in the face.

He should have been prepared. He should have acted reflexively but for some reason he didn't. He was half a heartbeat too slow. The look caught him, and the unearthly countenance stopped him dead.

*Isis*, Lord Byron had dubbed her, after the Egyptian goddess. Now James saw why: the strange, elongated green eyes . . . the wide mouth . . . the exotic lines of nose and cheek and jaw.

James felt it, too, the power of her remarkable face and form, the impact as powerful as a blow. Heat raced through him, top to bottom, bottom to top, at a speed that left him stunned.

It lasted but a heartbeat in time—he was an old hand, after all—and he averted his gaze. Yet he was aware, angrily aware, that he'd been slow.

He was aware, angrily aware, of being thrown off balance.

By a look, a mere look.

And it wasn't over yet.

She looked him up. She looked him down. Then she looked away, her gaze reverting to the stage.

But in the last instant before she turned away, James saw her mouth curve into a long, wicked smile.

# Chapter 2

And up and down the long canals they go,
   And under the Rialto shoot along,
By night and day, all paces, swift or slow;
   And round the theatres, a sable throng,
They wait in their dusk livery of woe,—
   But not to them do woful things belong,
For sometimes they contain a deal of fun,
Like mourning coaches when the
     funeral's done.

Lord Byron, *Beppo*

The two women giggled like schoolgirls as their gondola made its way through the sable throng clustered at the Fenice's rear door.

"Oh, but did you see Lurenze's face when he came back, and found the Russian count in his place?" said Giulietta. "Like a little boy with his pretty blond curls. He stood, so, with his mouth hanging open." She mimicked the prince's dismayed astonishment. "Poor boy. He was so disappointed."

"Boy, indeed," said Francesca. "He's like a

puppy—and I'm not sure I have the patience to train him."

"The young ones have so much energy," said Giulietta. "But too often they are clumsy."

"And they're in a great hurry," Francesca said. "Still, he's very beautiful."

"And he is a prince. And he has a fine fortune. And a generous nature."

"It would be a coup, I agree," Francesca said.

"And yet you hesitate. Is this because of the comte de Magny?"

"He has no power over me," Francesca said.

"You are not still angry with him?"

"I'm done with letting men tell me what to do—and he had the audacity to advise me about lovers. He even objected to the *marchese*."

"Bellaci? To what can anyone object? When I think of the jewels he showered upon you, I wonder how you could leave him."

"A year and a half in one man's keeping is long enough," Francesca said.

The longer an affair continued, the greater the danger of becoming attached. She'd never do that again.

"You don't miss him, your handsome *marchese?*" said Giulietta.

"When men are gone, I'm always glad they're gone," Francesca said. That included the two men in her life she'd truly loved: her father and her husband. "I will admit that Lurenze lacks their savoir faire. If a servant had spilled wine on Bellaci, for instance, he would have said something witty. Lurenze was thoroughly flummoxed."

"He was embarrassed because it happened in front of you," Giulietta said. "I felt sorry for him, yet I was amused, too. How precisely the servant aimed the wine! Almost I could believe he did it on purpose."

"I had the same impression," Francesca said. "Whose servant was it, do you know?"

"Who cares?" said Giulietta. "Did you notice his shoulders? *Buon Dio*." Though, after the long, rainy day, the night was cool, she fanned herself. "And his legs?"

"Oh, yes," said Francesca. "I noticed."

She'd noticed that the servant was magnificently formed. She'd noticed his broad shoulders and long, muscled legs, well displayed in the breeches and stockings of his livery. She'd noticed the way he moved—smooth and lithe as a cat—and she'd thought, *There isn't a clumsy bone in that body.* She would have noticed more, given a chance. The chance never came.

"I wish I could have seen his face," she said. "But it doesn't do to light the box too brightly."

"No, no, never bright," Giulietta said. "We must have the shadows, to encourage the intimacy, the seductive words, the naughty jokes. It is too bad he did not come back, to let us study him more. To speak for myself, I would have liked to study him with my hands—and perhaps my mouth."

"If he turned out to be ugly, you could put the towel over his face," Francesca said. "Ugly or not, it was inconsiderate of him to fail to return. He was a most welcome distraction from the others."

"Why is it the aristocrats never look like that?" said Giulietta.

"Because the aristocrats don't exercise their muscles with hard work," Francesca said.

"I would let him exercise his muscles on me," said Giulietta. "To keep them from going soft, you know."

Francesca's mind produced an image of naked masculine limbs tangled with hers. Heat swarmed over her skin. "You are the soul of kindness," she said, fanning herself. "Your heart is so charitable, you should have been a nun."

"I should have been a nun," said Giulietta, "but the habit is so unbecoming. And all the praying is bad for the knees. No, no, it would not suit me. I was born to be a slut."

"As was I," said Francesca. Resolutely banishing lewd images of excessively virile servants, she waved her hand. "Look at this. Were I not a slut, I should not be in the midst of this, laughing with my dearest friend."

After midnight, when the theaters let out and the parties began, the lights of hundreds of gondolas danced over the canals and candlelight twinkled in the windows of the palaces. Here, where no coach wheels and horses' hooves clattered over pavement, one moved in a quiet punctuated only by voices. Carried over the water, conversations ebbed and flowed around her, as though in a great drawing room.

But this was better than any drawing room, Francesca thought. One needn't play a part or make idle conversation. One might simply float upon the water, and on a clear night like this, lean out of the *felze's* open casement and look up at the

stars. One might, as she did now, hear voices singing and in the distance, the poignant notes of a vi-
olin. Even at its liveliest, Venice felt so much more
peaceful than other cities.

A form hurtled toward them out of the shadows,
sprang into the gondola, and folded up at the feet
of Uliva, the gondolier in front.

It happened so suddenly that Francesca was too
stunned at first to scream. Uliva reacted more
quickly. But as he and Dumini, in the rear, stopped
rowing, preparing to oust the intruder, a muffled
voice cried, "Have pity, I beg you, for mercy of
God."

The form rose to its knees. It proved to be a man
in a cape and a wide-brimmed hat. In the uncertain light of the gondola's lamp, Francesca could
not make out much of his features beyond noting a
long, thin, curling mustache and a pointy bit of a
beard. He put her in mind of a seventeenth-century
portrait of a nobleman she'd seen somewhere.

London? Florence? The Palazzo Manfrini? These
days one rarely saw facial hair on European men,
and certainly not in that curious style.

"I beg you most humbly, men of the paddles, do
not betray me," he said in thickly accented Italian.
"Please, I am of no harm." He pushed back his
cape and put up his hands. "No artillery. No sti-
letto. No pistol."

It was then he seemed to notice the two women
staring at him.

"This is a novel way of getting our attention,"
Francesca said calmly, though her heart pounded.
Venice was one of the safest cities in the world. But

no place was completely safe for women, she knew. She recalled her encounter with Lord Quentin in Mira, and what had happened afterward, and her uneasiness grew.

"Oh, speaking English, thank the saints," the stranger said, switching to that language. His version of it was as heavily accented as his barbarous Italian. "My Italian, not so good. My English less bad. A thousand pardons, *senoritas. Signorine.* Ladies, is my meaning. I have a little trouble, this is all."

Looking to Uliva, he said, "Perhaps you will make the paddle move more rapid, boat person?" He moved his hands in a rowing motion. "To make the boat go far away—yes?—before any trouble happens."

The large Uliva regarded him stonily. Behind the cabin, Dumini would be awaiting his partner's signal. Uliva could easily throw the intruder into the canal or knock him senseless with the oar. But while no one could determine the fellow's social position from his ridiculous accent, he had the unmistakable manner of the upper orders.

This didn't mean he was trustworthy. It simply made the gondoliers hesitate.

The stranger appealed to Francesca. "I know it is strange, my sudden appearing. But here is the cause: I visit the lady who has breasts of great beauty." He pointed. "There in that house she lives. But alas, the *esposo* of the lady—how is the word for him?"

"The husband," Giulietta supplied.

"That one," said the stranger. "He comes home

early because he has a discord—what is it when they scream at each other?—he has a disputing with his mistress."

"You mean a quarrel?" said Giulietta. She glanced at Francesca, her mouth twitching.

"The quarrel, yes," the man said. "Then with *me*"—he thumped his chest—"with *me* he makes the quarrel. What have I done? Almost no time he gives me to assume my *pantaloni*. How do you call them? My breeches, which they are down on my feet, so." He pointed to his ankles. "The *esposo* he shouts at me," he said indignantly. "He chases me with a knife very big."

Giulietta giggled.

Francesca couldn't help but smile. She and Giulietta had encountered his type before. Some of Lord Byron's romantic escapades were equally comical. She signaled the gondolier to proceed.

Uliva shrugged. This was Venice, after all. The vessel proceeded smoothly along the canal.

The stranger lightly tipped his hat, then kissed his hand to her. "You are so much kindness to come to my succor. So genteel. It is too shocking, what happens. My lady she is married, not a virgin. All the married ladies here, they have lovers, no?"

"A virtuous wife has only one lover," said Giulietta. "But sometimes the husband acts crazy, as though she had twenty. This one, it seems, was in bad temper because he quarreled with his mistress. It is most unusual, I agree, for the Venetian husband to make a fuss about his wife's *amoroso*."

"One or two lovers is normal for a married lady," said Francesca. "A wife with twenty lovers is a little wild, though. Then people talk. You must be new to Venice."

"Ah, yes." He smote his forehead, tipping the curious hat askew. "Alas, my so bad manners. I am Don Carlo Frederico Manuelo da Guardia Aparicio. But *you*." He pressed his hand to his heart. "No, do not tell me who you are. I am killed and you are angels in heaven . . . though I think," he added with a frown, "I did not expect to find myself in heaven. My mama always told me I would go to the other place."

"You'll see us there in due course, no doubt," said Francesca. "But for the present we remain in Venice. I am Francesca Bonnard and this is my good friend Giulietta Sabbadin, and you needn't worry about our husbands chasing you with big knives, for we are *cortegiane*."

"Ah, but of the certainty," he said. "So stupid I am. I should have seen at once—so much the beauty, so much the elegance, so much the costly gowns of the most fashionable." He kissed his hand to them.

"At any rate, I believe you're safe now," said Francesca. "Where would you like to get out?"

"It makes no moment to me," he said. He came off his knees and shifted to a sitting position as smoothly as the gondoliers' oars glided through the water.

She saw then, with shock, that he was bigger than she'd assumed. His long legs, angled to fit the small quarters, blocked the front of the *felze*. The shoulder resting against the frame of the open door was very broad . . . and familiar. She tried to recall where she'd seen him before.

The trouble was, Italy contained so many good-looking men—not to mention the countless paintings and statues of magnificent males. More than likely the physique, like the curious facial hair, called to mind a portrait she'd seen in somebody's *palazzo*.

In any case, she'd nothing to fret about, she told herself. This was merely a man lounging in a boat, merely a man at her feet—where she preferred them, by the way. Yet her heart beat fast, and under its pounding she was aware of a sharp pull in the pit of her belly.

*Not harmless,* she thought. *Not this one.*

Leaning back and tilting his hat over his forehead, he said, "I am content to go where you go, most beautiful ones. I am the courtesan like you. You will allure the men and I will allure the women."

It was true enough, James thought, as he watched them from under the brim of his hat. He'd whored before for his country and was doing it again. If he caught the clap and his pego fell off, well, too bad. He'd get no sympathy from his superiors. Men lost parts in war, didn't they, and he was a soldier, wasn't he, and better paid than any of them. That would be their attitude.

In any event, a man didn't get far in this trade if he couldn't improvise. Bonnard was clearly more cautious and mistrustful than her friend. She'd wound up as tight as a clock spring when he settled in the cabin's doorway, but his claiming to be a whore like them seemed to calm her somewhat. Now she was watching, waiting, deciding whether to have him pitched overboard or not.

He was watching and waiting, too.

"But you are a man," said her doe-eyed friend, Giulietta.

"Yes, thank the saints," he said. "But this night, if I run only a little more slow, I think I would not be all the man I was before."

"A courtesan is a *woman*," said Giulietta.

"What word then?" he said. "My English speaking, better than my Italian speaking, but still of no perfection."

Giulietta looked at her friend.

"The man prostitute," he prompted, "who costs very much. What is his name in English?"

"Husband," said Bonnard. And she laughed.

James sucked in his breath.

He'd heard about the laugh, and dismissed it as another of the myths men created to explain their stupidity about a woman.

He knew—*knew*—it was her art, yet the husky invitation in the sound caught him. It was a lover's laughter, hinting at private jokes amid tumbled sheets. It was the laughter of shared secrets, almost unbearably intimate.

It was like those sirens, calling to what's-his-name. Ulysses.

*Tie me to the mast*, he thought.

He recalled the look she'd given him at the theater, the smile as she turned away. It was the kind of smile Helen must have given Paris, the kind Cleopatra must have bestowed on Mark Antony.

Damn but she was good.

A challenge, then, and wasn't that what he wanted? Hadn't he balked at this mission at first because—among other grievances—he'd believed it a waste of his time? Hadn't he told his employers that any tyro could relieve a female of a packet of letters?

"Husband?" he said, pretending to be baffled. "But no, not to marry, you see, but only so." He made a hand gesture universally understood to indicate the carnal act. "To make happy the more old woman, who sometimes she is ugly, but very, very beautiful in the purse."

"Francesca teases you," said Giulietta. "She is speaking of *English* husbands. The English are crazy. She is English but she is only a little crazy." She looked to her friend. "Is there an English word? I cannot think of one. A hundred words for bad girls like us, but what is a man courtesan?"

"A penniless aristocrat," said Bonnard.

James suppressed a smile. Wit, of course. The best whores had it. The famous harlot Harriette Wilson had nothing remarkable in the way of looks apart from her fine bosom. Her great assets were her lively personality and her sense of humor.

So far, so good, then. If Bonnard had relaxed enough to ply her wit, he'd made progress.

"This is so true," he said gravely. "I have many brothers and sisters and I am one of the younger ones." That bit was fact, at any rate. "There is not enough money for everyone. And so I make my way in the world, you see."

"If you want to make your way in Venice," said Giulietta, "I will give you some good advice. Keep away from Elena da Mosta. She has the clap. She gave it to Lord Byron. This is why Francesca would not have him, though he was so charming to her and very sweet."

"He was charming and sweet to every woman he found attractive—and that meant nearly every young woman who crossed his path," said Bonnard. "How he could tell which one among the multitudes gave him gonorrhea is beyond my comprehension."

"But he loved Francesca very much," Giulietta said. "He wrote poems to her."

"He writes poems to everybody," said Bonnard. "That is how he converses with the world. That is how he experiences the world. Have you read his new poems?" she asked James, starting forward in her seat, her otherworldly face lighting up. "Are they not remarkable, so different from the others?"

The abrupt appeal, the sudden openness, took him unawares.

*Why, yes, they are,* he was about to say.

She made an impatient gesture. "But no, how could you have read them?" she said. "They've been published only in English." She sank back into the seat once more.

James swore silently. He'd come within a breath of betraying himself.

He'd read those new poems, and he'd been

amazed. They were so immediate, so conversational, and so completely different, he thought, from what he deemed the overwrought romanticism of *Childe Harold*. But he had no one with whom he could discuss them. In London, it would be different. In London one might easily find a group of gentlemen, a club, a salon, where people talked of poetry, music, plays, and books.

A man didn't find such people—or have time for literary discussions with them if he did—as he dashed from city to city, country to country, saving the world.

"She reads the poems to me, else I would not understand them at all," said Giulietta. "I speak English well, and practice with her all the time. But to read it hurts my head. The way the English spell: Where is the logic? Nowhere can I find it. They spell like madmen."

James nodded. "More easy it is to read Greek."

Bonnard had turned away. She leaned out of the open casement and looked up at the night sky.

Giulietta was chattering on amiably. James listened with a part of his mind. The rest was on her companion. Bonnard had put up her guard again and distanced herself from him. He could feel it, as palpably as if she'd thrust him away with her hand.

Very possibly, had she possessed the strength to throw him off the gondola, she'd do it. He was not sure what had happened, what had made her withdraw. All he knew was that he felt her mistrust humming in the air between them.

This was going to be a good deal trickier than he'd imagined.

This wasn't another Marta Fazi. This one was complicated. She had a brain and something more, though he wasn't sure yet what the *more* was.

He had no doubt now, though, that Francesca Bonnard was going to be a considerable challenge. He hadn't had a true challenge in a long time.

His heart went a little faster.

Perhaps this would be fun, after all.


Francesca finally got rid of their new friend at the Caffè Florian.

After the theaters emptied, the attendees often spent two or three hours at the coffeehouses. The Florian in the Piazza San Marco was the most popular with Venetians and visitors sympathetic to their cause. The Austrian soldiers and their friends preferred the Quadri, across the way. Like other social centers, the Florian offered the usual Venetian mix of classes and degrees of respectability.

Among other patrons this evening was the Countess Marina Querini Benzoni. Age might have withered her—she was sixty if she was a day—but it had not sapped her animal spirits or diminished her eyesight when it came to attractive, virile young men.

Three years ago, she'd attempted to captivate Lord Byron.

This night she pounced on Don Carlo.

Once the countess had the "alluring" Spaniard firmly in her clutches, Francesca told Giulietta it was time to leave.

As soon as they were out of the door Giulietta broke into giggles. "Oh, you are wicked," she said.

"He said he wanted to make an older woman happy," Francesca said as they started across the Piazza. "How lucky for him. He found what he was looking for without even trying."

"He would not have found her if you had not pushed into the crowd near her table," said Giulietta. "What is it? Did you not like him? I found him so entertaining. I like a man who makes me laugh."

"You like men," said Francesca, "generally speaking."

"And, generally speaking, you do not," said Giulietta.

"You know I'd rather have a dog," said Francesca. "But a dog won't support me in the style to which I've chosen to become accustomed."

"I thought Don Carlo was sweet," Giulietta said.

Francesca pointed to her head. "Too much pomade. When he took off his hat, I thought at first his hair was carved and painted on his head. What does he use, I wonder? Lard? His valet must apply it with a trowel."

That had given her a jolt: When he took off his hat in the coffeehouse, she saw thick black hair, plastered to his skull and gleaming greasily in the candlelight. The sight hadn't turned the Countess Benzoni's stomach, though. She probably hadn't noticed his head. His lower body was of far more interest.

"Madame."

Francesca turned. "Drat," she muttered.

The golden-haired prince of Gilenia strode toward

them, smiling. "At the last, I find you," he said. "Everywhere am I looking. I had the great hope of us to meet again at the Florian."

Losing his place to the Russian count had not dampened his ardor for long, it seemed.

Even in the uncertain light near the Campanile, the bell tower of St. Mark's Square, Francesca had no trouble discerning the happy sparkle in his eyes. Once upon a time, John Bonnard had looked at her in that way, and made her heart flutter. The moth to the flame. The old story. The old cliché.

Now she experienced an irrational urge to weep. John Bonnard was a treacherous man. This man was utterly guileless. She hated to disappoint him. It was like kicking a puppy.

But she wasn't sure she wanted him, and pity was not the way to commence an affair. In any case, she knew very well that if she made it too easy, he'd quickly lose interest.

"The café was so crowded and hot," she said. "And I'm fatigued."

Instantly his beautiful face was all concern. "But of course," he said. "This weather so strange in this place. One day so hot and the air like the soup. The next day, cold, with rain and wind. And everywhere madame goes, a crowd happens, to admire her. But please, you will allow me the honor so great, to escort you to your house?"

"Thank you, your highness, but not this night," she said gently. "Another time."

"I worry for you," he said. "These are times of too much danger. Everywhere is revolt, the insurrection. Only a short time ago is the Duke du Berri murdered."

"You are kind to worry," she said. "And you flatter me, putting me in the same category as the heir to the French throne." Lightly she patted his sleeve. His face lit at the touch.

Her conscience screeched.

"But please be assured," she went on, "I am in excellent hands. My gondoliers can deal with any would-be brigands or revolutionaries. Good night, your excellency."

She made her deepest curtsy, offering him a splendid view of her bosom. Giulietta did likewise. Then, while he was still blinking, dazzled by the display, she took Giulietta's arm, and walked on.

They soon passed the Campanile and turned into the Piazzetta San Marco, the smaller square between the Doge's Palace and the Zecca, the city mint. The area was far from deserted at this time of night. Now and again she nodded to acquaintances as they passed, walking to and from the landing place.

She was aware of Giulietta, unusually silent beside her, as they made their way to the gondola waiting at the water's edge.

Only when they were settled aboard the boat and gliding past the palaces bordering the Grand Canal did Giulietta speak. "Poor boy," she said.

"What would you have me do? Bed him out of pity?"

"I would."

"I can't," Francesca said. "I need a lover, a formal arrangement, not a night's amusement."

"I know. It is not good for one's reputation to take to bed every pretty boy—or man—who appears. Too easy, too cheap, we lose position. One becomes common, a mere whore, *una puttana*."

Francesca looked out at the boats passing, weaving in and out among their fellows, the lights of their lamps bobbing in the darkness. "Men are investments," she said. "One must choose carefully, and think of the future."

"You think Lurenze will lose interest as soon as he has bedded you?" Giulietta said. "I do not think so."

Francesca shrugged. "I'm not sure what I want at the moment. He isn't the only candidate."

"You seemed to enjoy his company before," Giulietta said.

Francesca looked at her.

"Before you saw the servant at La Fenice. He gave you ideas, I think."

"Of course he did," Francesca said easily. "As an amusing fantasy, yes. As a lover—impossible. Unless he's a jewel thief." She grinned. "A very *good* jewel thief."

Giulietta grinned back at her. Jewelry was a powerful form of financial security. Better yet, unlike bank notes, it was security one might display to the world. Francesca knew—and Giulietta understood—that Lord Elphick gnashed his teeth every time his wife sent him word of one of her acquisitions. It was one delicious form of revenge.

Thinking of him, she laughed, and Giulietta, knowing what she was thinking, laughed with her.

*A few hours later*

While Zeggio watched, fascinated, James stood at the mirror, carefully removing the thin mustache and beard.

"I've always found simplest disguises the most effective," James explained. "People sort strangers into categories—servant, foreigner, and so on. Remember, too, that they notice only what's unusual: a scar, a curious mustache, a flamboyant hat. The Florian was well lighted, and being indoors, I was obliged to take off my hat and keep it off. But Bonnard found my hair so revolting, she took no notice of my facial features. The next time she sees me, she won't know me."

Zeggio nodded. "She remembers the pomade, and the hair flat upon the skull. She does not know it curls."

Curl it did, in thick, crow-black ringlets. But at the moment, no one would guess that.

"What do you reckon about my hair, Sedgewick?" James said. "Strong soap, or do you want to try scraping it off first?"

"I reckon I wished you'd decided on a wig instead, sir," Sedgewick said.

"Too easy to lose in a tussle," James said. "I had no way to be sure her gondoliers wouldn't heave me overboard first and ask questions later. I think she's hired the biggest gondoliers in Venice. That Uliva? Hands the size of hams. Water wouldn't damage this, though."

"She must expect trouble, signore," Zeggio said. "The house is protected very well. Two porters.

One on the canal side and one on the land side. We have tried to get into it, but for us this is impossible. Even if we could get in, we do not know what to look for and where to look. How will you do it?"

"I won't," said James.

Zeggio's dark eyes widened. "No?"

James laughed. "She thought she was so clever, leaving me in Countess Benzoni's clutches. I could have escaped and followed La Bonnard—but to what purpose? When she wants to be rid of a man, she gets rid of him. She'd had enough of me. There was nothing to be gained by plaguing her. There was a great deal to be gained, though, by listening to what people said of her after she left."

"Prince Lurenze went after her," Sedgewick told Zeggio. "Where did it get him?"

James had not followed her but Sedgewick and Zeggio had. They blended in easily among the gondoliers and servants idling about St. Mark's.

"I took advantage of the opportunity she offered me," James said. "The Countess Benzoni is charming, lively, and most informative. I found out more from her in half an hour than I should have learned from Bonnard in a week. This, combined with my own observations, tells me what to do."

He looked up from the mirror into Zeggio's eager face.

*Once I felt the same zest for adventure, the same zest for the hunt,* James thought. *Where did it go? When did it go?*

"Everyone chases her," James said. "She knows how to deal with that. So she's going to chase me." He smiled grimly. "Until I catch her."

# Chapter 3

I'm fond myself of solitude or so,
   But then, I beg it may be understood,
By solitude I mean a sultan's not
A hermit's, with a haram for a grot.

Lord Byron
*Don Juan, Canto the First*

*Two nights later*

On nights like this Francesca truly appreciated her freedom. She had gone first to the theater, then to the Caffè Florian, and now—Giulietta having parted from her for an assignation—she was going home, where she might sit up for a time, reading.

She would not have to make conversation or stifle yawns. She would not have to be clever or amusing or enticing or even agreeable.

Tonight she need please only herself.

She sat in the gondola, her chin resting on her hand, watching the familiar line of *palazzi* near her house float past. It was delicious, sometimes, not to have to talk or even think, to simply savor the moment and her surroundings: the beautiful houses, which had stood here for centuries; the quiet of the canal, the same quiet it had known for centuries, too; the peace of this strange city.

None of the cities she'd visited since she'd left England had soothed her as Venice did. She had no trouble understanding why Lord Byron had been, in a sense, reborn here.

At present, she lacked nothing in her life, she thought. She was financially secure. She was free—in ways she couldn't have dreamed of in her old life. She had a friend in whom she could confide.

She needed nothing—except perhaps a lover who would give her a few hours' pleasure and go away and leave her in peace. Or perhaps a dog would be better, she thought with a smile. In lieu of carnal pleasure, a canine would offer unquestioning love and devotion.

But dogs could not buy her diamonds. Or rubies, emeralds, sapphires, pearls, peridots, amethysts, or any of their fellows.

She'd have to make do with a lover. She laughed softly at the thought.

As the gondola neared her house, she looked up toward the Ca' Munetti. Arnaldo had told her that the new tenant was hiring more servants. Several boats had arrived with supplies for the house. Of the tenant himself Arnaldo had learned little more. The gondolier Zeggio had claimed his master wished for privacy. He'd come to study with the monks and to concentrate on his work, whatever that was. He might go to the theater on occasion, or visit a church or a *palazzo*, to view the works of art. But he did not wish to attend the *conversazioni*—Venice's salons, or what was left of them—or go to parties or to the hotels to dine with friends.

He was reclusive, then, but not precisely a hermit, she decided. He was, her sources said, about Lord Byron's age but "perhaps more handsome." The shadowy form she'd glimpsed from time to time in the Ca' Munetti's windows was that of a tall man.

The rest was left to her imagination. And in imagining him, she lost awareness of her surroundings.

She heard the faint plash of oars but thought nothing of it.

The night was dark, and the gondoliers didn't see the danger, either, until a minute too late.

It happened so quickly.

A noise, the gondola rocking.

She looked to the front of the *felze* in time to see the man heave over the gondola's side, leap up at Uliva, and push him into the water. It happened in the blink of an eye. She tried to scream, but only a squeak came out. Her throat was tight and her heart beat so fast, she couldn't breathe properly, couldn't find the wind to cry for help.

She was aware of movement, more rocking. A *thunk*, then a splash. She scrambled up from her seat, but the attacker shoved her back into the cabin and fell upon her.

She punched and kicked but he was too big, a

great barrel of a brute. The stench of unwashed body clogged her nostrils.

His hands went round her throat. She clawed at them, struggled and squirmed, but it was like trying to move an elephant. She tried to thrust her knee in his groin, as she'd been taught to do. He was too heavy. She couldn't move her legs. He muttered an obscenity while his hands tightened round her neck.

James had come home half an hour earlier. He'd stripped down to shirt and trousers and donned his dressing gown. A glass of wine in his hand, he was standing at the darkened window next to Zeggio when it happened.

Zeggio had been watching the small boat—one house down from theirs—since midnight, he explained.

"I do not like it," he told James. "But I do not like to make trouble and call attention to us. What do you think, signore?"

"I don't like it, either," James said.

He'd scarcely uttered the words when her gondola swam into view. It was mere yards from the water gate of the Palazzo Neroni when the small boat moved out from the shadows.

James made out two figures in the rowboat.

It moved swiftly toward the gondola.

And swiftly attacked, taking the gondoliers unawares.

The man rowing the small boat reached over and grabbed the side of the gondola. He spread his legs to hold the rowboat steady while his accomplice climbed onto the gondola and made straight for the front gondolier. He pushed Uliva into the water and without the slightest pause, turned, hurtled over the cabin, and attacked the other gondolier, knocking him into the water.

Then he went for her.

It all took less than a minute.

But in less than a minute James was moving, throwing off the dressing gown and kicking off his slippers. He flung open the window, stepped onto the balcony, and jumped off.

Francesca's accoster grunted, relaxed his grip slightly, and began grinding his pelvis against hers. Despite the layers of clothes between them—her pelisse, gown, petticoat, and shift, and his filthy rags—she was all too aware of his erection . . . and how small a chance she had of stopping him from doing what he meant to do.

She was too afraid to be sickened, too busy gasping for breath and trying not to lose consciousness. He lay atop her, a great, stinking ox. His breath was foul, hot on her face.

She was dimly aware of sounds outside but her mind couldn't sort them out. She clawed with one hand at the thick fingers on her neck while with the other she tried to find something—a weapon of some kind, any kind.

James hit the water next to the rowboat. As soon as he came up, he caught hold of the side and heaved, throwing all his weight into it. The little boat tipped over, and the rower went over, too, with a curse and a shriek.

James pulled himself onto the gondola, and charged into the *felze*. The brute attacking her jerked up his head in surprise. James shoved his forearm across his throat and squeezed, trapping him tight in the crook of his arm. The villain was big, and he thrashed madly, but not for long. A few last, feeble twitches, and he went limp.

James dragged him out of the cabin and pushed him into the canal and watched the dark form sink beneath the water.

He returned to her. She sprawled half in the seat, half on the floor, her skirts bunched up above her garters, her stockings sagging. She was panting, one hand at her throat.

He reached to help her up. She recoiled from his outstretched hand. She rolled to one side, grabbing a bottle. She threw it at him. He ducked, and the bottle sailed harmlessly into the canal.

Relief coursed through him, as cool as the water streaming down his body. The black, consuming rage ebbed.

He set his fists on his hips and laughed. He had to. It was all too absurd, and he most absurd of all, in his shirtsleeves, dripping wet.

*"Ma amo solo te, dolcezza mia,"* he said.

But I love only you, my sweet.

*"Vai al diavolo!"* she gasped.

Go to the devil, in Italian with an amusing English accent.

"That," he said in English, "is both rude and ungrateful, after I have spoiled my best trousers on your account. Or perhaps you've reason to be ungrateful?" He pushed dripping black curls back from his face. "Did I mistake the situation, and interrupt a bout of lovemaking? Like it rough, do you?"

She scrambled up to a sitting position, tugging her skirts down over long, shapely legs. In the dim lamplight her face was ghostly pale, her eyes great, dark hollows in her face.

"Rough?" she said blankly. "*Rough?*" She shook her head, like one waking from a dream. "You're English?"

He was real. This was real.

She was cold and shaking and bile was rising in her throat. She was going to be sick.

Eyes fixed on the apparition before her, Francesca dragged in air and tried to make her mind work.

He couldn't be real.

Greek and Roman statues looked like that, not living men. Mythical gods and demigods looked like that, not mortal men.

But he was breathing. Hard. She watched his big chest rise and fall under his sopping shirt. The sodden linen was merely a veil clinging to his skin, hiding nothing. She could discern every taut line of muscle in his powerful shoulders and arms and torso. The wet trousers hugged a narrow waist and hips and long, muscled legs.

Very long legs. Had she ever met a man, a living man, as tall as this? Or did he simply seem so, towering over her as she lay sprawled in the cabin's seat?

Her first impression was of a handsome, strong-featured face, its expression so cold that it might

have been chiseled in marble. The forbidding countenance was at odds with the mop of wet curls
falling over his forehead.

She felt a wash of cold, then potent heat, a chill
again, and heat again. All the while her head spun,
trying to make sense of a world turned wildly awry
and trying to make sense of him, while he shifted
so easily from one language to another. At one moment he was indisputably Italian, in the next, incurably English.

She let her gaze drop to the hand he'd stretched
out to her. Now it hung at his side, a long, strong
hand that, only a moment before, had reduced a
great barrel of a man to a rag doll. He'd thrown
the big villain's body over the side as casually as he
might have flung a rat.

*Who are you?*

What *are you?*

She forced her gaze upward, back to his face, so
hard and pitiless a moment ago. It was still without warmth, though he'd laughed, and the smile
yet lingered at his mouth.

She wanted him to dive back into the water. He
wasn't human. He was a merman, part of a night-
mare she wanted desperately to wake up from. Let
him go back to his native element, let him vanish
like the apparition he had to be.

But he'd saved her life.

Whoever, whatever he was, he'd saved her life.

In all her seven and twenty years, no man had
ever come to her rescue before.

*Who are you?* she wanted to scream. What *are
you?*

But what came out was the silliest question of all: "You're *English?*"

James had already decided how to play it, though he hadn't planned for this scenario.

"To a point," he said.

She gazed dazedly about her. "I don't understand," she said. "Who were they? Why?"

Her voice was hoarse, and he knew that in better light, he'd see the imprint of her attacker's thick fingers on her throat.

He felt the rage rebuilding—the lunatic fury he'd felt a moment ago.

Lunatic, indeed.

He had a temper: He was half Italian, after all.

But temper—emotion of any kind—had no place in his work. Hotheads failed. Hotheads got their comrades tortured and killed. Hotheads ended up with missing digits, missing limbs. They were left to rot in rat-infested holes or buried alive or staked under the desert sun. Hotheads came to a thousand bad ends, and the end rarely came quickly and painlessly.

*Settle down*, he told himself. *Think*.

She, clearly, hadn't dreamt she was in danger. He, clearly, hadn't dreamt it, either. His superiors had offered no hint. She didn't understand. Neither did he.

Not that this would be the first time he'd been told only part of the story.

They always made it sound so simple—*Get the letters*—and it always turned into *un mare di merda*, a sea of excrement.

He scanned the immediate vicinity. "No sign of the would-be killers or rapists or thieves or whatever they were," he said. "No sign of their boat, either. With any luck, they've drowned."

He didn't tell her it wasn't good luck.

He didn't tell her he should have taken more care.

He should have used another method to immobilize the one he'd pulled off her. He should have made sure to keep him alive, to hold onto him and question him. James would have enjoyed the interrogation.

But there was the swine, chortling while he tortured her, choking her slowly and grinding his groin—doubtless crawling with vermin and disease—against her.

James had charged in like a mad bull.

So that one had got away—or, equally likely, was dead—and the other was either sinking to the bottom of the canal or had got away, too.

Clumsy work. Not setting a good example for Zeggio, going off half-cocked like that, a bloody damned Sir Baconhead, saving fair maidens from dragons.

Still, it was done and couldn't be undone.

James tensed as two heads popped out of the water. Then he recognized Uliva.

"Ah, here are your fellows," he said. "I guessed they'd be along soon enough."

The episode had taken a minute or two, start to finish.

He'd sized up her gondoliers the other night, and understood they were men to be reckoned with. The attackers probably hadn't known that.

Whatever the villains knew or didn't know, James couldn't leave it to the gondoliers to rescue her.

As it was, he might have reached her too late. It took no time at all to kill somebody, as he well knew.

He watched her two stalwart boatmen climb into the gondola. "Get the lady into the house, quickly," he told them in Italian. "Make sure to pour some brandy into her."

He moved to the side of the boat. It had drifted a ways from their respective domiciles, but not so very far, and this was not the Grand Canal but a *rio,* a smaller side canal. He was already wet. He'd a short, easy swim home ahead of him. The cold water would do him good.

He needed to get away. He wasn't happy with his performance this night. He'd had everything planned: their meeting and how he'd manage it.

He prepared to dive.

"Where are you going?" she cried. "Where's your boat? You're not going to swim, surely? Wait! I don't even know who you are."

He turned and gazed into her white, frightened face. He remembered the arrogant sway of her backside as she'd abandoned him in the Florian. He remembered the laughter, promising sin, and the smile, the devil's own smile.

He felt a stab, as of loss, though he'd lost nothing, though he had nothing to lose. Yet he turned away from the water and, with wry resignation, toward her.

"I'm the fellow across the way," he said.

*An hour later*

Francesca's neighbor was taller than she'd estimated, based on glimpses of a silhouette in a window. She could not have guessed how splendidly made he was.

At the moment, the leanly muscled body was not so plainly on display as it had been a short while ago. The recollection, however, was burned into her mind, and it made her go hot and cold again as, clean and dry and freshly clothed, he sauntered into the small parlor she reserved, usually, for her close friends.

He wore a curious combination of articles borrowed from the largest of her servants. The shirt and coat were too short in the sleeves, the waistcoat was too loose, and the breeches too baggy. The shoes were neither too large nor too small, but her discerning eye told her they did not shape properly to his feet. Yet he wore the ill-fitting hodgepodge with the same cool assurance he'd displayed as he stood in her gondola, half-naked and dripping.

Francesca could have changed into a dressing gown over one of her naughty negligees. She might have made herself more comfortable in dishabille. She was a harlot, after all, and need not play the modest lady.

Yet after a furious scrubbing to rid herself of the smell, the touch, the memory of the animal who'd assaulted her, she'd had her maid Thérèse dress her in a gown she might have worn when she had guests to tea.

Tonight—or this morning, rather—tea was laughably inadequate.

Arnaldo brought brandy. Her rescuer sipped his appreciatively as he gazed about the comfortably appointed room adjoining her boudoir.

She sat, supported by pillows, upon the sofa. " 'The fellow across the way,' " she said. She took a shaky gulp of her drink. "That is not the most enlightening introduction I've ever heard."

It was all she'd obtained so far. He'd hustled her inside, allowing no opportunity for questions because he'd been too busy ordering her servants about as though he were lord of the place.

Whatever else he was, he was without question an aristocrat.

"The gossip claims you are a member of the Albani family," she pressed on into the unencouraging silence. "A most distinguished family, they say. A pope or two in it, I'm told. But now you say you're English."

Glass in hand, he moved to a large portrait of her that hung on the *portego* side of the room. It was one of several the *marchese* had commissioned in the course of their relationship. This, the largest and most recent, was the only one he'd sent her after she ended the affair.

"My father is Lord Westwood," her guest said, his gaze still on the portrait. "My mother, his second wife, is Veronica Albani. They come to Venice from time to time. Perhaps you've met them?"

"I'm not usually invited to genteel gatherings," she said while she tried to place Lord Westwood. Once upon a time she'd had Debrett's Peerage memorized.

Once upon a time she'd understood the intricate family connections of Great Britain's aristocracy. She'd been John Bonnard's political hostess, after all.

She had no trouble at present remembering the names of those who'd cut her after the divorce—and that was everybody. At the moment, however, Lord Westwood was a blank to her. She had no idea where he stood in the hierarchy of noblemen: duke, marquis, earl, viscount, baron.

"I should hardly call my parents genteel," he said unhelpfully. He looked away from the portrait, studying her face, his own soberly critical. "An excellent likeness."

Under his quiet scrutiny she felt as awkward as a schoolgirl.

That was patently ludicrous.

*You're a notorious slut,* she reminded herself. *A demimondaine. A woman of the world. Act like one.*

"No one seems to know your name," she said. "It's most mysterious. What does it say on your passport, I wonder, and why does no one seem to know this simple thing?"

He shrugged. "Hardly a mystery. I've been in Venice for only a few days, and the curious can't have tried hard to find out answers. As you say, it's a simple thing, easy enough to find out. One need only ask the Austrian governor, Count Goetz, or his wife—or Mr. Hoppner, the British consul-general." He paused. "I'm James Cordier."

Then at last her mind made the connection. The Earl of Westwood's family name was Cordier.

"I am Francesca Bonnard," she said.

"That much I know," he said. "You're famous, it seems."

"Infamous, you mean."

His long stride brought him quickly across the small room to her. "Are you really?" he said. His eyes had widened with what seemed to be genuine surprise, and she was shocked to discover that they were not dark brown or black as she'd at first supposed, but blue, deep blue.

He sat in the chair nearest hers and leaned forward, studying her intently, rather as though she were another portrait whose quality he was assessing. "What dreadful thing have you done?"

Again she had to fight with herself not to squirm. Scrutiny from men she was used to. What she wasn't used to was being studied as though she were an abstruse line of Armenian. She felt stiff and uneasy. She was aware of heat spreading over her cheeks.

A blush, of all things! *She,* blushing!

She was disconcerted, that was all, she told herself. He wasn't what she was used to. He was reputed to be a scholar. He was reclusive. What surprise was it, then, if he was eccentric, too?

"Perhaps you don't go out much in Society," she said.

"English Society, do you mean?" he said. "No, I spend little time in England."

"I'm divorced," she said. "The former wife of Lord Elphick. It was a great scandal."

"And does he harbor ill will, do you think?" he said. "Do you suppose he might have hired men to kill you?"

Remembering Quentin's visit, and the sudden interest in those old letters of Elphick's, she'd considered the possibility and quickly discarded it. If Elphick had her killed now, he might get into trouble he wouldn't be able to get out of. She was no longer his despised slut of a wife. Here on the Continent she was a glamorous divorcée with important friends. Her untimely demise would cause an uproar. It would be scrupulously investigated. Not to mention that Elphick couldn't be sure what arrangements she'd made about the letters, in the event of her death. No, killing her was too risky for him.

"Good grief, no," she said. "I'm more useful alive. He looks so much nobler and more virtuous in comparison to his wicked wife. He can pose as brave and forbearing. No, killing me would spoil his fun."

"And dying would spoil yours, I reckon," he said.

Surprised, she laughed. She had not thought she could laugh again, so easily, so soon after a narrow escape from rape and a grisly death—but then she was resilient, wasn't she?

She became aware of an odd stillness about him that seemed to tauten the very air of the room. But she'd scarcely noticed it before it vanished.

"One's first theory is that they were robbers," he said. "But what a curious way to go about it. It would have been so much easier to knock you unconscious and strip off the jewelry and toss about your skirts for your purse. But this was meant to cause you as much suffering as possible in a short time. I saw it happen from my balcony, and it was plain that the assault was planned. Since violent crime is rare in Venice, one must conclude that this was deliberate, aimed at you. The motive, though . . ." He shrugged, in a most un-English way, drawing her attention to his big shoulders.

"You sound like a lawyer," she said tightly. "You seem to know a great deal about criminals."

"You sound like someone who doesn't like lawyers," he said. "You seem to know a great deal about them."

"I'm a divorced woman," she said. "My father was Sir Michael Saunders, the man who, single-handedly, nearly destroyed the British economy a few years ago. Yes, Mr. Cordier, I've had a great deal of experience with lawyers. I don't particularly like them. I don't particularly hate them, either. For a woman in my position, they represent an unfortunate necessity."

"Ah, yes," he said. "Your position. A divorcée."

"*Divorziata e puttana,*" she said tautly. A divorcée and a whore.

He leapt from his chair as though one of Satan's imps had pricked his arse with a hot fork.

"Good heavens!" he said. "I do beg your pardon. Am I keeping you from your work?"

That did it, finally. She stared at James, the green eyes huge in her face, shadowed and so vulnerable. He knew it was simply the aftereffects of looking death in the eye, yet it angered him. Before this, she had been so confident, so arrogant—

Then the too-fragile expression crumbled and she laughed, heartily and long.

His heart skipped a beat and another and went on so, beating raggedly.

He couldn't help that. He couldn't help smiling, either.

She was good, very good, and at last he was beginning to understand—in his gut, not simply in his mind—why she was so deuced expensive and why the men who could afford her paid without the smallest hesitation. This was a rare beauty with a rare exuberance.

She must be great fun in bed.

Small wonder the notoriously fickle Bellaci had kept her for so long.

"Keeping me from my work," she said, her laughter subsiding to a soft chuckle while the naughty glint returned to her green eyes. "I must tell Giulietta. She'll love that one. But no, Mr. Cordier, you are not keeping me from the streets, because I don't walk them. Besides, you may have noticed that Venice hasn't much in the way of streets. I'm the other kind of harlot. The excessively greedy kind. And I had planned to spend this night in bed—with a *book*."

"Then it's all too strange to me—at least to the Italian side of me," he said. "I shouldn't have imagined a woman of your quality would spend a night alone. But then, I'm still trying to imagine what would possess a man to divorce you. Was he enamored of his own sex perhaps? Or was it sheep he preferred?" He waved his hand, as though to dismiss the subject. "But it is none of my affair. I keep you from your book, and perhaps, after all, a book is preferable to a lover."

"Sometimes," she said, her mouth curving a little.

It was only a teasing hint of the wicked smile that sent electric shocks of anticipation straight into a man's bloodstream, to speed merrily to his reproductive organs.

The tiny smile was a devilish glimpse of things to come. It might be an invitation. It might simply be teasing.

Whatever it meant, it worked. His temperature was climbing and his brain was already turning over negotiations to his cock.

*Slow down, laddie,* he told himself. *You know better.*

He knew, far better than most men. He couldn't succumb. He couldn't let her have the upper hand. He'd already decided how he'd play this: hard to get.

"He divorced me for adultery," she said.

"Shocking," he said. "I should have thought he had a serious complaint: You'd put arsenic in his coffee or had his drawers starched or beat him at golf."

She shook her head. "I'm afraid not," she said. "I only thought of the arsenic after—and then it was too late."

"It's never too late for arsenic," he said. "What it is, is too slow. Unless you only want to make him desperately sick. Or to make sure he dies slowly and painfully. For fast work, I'd recommend prussic acid."

"You seem to know a great deal about these matters."

He remembered that she'd watched him kill a man—or nearly kill him. James was acutely, embarrassingly aware that he'd been too enraged to pay attention to what he was doing. He'd no idea whether the pig had been breathing or not when dropped into the canal. An unconscious man sinks more or less the same way a dead one does.

She was bound to wonder about a man who could incapacitate another with his bare hands. Clearly, she wasn't the sort who was callous enough not to wonder. He'd met far too many women who wouldn't wonder: Marta Fazi, most recently.

"I do know a great deal," he said. "In my youth, I fell in with a very bad lot." Absolutely true. He preferred to keep as close to the truth as possible. So much simpler that way. "The family packed me off into the army, where criminal and violent tendencies can be properly and gainfully employed." Also true.

"Violence, yes," she said. "But poison? I'd always heard it was a woman's tool."

"I come from a long line of poisoners," he said. "Mother's got some Borgia as well as Medici trickling through her veins." As he started to set down his glass on the table next to her, he caught a whiff of a light scent. Jasmine?

He carefully placed the glass and straightened, resisting the temptation to lean in closer, to find out if the scent was in her hair or on her skin. "And you, I see, come from a long line of women, eternally curious. I should be happy to . . . satisfy . . . your curiosity, but I am obliged to report the incident to the Austrian governor—as I should have done immediately. They are very strict, as you know, about their rules. Then I must be abroad early. The monks expect me punctually at ten. I shall send you my monograph on popular murder methods of the sixteenth century. My sisters say it makes excellent bedtime reading."

"Why don't you bring it yourself?" she said. "You might read it to me."

*In bed* was left unsaid.

It didn't need to be said. The smile lingered at her mouth and the green gaze slid over him, as smooth as water.

He wanted to dive in, even though he was sure she'd drown him there.

*Tie me to the mast,* he thought.

"*Devo andare,*" he said. I must go. "*Buona notte, signora.*"

"*Buon giorno,*" she said. "It's nearly dawn."

"*A rivederci,*" he said.

And before she could tempt him to argue whether it was night or morning or persuade him to watch the sun rise with her, he made his exit.

He was sweating.

# Chapter 4

'T is a sad thing, I cannot choose but say,
    And all the fault of that indecent sun,
Who cannot leave alone our helpless clay,
    But will keep baking, broiling, burning on,
That howsoever people fast and pray,
    The flesh is frail, and so the soul undone:
What men call gallantry, and gods adultery,
Is much more common where the climate's sultry.

Lord Byron
*Don Juan, Canto the First*

*The following afternoon*

Mr. Cordier's treatise had been delivered while Francesca was still abed, though not asleep. She'd spent most of the night—or what was left of it—awake, wanting to kill him—which effectively took her mind off the men who'd tried to kill *her*.

She wrote one short note to the comte de Magny, briefly explaining what had happened and assuring him she was unharmed. After telling Arnaldo to have it delivered without loss of time, she took up the treatise.

At present, still in her dressing gown, reclining upon the chaise longue of her private parlor, she read:

> *In fact, the second husband of Lucrezia Borgia was strangled because he had, quite innocently, become a political liability to her brother Cesare Borgia. The murder took place in the couple's apartments. Lucrezia did her utmost to save her twenty-year-old spouse, to no avail. Long afterwards, she remained inconsolable. Her father, sick of listening to her weeping, sent her out of Rome.*

"So that was my problem," Francesca muttered. "No brother."

"Signora, here is Signorina Sab—"

"Oh, get out of the way," Giulietta said, pushing past Arnaldo. She hurried to Francesca's side, knelt on the footstool, and took her hand. "It is all over Venice," she said. "Someone tried to kill you. It cannot be true."

Francesca threw down the pamphlet. "That much is true. Whatever else you've heard is bound to be less than accurate." In ruthless detail she described what had happened from the time the men had attacked to the moment Mr. Cordier had taken his leave.

Halfway through the recitation, Giulietta turned pale, but the story of Francesca's futile attempts to seduce Mr. Cordier revived her.

"I have to kill him," Francesca said. "It must be poison, though, because he's too big to strangle."

"Big and beautiful and he would not make love to you," Giulietta said with a laugh. "Who can blame you for wishing to murder him?"

Francesca had described him in mouth-watering detail: the thick, curling, raven-black hair; the eyes so shockingly blue; the athletic physique, the potent aura of masculinity.

Her mouth still watered, though she of all people ought to know better. She waved her hand dismissively. "I'll get over it. A temporary madness, perfectly understandable in the circumstances."

"He is beautiful. He saves your life. You are shocked and frightened. It is natural to want a big, strong man in your bed to keep you safe."

"And to help me forget," Francesca said. "What better than a bout of lovemaking to shut out unpleasantness? If only he'd obliged, I might have had a proper night's sleep."

"I understand," Giulietta said. "Everyone knows this happens. After a great danger, after a funeral, the lovemaking proves that we are alive. To me the puzzle is why he refuses. He desires men, do you think?"

"No." Francesca glanced at the small table placed, as always, near at hand. Today it held the wine decanter on its silver tray, along with two wine glasses, for she'd known Giulietta would arrive earlier than usual. Rumor traveled at a stunning speed in Venice.

In her mind's eye, Francesca saw Mr. Cordier's long-fingered hand as he set down his drink on that table. Recalling the quick, cool work he'd made of her attacker, she'd felt a chill—of fear or of excitement, she wasn't sure.

Then she'd felt his slight inclination in her direction, and the chill dissolved into a tingle of anticipation. But he'd straightened in the next instant, and withdrawn.

"Not that it matters," she went on, "because he won't get a second chance. A younger son, my dear? That would never do. He could never keep me in the style to which I've chosen to become accustomed, and I cannot lower my standards."

One standard being that Lord Elphick must get a stomachache when he learned who the latest lover was, instead of smirking at what he'd perceive as her downfall, the downfall for which he waited so eagerly. He'd still be waiting, she was determined, when he breathed his last—and, she hoped, agonizingly painful—breath.

"I cast lures at Mr. Cordier only because I was overwrought." She hesitated briefly before continuing, "I was grateful as well, naturally. Do you know, this was the first time in my life a man came to my rescue? Not one of the men I'd known during my Season or during my marriage made the smallest attempt to help me when my husband behaved so abominably. My father had already run away, leaving me to the wolves. Imagine the shock to my sensibilities, when a complete stranger risks his life on my account!"

Giulietta's brow furrowed. She rose from the footstool and turned to the small table. She picked up the wine decanter and filled the two glasses. She gave one to Francesca, then took her own and lifted it. "You are alive," she said. "For this I give your neighbor thanks."

Francesca raised her glass. "I'll be thankful for that, in any event."

They clinked the glasses and drank.

"But now let us set aside for the moment this provoking man who rescues you, and so stupidly declines to have his way with you," Giulietta said.

"Set him aside, indeed." Francesca gave a rueful laugh. "Easy for you to say. You haven't seen him yet. You haven't seen him *wet*."

"Sooner or later I will see him," Giulietta said. "Then I will understand why he made you break your rules. For now he matters only because he saved your life. To me the important question is, Who wants you dead?"


*That night, at La Fenice*

*La Gazza Ladra*. Again.

Lurenze. Again.

But not in the place of honor, James noted as he followed the Austrian governor Count Goetz into Mrs. Bonnard's box. In the choice seat, on Mrs. Bonnard's right, sat a tawny-haired Russian officer. To Mrs. Bonnard's left sat her little friend Giulietta. The two women had their heads together and whispered behind their fans.

The officer, who must have some understanding of the ways of women, made no attempt to claim her attention but chatted with the Russian consul, who sat nearby.

Lurenze, who obviously hadn't spent any time cogitating upon the conundrum that is Woman, sat halfway across the box. He watched her in the fixed way a dog watches at a table for a scrap to fall.

Exactly like a dog, he was not easily diverted. Goetz, whom protocol obliged to introduce James, tried several times before he succeeded in obtaining his highness's attention, and then the prince could barely conceal his impatience at the interruption. He did look at James, though, during the introduction, and let out a little sigh. James could guess what he saw: yet another rival.

But if his highness felt discouraged, it wasn't enough to make him leave. He forgot James as soon as the introductions were over and returned his adoring gaze to Mrs. Bonnard.

The women, James knew, were fully aware of his arrival. Though they did not turn their heads, he noted the subtle change in their posture, the coming-to-alertness that told him they were paying close attention to what went on behind them.

Ignoring his aide's whispered attempts to explain where Mr. Cordier fit in the English aristocracy, Lurenze addressed his lady love. "Madame, so crowded here it is. Perhaps you wish for some air."

"Thank you, sir," she said, throwing the briefest glance his way—and affecting not to notice James. "I don't find it stuffy at all."

"This is because you sit at the very edge," Lurenze said. "I observe this with great alarms. Count Goetz, you must explain to the lady of the danger, to make herself exposed. After what happens last night, it cannot be wise to appear where everyone can look."

"I want them to look," she said, turning a lazy smile upon the Russian beside her. "Let them see

I'm not afraid. Let them see that I will not hide or run away."

"I agree," James said. Suppressing a prickle of irritation—Did she smile at *every* male that way?—he made his way to the front of the box, Goetz in his wake. "For Mrs. Bonnard to hide herself would be a crime."

The two feminine heads turned his way in graceful unison.

"Mr. Cordier," Bonnard said coolly. "You have set aside your studies to visit us? How flattering."

"I have told him he must," said Count Goetz. "If not for him—"

"Let's not dwell on unpleasant subjects," James cut in. "Please be so good as to present me to the ladies."

"Yes, do, sir," said Bonnard. "Giulietta has been dying to meet my intrepid neighbor."

"Dying isn't strictly necessary," James said as he bowed over Giulietta's hand.

"He says that now," Mrs. Bonnard told her friend. "But you know what I had to do to get his attention."

Through this exchange, Count Goetz somehow managed to effect proper introductions.

"This is the man?" The officer, who turned out to be Count Vimstikov, rose. "Mr. Cordier, may I shake your hand? You have my gratitude. Indeed, I think I speak for everyone here—perhaps all of Venice—when I give you my heartfelt thanks."

Being an old hand, James had no trouble concealing his surprise. He'd been thanked before, yes, and often, usually in the form of money or valuables. Public thanks were altogether new to him.

True, he'd dutifully reported the crime not only to Goetz but to the British consul general, Mr. Hoppner. While James customarily worked behind the scenes, this was not the sort of episode—given the victim and its happening in front of a pair of gondoliers—one could keep secret in Venice. Besides, if it turned out to be an ordinary crime, unconnected with his assignment, the Austrian governor's men were best qualified to solve it.

Since everyone seemed to assume it was an ordinary if inexplicable crime, their thanking James was reasonable and normal.

He hoped they were right—that would simplify matters—but he doubted it. The crime didn't seem ordinary to him. Worse, it was completely unexpected. He'd received no hint that her life was in danger. He'd merely happened to be in the right place at the right time.

If he had not happened to be there . . .

But he shook off that thought as Lurenze at last remembered his manners and added his thanks to the general gratitude for the harlot's preservation.

"But these heroisms should not be necessary," his highness added. "For the woman alone to travel in the nighttime is always dangerous."

Count Goetz defended Venice's policing methods, concluding with, "This was a shocking aberration, your highness. I assure you that we are investigating." He approached the prince to explain exactly what was being done. The Russian consul joined them. National interests apparently led Count Vimstikov to graciously yield the place of honor to James, and join the others who surrounded the prince—and to his evident annoyance, blocked his view of his beloved.

James started to sit in the vacated chair but, "Not there," Mrs. Bonnard said, rising. "You had better take my chair and sit between us. Giulietta wants to feel your muscles."

Giulietta smiled sweetly up at him. "We argue that only men who work very hard have them. I must prove for myself."

"Well, if it's for *scientific* reasons," James said.

This set of chairs being drawn up close to the rail of the box, they had little space for maneuvering. He was aware of the swish of silk as Bonnard brushed against him. He caught her scent again, a gossamer-light lure inviting a man to discover its source. Her skin? Her hair? He had to concentrate hard to keep his head from inclining toward her neck. He focused on the pearls she wore, the size of quail eggs, and wondered how many men in the world, let alone in Venice, in this opera box, could afford her.

James hadn't much time to calculate the net worth of the males in the vicinity, because the *shush*ing started soon after he took his seat.

On stage, the evil mayor was about to ravish poor Ninetta.

This was one of the good parts.

Mr. Cordier was the only man in Francesca's opera box who was truly paying attention to the opera. The rest merely bided their time, keeping silent only because the Italians would kill them otherwise. Not until the proper moment—when the audience in loud bravas or bravos or hoots, catcalls, and fruit and vegetable missiles, gave its opinion of the proceedings—not until then might normal activity resume.

Her neighbor's attention remained on the stage well after everyone else's had left it, however. This gave Francesca far too much time with nothing to distract her from her pulsing awareness of the size of him and the scent of him and the sheer maleness of him, mere inches away.

He was, beyond question, the most masculine male there. She had no doubt the others knew it, too.

*Men are like wolves and dogs,* her mentor, Madame Noirot, had told her. *Some are leaders; some are followers. You will notice how one man arrives upon the scene and the others defer. Either that, or they fight for position. The man you want is the one who is most powerful, the one to whom the others defer.*

At the moment, Francesca was well aware that the most powerful male in the Fenice sat beside her.

Ignoring her.

She was not used to being ignored, and that was only the start of her vexations. Equally galling was his becoming completely engrossed in the opera, as she always wanted to do but must not, because to sit rapt through the whole performance was gauche.

He cared nothing for what was or wasn't gauche.

But he had all the advantages: He was (a) an aristocratic male, and they all did as they pleased, (b) a scholar, and they were allowed to be eccentric, and (c), most important, the man at the top of the male pecking order, who answered to nobody.

A younger son was not at the top for her, she told herself, even though his presence diminished every other man about him.

He was not at the top for her, despite his broad shoulders and rampant masculinity and wicked black curls begging her fingers to come and play.

He was not at the top for her, even if he had saved her life. He'd had his chance to enjoy her gratitude, and he'd declined. No man got a second chance with her.

She rose.

All the men rose as well—he, absently, still watching events unfolding onstage. She resisted the childish urge to swat him with her fan—or a chair—and made her way to Lurenze. At her approach, the other men gave way, and the prince's beautiful face lit up like the sun.

She gave him her most dazzling smile.

James found Giulietta amusing. In ordinary circumstances—for instance, had he been one of these other men—he would have preferred her uncomplicated good nature to the mysteries and moodiness of her friend.

But James was not yet permitted an ordinary life. When he had one, it would be in England. And when he chose someone cheerful and uncomplicated, he'd choose a fresh young maiden who'd brighten rather than add to the murk within him. She'd remind him that not all of life—or even most of life—was about deceit, treachery, greed, and unnatural deaths. She'd prove to him that not everyone spent his time navigating *un mare di merda*, as this mission was rapidly becoming.

He was still, as usual, trying not to drown in that sea. And so he couldn't simply turn his charm upon Giulietta and look forward to a cheerful romp between the sheets.

He was obliged to play cat and mouse with her provoking friend, who was now getting Lurenze's hopes up, not to mention other parts of his anatomy.

"You resist her but you want her," Giulietta whispered behind her fan.

"What man doesn't want her?" James said with a shrug. "I wonder how you can be friends with her."

"Most of the time we do not like the same kinds of men," she said. "For instance, for myself, I like Lurenze very much more than she does."

"He is deemed classically handsome, I believe," James said. *He reputedly has brains the size of a squirrel's, but he's the prettiest squirrel-brain in town.*

"He is so sweet, an unspoiled child," said Giulietta. "That is so rare."

"That won't last long," James said.

"I know," Giulietta said wistfully.

"I collect you deem it unethical to poach on your friend's preserve," he said. "Even though it's a vast preserve. I should think there were plenty of men to go around, and she wouldn't miss one or two or ten."

"She would not mind but he can see no one else," Giulietta said. "His life has been too wholesome, you see. And so he finds attractive the women who look dangerous, exotic. Alas, I am cursed with a face like a child."

"Not always a curse, surely," James said. "Some men find a wholesome countenance appealing." *I certainly do.*

"But not he," she said. "Stupid boy! He cannot guess what fun we could have, how much I can teach him. But she will break his heart. I know, sooner or later, someone must, and she at least would not be cruel—and yet I cannot help dreaming a little, of what might be."

"You weren't dreaming of killing off the competition, I trust," James said.

She looked at him, the doe eyes incredulous. "You mean Francesca? You think I would send those animals to kill my friend—because of a *man?*"

It was amazing how much scorn a woman could pack into the three-letter word *man.*

James laughed. "There's a setdown if ever I heard one. Men are so far beneath contempt that they're not worth killing."

"You must not misunderstand," she said. "Mine is not a gentle soul. I am Italian, through and through. If I learn who this was who tried to kill her, this one I would kill—man or woman. I would do it with a smile, too, upon my so sweet and innocent face. And even the Austrians would not convict me."

"Mrs. Bonnard has no idea, it seems," James said. "She insisted it wasn't her husband."

Giulietta shook her head. "I cannot believe it is he. They play a game—and to kill her is to admit he loses."

"A game?"

Giulietta looked away, fanning herself. "That is private, between them."

"But you know."

"If you wish to know, ask *her*," Giulietta said.

Francesca allowed herself a quick glance at the front of the box, where Mr. Cordier and Giulietta were engrossed in their tête-à-tête, their two dark heads bent together. She felt a sharp stab, too much like an emotion she hadn't experienced in years and which she'd believed herself immune to. What she felt was mere pique, she told herself, not jealousy. Giulietta was welcome to him.

Francesca turned back to the prince. "Perhaps, after all, I am a little foolish," she said.

"This is impossible," he said gallantly.

She rearranged her posture to offer him a better view of her breasts. "One doesn't wish to seem cowardly," she said. "I've always believed in facing whatever trouble came my way. Still, I've never been in quite this situation before. It's possible I'm not thinking logically. Perhaps there is a chance of trouble—a small one, I don't doubt, because the Austrians are notoriously efficient."

"Notorious, yes," Lurenze said in an undertone. "Always marching, so stiff. So many rules. Everything must be so. I tell them jokes. They never laugh. They are too much like my father."

"I am sure they will find these bad men very soon," she said. "Venice is so small. No one can keep secrets here. No one can hide for very long, and the Venetian Lagoon is well patrolled. Still, they haven't yet found the villains—or their bodies," she added, as her mind painted a vivid image of her attacker, his thick neck caught in Mr. Cordier's crushing grip. "Until that's settled, perhaps it would be wiser not to invite trouble. Perhaps I should not travel without a male escort—at least for the time being."

"Madame, we are in complete accord, in this, as in so much else. If you . . ." He trailed off, his smile fading as his gaze slid away from her face and traveled upward.

At the same moment she became aware of a large body behind hers, though she couldn't see it without turning her head, which she refused to do. She felt it, though, the awareness thrumming along her nerve endings.

"Mrs. Bonnard, a word, if you please." The deep voice behind her carried the unmistakable and unfakeable accents of the English privileged classes.

She turned her head a very little bit, offering only her profile, and said coolly, "Only a word, Mr. Cordier? What word can that be, I wonder?"

He bent and brought his mouth close to her ear. "*Andiamo*."

At the sound, so inexpressibly Italian, so intimate, tiny electric shocks danced over her skin.

She squelched the irrational thrill, reminding herself that there was nothing romantic or even intimate about a man telling a woman, *Let's go*.

She turned to stare him down, no easy task when the deep blue eyes—not in the least abashed or apologetic—stared right back, and she was placed in the undignified position of tilting her head back to look up.

"To put it in a nutshell," he said. Unhurriedly he straightened. He smiled a very little, as though at a private joke.

She looked away in time to see Lurenze's uneasy expression turn to obstinacy. He was a prince, after all, and as naïve as he was, surely he knew how to put an upstart in his place.

"The opera isn't over, Mr. Cordier," she said, refusing to adopt his confidential tones. They shared no secrets, would never do so. "I'm not ready to leave."

"Madame is not ready to leave," said Lurenze.

Cordier ignored him. "Use your head, madam," he said. "In the crush when everyone else leaves, any villain might easily accost you and escape in the confusion. You can always see the opera at another time, if you're wild to find out how it comes out. Or I can tell you."

She did not tell him that she knew how it came out, having seen it more times than she could count.

"I'm not a coward and I won't run away," she said. "I refuse to let my life be ruled by a lot of criminals."

"Madame does not wish to leave at this moment," Lurenze said. "When she so wishes, I shall escort her to any place of her choosing. Count Goetz will supply the soldiers to guard."

Cordier finally looked at him. The prince reddened under his gaze but showed no signs of backing down.

"You are exceedingly gracious to offer, your highness," Cordier said. "But even if it were not beneath your dignity to play guard dog, I know you would not wish to endanger her inadvertently."

Lurenze stiffened as though he'd been slapped. "Endanger? What is your meaning?"

"It is possible that the attack was the work of insurrectionists, revolutionaries," said Cordier. "As your excellency knows, such persons choose important targets, celebrated people. You are a prince, heir to the throne of Gilenia, whereas I am of no importance whatsoever."

"I will agree that Mr. Cordier is of no importance whatsoever," Francesca said. "Nonetheless—"

"Excellent," said Cordier. "I'm glad we're all in agreement."

She opened her mouth to retort, but his large, firm hand wrapped about her upper arm and exerted a light but inescapable pressure. She looked down at his hand, then up at him. In a properly ordered world, the look she gave him would have shriveled him to a husk that would burst into flame, leaving a tiny speck of ash behind.

He did not regard her at all. He was nodding at Lurenze and saying something in Russian to Vimstikov. All the while, the big hand continued to exert its inescapable pressure. To her fury, the light touch was sufficient to lift her from her chair and push her to the door.

"Cordier," she said between her teeth. "If you do not let go of me I will kick you where it hurts, and do it hard enough so that you won't soon forget it."

"Are you always this thick?" he muttered. "Isn't it obvious? I'm trying to help your little friend."

# Chapter 5

The sun set, and up rose the yellow moon:
    The devil's in the moon for mischief; they
Who call'd her CHASTE, methinks, began
        too soon
    Their nomenclature; there is not a day,
The longest, not the twenty-first of June,
    Sees half the business in a wicked way
On which three single hours of
        moonshine smile—
And then she looks so modest all the while.

Lord Byron
*Don Juan, Canto the First*

*T*he dirty truth was, James wasn't thinking clearly.

At one point he was listening to Giulietta, trying to learn what he could about her friend. But behind her, at the corner of his vision, sat the friend and Lurenze. James caught scarcely one word in ten of their conversation. He didn't need more to grasp the meaning. He was aware of Bonnard leaning toward the prince to give him an unobstructed view of her breasts. James heard clearly enough the change in her tone, how it became softer and more seductive.

Then he was murmuring polite excuses to Giulietta, and rising from his seat and walking toward the pair: the dark head, glimmering with pearls, bent so close to the fair one, as though they were sharing secrets.

He saw Bonnard applying her siren's arts to the young prince and her victim practically wriggling with delight, like a puppy having his belly scratched.

James found himself one furious heartbeat away from lifting her out of her chair and carrying her bodily from the opera box.

Luckily, lying was second nature to him, costing him nothing. A conscience was something he'd owned at one time, but it was a very long time ago, and he couldn't remember much about it.

The lie had worked, and that was what mattered. Though he could feel her anger pulsing in the air between them, she did not threaten him or argue as they left the opera box. When she encountered acquaintances on the way downstairs, she appeared completely at ease, chatted briefly, and left them smoothly.

Like so many of her ilk, she was an excellent actress. She might be longing to plunge a dagger into his black heart but she made a good show of going with him peaceably out of the theater.

When they stepped out into the night, James was relieved though not altogether surprised to find her boat in readiness. Her gondoliers were reliable men, Zeggio had confirmed. Their ancestors had served Venice's great families for generations, protecting them from treachery both political and personal. Thus, when James said quietly, "Don't take the usual way," Uliva didn't seek confirmation from his employer but simply nodded.

Soon they were making their way along the Rio delle Veste past the crowd of vessels converging at the Fenice's rear door.

Mrs. Bonnard settled into her seat in the posture he remembered from the time he'd played Don Carlo. She leant her elbow on the edge of the open window, rested her cheek on her knuckles, and looked out at the passing scene.

She was shutting him out, as she'd done then.

He wished he could shut her out. He'd closed the door unthinkingly. The space inside the cabin had shrunk and, even with the windows open, felt too small, too close.

Though the gondola glided smoothly through the water, now and again a movement brought her hip against his, her shoulder against his upper arm. The skirt of her silken gown slid against his trousers. The breeze gently entering through the casements traveled toward rather than away from him, carrying her light scent to his nostrils.

He needed a distraction. An argument would do admirably. But he refused to be the one to break the silence. He stared hard at the pearl and diamond bracelets hanging upon her gloved wrists and tried to occupy his mind by calculating their worth.

Finally, when they were clear of the theatergoers' boats, she said in a bored voice, "So, you were helping Giulietta. How gallant of you."

"I thought you needed only a hint," he said. "It was hard to believe you meant to keep the boy prince to yourself, since you don't really want him."

"It's unwise to let men believe one wants them," she said. "They only presume."

The scornful glance she threw him was as easy to read as a tavern sign.

He told himself to ignore it. He couldn't. "You mean me. I'm presumptuous, you've decided."

"You seem to be under the misapprehension that I've been languishing for your company," she said. "Let me quiet your anxieties. Last night my mind was disordered by shock and my reason overcome by gratitude. Such is not the case tonight. You lost your one and only opportunity with me."

"That is not why I removed you from the theater," he said.

"It wasn't because of Giulietta," she said. "That was a thin excuse if ever I heard one—as thin as the one you gave Lurenze."

He'd no reason to feel embarrassed, James told himself. He lived on thin excuses.

But as easily as he might find it to lie to everyone else, he was unable to lie to himself. He couldn't pretend he didn't recognize the real reason he'd dragged her away. That she recognized it, too, made the heat race up his neck. He felt like a fool. No, it was worse than that: He, a professional, had let himself turn into the impetuous boy he'd been a lifetime ago.

Meanwhile she remained unmoved, her silken cheek still upon her hand, her green gaze shifting lazily from the scene outside to him.

"And you were toying with Lurenze in hopes of making me do exactly what I did," he said.

To his surprise, she smiled. "It worked, did it not? Men are so easy. They're so competitive."

James made himself smile, too. "So true. We'll fight over anything, even if we don't really want it."

"If you're trying to crush my vanity, you must do better than that," she said. "Pray recollect that I am a divorcée, Cordier. I've been insulted and slandered by experts."

He felt a sharp inner twinge. It couldn't be his conscience, since he'd left his in France ten years ago. It was . . . irritation. "Pray recollect that I'm not a coddled royal of one and twenty, Mrs. Bonnard, but a man of one and thirty who's seen something of the world. You are not the first woman who's tried to drive me to distraction."

"I haven't begun to try," she said. "When I do—if I do—you'll know it."

"You tried your damnedest last night."

Her sleek eyebrows went up. "You think that was an effort?"

"I know a lure when I see one."

"All I offered was a mild yes," she said. "Very mild. Only the first notch above a no. Were I to make an effort—and no great one, either—you'd never withstand it."

James recalled the siren laughter. He felt a prickle of uneasiness but he shook it off. "You have a high opinion of yourself. But the king's ransom in pearls you're wearing is not proof that you are irresistible, only that some men are weaker than others."

Some man had been weak, indeed. He shifted

his gaze from her haughty countenance to the top and drop pearl earrings, then down to the two pearl necklaces circling her throat. From the upper, shorter one dangled pear-shaped drops of graduated size, the largest at the center. It pointed to the space between her breasts, whose rapid rise and fall told him she was not so indifferent as she pretended. The low-cut gown, of silk the color of sea foam, reminded one of the pearls' watery origins. The pearl and diamond bracelets at her slim wrists glimmered against the butter-soft gloves.

The jewels alone constituted a cruelly arousing sight for a man who was a thief at heart. It was maddening that he couldn't simply steal them and have done with her.

"You don't think I could bring you to your knees," came her voice, cool and taunting. "Would you care to make a wager?"

His attention snapped back to her face.

The tension in the *felze* increased by a factor of ten.

"I don't wager with women," he said. "It's unsporting."

"Men so often say that when the truth is, they can't bear the mortification of losing to a woman."

"I don't lose," he said.

"You will," she said. "Let me see. What shall it be?" She closed her eyes briefly, thinking. When she opened them, they glinted. "I know. There's a peridot parure at Faranzi's shop that took my fancy."

"Merely peridots? You don't rate your powers very high."

"I'm rating your income," she said. "You'll find these peridots painfully expensive. You'll have to borrow to pay for them. But they aren't beyond the borrowing abilities of one of Lord Westwood's younger sons."

"I see. You wish it to be not merely a costly wager, but a painful and humiliating one."

She nodded. "Well?"

"And if you lose?"

"I won't," she said. "But if it soothes your masculine pride to imagine you'll win, then by all means choose a forfeit."

*The letters,* James thought. *The reason I'm obliged to tangle with you. All I want is the damn letters, curse you.* But even if that had been completely true, if the letters were all he wanted, it was the one forfeit he couldn't ask for.

"The peridots," he said.

That did surprise her. She took her hand away from her cheek and tipped her head to one side, studying him.

"They'll be a gift to my betrothed," he said.

She blinked. "You're betrothed?"

It was an easy lie, too easy. He was far too angry to utter it. "Not yet," he said. "But before too long. It will be a fine symbol for my bride-to-be. It will signify my ability to defend my principles and honor in the face of all-but-irresistible temptation."

Her exotic eyes narrowed. "There'll be no *all-but* about it."

"We'll see," he said. "Name your time and place."

She glanced out of the window. "Now," she said. "We've plenty of time before we reach my house. This shouldn't take so long, at any rate."

Her confidence—hell, her insolence—was beyond

anything. It was infuriating. Knowing he was in a temper, he should have held his tongue. He should have given himself time to cool down and think. But he was too angry—with her, with himself.

"Do your worst," he said.

Francesca couldn't remember when last she'd been so furious.

She'd made a fool of herself last night, and now he presumed she was his for the taking—if and when he felt like it.

To him, she was merely a whore.

*You are,* a rational voice within reminded her. *You chose to be.*

True enough. Nonetheless, the pearls he called a sign of men's weakness were in fact a sign of respect, a sign of her power.

Since she'd left England—that frigid island of provincials, Puritans, and hypocrites—no man had shown her disrespect . . . except this one.

An Englishman, naturally. Half an Englishman, to be precise, but half was more than enough.

He needed desperately to be taught a lesson.

Unhurriedly she slid shut the casement beside her and closed the blinds. She reached across him, letting her bosom brush against his chest, and closed the window and blinds on his side.

As she moved back to her place, she felt his chest rise and fall a little faster than it had done a moment earlier.

She folded her hands in her lap. "There," she said. "No one can see."

"There won't be anything to see," he said.

"We'll see," she said.

She looked down at her hands. She looked at them for a while, making him wait.

Since he sat to her right, she started with her left glove. She slid it down toward her wrist until it bunched against her bracelets. She tugged on the thumb, the index finger, and so on, each finger by turn. She did it in a leisurely way, as though her mind were elsewhere. Then she drew off the glove, pulling it gently through the bracelets.

She dropped the glove into her lap.

She didn't look at him. She didn't have to. She knew he was riveted on her hands. She knew he was breathing faster and harder and trying not to.

She went to work on the other glove, again, slowly, casually, in the way she might if she were alone in her boudoir. Undressing.

She let the second glove drop onto her lap.

She adjusted the bracelets, letting her fingers trail lightly over the pearls and diamonds circling her now-naked wrists.

She lifted her hand.

He tensed.

She didn't touch him.

She touched herself, bringing her index finger to her right ear. She made a light path along the curve of her ear and behind it, lingering at the place below her ear where she liked to be kissed.

She felt him shift in his seat.

She ignored it. She pretended she was alone, enjoying her treasures, herself.

She drew her finger down over the earrings, caressing the round top and the pear-shaped drop, savoring the feel of these, the most sensuous of gemstones.

She let her hand glide down over the upper necklace, and enjoyed the feel of the large pearls under her fingers. Back and forth, back and forth she went, then down, to fondle the immense pear-shaped pearl at the center.

And down further still she went, to play with the other necklace. And down again. This time she slid her hand over the silk of her bodice, making the fabric whisper. Then lightly she cupped her breast.

He made a sound, deep in his throat.

She didn't look at him. She watched her hand as she might have done had she been alone . . . touching herself.

She drew her thumb along the edge of her bodice, slowly, back and forth, tracing the swell of her bosom.

Then she lightly pushed the edge of the bodice down, baring another inch of skin.

His breath came out in an abrupt *whoosh*.

"*Diavolo!*" he growled.

His arm wrapped about her waist. He pulled her onto his lap. He grasped the back of her head and brought her face close to his.

It happened so fast, faster than she'd expected. She wasn't ready. She wasn't done yet.

"I'm not done y—"

His mouth silenced her. It was warm and stubborn and very, very angry.

She brought her hands up to his chest and pushed. *I'm not done yet.*

"I'm n—"

But she forgot the rest, because his mouth was so warm and sure and . . .

And then her hands went limp, her mind clouded, and everything turned hot and confused, and she was swimming in awareness.

She could smell him. Man smell. The tang of shaving soap and starch and freshly laundered linen. The damp Venetian air clinging to the wool of his coat. All of it mixed with the scent of his skin.

She could feel him: the big, warm, powerful body under the civilized trappings. She could feel the tension in his powerful thighs. She was aware of the heat beneath her, of his arousal.

Something kicked, low in her belly, and heat uncoiled there, serpentlike.

Her hands slid up, to grasp his shoulders, then up again to find the thick black curls, where they tangled. She held him thus, as he held her, and kissed him back, as stubborn and angry as he.

Stubborn and angry and hot and wanting.

His tongue pushed for entry and she gave way, and the taste of him was dark and wicked and exactly what she wanted. He tasted like every sin she'd ever been warned against and committed, every rule she'd learned and broken.

She was distantly aware of sound, a drumming, but there was drumming within, and she didn't know, didn't care, which was which.

She cared about his hands, the long fingers moving down her neck, sliding over the pearls, and over her skin and down to the place where she'd silently invited him a moment ago. He pushed the bodice down and cupped her breast. He broke the kiss and bent his head. She arched back, to give him room. He kissed her once, long and hard, upon the breast he'd bared, then again, long and hard upon the other.

Then he lifted his head and looked at her, his blue-black eyes glittering in the lamplight.

"You're a very bad girl," he said hoarsely.

He lifted her up and dropped her back into her seat. Not gently.

Hot need bubbled into rage. She almost bounced up from the seat and wrapped her hands around his throat . . .

A modicum of sense remained, though, pointing out that he was too big for her, and the attempt would only make her look more ridiculous than she felt already.

She became aware once more of the drumming. Her heart was pounding with balked lust, with fury, but that wasn't what she heard.

It was rain, beating on the cabin roof.

He opened the blinds and peered out.

"Home," he said, his voice thick. "You lose, *cara*."

Home? Already?

She yanked open the blinds.

Her house.

She blinked in disbelief.

She looked at him, but he was still gazing out of the window.

"*Maledizione*," he said.

She leaned forward to see.

A large, ostentatious gondola waited at the open water gate, lamps ablaze, as were all the lamps in the *andron*.

She could see, within, Prince Lurenze standing near the gates. With him stood Count Goetz.

Cordier turned to her and started to pull up her bodice. She slapped his hands away and quickly covered herself.

She smoothed her skirts and her expression. When the gondola stopped, she was ready. She let Cordier hand her out of the vessel but she pretended she had eyes only for Lurenze. She gave the prince her warmest, most intimate smile and addressed him as though only he mattered, as though the others didn't exist.

"What an agreeable surprise," she said. "Or ought I not to be surprised? Had I scheduled a *conversazione* and forgotten it in all the recent excitement?"

"No, madame, not at all," said Goetz. "We are here because we did not wish to lose a minute in informing you."

His highness only nodded. No doubt he was gathering his wits, which her smile must have scattered.

"A moment after you left with Mr. Cordier, I received a message," the governor went on. "A man was captured on his way to the mainland in a stolen gondola. We have reason to believe this may be one of the men who attacked you. Mr. Cordier, we have him in custody. I must ask you to come to identify him, to spare the lady this distressing task."

"All is well," Lurenze told her. "You must have no fear, madame. I remain to protect you—like the guard dog." He shot a defiant look at Cordier.

The defiance couldn't quite mask the prince's uncertainty. He had reason to be unsure, she knew.

She'd rejected all of his previous efforts to protect her.

She moved to him. "You are exceedingly kind, your highness. Thank you. I shall be very glad of your company."

His grey eyes lit. The corners of his beautiful mouth turned up, transforming his expression to pure, unmasked, unashamed happiness.

How could she help smiling up into that face, at so much sweetness?

She glanced at the governor, making it seem that she could scarcely tear her gaze away from Lurenze. "Until next we meet, Count Goetz," she said. He bowed.

She turned away and took Lurenze's arm. "*Addio*, Mr. Cordier." She tossed the dismissal over her shoulder and went on to the stairs with Lurenze. She didn't look back.

*Later, at the Doge's Palace*

James fervently hoped the Austrians had the right man in custody because he needed, very badly, to hurt somebody.

He'd come within a gnat's testicles of losing his wits entirely and taking Bonnard then and there, in the gondola.

You'd think he was a schoolboy with his first tart.

It was the great pearl, tapping against his head as he was losing himself in the silken smoothness and warm fragrance of her breasts. If that light tap hadn't recalled him to the moment, made him remember where he was, who she was, what he was about . . .

His face burned, recalling.

*Imbecille!* he berated himself. *Idiota!*

A fine way to play hard to get.

She would have had him, proved her point, and tossed him aside. She had much larger fish in her nets.

Peridots, indeed. Mere baubles to her, though the set she had in mind would no doubt send the typical younger son deep into the nets of the moneylenders, from which he might never disentangle himself.

Still, he had managed to save himself. He had won, and she was furious. Had Goetz not turned up, with the goggle-eyed boy, James might have provoked her to extend the wager.

*I'll give you another chance,* he could have said. Then she might have invited him into the house, and—if he were clever and careful—into her confidence.

But no. Instead, he must spend hours in officialdom, trying to extract information from a ruffian while concealing from the Austrian governor his true purpose.

Such were James's thoughts as he and Count Goetz made their way through the Ducal Palace. En route here, they'd discussed how they would deal with the suspect, and James had succeeded in making Goetz believe the resulting plan was Goetz's. Now, having traversed a dark, narrow passage from the great council chamber, they stood in the State Inquisitor's room.

It was not a happy room. Even one whose nature

was not fanciful would sense its dark history, as though the souls of all who'd suffered here haunted it.

Fear was an old but reliable tactic, as the Austrians clearly understood. To strike terror into their prisoner's heart, they'd lodged him in the *pozzi*, the "wells." The narrow, dark, dank cells had once held great crowds of those who'd run afoul of the Venetian Republic. Nowadays, it was a lonely place.

While James and Goetz waited for the man to be unearthed from the prison depths, the governor showed James about this part of the Ducal Palace.

At last the prisoner entered, with guards fore and aft—an unnecessary precaution, given the heavy chains about his ankles.

James stood in the shadows, as he and Goetz had agreed. The prisoner took note mainly of the governor, disregarding James as merely a minion. The interview proceeded in Italian.

It did not proceed very far. For one, the southern dialect the suspect spoke was nigh impenetrable to the governor and difficult even for James. For another, the fellow—who gave his name as Piero Salerno—claimed to know nothing about any lady. He had fallen off a fishing boat, he said. He wasn't trying to steal the gondola. He'd only climbed into it because he was tired of swimming.

That was his story. It made no sense whatsoever and he couldn't be made to budge from it.

Goetz sighed and turned to James. "Sir, do you know this man?"

The prisoner started, apparently having forgotten anybody else was there. Now he craned his neck forward and squinted into the shadows where James stood.

Though parts of the chamber were dark, as James had advised, the place to which they'd led the prisoner was well lit. Even in poorer light, James would have known the man. He'd seen this face only briefly, but it was his business to notice and remember details.

"This is the one," he said.

He stepped out of the shadows.

Piero shrank and took a hasty step backward. One of the guards prodded him back into place with his bayonet.

"What a pity," James said. "I was hoping for the other one. All this one did was row the boat."

"He is an accessory," said Goetz. "The penalty is the same."

"But if he cooperates?" James said. "Perhaps if I spoke to him alone, he would be more confiding."

Piero's eyes widened. "No!" he cried.

He had not gone far last night, then. Judging by his reaction, he'd seen what James had done to his large friend.

James smiled at him.

Goetz signaled to the guards. The three of them exited the room, leaving James alone with the prisoner.

Speaking in the plainest and simplest Italian he knew, James said, "This has not been a happy night for me, Piero. I had to leave the opera before it was over—I must abandon *Rossini*, of all things! One woman complains to me about her man problems until my ears ache and the other woman is breaking my balls. I didn't want to come here in the first place. I have better things to do. Lying little mounds of filth like you are sucking from me time I shall never get back. I am not in a good mood and I want to hurt someone. You're not my first choice, but you'll do, you ugly little pile of shit."

He advanced. Piero tried to back away, but he stumbled on the manacles and fell.

James grabbed one arm and hoisted him up, pulling hard enough to make the prisoner shriek. "I can pull harder than that," James said. "I can pull it right out of the socket. Shall I demonstrate?"

Piero began to scream. "Help! Help! He will kill me!"

He tried to run to the door, but stumbled again. When James reached down to pull him up, the man tried to scramble away on his backside.

"None of them care if you scream, you reeking pustulence," James said. "No one cares if I kill you. It will save the government the cost of a trial and execution. But I'll give you a kind warning: After the troublesome women, this noise you make is not improving my humor."

Once again he jerked the man to his feet. This time James held onto his arm, squeezing hard. Piero whimpered.

"The way to improve my humor," James said, "is to tell me who you are, who your friend is—or was—and why you attacked the lady. I shall give you to the count of three to begin putting me in a better frame of mind. One. Two."

"We do it," the man said. "We attack the whore."

James squeezed harder.

Tears started from Piero's eyes. "The one you throw in the water is Bruno. I hide and wait for him but he never comes. Then I think you have killed him. And so I steal the gondola and try to go back."

"Never mind that," James said. "Why did you come here in the first place?"

"To steal. This is what we do, Bruno and me. We have some trouble in Verona, and so we go to Mira. The whore was there, for the summer holiday. Everyone talks of the jewels she has. But then, she moves from the villa there back to Venice. And so we come to Venice, because it is easier to follow her here than in the little village, where everyone watches everything. We come to Venice, and then we wait for the right time."

Once he'd begun talking, he babbled on and on. But most of the rest he had to say was irrelevant

All the way to Venice, simply to steal? That made no sense to James. Crime was far easier elsewhere in Italy—in the Papal States, for instance, where corruption was rife. Or farther south, in the Kingdom of the Two Sicilies. But to come here, where the Austrians ruled? It made no sense.

Still, Piero would not budge from his story. It was theft, mere theft, he insisted. Bruno had only decided to make some fun with a little rape. He'd choked the English woman to keep her from screaming, Piero claimed. "She's a whore. This is what they like, as everyone—"

James flung Piero away from him so violently that the man tripped and fell.

This time James left him where he was.

If he touched the swine again, he'd kill him.

# Chapter 6

And even the wisest, do the best they can,
   Have moments, hours, and days, so unprepared,
That you might 'brain them with their
    lady's fan;'
   And sometimes ladies hit exceeding hard,
And fans turn into falchions in fair hands,
And why and wherefore no one understands.

                   Lord Byron
          *Don Juan, Canto the First*

*J*ames wasn't as easily finished with the business as he was with Piero. The governor kept him at the Ducal Palace past dawn, dotting every *i* and crossing every *t*.

James would have returned to Bonnard's place even at that indecent hour, but he was too conscious of the combined stench of Piero's unwashed body and whatever noxious fumes the swine had acquired from the prison, all of which clung to James's clothes.

He went back to the Ca' Munetti instead. His

servants being up and about by this time, he had not long to wait for a bath. After this, he gave Zeggio and Sedgewick a brief summary of his interview with Piero.

Then James went to bed, telling himself that once his head was clear, he'd find a way through the present difficulty.

He slept for only a short time, because of a dream. It started out splendidly, with Bonnard naked and hurtling herself at him, wrapping her arms about his neck and pressing her luscious body against his. Then Lurenze appeared, and she pushed James away and threw herself at the prince instead.

James woke abruptly, aware he wasn't alone.

He hauled himself up to a sitting position. Sedgewick and Zeggio stood in the doorway, wearing matching worried expressions.

"What?" James said. "What?"

"You was yelling, sir," said Sedgewick apologetically. "Which you never does, as I was telling Mr. Zeggio here. But it was in Italian, and I couldn't make it out."

"I tell him, all you say is, 'Come back here, you she-devil,'" said Zeggio. "I tell him this is no cause for alarm. It is a dream, nothing more."

"But you was at them posies last night, sir, and—"

"*Pozzi,*" Zeggio corrected. "The prisons, very deep in the ground, like wells."

"It give you the heebie-jeebies is what I reckoned, sir. On account of that time you was in Paris in that hellhole—the one where them filthy frogs tortured you. Which is why I said we oughter wake you up. But you woke up on your own."

James had spent nearly a year recovering from the French interrogation. It was a long time ago: ten years. Pain was easy to forget but every other grim detail remained etched in his memory.

He wasn't the only one who'd been betrayed, but he was one of the lucky ones. Two of his associates had been tortured to death. His scars—the visible ones—had faded. His nails had grown back. And he'd gone back to work, determined to settle scores. But he'd been so much younger then. Now, it would take him years to recover—if he did recover, which was by no means certain. Now he understood, too, that the trail of betrayal was not simply tangled but endless.

*I'm getting too old for this,* he thought.

"Find me something to wear," he told Sedgewick. "And get my shaving things."

He shaved and dressed quickly, as always. Lingering over his toilette was not in his style.

He was halfway through his breakfast when Zeggio, who'd been sent to ready the gondola, reappeared with a small parcel.

"A maid brings it," he said. "From Signora Bonnard, she says."

James stared at the elegantly wrapped parcel.

He set down his coffee, took it, and unwrapped it.

He recognized the shape of the box.

Grimly he opened it.

He didn't need to look up to be aware of Sedgewick and Zeggio, who'd crept closer. They looked down at the contents, then at his face.

He did not throw the elegant box across the room. Peridots were not pearls, diamonds, or emeralds, true. On the other hand, good specimens did not come cheap. Royalty wore peridots, he knew, and this set, the well-cut stones bordered with brilliants, was worthy of a queen. He simply sat, staring at it, seething, though he had no reason—no sane reason—to be angry.

This was a taunt, nothing more. The wager didn't signify to her. The price of the peridots was laughable. That was the message he read in it. He'd been merely a diversion to her, a game to while away the journey—at the end of which she had more important prey.

When he could control his voice, he said, "A little wager, that's all. Mrs. Bonnard certainly pays promptly. She must have had her servant waiting at the shop door for it to open."

"Very fine articles, those are, sir," said Sedgewick.

"Indeed they are," James said. "Most sporting of her. I must thank her. Personally. Zeggio, I thought you were readying the gondola."

Though he spoke calmly and quietly there was something in his tone that made Zeggio hurry from the room.

The something made Sedgewick's brow furrow. "Sir," he began.

James held up his hand. "I'll deal with this," he said.

"Yes, sir," Sedgewick said.

"At least I've learned one thing," James said.

"Yes, sir. It were a robbery, nothing to do with—"

"I now understand why Elphick divorced her," James said. "What I don't understand is why he didn't strangle her."

*Palazzo Neroni, a short time later*

Francesca was naked.

Or so, at least, would respectable persons describe her—for there was, they would scold, far too much of her on view.

Not only had she failed to don a proper morning gown but she wasn't even wearing decent nightclothes.

Instead of the frumpy cotton nightdress virtuous women wore to bed, she'd donned a shift of exquisite pale yellow silk. Pink silk ribbons tied the deep neckline closed. A pink silk ribbon drawstring tied under her breasts. Over the nightdress she wore a silk dressing gown of a paler shade, closer to the color of cream. In contrast to the simple shift, this was trimmed with miles of ruffles and lace and shimmering embroidery dotted with seed pearls.

As she entered the Putti Inferno, she regretted not having ordered breakfast served in the intimacy of the room adjoining her boudoir.

Well, too late. She must shock the plaster and painted children.

Ignoring them and the pudgy little fingers pointing at the great whore in the room, she directed her gaze to Lurenze, who'd risen, his face lighting up, at the sound of her footsteps. Then his eyes opened very wide, and his mouth fell open. He put his hand to his heart. He murmured something in his own language.

"Good morning," she said, with a small, intimate smile.

Arnaldo was there to pull out her chair, luckily, for his highness was temporarily *non compos mentis*.

After a moment's delay and more murmuring to himself, he strung some English together. "You look like—like a—a froth," he said. "Never have I seen anything so beautiful. In my country, the women do not dress so—so—so showing of their beauties."

"They don't do it in my country, either," she said.

"I am glad we are not in your country or in my country," he said.

Francesca became aware of distant sounds, coming from the *portego*. Arnaldo poured her coffee and went out.

She sipped her coffee. She nibbled on a pastry, then put it down because her hands were shaking.

Her heart was beating hard but she went on bestowing sleepy smiles upon Lurenze while she dropped a few innuendoes that went over his golden head.

Arnaldo returned. "Signor Cordier has arrived, signora," he said. "Do you wish I tell him to come another time?" The servant did not so much as glance at Lurenze when he said this.

"No, send him up," she said. She did not add, *I've been expecting him.*

Arnaldo went out.

"I'll wager . . ." She began. Then she paused, her smile widening. She couldn't help it. She'd lost the wager, but Cordier would learn what sort of game-ster he played with. "I daresay," she continued, "Mr. Cordier has come to tell us what transpired last night with the man who was captured."

"I wondered when word would come," said Lurenze. "So long it takes. Almost I am thinking it is time to send a servant to him for the explanation."

"Legal matters always take a ridiculous amount of time," she said. "Rules and regulations. Papers to sign."

"So true it is," said Lurenze. "Sometimes, the signing of the papers makes me like a wild man. So many rules. Then all the protocols, to talk to this one, that one. To listen while this one complains and another one wishes to make me do this or that. But when I rule Gilenia, only worse it becomes. I must study madame, who is so patient and gracious."

"You bring out the best in me," she said.

He flushed with pleasure.

How easy it was to please him!

She reached across the little table and laid her hand over his. "You are so good," she said. "I don't know how you came to be that way, but please don't change."

"Good?" he said with a laugh. "But I did not come to Venice to be good."

"You came to be naughty," she said. "I quite understand. But one might be naughty and still"—she stroked his hand—"keep goodness in one's heart."

Arnaldo came in. "Signor Cordier," he said.

Close behind, like a great, ominous shadow, loomed Lord Westwood's troublesome son. He strode in, carrying the parcel she'd sent.

A dangerous glitter came into his blue eyes as his gaze went from her to Lurenze's flushed and happy face, then to her hand, resting on the prince's.

*She's a professional*, James reminded himself while he said the polite thing and she said the polite thing and the ecstatic Lurenze was all princely cordiality.

*You're a professional, Jemmy*, he told himself. *Act like one.*

And so the question naturally arose, What would be the most professional way to kill Lurenze?

Slowly Bonnard withdrew her hand from the prince's. "We've only started breakfast, Mr. Cordier. Won't you join us?"

It must be noon at least, probably past it. James had not bothered to consult a clock before he left his house, but the sun told him it was midday. He told himself not to imagine what they'd been doing since he left them . . . not to imagine how they'd spent the night . . . not to picture the pair of them, tangled among the bedclothes, lazing in bed as the morning sun poured through the windows.

It was hard not to imagine, given the fluffy lot of nothing she was wearing.

Arnaldo brought a chair to the small, intimate table . . . set for two. He set another place.

James sat.

Bonnard gave Lurenze a sultry smile. The prince smiled back at her, thoroughly pleased with himself.

And why shouldn't he be? Last night, James had done all the hard work of getting her heated up. All his highness had to do was finish the job.

James became aware of his fingers tightly clutching the parcel in his hand. He laid it on the table.

Lurenze stared at it. "You bring a gift for madame, I see."

"Not exactly," James said.

"What's wrong, Mr. Cordier?" she said. "Is it not what you asked for: the perfect gift for your betrothed?"

"You are betrothed?" Lurenze said. "I congratulate you!"

"I am not betrothed," James said.

"Not yet," said Bonnard. "But he wishes to be prepared."

Lurenze nodded. "For me, all is prepared. Soon I shall be betrothed. The girl is not yet decided. One of my cousins, perhaps. Or else a girl of a great family of Italy or Russia or Hungary or one of those places. Half the world they want the alliance with my country, but the Russians plague me most. I wish they would leave me in peace but it cannot be. Alas, the man of my position cannot marry where is his heart."

He gazed soulfully at Bonnard.

She gazed soulfully back at him.

*Excuse me while I vomit*, James thought. He rose.

"Well, then, good-bye," he said.

The Cleopatra eyes widened.

Ah, she wasn't prepared for that. She thought she could torment him for as long as she liked.

*Sorry, cara. I've been tortured by experts.*

"But you haven't touched your breakfast," she said.

"But what of the man who is captured?" said Lurenze. "Did you not come to report of this, to put madame's mind at the ease, I hope?"

Damnation. James had forgotten about Piero. He'd forgotten everything he was supposed to remember.

It all went out of his head at the sight of Lurenze's classically handsome, beaming countenance . . . those guileless grey eyes, which had scarcely seen the world, let alone beheld any of its treacheries and horrors . . . his pure happiness at having the woman he wanted . . . his pleasure, untouched by doubt or painful experiences, by betrayals . . .

And she, stroking his hand, encouraging his delusions . . .

*No excuses, Jemmy. You're letting your cock do your thinking for you.*

"I didn't want to spoil your breakfast with unpleasant subjects," he said.

"On the contrary," she said. "My appetite is bound to improve, if any progress has been made in this matter."

She gestured for him to sit down.

James remained standing. He would not stay a minute longer than necessary. He needed to get away and repair his brain.

"The man in custody is the one who rowed the boat," he said. "He confessed. They were after your jewelry. But the other one, apparently, thought it would be fun to rape you as well. His accomplice claims he was not trying to strangle you, only to keep you quiet."

Her hand went to her throat, involuntarily, he could tell. It was as instinctive a reaction as the color washing out of her face.

James's reaction was instinctive, too. He caught her as she began to slump. He lifted her from the chair and carried her to the sofa.

Lurenze, startled, took a moment to react. But before he could shout for servants, James said, "Excellency, pray dip a napkin in water."

The prince quickly did as he was told and hurried to the sofa, where James sat, his hip against hers. He took the wet cloth and dabbed her forehead, her temples, her cheeks.

Her eyes fluttered open. She stared at him. In the noontime light, he could make out the flecks of gold in her green eyes.

"Good grief," she said. "Did I faint?"

"Perhaps, madame, this was too much excitement for you, so soon after rising from the bed," Lurenze said. "I am so stupid. Why do I not think wisely, to tell Mr. Cordier to wait until you have something to eat? All you have is one small piece of pastry, and only two bites from this do you take."

"Perhaps you're right," she said. "But how embarrassing! I've never fainted before."

"*Mi dispiace*," James said. "I do apologize."

*Imbecille*, he rebuked himself. *Idiota*.

He had no conscience, true. The trouble was, he'd let his emotions rule his brain, on about a dozen counts.

He'd been callous, deliberately so.

He'd been there. He'd seen what she'd endured, how shocked and frightened she was. Now, in the bright light of day, he could see the faint marks on her neck.

The trouble was, he could see Lurenze, too, almost visibly floating on his cloud of post-coital bliss.

"But this is good news, yes?" Lurenze said. "One man is found. He is in the prison. The other one, too, they will find soon, unless he is dead and the sea has carried him away. You must be comforted, madame. No one will allow you to come to harm. I keep the guard in the night, and here is Mr. Cordier to take my place."

James blinked and looked up at him. "Take your place?"

"But here are you, and what is it more important for you to do?" said his highness. "Me, I would not leave madame alone, but my life is not mine to live as I wish. I must give the audience to these Russians who plague me. I do not mind to keep them to wait some hours, but I must appear to them before the time of dinner, when I have the engagement, also impossible to avoid. The Bavarians make a great dinner in my honor, where I must show myself. I must have clothes fresh and my face to be shaved." He rubbed his jaw. "Madame is so patient. She makes no grievance. But the pricks of the beard are not agreeable to the ladies, I know."

A short while later—after he'd reminded James several times to make sure madame ate properly— his highness departed.

By this time, madame had fully recovered. She left the sofa and walked with Lurenze as far as the door to the *portego*, where she gave him a kiss on the cheek. He reddened with pleasure. Then he took her hand and kissed it, not like a boy but like a royal and a man of the world.

Then, finally, he was gone.

She did not return to the breakfast table but sauntered past James to the window.

The noonday light made the seed pearls shimmer. The light also rendered her garments—such as they were—nearly transparent.

Though the dressing gown glimmered in the light, and the ruffles danced with the slightest movement, he could clearly discern the shape of her breasts. His hands cupped involuntarily, recalling the way they fit his hands, their smoothness, their firmness. He had no trouble remembering the warm scent of her skin. If he'd been a dog, his nose would have quivered. As it was his brain was closing the thinking door and preparing to hang the "Closed" sign on it.

He tried to look away but his gaze helplessly slid lower. He could discern the outline of her hips, her long legs.

"What are the chances of their finding the other one?" she said.

"The other one?"

James dragged his attention upward, to her profile. She was looking out of the window.

"The other criminal," she said.

"Bonnard, put some clothes on," he said.

"No," she said.

"You're doing this on purpose," he said.

"Yes," she said.

"To punish me," he said.

"Yes."

"You knew I'd come."

"Yes."

"That's why you sent the peridots."

"Yes."

"And you bedded him for spite."

She turned her head then, and looked at him. "Oh, no," she said. "I never bed anyone for spite. I'm a businesswoman."

"He doesn't know that! He's over head and ears in love with you!"

"Ah, yes. First love. There's nothing quite like it. What does Byron say? 'But sweeter still than this, than these, than all,/Is first and passionate love—it stands alone,/Like Adam's recollection of his fall;/The tree of knowledge has been pluck'd—all's known—'"

"'And life yields nothing further to recall,'" he continued, "'Worthy of this ambrosial sin, so shown,/No doubt in fable, as the unforgiven/Fire which Prometheus filch'd for us from heaven.'"

While he quoted the lines from *Don Juan*, her expression changed, and the color came and went in her cheeks.

"Is that how it was with you the first time you loved?" he said. "Sweet? And because you had a rude awakening are you compelled to pass the favor—and the poison—on to the next innocent?"

"How tender your heart's become on his account," she said. "Your brain must be tender, too, if you take me for an idiot. You don't give a damn about him. You're only vexed because you tried to play games with me and lost. I know games you never dreamed of, Cordier. And I always play to win. I tossed the bait and you chased it, the way a dog chases a stick."

In an angry swirl of ruffles, she swung away from the window and strode to the table. She picked up the jewelry box and threw it at him. Reflexively he caught it.

"But now I'm bored with this game," she said. "Go home, little dog, and take your toys with you."

He looked down at the box in his hand. He looked up at her haughty face.

Francesca held her breath.

She'd gone too far. He'd throw her through the window. He was strong enough to do it.

And she wasn't sure she could blame him.

She braced herself for she knew not what: if not strangulation or a trip through the window into the canal, then another flaying from that cold, cutting tongue of his.

He couldn't know how deeply he'd cut with his remarks about her first love. Or perhaps he did know.

Very slowly, he set down the jewelry box on the table.

She thought of edging toward the bell, to summon help.

He started toward her.

She froze.

"You," he said. "You." Then he stopped, and put his hand to his head. His shoulders began to shake.

He let out a great crack of laughter, sudden and sharp as a pistol shot.

She jumped.

He laughed, turning away from her.

She only stood where she was, staring.

"*Diavolo*," he said. He shook his head. "I'm going now." He walked to the *portego* door, still shaking his head. "*Addio*," he said.

And out he went, taking the jewelry box with him, and leaving her still staring after him.

She stood for a moment, clenching and unclenching her hands. Then, "You conceited, arrogant beast," she said. She marched to the door and through it into the *portego*.

She'd had enough. This was the last time he'd turn his back on her, the last time he'd walk out on her.

She knew ways to stop men in their tracks, and he—

She stopped in her tracks.

Two men stood not twenty paces away. At the sound of her angry footfall, both turned and looked at her.

One was Cordier.

The other was a few inches shorter, and about three decades older.

"Madame," came a voice to her right. Belatedly she noticed Arnaldo. She must have walked straight past him as he was coming to announce the new visitor. He cleared his throat. "The comte de Magny," he announced.

"*Ma foi*, Francesca," said the count. "Have you taken leave of your senses, child, to run about these drafty corridors naked? Go put some clothes on."

"Monsieur," she began.

"Run along, run along." He waved his hand. "I will entertain your friend."

# Chapter 7

Yet he was jealous, though he did not show it,
For jealousy dislikes the world to know it.

Lord Byron
*Don Juan, Canto the First*

$\mathcal{M}$onsieur de Magny was not the feeble old man James had envisioned. The count stood only a trifle under six feet tall, and the gold-knobbed cane he carried was merely a fashion accessory. Deep lines marked his patrician countenance, mainly at his eyes and mouth and above the bridge of his long nose. His wavy brown hair was streaked with silver. His brown eyes held a gleam—of humor, cunning, or cruelty, James couldn't be sure.

He could be sure that monsieur spent a good deal of time and money on his appearance. He was elegantly turned out, his linen starched within an inch of its life. A gay profusion of chains, fobs, seals, and medals adorned his waistcoat.

"You are not obliged to entertain my caller, monsieur," Bonnard said. "Mr. Cordier was leaving."

"Cordier?" said Magny. "I know this name."

Who didn't? James wondered. His family, on both sides, was old and extensive. His father and mother were well known in Europe's courtly circles. Lord and Lady Westwood had always spent a great deal of time abroad. Even in wartime, they'd refused to remain safely at home.

"The name is French but you are not," Magny said.

"Not our branch," James said. "Not for some centuries. My father is the thirtieth Earl of Westwood."

The count nodded. "A family of Normandy."

"A very *large* family," Bonnard said. "Mr. Cordier is one of several children of the second marriage."

*Merely one of those extraneous younger sons, hardly worth knowing*, her tone said.

The count gave her a look James couldn't read.

"And he's leaving," she said.

"Not quite yet," James said. He patted his coat as though looking for something. "I seem to have left my pocket notebook in your bedroom."

Cold green murder glittered in her exotic eyes. "That's impossible," she said. "You were never—"

"There's no need to summon a servant," he said. "I can find it myself."

"You don't know the way," she said.

"Don't be silly," he said. "I wasn't *that* drunk last night, *mia cara*. I'm sure I can find my way . . . back." He moved to her. "But since you're going to get dressed anyway . . ." He offered his arm. He smiled down at her.

She smiled up at him. He remembered the serpent on her back, a cobra. Had she owned fangs, she'd have bared them. She took his arm, though.

"Cordier," she said in an undertone, "I'm going to make you very, very sorry for this."

"Oh, good," he said, not troubling to lower his voice. "That sounds like fun."

Her bedroom, James discovered, comprised a set of apartments on the other side of the *portego* at the courtyard end of the house. The parlor in which she'd first tried to seduce him opened into a sitting room or boudoir. This in turn gave way to another set of rooms. Her bed stood within an alcove. Curtained, arched doorways on either side led to other, smaller rooms, one clearly a dressing room.

Like the parlor, these rooms were modestly decorated by Venetian standards. The color scheme was lighter: soft pinks and greens, gold, and white. There was not a *putto* in sight. Instead, several choice landscape paintings adorned the walls and small circular scenes of mythical beings, framed in swirling gilt, appeared on the ceilings.

He saw no portraits of anybody, including her, but numerous other signs of her. A stack of books stood on the stand by the bed. Her toiletries were tumbled about a delicately carved writing desk in the boudoir. There, too, the pearls—those magnificent pearls!—lay as well, spilled carelessly among combs and jars and bottles.

As was the case with the beds in his *palazzo*, hers was not curtained. Nothing concealed the rumpled bedclothes from view. This wasn't the only evidence of what had passed last night. Her clothes were strewn about the room. A sea green silk slipper lay on its side near the bed. Another lay upside down under the desk chair.

He remembered the way she'd teased off her gloves—and remembering was a mistake, because he promptly envisioned her discarding the rest of her garments under Lurenze's delirious gaze.

Now Magny was here. His easy informality and assumption of command left James in no doubt of their relationship.

His head began to pound.

"How many lovers do you have, exactly?" he asked as he closed the door behind them. "And how many of them know about the others? Does Magny know about Lurenze? Does Lurenze know about him? Is there anyone else I ought to know about? I should hate to say the wrong thing, inadvertently."

"No, you'd rather say the wrong thing deliberately," she said. "Were you looking to start a fight, perhaps, with a man old enough to be your father?"

"I shan't ask what you'd want with a man old enough to be *your* father."

"Oh, don't be shy, Cordier. Ask away."

She began untying the dressing gown.

"There's a screen," he said, pointing to a handsome one, painted with a pastoral scene of shepherdesses and lambs. Behind it, he supposed, was a commode and a washstand. "Why don't you pretend to be modest and undress behind it? Or, here's a novel thought: What about undressing in the dressing room?"

"How curious," she said. "Most men would give a great deal to watch me undress."

"That's the trouble, you see," he said. "So many men have."

"And yet you won't go away," she said. "Curious."

He stalked to the nearest window and stared out. "We need to talk."

"Is that what we need to do?"

He fixed his gaze on the well head in the courtyard. "We do need to talk, reasonably and rationally. But you are so provoking. Do you recall my asking why Elphick divorced you?" He didn't wait for her answer. "I couldn't believe a man would give you up simply because you were not perfectly faithful. Even English gentlemen usually overlook their wives' peccadilloes in order to save face publicly and maintain a semblance of peace privately. Such indiscretions are rarely a secret in the Beau Monde, I know, but that is a small, closed circle. Why should a gentleman seek a divorce—and let every street sweeper and pie seller know he's a cuckold?"

"You might ask His Majesty King George IV the question," she said. "He was more than happy to have Queen Caroline's dirty linen washed in public not many weeks ago."

"Kings are another species," he said. "In earlier times, they sent adulterous wives to the chopping block—the penalty for treason."

"That's how men view it, isn't it?" she said. "Treason. Women are mere vassals, property. When we vow to love, honor, and obey, it must be blind obedience. I had not realized that, and Elphick did not understand what sort of woman he'd married. You make the matter unnecessarily complicated and mysterious, Cordier. The reason he divorced me is simple enough. You've seen for yourself: I'm impossible."

He swung round to look at her. She'd thrown off the dressing gown. She stood defiantly in a flimsy yellow and pink nothing, the lewdest nightdress he'd seen in all his life, and he'd seen more than his share of women's lingerie.

His heart instantly doubled its tempo, and its fierce beat sent blood rushing straight to his loins.

His mind started to close down.

*Don't, Jemmy. Don't muck it up again.*

But there she was, all creamy smooth and sinfully curved under a mere wisp of cloth. He could clearly see her nipples thrusting against the thin silk.

*You've been tortured by experts, laddie. Pretend it's torture.*

Given a choice, he'd rather have his nails pried off.

He set his jaw. "We need to talk," he said, "but you insist on provoking me. With excellent success, I might add. The trouble is, it's only a game to you. All you want is to make me crawl and beg."

"That's not *all* I want," she said. "But I should enjoy it."

"I'm not saying I wouldn't enjoy it, too," he said. "But then you'll throw me away, which is *not* to my liking. Look at the way you treat those pearls, those splendid pearls." He nodded at the tumble of jewelry on her dressing table.

"I ordered my maid to stay out of this room until sent for," she said. "Call me old-fashioned, but I dislike having servants come into my bedroom as they please, regardless of who is there."

"Old-fashioned," he said. "*Old-fashioned?*" He laughed. "By gad, Bonnard, you are a precious jade. For the first time in my life, I harbor fantasies of killing all of my older brothers, that I might be taken seriously as a lover."

"According to your treatise," she said, "that course of action would not be unprecedented."

She made him laugh. She made him furious. She made him crazy. He was half Italian. How could he keep away?

He closed the distance between them. He wrapped one arm about her waist. With his free hand he clasped the back of her head. "You are wicked," he said.

"Yes," she said.

"All you'll get from me is a kiss or two," he said. "I'm not one of your baubles. You won't use me as you use your jewelry. I won't be used, to prove whatever it is you want to prove, and cast aside."

"That's what you think," she said. She tilted her head back. She smiled the long, slow, lazy smile.

"First thing I'm going to do," he said, "I'm going to wipe that smile off your face."

He'd drive her boy prince out of her mind, make her forget he'd ever existed. James knew more about women than the sheltered Lurenze would ever learn, if he spent a lifetime studying nothing else.

He kissed her, but not on the wicked smile. He kissed her temple, and one spot at the top of her cheekbone. Then, remembering what she'd done last night, he followed the path she'd traced with her finger, around the delicate curve of her ear, and down. He pressed a tender, lingering kiss upon the spot where she'd paused.

She trembled.

Then, so did he.

Lightly, so lightly, as though she were the innocent girl he'd been dreaming of for years, he made his way down her neck. With his mouth, he moved the edge of the nightdress aside and kissed her shoulder. He made a necklace of kisses where the pearls had hung last night. He followed the path she'd drawn at the upper swell of her breasts. He knew her heart beat faster, as his did.

She tried to remain still, but he felt the tiny shudders she couldn't suppress. She couldn't hide, either, the quickened rise and fall of her bosom as her breath came and went, faster and faster. She couldn't mask the heat that deepened the scent of her skin, with its dizzying mixture of jasmine and woman.

He wanted to lose himself in her scent, in her. He wanted to forget everything else, to heed only this siren's call.

*Tie me to the mast.*

He lifted his head.

Her eyes slowly opened. Her gaze, unfocused, drifted to his.

She cupped the sides of his face. "Beast," she said, her voice husky.

"Tame me, then, beauty," he said. "I dare you."

He dragged his hands down over her breasts, to linger at the perfect inward curve of her waist, then down, to savor the sweet flare of her hips.

*This isn't why you came*, the voice reminded,

the inner voice that had kept him alive for all these years.

He knew he hadn't come for this. He knew it was only a means to an end.

Yet the light touch of her smooth hands held him. She held him, too, with her softened gaze . . . and with the ghost he saw in those hazy green depths: the shadow of another girl, one not so cynical and sublimely self-assured. He saw a lost soul, an innocent who might believe anything, and who was capable of trusting absolutely.

He told himself this was mere fancy, and he was getting soft in the head because he was so hard lower down, but he felt a stab, in the heart he couldn't afford to have.

To shut out the feeling, to shut out the troubling vulnerability he saw in her eyes, he kissed her.

It was long and deep, passionately deep, and still she held him so gently, her hands framing his face as though she'd hold him forever this way, as though the easy yielding of her mouth wasn't surrender but an invitation, beckoning him into a place that had no way out.

He knew there were no forevers and there was always a way out, yet he lost his way, lost his balance. He lost the warning voice, his guide. His senses filled with her, with the taste and scent of her. The silk slid under his hands as they moved over her, learning the rich curves of her body. She moved under his touch, urging him to fill his hands with her, to fill his world with her, leaving room for nothing else.

His inner guide would have told him this was

merely the harlot's art, but he'd lost his guide. All he could find was the warm, inviting woman in his arms . . . the scent of jasmine mingled with the scent of her skin . . . the warmth of her body under the silken veil . . . the fullness of her breasts against his chest . . . the softness of her belly as she pressed against his swollen cock.

His hands fisted in the silk at her hips and he pulled up the shift, inch by inch, while the kiss went on, the game of seduction deepening and darkening into pounding need.

He pulled the garment up to her hips and let the fabric slither over his hands while they slipped underneath to travel over her velvety skin: the tops of her thighs, the smooth curve of her bottom. He slid his hand between her legs, and she broke the kiss. She made a sound, like a sob, and trembled.

She was damp and ready and he could have her now, as every animal instinct roared at him to do.

But winning was a driving need, too, and stronger than any other.

*I'm better than any of the others. I'm the one who'll make you surrender, completely.*

He slid his fingers through the soft curls and cupped her. He let his fingers stroke, gently and lightly at first while he listened to her sighs. As she moved more urgently against his hand, he responded, giving her more, but little by little. He wanted to be done. He wanted to make her his completely. But he wanted, even more, her surrender, and so he made himself take his time pleasuring her.

Her head drooped against his chest. His heart

pounded so hard it must deafen her. But her heart must be pounding, too, because her breathing came faster and faster. Her body shook, and she gave a little cry.

Then at last she sank against him, shaking.

He drew his hand away and wrapped his arms tightly about her, crushing her to him.

He lifted her up, to carry her to the rumpled bed.

Then he set her on her feet again.

From somewhere in the distance came sounds: voices, the click of heels on the *terrazzo* floor.

He heard the sounds without fully realizing and he reacted without thinking, training and experience coming to the fore. He'd learned to detect a footfall from several rooms away, through closed doors, upon carpets. He had the senses of a cat, some of his colleagues said.

If he was a cat, he'd been doing a fine imitation of a blind, deaf, and lame one.

He put her away from him, aware of her eyes and the flash of emotion in them. Anger? Hurt?

It lasted but an instant, until she noticed the sounds, too. Her gaze shot to the door.

The voices coming from the *portego* became plainly audible.

A female servant was saying, "But of course, *monsieur le comte,* I will remind the mistress that you are waiting."

"I'll remind her myself," said monsieur.

Francesca wasn't ready.

She was shattered, lost.

She didn't understand.

She understood pleasure. She'd studied how to give and receive it.

She'd learned, as well, to keep the upper hand, never to yield altogether.

She'd surrendered completely to him after a laughably short struggle. He'd touched her, kissed her, and her strength, her hard-won strength, seeped away.

Heart beating too fast, much too fast, she looked about her and tried to think.

She was aware of his bending down and picking up something. She made herself focus. Her dressing gown. Yes. She must . . . cover up.

He tossed it to her. She hastily thrust her arms through the sleeves while he returned to the window and clasped his hands behind his back.

The door opened.

The maid came in, the older man close behind her.

Francesca had to struggle before she could find the casual words she needed: "There you are, Thérèse." Her voice sounded strange, not her own. Too high-pitched. She took a quick breath and went on, "What was I thinking of, not to send for you? It is not as though I can dress myself. But having all these gentlemen stomping about the place is so distracting."

Magny's brow furrowed.

"Well, then, I shall take my leave," Cordier said.

"You found your notebook, I trust," said the count.

Cordier patted his breast pocket. "Yes, I did, at last." He looked at Francesca. "What a strange place for it to end up in, eh, *cara*?"

*Cara.* What a joke. She wasn't dear to him at all, merely a conquest. An easy one, more shame to her.

Beast.

He took a polite leave of Magny and an impolite one of her, catching up her hand and planting a wet kiss between the rings on her middle and third fingers.

She wanted to weep.

She wanted to kill him, to hurl a dagger into his back as he walked away, through the door.

She listened to his footsteps fade away.

Monsieur gave her one of his looks, then stalked to the window. He clasped his hands behind his back, exactly the way Cordier had done.

Trying to block out from her mind all else Cordier had done, Francesca walked past the count into the dressing room.

Thérèse followed, leaving the door open. She'd been with Francesca since the early days in Paris. Being French and eminently practical, the haughty maid was not in the least troubled by her mistress's morals or lack thereof. To Thérèse, what mattered were Francesca's hordes of admirers, her wealth, and her jewels. Not another lady on the Continent, save a few royals, could match the mistress in this regard. Furthermore, one of madame's grandmothers had been a French aristocrat.

All these factors made Thérèse fiercely protective of her position. No bribe was great enough, no one important enough to pry from her a syllable of her mistress's secrets. None of madame's suitors received special treatment, no matter who they were. Madame ruled. Thus Thérèse would not close a door when a man was present or make herself scarce unless told to do so. And, most conveniently for Francesca and her guests, the maid condescended to understand and speak only as much English as she deemed absolutely necessary to performing her duties. She was equally scornful of Italian.

Magny took no more heed of Thérèse than she did of him. All the same, he spoke in English. "You should not have left Mira. I told you this was an unhealthy time to come to Venice."

"You should not have come," Francesca said, watching Thérèse fill a wash basin. She wished it were possible to scrub Cordier's touch away. She wished she could cleanse herself of the weakness he'd somehow uncovered.

"That was the whole point of my note," she went on. "It was supposed to reassure you. I knew you'd hear stories—and of course they'd be horribly exaggerated. I was sure you'd hear I'd been murdered. I know what gossip is like, especially in country villages."

"Speaking of gossip," he said.

"Gad, I knew this was coming," she muttered.

"I hear stories," he said, "of you and Lurenze. But when I arrive, I find an Englishman. Do you know who his father is?"

"I never met Lord Westwood," she said. "Elphick and he did not travel in the same circles—though I don't doubt that my former husband tried as hard as he could to worm his way into those exalted circles."

"Westwood is a great hero, especially to the French aristocracy. One cannot count the number of heads he and his lady saved from Madame Guillotine, at great personal risk."

The image jumped into Francesca's mind, as it had done time and again: Cordier lunging into the *felze* and wrapping his arm around the villain's throat . . . the brute struggling helplessly, futilely . . . then going limp.

"Taking risks runs in the family, then," she said. "Apparently Cordier jumped from one of his balconies into the canal to save me. Still, I should distinguish between physical daring—or recklessness is probably more like it—and heroism. He's a black sheep. He told me so himself."

She heard a long, loud sigh. She glanced toward the doorway but Magny was not there. No doubt he still stood at the window, looking—or glaring—out.

"I won't ask what goes on between you," he said.

"What else?" she said easily. "Games."

She could not have guessed how dangerously sweet a game Cordier could make it. She could not have guessed how the light caress of his lips upon her skin could touch something hidden deep within her, a part of her being she'd buried long ago. It was as though he'd reached straight down into her soul and turned her inside out.

He'd remembered everything she'd done last night when she'd tried to seduce him. Everywhere her fingers had gone, his mouth had gone. He'd done what she'd silently invited him to do, but what he'd done to her was not what she'd bargained for.

He'd touched her and kissed her exactly as she'd instructed. And he'd made a shivering wreck of her—she, who was an expert at the give and take of dalliance. But his mouth took possession of her so easily. His touch simply stripped her, leaving her naked and blind with longing. He'd pleasured her—and she liked to be pleasured—but this was not the same. He'd cracked something inside her and she'd come within an eyeblink of weeping. She didn't understand and wasn't sure she wanted to understand.

Why the devil hadn't he been quicker? Why hadn't he thrown her on the bed and had his way with her . . . and let her have her way with him, let her simply enjoy his big, strong body?

*Beast*.

"I do not wish to know," Magny said. "I find it is better not to know. But if you own a particle of common sense, child, you'll send this one about his business. I survived my trials and lived this long because my judgment of men is keener than most. This one, I promise you, *ma cherie,* is trouble."

The man who was trouble retrieved the jewelry case from the table in the *portego* where he'd tossed it shortly after leaving madame and a moment before Magny appeared. This time James didn't pause but continued through the archway, and down the stairs to the *andron*.

He fixed his attention on his surroundings, taking in every detail. Though he'd come this way before, it was the first time he'd done so in broad day. He could only hope his years of training had survived the tempest that was Francesca Bonnard, and he'd remember, once he calmed down, every detail of the rooms he'd passed through this day.

He had to hope that some part of his mind had paid attention, while the rest of it was roiling with anger, jealousy, lust, frustration, and several other emotions he'd rather not examine too closely.

If all else failed, he'd have to search the house. In such a case, it was best to have a mental picture of the likeliest hiding places. Searching, however, was the method he'd hoped to avoid. On the occasions when he had to turn burglar, he preferred to know exactly where to find what he was looking for.

That was not the case here. Though, like other Venetian *palazzi,* hers was fairly simply laid out, the house was large, containing all too many possible hiding places. With most people, he could easily deduce where they'd keep precious items, once he understood how their minds worked. The trouble was, he could not unscramble the workings of a woman's mind while she was scrambling his.

He swiftly made his way to his waiting gondola. Sedgewick and Zeggio, who'd been talking softly, looked up at the same time. Both faces were wary.

*They think I've taken leave of my senses*, James thought, *and they're not wrong.*

He told Zeggio to take them to the island of San Lazzaro.

James needed to clear his head, and he was sure that would happen more quickly once he was out on the water, several miles from Venice—and from her. The tiny island, once a haven for lepers, was now home to the Armenian monastery where Byron had studied.

A monastery, at the moment, sounded like heaven.

# Chapter 8

Oh Pleasure! you are indeed a pleasant thing,
    Although one must be damn'd for you,
        no doubt:
I make a resolution every spring
    Of reformation, ere the year run out,
But somehow, this my vestal vow takes wing,
    Yet still, I trust it may be kept throughout:
I'm very sorry, very much ashamed,
And mean, next winter, to be quite reclaimed.

Lord Byron
*Don Juan, Canto the First*

"You should not have come," Francesca again told Magny as she emerged from the dressing room.

He'd left the window and planted himself on a chair in the boudoir. His hands folded upon the elaborate gold knob of the walking stick propped between his legs, he glowered at the floor.

"I hear things," he said. "They make me think you've taken leave of your senses."

"You are at liberty to think what you like."

She walked to the writing desk she often used as a receptacle for odds and ends of jewelry, scarves, gloves, creams, and lotions. She sank into the chair, and hunted through the bric-a-brac for her note paper and pen. "I will not allow any man to rule me. If that was what I'd wanted, I'd have remarried."

"Thérèse, do gather up those pearls and put them away properly," he said. "For God's sake, Francesca, let the girl tend to your jewelry. What has come over you, to make you so careless?"

*Look at the way you treat those pearls, those splendid pearls*, Cordier had said. *I'm not one of your baubles. You won't use me as you use your jewelry. I won't be used, to prove whatever it is you want to prove, and cast aside.*

Men used women, but when the tables were turned . . . oh, that was another matter altogether. That was a capital crime.

"Take them," Francesca told her maid. Though Thérèse ignored the count, she was no doubt itching to do as he commanded.

Francesca pushed a jar of powder aside. "Ah, there's a pen." She took it up, separated the inkwell from the other little jars and bottles, and cleared a space on the table. She found a few sheets of note paper under a scarf.

Magny knew better than to ask to whom she was writing. He knew she'd only tell him it was none of his affair.

"I understand they've caught one of the men," he said after a moment's thunderous silence.

"Footpads," she said. She shuddered involuntarily.

She gave a short laugh to conceal it. "Or are they *float*pads in Venice?"

"It does not amuse me," he said.

She shrugged. "They'd heard of my jewelry. That's what they wanted—and to entertain themselves by tormenting a helpless woman."

"Is that what the governor believes? Is that what *you* believe?"

She paused, the pen in midair. She turned and looked at him. "The man was already in custody," she said. "He's sure to be executed. Why should he lie? What had he to lose by telling the truth?"

"I don't know. I cannot help thinking it had to do with that business earlier in the summer."

"Lord Quentin," she said grimly. She turned back to her note.

She didn't know how Quentin had learned about the letters she'd taken from the locked drawer in her former husband's desk. She didn't know how Quentin had obtained the fragment he'd shown her, so startlingly like those she had. It sounded, however, as though he'd made the discovery not very long ago.

*The matter has puzzled us for some time,* he told her. *But it was only recently that we've begun putting the puzzle pieces together.*

The puzzle pieces indicated that Elphick was what she'd suspected him to be five years ago: a man who worked for his country's enemies. But five years ago no one would have believed her. With the appalling accusations he'd made during the divorce, he'd destroyed her credibility—that was to say, what little credibility remained, after her father had swindled half the Beau Monde.

Her own lawyers, to whom she'd shown one of the letters, had told her they'd do her more harm than good, either during the criminal conversation case John had brought against her lover, Lord Robert Meadows, or during the divorce proceedings. John's lawyers would have no trouble making people believe the letters were the inventions of a vindictive, amoral woman.

They'd had no trouble, she'd discovered, making the world believe the worst of her, in any case. Her father had made that all too easy for them.

She'd not been without sin, true. She'd served her faithless spouse as he'd served her. But no one cared about a man's infidelities, even when they were beyond counting. Meanwhile, by the time John was done poisoning everybody's mind, her one spot of mud—one affair, undertaken when she was maddened by heartbreak and rage and longing to get even—had grown into a reeking cesspit.

Like father like daughter, all of England believed. Even her lover, embarrassed by the crim con case and sickened by the stories, abandoned her.

Lord Quentin had urged her to entrust the letters to him. She remembered the exchange very well:

*You must have heard the rumors,* he said. *Elphick has hopes of becoming our next prime minister.*

*Some would say that England will get the leader it deserves,* she answered.

*If the man's a traitor,* his lordship said, *isn't it long past time he paid the penalty?*

*Hanged, drawn, and quartered, do you mean?* she said. *But is that punishment enough? Why don't you leave it to me?*

She didn't add, *Why should I trust you?*

For all she knew, Quentin was one of Elphick's pawns. For all she knew, every word Lord Quentin uttered was part of an elaborate lie concocted by her former husband, a brilliant liar.

Quentin had returned several times, until at last she'd told the servants he was not to be admitted.

Some weeks later, her villa was searched. It was efficiently done. The signs were not obvious. But Magny had noticed, and once he pointed out the signs, so had she.

He'd warned her that her bank accounts and the contents of the bank vaults would probably be scrutinized. Government agents could get in wherever they liked, and Elphick had built up a network of allies in government. Magny had offered plenty of advice. Too much. The matter had made him finical and meddlesome. Since she'd decided years ago that no man, ever again, would control her, they'd quarreled, repeatedly.

And so she'd left Mira.

Magny's voice ended her brief journey into the recent past. "You never let me help you," he said.

"Make decisions for me?" she said without looking up. "No, thank you, sir."

"Francesca, this is absurd. Let me take you back to Paris."

"My enemies can find me as easily there as here," she said, "if that's what worries you. I'm not worried. They dare not kill me until they find what they want, because they don't know what arrangements I've made in the event of my untimely demise. They cannot risk those letters being published."

"Francesca."

"I have letters to write," she said.

*Sunday night*

When Marta Fazi learned that Piero had been taken into custody and Bruno had disappeared, she smashed several more madonnas, had a weeping fit about her lost emeralds, and vowed revenge on everybody who'd ever annoyed her. Then, as was usual with her, she abruptly became completely calm again. Plan A—using bullies to terrify the Englishwoman into handing over the letters—having failed, she swiftly devised Plan B. Then she went out in search of lackeys to replace the pair she'd lost. This was difficult in Venice but not impossible. Everywhere, Marta had learned, a strong-willed woman could find weak-willed men to do her bidding.

It was true that Venice was not the most welcoming place for criminals. This didn't mean it hadn't any. As was the case in more lawless cities, it had a population of desperately poor persons and desperate neighborhoods in which they lived. In such places, crime flourished, and as long as the criminal element confined itself to stealing from and cutting one another's throats, nobody bothered about them very much.

The difficulty was not in finding ruffians but in

finding ruffians whose speech she could understand. The Venetians definitely didn't qualify. For all she understood of their language, they might as well have spoken Chinese.

Luckily for her, people came to Venice from everywhere. It had its Albanian, Armenian, Greek, Turkish, and Jewish communities. It had drawn, as well, its share of outcasts from other parts of Italy, including regions where she'd lived. Among the ne'er-do-wells who met her requirements were a handful willing—for a price—to venture outside their neighborhoods and risk the attention of the Austrian soldiers. The price, as one would expect among the poor and desperate, was quite low. It didn't take Marta long to find what she needed.

*Three o'clock in the morning,*
  *the following Tuesday*
*Caffè Florian, Piazza San Marco*

At this hour the coffeehouse's rooms were thin of company. Customers were drifting away, either homeward or to other entertainments.

Francesca and Giulietta remained, though, sharing a table with Lurenze—and, for once, no one else. He'd contrived to shed the various diplomats and most of his retinue, except for a few bodyguards trying to be unobtrusive here and there: some inside the café, others outside, loitering about the entryway.

At the other end of the same room, most of the remaining patrons were gathered about the

Countess Benzoni. Don Carlo was not among them. Francesca wondered if he'd decided Venice had insufficient quantities of the "the more old woman, who sometimes she is ugly, but very, very beautiful in the purse," and had taken himself elsewhere.

She'd decided to take herself elsewhere, and was debating how best to discourage the prince from following, when the atmosphere of the room changed. She looked up as Cordier came through the door.

He was dressed in a black tailcoat worn open. Over the frilled white shirt and black underwaistcoat he wore an embroidered waistcoat, from which hung a gold watch chain and fob. His immaculate neckcloth was tied with a simple knot. Close-fitting, light-colored evening trousers displayed long, muscular legs. The black pumps, black hat under his arm, and white gloves completed the picture of the proper English gentleman. His air and the way he moved, as lithe as a panther, told another story.

She remembered Magny's warning: *This one, I warn you*, ma cherie, *is trouble.*

Trouble did not look her way but made straight for the countess.

To Francesca's exasperation, all the men in the group made way for him, including the countess's lover, the Cavalier Giuseppe Rangone.

Francesca returned her attention to Lurenze, who was describing a miniature recently presented to him, of a Bavarian princess, one of the hordes proposed as the next Queen of Gilenia.

That was to say, Francesca tried to attend to Lurenze. Her gaze kept reverting to Cordier. Though far from flamboyantly dressed, he was impossible to ignore. For one thing, the café was thinly populated. For another, he stood at least a head taller than those about him . . . except when he was bowing over one of the women's hands or whispering something to make them smile or—no small achievement in that group—blush.

A plump masculine figure hove into view, blocking the scene at the other end of the room.

The approaching fellow paused at Francesca's table. He carried a covered tray.

"What is it?" Lurenze said. "Trinkets for ladies?"

"In a manner of speaking," Giulietta said. With an impish glance at Francesca, she signaled the vendor to uncover the tray.

He did so, and Lurenze leaned forward to peer at its contents. He instantly recoiled, as though it had been filled with rats, and waved his hand. "No, no! Are you mad? Cover those things! Be off with you!"

When he chose, Lurenze could be imperious. The vendor hastily threw the cloth over the tray and started to back away.

"No, please wait," said Giulietta. With crooked finger she summoned the vendor. She turned a limpid, doe-eyed gaze upon the prince. "This is most important, your illustriousness. These are cundums."

"I know what they are," Lurenze said. "I am not a child. But you—please not to speak of this in a place so public. It is most improper of this man to come before ladies."

"It is always improper for the man to come before the lady," said Giulietta.

Francesca laughed.

After a moment's cogitation, Lurenze understood the joke. "Oh, she is wicked," he said, clearly torn between mortification and amusement. "Someone must wash her mouth with soap."

"But your radiance, the cundum is most useful," Giulietta said. "You would not wish to have a deformed heir, or an idiot to succeed to the throne of Gilenia—or perhaps to have no successor of any kind. These are some consequences of the pox. Also, to go mad and have ugly sores on the face, not to mention warts on the manly organ."

His fair countenance instantly turned rosy. "Signorina Sabbadin, I promise you, I do not consort with persons who carry these diseases," he said.

"But what of Lord Byron?"

His eyes opened very wide. "Lord Byron? *Lord Byron*? What is this you say? He is a *man*! A man does not consort with men. It is unnatural!"

"He is a great poet," said Giulietta. "Yet even he, an intelligent man of letters, received an unwanted gift from a highborn lady."

"I could name several ladies in England who received similar gifts from titled gentlemen of their acquaintance," said Francesca. *With any luck, a lady will be so accommodating as to pass on the gift to Elphick.*

Lurenze's gaze went from her to Giulietta. Then it settled upon the cundum seller, patiently waiting.

"Very well," said the prince. "I do it for my posterity."

"Show his excellency your wares," Giulietta briskly told the vendor. "The good ones. Underneath."

Obediently, the man lifted out the first tray, to reveal the articles below, in their thin paper packets.

Lurenze peered at them for a time. Then he reached for one.

"Not that one," said Giulietta, nudging his hand away. "This one." She picked up one of the larger packets and took out the cundum. The ribbon with which one tied it onto the penis was deep red. The prince's color, which had begun to return to normal, instantly matched the ribbon.

"Is this the largest one you have?" Giulietta asked the seller. "A prince is more magnificent, you know, than the ordinary gentleman."

"Signorina, I promise you, this will accommodate the greatest size," said the seller. "These are of the finest quality, of the intestine of the sheep."

Her face grave, Giulietta tugged on the cundum. Then she stuck her dainty hand into it, as though it were a glove. She held up her sheep-gut-encased hand. "Do you think this will be large and strong enough, your sublimeness?" she said.

Lurenze studied it, eyes narrowed. Then, "I cannot be sure," he said. "Pull it over your head."

His eyes crinkled at the corners and he laughed, so heartily that Francesca had to laugh, too. Giulietta joined in.

Every head in the room turned their way.

Including, at last, Cordier's.

James did not want to look. If he didn't, though, he'd be the only one.

There were the three of them, laughing while a vendor pressed his wares upon them.

Bonnard dripped rubies this night. Along with the gems hanging from her ears and throat and wrists, she wore a magnificent ruby-colored cashmere shawl. It had slid from her shoulders, revealing the deep neckline of a jade green gown of a thin fabric—possibly silk or a crepe of some kind. Metallic thread in the embroidery made it shimmer when she moved. It fell from the high waist in numerous thin pleats, like certain draperies he'd seen on women in Egyptian tomb paintings. The pleats clung in a perfectly obscene manner to the curves of her hips and long legs, of which he had a mouth-watering view from this angle.

He remembered the green evening slippers he'd seen flung about her bedroom in gay abandon, and he grew impatient. He had to concentrate all his will on *not* stalking down the long room and dragging her up from her chair and away from the company.

The company, meanwhile, merely watched the group at the other end of the room for a moment or two before returning to their conversations.

The Countess Benzoni said to him, "We cannot expect his highness to tear himself away from that pair. They are too amusing. Have you attended Signora Bonnard's *conversazione*, Signor Cordier?"

He didn't say Bonnard hadn't invited him to one of her salons. He said, "I have been in Venice for only a week."

"Once upon a time, you might choose from scores of *conversazioni*, every day of the week," she said. "When Lord Byron first came here, only two remained: mine and the Countess Albrizzi's.

But then Signora Bonnard arrives, and hers become his favorites. She has the joie de vivre. In addition, she is well read."

"No one is more beautiful and clever than you, my soul," said Rangone, the countess's devoted *cavalier servente*.

"So you say, but when she laughs, you turn your head, exactly the same as the other men," said his beloved.

A little while later, Mrs. Bonnard laughed again. Turning toward the sound, James saw her leaving with her two companions. A few minutes and what seemed like an endless series of farewells later, he slipped out of the door after her.

He discovered the trio nearby, only a few yards from the Florian. Mrs. Bonnard was looking across the way, up at the Torre dell'Orologio, the beautiful clock tower at the northeast corner of the Piazza.

Above the tower, a few wispy clouds drifted across the night sky. The moon, which had only recently passed its full, shone brightly, and the stars were out in force. The square was well lit, too. All the same, James couldn't read her expression.

Giulietta had her hand over her face, and as he neared, he heard her giggling. As always, people came and went. Even in decline, Venice never slept.

None of the three seemed to notice James's approach. Lurenze was saying something and gesticulating.

Then Bonnard turned her head. James saw her posture stiffen as she spotted him. He felt himself tensing, too, with anticipation.

He sauntered to the group. "Everyone in the *contessa's* circle was wild to find out what was so humorous," he said. "You were all so merry."

"Cundums," said Giulietta. She went off into whoops.

"Signorina Sabbadin enjoys to make me blush," said Lurenze. "I tell her, in my country, we are shy to speak of such matters. To say them in the company of the woman is unheard of."

"But we are not in your country, your supremeness," said Giulietta.

"For this I am most thankful," the prince said with a smile. "But you—it is too shocking what you do and say. You are a naughty child."

Instantly her merriment vanished, and her sweet face turned cold and austere. "I am no child," she said. And off she went, a compact bundle of outraged womanhood, storming across the square, hips swaying, nose aloft.

Lurenze looked from Bonnard to James. "What is it I say?"

"I don't know," James said. "Italians are so passionate. I hope she doesn't throw herself into the canal."

The prince's innocent eyes widened. "Oh, but no. This is unthinkable."

Bonnard opened her mouth, but his highness had already dashed away after Giulietta.

Madame watched them go. "She may be Italian," she said, "but she is no more likely to throw herself into the canal than I am, as you are undoubtedly aware."

"You're so thick," James said. "You know she did that to get him to go after her. I was merely helping. Are you going to be cross? Had you meant to keep him all to yourself?"

"I had," she said. "But then I saw you. What, I asked myself, would I want with a beautiful young prince, the possessor of mountains of money he's desperate to spend on wicked women, when I might spend my time with an ill-mannered, impecunious younger son who begrudges me a few peridots, stirs up trouble with my friends, and can't make up his mind what he wants?"

"Did you miss me, *cara*?" he said. "It's been three whole days and more."

"So long?" she said. "It felt like three minutes. It seemed I'd hardly got rid of you—and here you are again."

"If that's how you're going to be, I won't take you up to the top of the Campanile," he said, with a nod in the direction of the brick bell tower straight ahead.

"I am desolated," she said. "I wonder if I can find the strength to pick up the shattered pieces of my life and go on."

"Have you ever been to the top of the Campanile at night?" he said.

"I doubt anyone has since Galileo went up to discover that the world was round," she said. "It's closed at night these days. There's a guard." Yet her gaze strayed upward and a gleam came into her eye.

"It's a perfect night, but the sky will be lightening in an hour or two," he said. "We'd better make haste." He took her hand.

She tried to pull away but he kept a firm grip and started walking toward the bell tower.

She wisely gave up struggling. "I refuse to wrestle with you in St. Mark's Square," she said.

"Good, because you'll lose," he said. Her gloved hand fit comfortably in his. He remembered her peeling off her gloves. Heat arrowed straight to his groin.

"If we do get to the top of the tower," she said, "the first thing I'm going to do is push you off. But you needn't worry, because we won't get in. The watchman's bound to be Austrian, and you know what sticklers they are for rules."

"Stop talking," he said. "You'll need your breath for the climb."

Francesca was out of breath before they started.

It was because her hand was folded in his, so big and warm and sure. The last time she'd walked hand in hand with a man was early in her marriage, in the days when John Bonnard was so tender and affectionate, when she seemed to be falling in love with him over and over.

Her eyes stung and she blinked hard, grateful for the night and the deep shadows at the back of the Campanile.

On the verge of tears, ye gods! What need had she to weep, after all this time?

Yet when Cordier released her hand, to speak to the guard, she felt bereft, and her eyes itched.

*Stop sniveling*, she told herself.

She heard Cordier's low murmur, the guard's

answer. It didn't last long. He returned to her, reclaimed her hand, and grinned, so cocksure.

"He's Venetian," he said. "When he saw I had a beautiful woman with me, he wanted little persuading."

She supposed Cordier's speaking Italian like a native had more to do with his persuasive powers than the Venetian's romantic streak. As well, a coin or two could work wonders, even, sometimes, among the supposedly rigid and incorruptible Austrians.

"There's another watchman at the top," she said. "That one will surely be Austrian."

"His job is to look out for riots, fires, invasions, and such," said Cordier. "He might search us for weapons. Would you mind being searched?"

"That would depend," she said, "on whether he was young and handsome."

"Well, then, we'll see," he said. "Shall I race you to the top?"

"It is typical of a man to suggest such a thing," she said. "You in trousers, and I incommoded by skirts, petticoats, and stays."

As the guard opened the door, Cordier bent to whisper in her ear, "We can always *take them off.*"

Tiny electric shocks darted up and down her spine.

She stopped short.

He laughed and tugged her inside.

And she went, fool that she was, because it was a starlit night, and the bell tower was forbidden, and the last time she'd climbed to the top was in daytime, and she'd been one of a crowd of tourists.

. . . and because he'd taken her hand and she wanted to go wherever he took her. It was only lust, she told herself, and the sooner she exorcised that demon, the better.

Dawn was an hour or more away, and the moon and stars, pretty enough in the heavens, made no impression upon the tower's interior, though James was able to discern the outlines of its arched windows. He might have asked the guard for a lantern or torch but he neither needed nor wanted additional light. He'd had never had a problem finding his way in the dark, and in the present case, he'd only one way to go: up the gentle, winding incline of the ramp.

He was more comfortable in the darkness, in any event. And this night he had her hand in his and he could hear the soft rustle of her garments as she walked with him. Sometimes her skirts brushed his legs. Sometimes, too, the scent, tantalizingly faint, drifted to his nostrils, of jasmine and her.

"Is it in your clothes?" he said. "The scent? Jasmine, it seems like, but with another note I can't identify."

"Thérèse puts sachets in my wardrobe, amongst my gowns, my undergarments, my gloves and handkerchiefs," she said. "It is not enough, you see, to dress beautifully. A great whore must have her own distinctive scent."

"Are you a great whore?" he said, refusing to let his mind linger on images of her bedroom, with the various articles of clothing strewn about, the so-feminine jars and bottles with their gold caps and swirling gold lettering. Above all, he would not let himself imagine her undergarments or recollect the salacious excuse for a nightdress she'd worn. "You keep your other lovers wonderfully secret, then, because I count only two so far—well, three, if we include me."

"You are not included," she said. "You are an aberration."

"Very well. But in Italy, respectable matrons might have two lovers and perhaps an aberration or two."

"I'm not Italian," she said. "I'm English, and a divorcée."

"When in Rome," he said, "it's best to do as the Romans do. In Rome—in Italy—in nearly every nation of the Continent, you are a pitiful excuse for a whore."

"Don't be absurd," she said. "I'm a magnificent whore. I have the jewels to prove it."

"A magnificent businesswoman, certainly," he said.

"I learned from the best," she said. "In Paris. Fanchon Noirot."

He gave a soft whistle. "I've heard of her. She must be sixty."

"Sixty-five—and living a luxurious retirement with a devoted lover. That is one harlot who did not end up in the gutter."

He paused. "By gad, Bonnard, you went about this methodically, I see."

"You may read all about it in my memoirs," she

said. "I plan to write them when I'm forty: before all the main characters are dead and while they're not too old to be embarrassed—or amused, as the case may be."

"Will I be in them?"

"Probably not," she said. "I plan to forget you by tomorrow."

"In that case, I'd better make the most of today," he said. He squeezed her hand, and continued up the winding ramp.

# Chapter 9

The moment night with dusky mantle covers
    The skies (and the more duskily the better),
The time less liked by husbands than by lovers
    Begins, and prudery flings aside her fetter;
And gaiety on restless tiptoe hovers,
    Giggling with all the gallants who beset her.

Lord Byron, *Beppo*

He was like a cat, Francesca thought. Though they made their way through a nigh-impenetrable gloom, Cordier never hesitated, never stumbled.

There was not a clumsy bone in that body . . .

Something flickered in the back of her mind, but it was as fleeting as the light of a firefly.

It left her uneasy, though, and as they neared the belfry, she became conscious, at last and far too late, of being utterly alone with a man she didn't really know. She remembered, at last and far too late, that a man had tried to kill her a few days earlier . . . and another man, with a legitimate title and connections to the British government, had had her house searched some weeks ago. She remembered, at last and far too late, how shockingly strong this man was. He might easily pick her up and toss her through one of the arches onto the stones below.

Her heart thudded. She told it not to be ridiculous. She was letting Magny's fussings and alarms prey on her mind.

"Why?" she said. "Why did you take it into your head to ascend the Campanile in the dead of night?"

"I had a fancy to see Venice by starlight, with a beautiful woman at my side," he said.

"There were beautiful women among the Countess Benzoni's coterie," she said. "Giulietta is beautiful. You could have been quicker off the mark and chased after her."

He sighed. "I know. The trouble is, you're the only one I can see—and for some mad reason, you're the only one I want to climb to the top of this bell tower with. Strange, isn't it?"

"Not at all strange," she said. "You're infatuated with me. It happens all the time."

He laughed—and tripped, tumbling forward. She shrieked, and tried to yank back on the hand gripping hers, before he could pull her down with him. But he easily and quickly righted them both, and told her to hush.

"I forgot," he said. "There's a stairway here."

The noise they'd made alerted the watchman. The small, dark figure, carrying a lantern, bustled out from wherever he'd been keeping himself and demanded to know who was there.

Cordier had no more trouble with him than he'd had with the guard at the bottom. He talked, the man answered, and so it went, back and forth in the friendliest way. He showed the ticket the guard below had given him, and dropped a coin into his newfound friend's hand. Chatting amiably, the watchman led them up another set of stairs, opened the door to the upper gallery for them, then went back to his interrupted nap.

"I'm not infatuated," Cordier said as he led her to the edge of the stone balcony.

*Perhaps you're not, but I am,* she thought.

"Stop talking," she said.

She didn't want to talk. She didn't want to think. She wanted to put everything else from her mind and simply drink in this moment, and the view of this magical place.

The sky was showing the first signs of lightening but stars still hung in the heavens. Below, the city was a dark fairyland dotted with faintly twinkling lights. She moved along the balustrade, enchanted, as she gazed at the world below her and beyond. The lagoon twinkled, too, reflecting the fading starlight and the lights of the boats, and perhaps the sun as well, still lurking below the horizon.

"This is the way deities see the world," she said softly. "We're merely specks to them."

The people in the square below were dark, moving specks against the silver and shadow of their surroundings. She looked for the labyrinth of canals, but at this height, the city's domes, towers, and palaces concealed them. She knew the snow-capped mountains were out there, too, but at present the darkness hid them. She supposed they'd gradually appear when the sun rose, if the day continued as clear as the night had been.

But the mainland's distant heights weren't what captivated her. It was the lagoon and the islands scattered upon the glistening water and the boats plying among them, already busy at the first promise of daybreak.

She drank in the sea air. "This is what heaven ought to be like," she said. Then her throat ached and her eyes filled, and to her chagrin, she started to cry.

James was not the type of man to be alarmed by women's tears. He had what seemed to be an infinite number of sisters as well as aunts and nieces and female cousins beyond counting.

But those were his sisters and aunts and nieces and female cousins.

He left the wall he'd been leaning on and went to her. He pulled her into his arms. "*Per carità,*" he said. "For pity's sake, what is it?"

She bowed her head upon his chest and wept, not gently but in harsh, racking sobs he recognized as the deepest grief.

His heart pounded. "Come, Bonnard, you mustn't take on so," he said with forced lightness. "I know your love for me is nigh unbearable, but still . . ."

She gulped, and sobbed some more.

He tightened his hold of her. "I beg you will not throw yourself over the railing. I'm not worth it."

She looked up at him. Tears glistened on her lashes. A tear trickled down the side of her nose.

"Really, I'm not," he said.

"*Cretino,*" she said, her voice clogged with tears. "If only I were big enough to push you over the balustrade."

You'd think it was an endearment, to be called a cretin, for relief washed through him, sweet and cool as the breeze coming off the water.

"I need a handkerchief," she said, in the same watery voice. "Or may I wipe my nose on your neckcloth?"

"No," he said. "I should do anything for you, *mia cara,* but a man's neckcloth is out of bounds."

He let go of her in order to hunt for his handkerchief. By the time he'd fished it out of his tailcoat pocket, she'd unearthed her own: a tiny square of tissue-thin linen surrounded by about six yards of lace.

She dabbed her eyes with this useless bit of froth and daintily wiped her nose.

He put away his handkerchief. "Wipe your nose on my neckcloth, indeed," he said. "You do believe I'm infatuated, don't you? Well, let me explain something to you, Goddess of Beauty, Wicked Harlot, Queen of the Nile, and whatever else you imagine yourself to be—"

"You're a man," she said. "You don't know anything. Not a damned thing."

She threw one gloved hand up in the air in a queenly gesture of dismissal and walked away to the stairs.

"Exits," he said. "These women are always making dramatic exits." He followed her, singing Figaro's lines, "*'Donne, donne, eterni dei,/Chi v'arriva a indovinar?'*"

Women, women, eternal gods,/Who can fathom their minds?

Without hesitation, she answered—not in the soprano meant for Rosina but in a husky alto, "*'Ah, tu solo, amor, tu sei, /Che mi devi consolar.'*"

Ah, you alone my love, only you, /Can console my heart.

His heart skipped a beat, and another.

He followed her down the stairs. "There, you see," he said. "That's the trouble. We have too much in common. You know Rossini. You know Byron. Or at least, the same bits I know."

"Half the world knows those bits of Byron," she said. "Half the world has *The Barber of Seville* by heart. Keep looking for reasons, Cordier. Keep trying to explain why you can't keep away from me. You're the same as Lurenze. Infatuated. The difference is, he's man enough to admit it."

James was not infatuated. He knew what that was. He'd fallen over head and ears in love with the wrong sorts of girls numerous times in his mutinous youth.

"It's lust, you stupid female!" he said. "What Lurenze feels is the normal hankering of a healthy young man for a beautiful woman. In his case, it's more intense than usual because they've kept him in the royal nursery for so long. What you see in his case is years of pent-up need for a good plogging."

"A plogging?" She laughed the wicked laugh that made his skin prickle and his prick come to attention. "A right good rogering, do you mean? You're ridiculous, Cordier, do you know that? You took me to the top of the Campanile on a starlit night. It was romantic. So romantic that I wept. I shall probably start blubbering again now—because my heart aches—with pity, because you are such a hopeless, utter blockhead."

She moved along the outer edge of the bellfry, looking out through the arches.

He clenched his hands so hard that the nails dug in. He looked down at his hands. Carefully he unclenched them. What was the matter with him? He had no reason on earth to be in a turmoil, he told himself. None at all. She was right. This was supposed to be romantic. He was supposed to win her over, win her trust. He knew exactly what he was doing. He was doing his job.

But matters were not proceeding as they ought.

For about the hundredth time.

He'd *tripped*. He never tripped.

He was getting dull, clumsy, and stupid—and no wonder. He was tired and disgusted and should have gone home months ago. He was worn out, used up.

What he was *not* was infatuated.

"I know what you want," she said. "You want the upper hand. Abandon that hope, my dear. I did not come this far and achieve all I've achieved by letting anyone have the upper hand."

That surely included Elphick, James thought. Were the letters her way of maintaining the upper hand with her former husband? Was that why she'd so obstinately refused to admit she had them?

He didn't want to ask, even if it had been wise to do so. He didn't want to think about Elphick and those accursed letters.

He crossed to her and stood behind her.

She was looking down on the Piazzetta.

He looked over her shoulder, to see what she saw: not simply the square below but the city surrounding it, the gold domes faintly glowing in the pale promise of sunrise. Beyond it the lagoon's islands lay scattered upon the glittering water.

He felt a queer constriction in his heart. He had not wanted to come here. To him, Venice was a city in decline, a melancholy place. But at this moment, gazing over her shoulder and seeing it through her eyes—the eyes of one who'd found refuge here—he felt its enchantment.

"I'm not a blockhead," he said.

He let his hands rest alongside hers on the stone railing, his arms boxing her in. He drank in her scent, mingled with the scent of Venice, and that of the ancient stones about them and the metallic smell of the great bells over their heads. His head bent and he pressed his lips to her neck, then, lingeringly, to the special place below her ear.

She shivered, then ducked under his arm, and slipped away, laughing.

The beckoning sound echoed through the belfry.

"You're an abominable tease," he said.

"So are you," she said.

He strode to her and pulled her into his arms, "I'm done playing games." He shouldn't be done. He had work to do and the games were part of the work. But his arms were full of her, full of whispering silk and the scent of jasmine and the feel of warm curves and velvety skin, and he didn't want to think about his work.

His lips had only to touch hers and the heat, never fully suppressed, rushed through his bloodstream, melted his reason, carried off his guardian common sense, and left him stupid and wanting.

She twisted free. "I'm not."

She danced away, humming. He followed her. She began to sing. He knew the words. As she'd said, who didn't? From *The Barber of Seville*. The aria, *Una voce poco fa*. Meant for a soprano, it sounded far more suggestive at her lower pitch.

"Docile?" he said. "Respectful? Obedient? You?"

"*Dolce, amorosa*," she sang.

"Sweet and loving? I think not."

"*Ma se mi toccano /Dov'è il mio debole, /Sarò una vipera, sarò.*"

But if my will is crossed, I can be a viper.

"That's more like it," he said. "A viper, indeed." He recalled the snake tattoo on her shoulder blade. "That would explain the . . ." He caught himself in time.

He'd seen the tattoo only once, at the Fenice, when he'd been disguised as a servant. Even her nightdress—or shift or whatever that indecent silk thing had been—concealed it.

*Clumsy, clumsy.*

But she seemed not to notice. Perhaps she hadn't

heard. She was humming, still keeping a distance from him, moving from one arch to the next.

"*Cara,*" he said.

She put up her hand. "Don't call me that. No endearments, even in fun."

"Bonnard."

"Not that, either."

"Francesca," he said, and his face heated—as though he were a boy who'd done something thoroughly outrageous. When had he blushed last? But her name fit on his tongue the way her hand had fit in his, the way her body fit against his. "She-devil."

She laughed softly but she stopped and leaned upon the wall, looking out.

He went to her. Once again he rested his hands on the wall, caging her between his arms. "Let's try this again," he said.

She shook her head.

He kissed her neck. She shivered and tried to slip away but this time he nipped her neck. She stilled.

He gently bit her ear, and she trembled.

He slid his tongue down the side of her neck, to her shoulder. He kissed her, and when she trembled, he bit her.

"Oh," she said softly. "Beast."

"Your beast," he said. He tugged down the neckline of her gown, baring more skin, and followed with his mouth, making a slow trail of kisses to the top of her arm.

He tasted the cool night air on her skin, inhaled the mingled scents of jasmine and the salt breeze of the lagoon and the teasing notes he'd never been able to find a name for, which must simply be some essence of her. The mixture filled his mind, filled the world, and became a sea in which he was ready to drown. Everything about her lured a man to destruction.

He ought to be immune to her allure but he wasn't.

At this moment, he didn't want to be.

He wanted her, that was all.

His moved his hands over her bodice. He wanted skin under his hands. He wanted to cup the soft swell of her breasts. His mind was thick but a modicum of reason remained, enough to remind him where they were. They stood in a corner of the belfry, deep in the shadow of one of the columns. Even so, it was a public place, and the sky was lightening. He drew her shawl up over her shoulders and used it as a curtain while he loosened her bodice and bared her breasts, so warm and smooth and soft. He let them spill into his hands. She squirmed against him, pushing her backside against his groin.

He lightly bit her neck, to hold her still, and dragged up her skirts and petticoats. "You're a bad girl," he whispered. "A very bad girl."

"Oh, yes," she said. "I certainly am."

Francesca was a very bad girl, and that, she told herself, was what she wanted to be.

She only wished . . . but no. It was maudlin and stupid to wish the past undone, to wish to start fresh, with a clean slate. She couldn't wish it now, for this moment was too darkly, wickedly magical.

Her eyes drifted open. Below, all of Venice spread out before her like a jewel box spilling its treasures: the firefly lights, the glitter of golden domes, the boats dancing on the glistening sea. She drank in the salty air and the scent of the man behind her. She heard the whisper of silk as he lifted her skirts. A good girl would make him stop but she wasn't a good girl and didn't want to be. She was bad, very bad, trembling with need, with impatience, while his hands slid over her thighs, over her naked bottom, and finally, between her legs.

She couldn't pretend to play cat and mouse anymore. She couldn't pretend she was playing at anything. The truth was too obvious. She couldn't hide her heat from his questing hands. She'd been ready even before he touched her. She'd danced away, but it was all pretense, masking desperation . . . infatuation.

She wasn't a man. Unlike him, she had a very good idea what her trouble was.

She didn't want to think about it. Not now.

She was a deity looking down on all the world, and for this moment, she had all she wanted: his touch, his kisses, the teasing nip of his teeth, so playful and so knowing . . . his long, clever hands touching her. And at the first intimate touch, her knees gave way. If not for the stone balustrade bracing her, she'd have sunk to the floor of the belfry.

Desire was an ache, a nagging pull in the pit of her belly. She squirmed against his hand but it wasn't enough.

*Please. Now, please.*

She wouldn't beg aloud but he understood. She heard the rustle of clothing as he bared himself. He pressed against her and she gasped. He was big and hot and she had an instant of panic—absurd panic, as though she were still a girl.

He pressed one hand to her back, gently pushing her down, angling her as he wanted. His fingers slid over her, where she was slick, all too ready. He touched her, parted her, then he pushed inside her. She gasped, and the sound slid into a sigh. Pleasure blossomed inside her, in a great surge of feeling, like the mad swell of the overture of *La Gazza Ladra*. It was like the aching joy the music brought her, and she thought she'd burst with happiness.

*Oh, yes, oh, yes.* It seemed she'd waited all her life for this.

She felt his mouth at her neck while he moved inside her. She turned her head and he understood, and kissed her, long and deep and with a strange tenderness that made her ache. But the ache for release was stronger, and she moved with him while sensations pounded through her, wild and unfamiliar. Her heart was too big, swelling in her chest, beating too hard. She tried to find her way back, to regain control, her precious control, but she couldn't find her footing.

It was too late for control. She'd wanted him from the moment she'd met him, and all she could do now was want him to be hers. All she could do was own him for this moment and want to be his, only his. She gave herself up to the wild, mad happiness, rocking with him as his thrusts grew fiercer and faster, until at last the world exploded.

The ground seemed to shake beneath them, and it was a moment before she recognized the vibration and the deafening clang of the bells ringing above their heads. He laughed and covered her ears. She laughed, too. She couldn't help it. Then she opened her eyes and looked out and saw on the horizon the small red arc of the rising sun.

She felt his warm breath at her ear. "Tell me, *mia vipera,*" he said hoarsely, "is this romantic enough for you?"

It was far too romantic for James. He told himself it was too much, so ridiculous: the bells ringing as they climaxed, the sun bursting up from the horizon.

But in the golden afterglow of lovemaking, he could only laugh as he helped reassemble her garments and smooth petticoats and untwist skirts. He could only laugh, when in the midst of doing so, she told him to pull up his trousers.

He looked down and discovered he was growing aroused again. He thought about England, pulled up his undergarments and trousers, stuffed his shirt inside, and concentrated on buttoning the flap. "By gad, you are a precious jade," he said.

"I had no idea I was a miracle worker," she said. "That is a remarkably quick recovery for a man of your age."

"*My* age? What about Magny?"

"What about him?" She was rearranging her breasts in her bodice.

"He's old enough to be my grandfather."

"Surely not that old," she said. She frowned

down at her bosom. "Are they even? This is my favorite corset, but if my bosoms are not arranged just so—"

"They're splendid," he said. "Everything about you is splendid. But I'm not infatuated."

She moved to him. She smiled. She reached up and patted his cheek. "If that's what you want to believe, *mio caro,* I haven't the heart to disillusion you. Especially not now. It really was quite wonderful, inexpressibly romantic, and dreadfully naughty. A perfect combination—and an experience I shall not soon forget. *Grazie tante, amore mio.* But it's long past time I said good-bye."

She turned and moved swiftly away.

Thanks very much? Good-bye?

He was slow to react, his mind still in a post-coital haze. He stood for a moment, staring in disbelief at her retreating back. Then he started after her.

"Plague take you, Bonnard."

"Don't call me that." She moved quickly down the stairs.

"Francesca."

"Don't follow me. The sun is up, and you don't want all of Venice to see you looking like a love-sick puppy."

*Lovesick puppy?*

He came to a dead stop. "I am not—"

"It was great fun but it's done," she said, never turning her head. She flung up her hand in that aggravating gesture of dismissal. "*Addio.*"

# Chapter 10

Oh Love! How perfect is thy mystic art,
  Strengthening the weak, and trampling on
    the strong,
How self-deceitful is the sagest part
  Of mortals whom thy lure hath led along—

Lord Byron
*Don Juan, Canto the First*

*I*f one could not obtain the upper hand, the next best thing was to pretend one had it.

Francesca left with a mocking wave and a mocking smile that dissolved as soon as she started down the ramp.

She feared he'd follow her.

She feared he wouldn't.

She made herself hurry away, because she was too strongly tempted to linger, to find out whether he'd pursue her or not. If he did pursue her, she was too strongly tempted to let him catch up with her.

Games, stupid games. You'd think she was a dewy-eyed miss from the schoolroom, expecting her swain to chase after her.

Though she'd been no dewy-eyed miss when her marriage began to fall apart—or her dream of marriage, at any rate—she'd expected John Bonnard to hunt her down and wrench her from the man into whose arms she'd gone for consolation. She'd expected to make John jealous, to hurt him the way he'd hurt her.

But he wasn't jealous or hurt.

He was disgusted.

*You filthy slut. You've no more morals than your father. No wonder he was so generous with the marriage settlements. He feared he'd never get you off his hands in time, before the world discovered what you were.*

Her eyes burned and her face as well. Inside she went cold, cold as death, then hot with shame, her heart pounding as it had done that day, that terrible day when she saw all her husband's love curdle into hate.

Light filtered through the windows of the Campanile but she couldn't see through the haze of rage and misery. She stumbled. She flung her hand against the wall and regained her balance.

"Idiot," she muttered. "Break your neck, why don't you? And give Elphick cause to celebrate."

This was what happened when one gave way to feelings, she told herself. Emotion took over. One became maudlin, fretting over the past. The husband she'd loved so dearly, so deeply, had called her a slut, a whore, and worse.

Very well. She had become a whore. A magnificent one.

No sniveling now. She'd made a fine exit. She would not spoil it by hesitating or hoping. She would not spoil it with old grief and grievances.

She hurried down the ramp as quickly as skirts, petticoats, and stays permitted.

When she left the building and came out into the square, she slowed only enough to preserve her dignity. In the early morning, the small square was as busy as its larger counterpart.

She made her way past the Ducal Palace to the Molo, where her gondola waited.

Uliva, who was awake, woke up Dumini, who was not. Whenever the gondoliers had a long wait, they took turns napping, so that one was always on the alert.

"Take me to Signorina Sabbadin," she said.

From the top of the belfry, James watched her cross the Piazzetta. No matter what she said, no matter how angry he was, he should have followed her, if only to see her safely home.

It was no good telling himself how small the chances were of anyone's attacking her at this time of day. The place was abustle with vendors and others who had their livings to get and could not lie abed until noon. Along with the worker ants were those straggling home after enjoying a night and early morning of dissipation.

"Unlikely" wasn't the same as "impossible." If someone did attack her, what excuse would he offer his superiors?

*Sorry, but she hurt my feelings. Then she threw me into a mindless rage. I dared not follow her because of the strong chance I'd strangle her—and throw her luscious, lifeless body through the nearest window.*

"What an idiot," he said. "What a complete, utter imbecile."

He'd ruined everything. He was supposed to make her chase him. Instead, he'd given in to the impulse of the moment—No, it was worse than that: He'd given in to the little brain between his legs. He'd given her what he wanted and what she wanted—and that was all she wanted, obviously—and now she was done with him.

*Ciao, cretino. I'm off to drive a French count mad. And a Gilenian prince. And perhaps some Russians and Bavarians, and maybe I'll have a gondolier for dessert.*

"So what does that make me?" he muttered. "The hors d'oeuvre?"

He stomped down the stairs, down the ramp, out of the Campanile, and along the same route she had taken. All the way he cursed himself, under his breath, in Italian, in English, and now and again, for a change of pace, in French, German, Russian, and Greek.

When he reached his gondola, Zeggio reported that he and Sedgewick had seen the signora. She'd ordered her boatmen to take her to her friend's.

Perfect, James thought. She and Giulietta would compare their experiences. Giggling.

"Sir?"

James looked up.

Sedgewick and Zeggio were exchanging that look again.

"Where to, signore?" Zeggio said.

James climbed into the gondola. "San Lazzaro," he said. "The monastery. This time I'm joining up."

It was an inhuman hour of the morning, but Francesca was too desperate to think of that.

She had second thoughts when she reached Giulietta's house and saw the large, familiar gondola moored there. However, before she could tell Uliva to set out for home instead, a gentleman stepped into the boat. It promptly pulled away from the water gates.

Moments later, the gondola passed hers. She made herself give a cheerful wave. The man inside turned a brilliant shade of red but doffed his hat with princely aplomb. The early morning sunlight turned Lurenze's curls to a pale, sparkling gold.

Not many minutes thereafter, Francesca was shown in to Giulietta's boudoir. She sat at a little table by the fire, stirring a spoon round and round her coffee cup. At Francesca's entrance, her faraway look vanished.

"Well, I can see you had your fun," Francesca said as she entered. "His highness was leaving as I arrived."

Giulietta shrugged. "I made him buy the cundum. I had to show him how to use it." She ordered more coffee and bade Francesca sit down and have something to eat.

Francesca sat down, and promptly burst into tears.

Giulietta bounced up from her chair and moved to put her arms about her friend. "But what? What is wrong? Did you not want to be with Cordier?"

Francesca pulled out her damp handkerchief and stared at it. A lot of useless decoration. Why hadn't she taken Cordier's when he offered? She could have taken it home with her and kept it as a souvenir.

The thought made her sob afresh.

Giulietta stuffed a napkin into her hand. "What?" she said. "What is wrong? You never weep. Are you pregnant?"

"N-n-no." Francesca wiped her eyes and nose on the square of linen.

"You cannot be weeping about the prince," Giulietta said. "Please tell me this is not so. I thought you wished to go with the other one. You *looked*—"

"That's why you took that sudden temper fit and stormed away?" Francesca said. "What if Cordier had come after you instead?"

"But why should he? He was not the one who hurt my so-delicate feelings. It is Lurenze who calls me a child and so it is he who must chase me, and when at last I let him catch me, he says he is so very sorry. At first I am haughty and angry but by degrees I let him melt me, and then I say sweet things to him. And then . . . but you know how it is done."

"Not so well as some people, it seems," Francesca said. "Cordier was positive you wanted Lurenze to pursue you, and decided to help. Well, you and Cordier are mighty considerate of each other."

Giulietta returned to her chair. "But you know I want Lurenze," she said. "And I know you do not care about him. You want Cordier."

"But he's a nobody!"

"Why is it wrong to take a nobody for a lover once in a while?" Giulietta said. "Especially this one. He is not the waiter in the café or the handsome fisherman or flower seller. He is the son of an English nobleman. His mother comes from an old and very great Italian family. Everyone knows them."

"But in England Cordier is merely a younger son," Francesca said. "Younger sons never have any money to speak of—not real money. He can't afford to buy me treasures that will make Elphick gnash his teeth."

The coffee arrived then.

After the servant had gone and after she'd made Francesca eat half a breakfast pastry and drink some coffee, Giulietta said, "I understand the vendetta. In your place, I would have killed the brute of a husband. Or better, I would arrange for others to take him to a place where he is made to die slowly and in terrible pain. But your way is more inventive and more fun for you. Now, though, the fun is not there. It is stupid to hurt yourself to hurt a man far away on a cold little island. If you want Cordier, have him—and to the devil with Lord Elphick!"

Francesca gulped coffee. "I had him," she said.

Giulietta's face lit. She grinned. "Ah, now I see. It was good?"

"It was in the belfry of the Campanile San Marco," Francesca said.

"The belfry," Giulietta echoed softly. "Ah!"

Normally, Francesca would describe her experience in minute detail. This time she could not think what to say. She could not find the words to describe what had happened. The magic. The surge of feeling like that made her feel as music could make her feel. But more so.

She said, "It was very romantic."

"Ah, yes."

"And silly. But romantic." She told about the bells ringing and the sun coming up.

"Yes. He makes you laugh," Giulietta said.

"He makes me cry, too. He makes me . . ." Francesca hesitated. But she always told Giulietta everything. "When I'm with him, I remember who I used to be," she went on. "Everything comes back." Over her heart, she made a churning motion with her hand. "Feelings. Too many. I don't know what to do. I cry. I'm angry. I'm sick, heartsick. I want to put my head on his chest and—and I want him to put his arms around me and hold me and say he understands . . . and I want to trust him." She swallowed. "Is that not mad? I met him only five days ago."

"But he saved your life," said Giulietta. "That is how you met him—when he risked his life to save yours. What could be more stirring of the emotions than this? And what is the better way for a man to earn the trust of a woman? What is the better way for anyone, man or woman, to show what words by themselves cannot prove?"

"Magny doesn't trust him," Francesca said.

"Magny is very wise," Giulietta said. "But he is not all-knowing."

"No, he isn't," Francesca said. "Yet I can't help feeling he sees more clearly than I."

The servant re-entered. One of Signora Bonnard's servants was here, he said. He was sorry to interrupt the ladies, but the matter was most important.

James had calmed down enough to realize he needed a bath and a change of clothes and breakfast, all of which meant returning to the Ca' Munetti. He needed sleep, too, but he could do that in the gondola on the way to San Lazzaro.

He was finishing breakfast when Sedgewick came in, frowning.

"Sir," he said, "something's happened across the way."

"Nuns?" Francesca said incredulously. "Are you sure?" She stood in the Putti Inferno, looking about her.

This time she didn't need Magny to point out the signs. This lot had tried to be careful, too, but they weren't as good at it as the ones who'd come to Mira.

Her servants had noticed odds and ends out of order. They'd put this together with the fact that all of them had fallen mysteriously ill during the night—a few hours after supping with three nuns.

"They come a little while after you go to the theater," said Arnaldo. "They are from Cyprus, they tell us. They are lost. They have wandered for hours. They have little money. They are hungry." He lifted his shoulders. "What can I do? Holy sisters. How can I send them away? And so we share with them our supper."

A short time later, all those who'd shared in the supper—which was all the servants who lived in—became ill.

"At one moment, they are taking care of us," Arnaldo said. "This much I remember. I think, 'Why are the nuns not sick?' But then my head is so heavy and I must lie down. I sleep. I wake only a little while ago, and they are gone. Before too long I discover that all of the servants were the same. No one was well enough to watch the house. And soon we see that someone has been searching. Who else but these nuns? We think nothing of value is missing but we are not sure. This is why I send servants to find you. Do you wish for me to send one of the men to tell the governor what has happened?"

"No!" The last thing Francesca wanted was the Austrian governor poking his nose into this. "Send to the comte de Magny."

Arnaldo tried to put James off. "The signora is not receiving visitors."

James was not in the most patient or rational frame of mind. What he saw was not a butler doing his duty but an obstacle in his path. What he wanted to do was pick up the obstacle and throw it aside.

He told himself not to be an idiot. He reminded himself that he'd learned, a long time ago, that there was a time and a place for violence. He knew perfectly well that this was not the time or place.

He was angry because he hadn't been prepared for this possibility: that someone would not only dare but succeed in invading Bonnard's well-guarded house. That was not Arnaldo's fault.

And so, in smooth, idiomatic Italian, James thanked him for his devotion to the lady—and walked past him, into the most feverishly decorated drawing room in all of Italy—and that, James knew, was saying something.

"Thank God all the *putti* are still here," he said. "When I heard something had happened, I thought for sure the children had all flapped their little wings and flown away."

She started toward him and for a moment he thought she would throw herself into his arms.

But she stopped short, got as stiff as a poker, and said, "I am not receiving visitors."

"I heard you've had a visit from burglars," he said.

Her jaw dropped.

"Word travels quickly across a canal," he said. "My gondolier had it from one of the market boats who had it from your cook."

He looked about him. "Not amateurs, clearly," he said. But of course they weren't. Amateurs would never have made it past the porters. "What made you suspect?"

"It was the servants who were suspicious," she said. "I arrived only a short time ago. Not that it's any of your affair."

Arnaldo, who'd followed James into the room, said, "We see that some objects and some furniture are not in the proper place, signore."

She threw up her hands. "Does everyone cater to you?"

"It's my charm," James said. "Irresistible."

She turned away and threw herself into a chair. She waved at Arnaldo. "Go ahead, then. Tell him."

In rapid Venetian—which James could barely follow—and in considerable detail, Arnaldo told him.

"Nuns?" James said. A cold knot formed in his solar plexus. "From Cyprus?"

He knew that Venice had once been the center of a vast trading empire. People came from every corner of the globe, even in these unhappy days. The Armenians had their own church. So did the Greeks. The Jews had several synagogues.

Nuns from Cyprus would be nothing out of the ordinary.

The trouble was, he was aware that so-called nuns from Cyprus had been responsible for several spectacular thefts in southern Italy in the last year. It was one of these thefts that had brought James to Rome, and his encounter with Marta Fazi—the ringleader . . . who was mad for emeralds. If she hadn't been mad and thus indiscreet, flaunting them in very public, if low, places, they might have gone missing forever.

But Marta was supposed to be in prison. Her gang had been broken up. Was this the work of an imitator? A coincidence?

Arnaldo must have finally noticed the baffled expression his listeners wore, because he reverted to Italian when he answered, "Everyone knows this accent. In Venice we hear it almost every day."

James recalled the trace of foreign accent in Marta Fazi's speech. She'd been born in Cyprus.

Anyone could claim to be from Cyprus. But the accent was distinctive, to Arnaldo at least.

The chances of this being a coincidence or the work of imitators were shrinking by the moment.

Someone could have got Marta out. She'd been imprisoned in Rome, and the Papal States were notoriously corrupt. Powerful friends with money could have arranged her release.

All while James's mind was scrambling through details and arranging them and making its way to the logical conclusion, he maintained his calm, casual pose.

"Your jewelry?" he said to Bonnard. "Gone, I daresay?"

She blinked at him. "*My jewelry?*"

"That's what Piero said they were after the last time," he reminded her. He'd doubted the story then, both logic and instincts telling him there was more to it than Piero told. Now a pattern was emerging. It wasn't pretty. "Your jewelry's become famous among the thief community, it seems."

She bolted up from the chair and hurried from the room.

James followed her.

Francesca's private quarters were not so neatly searched as the other rooms. She felt chilled as she took it in: The mattresses hung partly on, partly off the bed. The bric-a-brac of her dressing table was tumbled about, and some of it had fallen to the floor beneath.

This was nothing like what had happened at Mira. Then the intruders had left very little trace of their doings.

This was . . . disturbing.

Thérèse stood on the threshold of the dressing room. She was weeping.

Francesca had never before seen her maid shed tears. It had not occurred to her that the haughty, self-sufficient lady's maid was capable of weeping.

"Thérèse?" Francesca said, and went to the maid and put her arms about her shoulders. "Are you all right?"

"Oh, madame." The maid turned and pressed her forehead against Francesca's upper arm and sobbed.

"It's all right," Francesca said. "Everyone was sick but no one was hurt."

Thérèse lifted her head, wiped her eyes with the back of her hand, and said in rapid, angry French, "It is despicable. Filthy brutes. To dare to touch your beautiful gowns, your jewels—"

"Gone?" came a masculine voice from behind them.

For a moment, shocked at seeing Thérèse in tears, Francesca had forgotten Cordier was there.

Tearful or not, Thérèse ignored him, as she always ignored the men in Francesca's life. "They throw everything everywhere," she said. "They empty your jewel box on the floor." She nodded at the dressing room's interior.

Everything was on the floor. Including her jewelry.

"That's interesting," Cordier said. His voice

came from much nearer behind her. He was looking over the maid's head into the dressing room. "They didn't take the jewelry. What on earth could they have wanted, then? Those memoirs you mentioned? Had you started writing them already?"

This had nothing to do with the memoirs Francesca doubted she'd ever write. It had nothing to do with simple robbery, either. Ordinary robbers did not throw expensive jewelry on the floor and leave it there. They—whoever they were—were after something far more valuable: the letters.

Francesca shook her head. She spoke lightly while her heart beat too hard. "Perhaps someone simply dislikes me. Perhaps it's a prank."

"An elaborate prank," he said. "Dressing up like nuns and poisoning your servants."

"It's very strange they didn't take the jewelry," she said. "Perhaps they truly were nuns. Who else could exercise so much restraint, and leave my pearls and sapphires behind?"

There they were, glinting up at her from among heaps of dresses, petticoats, corsets, chemises, gloves, and stockings.

Like a taunt. She'd taunted Elphick with reports of her jewels, her conquests. He'd taunted her, too, with his achievements, his conquests. A game, not very mature, perhaps.

Now it had turned ugly.

"Perhaps the nuns did this as a warning to me to mend the error of my ways," she said. "Or to tell me that all is vanity or some such sanctimonious rubbish."

"Your letters," the maid said, moving into the dressing room. "The box where you keep them is there, on the floor, madame, but I see no letters, no papers of any kind."

It was impossible, James told himself. Had she kept Elphick's incriminating letters in so obvious a place, Quentin's men would have found them when they searched her various residences.

They had searched the obvious places and the not-obvious places. Agents had obtained access to all the banks with which she did business. In the vaults they'd found jewelry—saved against the rainy day that often came to harlots as age took its toll—and her will and various financial and legal papers, but not the letters.

If it had been as simple as opening a portable writing desk or looking for secret pockets in her clothing or the bed curtains or hidden compartments in the furniture and such, they would not have needed James Cordier.

Yet he heard her sharp intake of breath and was aware of how she struggled to maintain her composure. She knew she was in trouble. The trick would be getting her to admit it.

"This grows more absurd by the minute," she said. "It's impossible to try to determine what's gone and why in this chaos. Summon some maids to help you restore order here, Thérèse. Then you can make a list of what, if anything, is missing. Whatever these naughty nuns were up to, I shall be much amazed if they left without taking a single piece of jewelry."

The maid went out.

"Maybe someone believed you'd started writing your memoirs," he said.

"That makes no sense," she said. She swung away from the doorway and moved to the mangled bed. "I've been at this for less than five years. My affairs are not secret. Far from it. I am not only a magnificent whore but a flamboyant one. No back doors or back stairs for me. Anyone who wants to know about my lovers might read about them in the newspapers. In fifteen or twenty years the participants might find the revelations embarrassing. At present, however, they are more likely to consider a liaison with Francesca Bonnard a badge of honor. You see, though you do not appreciate me properly, others do."

"I appreciate you," he said. "I thought I proved that a very short time ago. In the Campanile. Or have you forgotten already?"

The green eyes flashed up at him. "Cordier, you are an utter blockhead."

"I know," he said. "I should not have let you run away."

A shadow came into her eyes, then, and he thought he saw the girl again, the girl who could believe, who could trust. But she vanished in the next instant. "I did not run away," she said. "I was done with you. I left."

"I'm not done," he said.

"I don't care," she said.

*How do I make you care?* he wanted to ask.

"I do," he said. "I'm worried about you. A few days ago, someone tried to kill you."

"To rob me," she said.

"A few days ago you were assaulted," he said patiently. "Last night, your house was ransacked."

"Searched," she said. "So far, all that seems to be missing is some correspondence." She smiled thinly. "And very amusing reading it will prove to be, to whomever has it."

"Love letters?" he said.

"Oh, no," she said. "They're from my husband."

The bedroom door flew open and Magny stalked in, followed closely by a protesting Thérèse.

"Madame, I have told him you are engaged," Thérèse said.

"*Allez-vous en,*" Magny told the maid.

She did not so much as look at him.

"Do proceed, Thérèse," said madame. "I know you wish to put everything in order."

Nose aloft, Thérèse walked past monsieur into the dressing room.

"Your servants are abominably insolent," Magny said.

"My servants are loyal," Bonnard said.

"If you did not want to see me, why the devil did you send for me?" he said, throwing a glare in James's direction.

"I did want to see you," she said. "I do not want you ordering my servants about. That is the trouble. That is always the trouble. I should have remembered. What the devil was I thinking of, to seek your advice?"

"What were you thinking, indeed? Here is Monsieur Cordier to—" Magny made a dismissive gesture. "To do whatever it is he's here to do."

"I'm not sure there's anything I can do," James said. "For some mad reason, a lot of nuns made off with her husband's not-love letters."

"Letters?" Magny said. "But that—" He broke off, walked to the door of the dressing room, and glared at the maid. She turned her back to him and went on folding garments.

He came away from the door. "I have seen enough, Francesca. You're moving out of this place and coming to live with me."

"We tried that," she said. "Twice. It was disastrous both times."

"What else could it be?" said James.

Magny glowered at him.

James ignored it. "Come live with me, then."

Magny stared at him. So did she.

And it seemed for an instant, as though they wore exactly the same expression. Then the ghost came into her eyes. "Why?" she said.

"Because I'm worried about you," James said. "And because it's a much shorter way to go—merely across the canal. And because . . ." He paused. "Because I'm infatuated."

"I am going to be sick," Magny said. He threw up his hands and left the room.

Bonnard watched him go. "He isn't romantic," she said.

"Neither am I," James said. "If I could devise a less sickening reason, you may be sure I'd use it. But the fact is, I want to knock him down."

"A great many people feel that way," she said. "Including me."

"In my case, it seems to be jealousy," he said.

She turned away and moved to the dressing table. She righted a toppled jar. "You do understand that jealousy is absurd in my case? I don't belong to any man. That's the trouble with living with a man. When a woman takes up residence under his roof, he assumes she's one of his possessions. I'm nobody's possession."

"Very well," he said. "We can discuss terms, if you wish."

"There are no terms," she said. "I am not coming to live with you."

"Then I'm moving in here," he said.

She paused in her fussing over the bottles and jars—the fussing that rightly was Thérèse's province —and turned. She set her hands on the dressing table and braced herself on her arms. She smiled. "No, you're not."

"Madame."

Thérèse emerged from the dressing room, a velvet box in her hand. "The emeralds are gone," she said.

# Chapter 11

A long, long kiss, a kiss of youth, and love,
    And beauty, all concentrating like rays
Into one focus, kindled from above;
    Such kisses as belong to early days,
Where heart, and soul, and sense,
      in concert move,
    And the blood's lava, and the pulse a blaze,
Each kiss a heart-quake,—for a kiss's strength,
I think, it must be reckon'd by its length.

Lord Byron
*Don Juan, Canto the First*

*J*ames was putting puzzle pieces together. He
didn't like the looks of any of them.

Letters had been stolen.

And emeralds.

The robbers had taken the wrong letters, apparently. Bonnard would not be so amused—and he
was sure she hadn't feigned that—if they'd taken
the right ones. But what was in the wrong ones, to
amuse her so?

Or was she simply amused at the error?

He wasn't.

Someone who did not read very well in the first place and who understood very little English in the second, might easily make the mistake.

That someone needn't be Marta Fazi. Who else, though, besides Marta, was demented enough to take emeralds and leave diamonds, rubies, pearls, and sapphires behind?

The logical conclusion was, someone had sent Marta to retrieve the letters. The someone had overestimated her intelligence and underestimated Bonnard's.

Her former husband?

*They play a game,* Giulietta had said of Bonnard and her former spouse, *and to kill her is to admit he loses.*

The trouble was, bringing crazy Marta Fazi into the business indicated a willingness to kill. James tried to remember if he'd heard of any connection between Fazi and Elphick. Nothing came to mind.

Was he completely wrong? Was there something he ought to see that he couldn't? If so, it was not surprising. He was stumbling in the dark because he didn't understand the game Bonnard played with Elphick. And he'd keep on stumbling until he put an end to the game she played with James Cordier.

He turned to Thérèse and gave orders in the French he'd perfected decades ago, the impeccable accents that had spared him decapitation on more than one occasion.

"Madame requires a bath," he said. "While that

is in preparation, have servants repair her bed. While they do this, you will restore order to the dressing room and carry out the inventory madame ordered. She will expect you to list every missing item, no matter how unimportant. After madame has bathed and rested and is properly supplied with correct information, she will decide how to proceed."

Thérèse bowed her head. "*Oui, monsieur,*" she said. She hurried from the room.

Bonnard stared after her. Then she stared at James. "Who *are* you?" she said. "A long-lost Bourbon? She won't heed even Magny, yet she heeds you."

"It's my charm," James said. "Irresistible."

Her beautiful eyes narrowed.

"I told her to do precisely what she wanted to do," he said. "She's too worried about you to pay proper attention to your belongings. Once you've bathed and rested, she'll be able to concentrate on her work. Likewise, you can't be expected to think clearly until you've had time to recover."

"From staying out all night?" she said. "I'm used to that."

"From the shock."

"It's true I'm still reeling at the idea of nuns as burglars."

"Those weren't real nuns," he said. "And it wasn't a simple robbery. What is this about, Bonnard?"

She shrugged, and picked up a bottle from the floor.

He moved to her. "How stupid do you think I am?" he said. "I know something is going on here.

What are you hiding? How can I help you if you won't tell me anything?"

"Where did you get the idea I needed help?"

"A pair of nasty brutes assaulted you last week, supposedly for your jewelry—"

"Supposedly? Aren't you sure? You told me that the one who was captured said it was an attempted robbery."

"A few days after that attack, your house is searched," he said. "How much more evidence do you need that something is wrong? Why should someone make off with your husband's letters?"

"And my emeralds," she said. "Maybe something alarmed the naughty nuns when they were ransacking my dressing room, and they simply snatched up what was at hand. They might have mistaken the letters for bank notes." Maybe they thought they were passionate love letters and they could sell them to the scandal sheets. If so, they're in for a disappointment. They've stolen a lot of boring boasting and name-dropping—"

"Francesca."

"It's none of your affair!" she snapped. "I don't want your help!"

"You're behaving like an idiot," he said. "Are you pregnant?"

The bottle shot toward his head. He ducked. It struck the back of a chair, and toppled to the floor, unbroken. It must be a heavy little bottle. If he hadn't ducked, it might have cracked his skull open.

"Pregnant?" she cried. "Pregnant? Why not ask if it's coming to that time of the month?"

"Well, is it?" he said.

"You stupid, stupid man! I'm not pregnant. It's not coming to that time of month. I'm tired and dirty and I want a bath. And some sleep. And I want you out of my house. *Va via!*" She flung up her hand in that provoking backhanded gesture of dismissal.

He shook his head and rolled his eyes toward the ceiling and its cavorting mythological beings. Hadn't he told her, a moment ago, that she needed a bath and rest?

He strode to her, and scooped her up in his arms.

"Put me down," she said.

"I'm going to give you a bath," he said. "I'm going to throw you into the canal."

Francesca did struggle but it was pointless. The brute who'd tried to strangle her was three times her size, and he'd struggled with this man to no avail.

She remembered how easily Cordier had subdued him, how effortlessly he'd tossed him into the canal.

"You wouldn't," she said.

He didn't answer, only strode out of the bedroom and down the *portego* toward the canal-facing windows. With their balconies. Directly over the canal.

"Can you swim?" he said.

"Yes."

"Then you've nothing to worry about, have you?"

"Cordier," she said.

"The water is cool and refreshing at this time of year," he said. "Exactly the sort of thing you need to clear your addled little head."

She was addled, she knew, and she'd been an utter bitch as well.

She laid her head on his shoulder. "I'm sorry," she said. "I'm . . . emotional, I know."

"No, you're insane," he said.

"I don't want to care for you," she said.

He kept on walking. "Honeyed words will not work," he said. "I wasn't born yesterday."

"Oh, very well, then," she said. "Drown me. It'll be a relief."

"No, it won't. You know how to swim, you said. Besides, you're beautiful. A romantic Venetian is sure to fish you out before the tide carries you out to sea."

She tightened her arms about his neck. "I'm sorry," she said. "Don't be angry with me." She felt the tears trickling from her eyes. Again. This was horrible, worse than she'd supposed—and she'd thought she'd supposed the worst.

She was afraid of losing him. She must be mad. She hoped she was. The alternative was too ghastly to contemplate. Five days! She'd met him only five days ago!

"I'm immune to tears," he said. "I'm doing this for your own good."

"I'm g-going to s-scream for help," she said. "The s-servants will c-come to my r-rescue."

"They'll have to be deuced qu-quick," he said mockingly.

They'd reached the *portego* windows.

"Cordier."

The arm under her knees shifted slightly, and he put his hand on the window handle.

"You won't do it," she said.

"Watch me," he said.

She was aware of heads popping out of doorways. "The servants won't let you," she said.

"Yes, they will," he said. "They're Italian. They'll understand perfectly."

He opened the tall window and carried her through it. The balcony was narrow. It wanted only a step to carry her to the edge. He set her down on the wide stone railing.

She locked her hands behind his neck. "If I go down, you're going with me," she said.

He reached for her hands.

He'd have no trouble getting free of her.

And that was the trouble.

She let go of him and quickly, before she could think twice, turned.

And jumped.

"*Merda,*" she heard him say.

It did not take very long. Merely a lifetime while James's heart stopped and he blinked in disbelief, while he uttered the one word and pulled off his shoes. Merely a lifetime passed while he plunged in after her.

He caught hold of her before she could swim away—or attempt it: a considerable challenge, given the impediments of skirts and petticoats and stays. He dragged her the few feet to the water gates, wrenched them open, dragged her inside, rose, hauled her upright, and shook her.

"Don't ever." Shake. "Do that." Shake. "Again."

She stood, dripping, looking up at him, her green eyes so soft, filled with the ghost.

"Don't look at me that way," he said.

"I'm not," she said.

He pulled her into his arms. He kissed her wet forehead, her nose, her cheeks. He dragged his hands through her sopping hair while he waited for his heart rate to return to normal. It wouldn't, just kept thudding unevenly, with panic and anger and he didn't know what else. He didn't know how to stop it. He didn't know how to feel in control again.

Then his mouth came at last to hers and he kissed her, like the drowning man he was. It was deep and hot and ungentle, and she kissed him back in the same ferocious way.

She was bold and unafraid and shameless—the exact opposite of what he wanted. Nonetheless he wanted her, and the fierce kiss left him weak in the knees.

Yet all the while he was still himself, still aware of where they were. He knew he couldn't let his brain go weak as well. Not now. For her sake he must keep his wits about him.

Oh, yes, and for king and country, too.

The last thought was as bracing as a slap in the face.

He drew away. "I should have stayed where I was and waved good-bye," he said. " '*Ciao,*' I should have said. I should have waved and thought, *good riddance*. That's what I should have done. You are nothing but trouble."

She flung her arms around his waist and held him tightly.

Then he was done for, king or not, country or not.

"You smell like canal," he said. "You really need a bath."

"So do you," came her muffled voice from his waterlogged coat.

"How big is your bathtub?" he said.

"I'm a great whore," she said. "What do you think?"

It was only a short distance to the bathing room, which Francesca had created from one of the cozy rooms on the mezzanine, between the *andron* and the *piano nobile*. The tub was very large, as befitted a courtesan, but she had not yet entertained a man here while bathing.

A small window let in light from the courtyard. Even when the sun was at the best angle this room was one of the darker ones in the house. A servant was lighting candles as they entered. He'd already lit the fire in the fireplace.

The light flickered over what she thought of as a most luxurious cave.

The tub stood to one side of the fireplace. A Roman-style couch stood on the other. Soft towels, neatly folded, stood in heaps on tables nearby.

She'd furnished the room in the style she'd seen on mosaics from Roman times, to go with the frescoes. Instead of the *putti* and saints and martyrs prevalent elsewhere, the flickering candlelight here revealed gods and goddesses, nymphs and satyrs, food and wine, dancing and lovemaking. Incense burned in the braziers, as it had done in the old days of the Republic.

This room was private, a refuge. She never brought company here.

The servants had already prepared it for her, though. In the circumstances, it was irrational as well as inconsiderate to make them labor again, this time hauling water all the way up to the *piano nobile*. She was cold and wet. Cordier was cold and wet . . . and what did it matter if she let him into her sanctuary? What was the point of trying to keep him out of any corner of her life?

"You're full of surprises," he said, looking about him. "I'd expected to see a tub wheeled into your boudoir or bedroom."

"There's a smaller tub upstairs," she said. "It's mainly for the benefit of gentlemen who might wish to watch me bathe. But this room is for me."

The servant went out and Thérèse hurried in, carrying a basket of soaps, creams, and perfumes. Over one arm hung a dressing gown. She looked hard at Francesca, glanced at Cordier, and compressed her lips. "Madame will take cold," she said.

"I'll see that she doesn't," Cordier said. He took the basket and dressing gown from her. "Madame pleases to drive me mad—"

"Monsieur pleases to provide me the same service," Francesca said.

"Nonetheless, I shall see that she comes to no

harm," Cordier said. "You may go now. She'll scream if she needs you."

Thérèse looked to Francesca. "You may go," Francesca said.

The maid went out.

"Every member of the household knows what happened," he said. "It will be all over Venice in five minutes."

"You upset me," she said.

"The feeling is mutual," he said.

"I don't like to be upset," she said.

"Who does?"

"I have spent the last five years arranging my life to keep that from happening," she said.

He inspected the jars and bottles and soaps in the basket and removed one bottle before setting down the basket on the table close by the tub. He unstopped the bottle, sniffed it, then sprinkled a few drops into the tub. "I'm beginning to understand," he said.

"You're a man," she said. "It's impossible for you to understand. Men have all the power. Men control everything. They make the official laws and all the ordinary and unofficial rules. They—"

"Your husband broke your heart," he said.

What was she to do? Lie and lie again? Pretend, endlessly pretend? That worked well enough with everyone else, but with this man the pretense made her sick and confused.

"Yes," she said. Her shoulders sagged. She was weary, so weary.

"Come here," he said.

She went to him, of course. That was all she

wanted to do: to go to him, to feel his arms about her.

But he didn't pull her into his arms. He turned her around and unhooked the back of her gown. "You look like Isis in this gown," he said. "After she fell into the Nile."

In spite of the weariness, in spite of old wounds, she smiled. "Did she fall into the Nile?"

"Or was she pushed? Who knows?" He untied the waist, and the gown drooped. If it had been dry, it would have slid down. "I like this garment construction," he said. He tugged gently, drawing the gown down over her hips.

"It was a beautiful gown," she said. "Dry, it whispered over my petticoats as it slid to the floor."

It wasn't dry now, though, and he had to help it down. Once past her knees, it fell to the floor with a most unseductive *plop*.

He went to work on the wet strings of her petticoat. "I'm sure you don't like being wet and bedraggled any more than you like being upset," he said. "You should have thought of that before you jumped into the canal."

"You were going to throw me in."

"And you jumped to rob me of the pleasure?"

"I wasn't thinking clearly," she said.

"As I believe I pointed out to you. More than once. *Al diavolo!*"

"What's wrong?"

"These strings are impossible," he said. "By the time I've got them and your corset string untied, you'll have pneumonia. And the bath will be cold.

I'm cutting them. It's not as though you can't afford to replace them, what with your being the great Whore of Babylon and all, and rich as Cleopatra besides."

Her chest heaved.

"Don't cry," he said.

"I'm n-not," she said.

She felt the strings give way.

He swiftly stripped off the petticoat, stays, and shift. She stood only in her soaked stockings and garters, and her water-stained slippers.

She heard him suck in his breath.

She turned toward him.

He stood, looking at her, up and down, up and down. He had a penknife in his right hand.

"I'm going to faint," he said.

"Don't be silly," she said. "You've seen lots of naked women."

"I'm not silly," he said. "I'm half Italian, and you . . ." He drew his left hand down over her breast. "I think you must be the Eighth Deadly Sin. And well worth an eternity in Hell." He knelt, slid the penknife between her leg and the garter, and slit it. He peeled the stocking down, slipped off her shoe, and drew the stocking over her foot. He kissed her knee.

Her legs trembled. She set her hand on his shoulder to brace herself. He slit the other garter and performed the same ritual.

"I can think of a great many things to do at this moment," he said, stroking her thigh. "But the bath will grow cold, and you do smell of canal, and so do I."

He rose, set aside the knife, and began to work his way out of his sopping coat. The garment fit, as it ought to do, like skin.

She moved to help.

He waved her away. "Get in the tub," he said.

"You'll never do that alone," she said. He probably needed two servants to get him out of it.

"Watch me," he said. "Get in the tub."

She climbed in, and groaned involuntarily. It was beautifully warm and smelled like a lemon grove.

She closed her eyes and leaned back, resting her neck on the thick linens with which the servant had draped it.

"This is a wonderful bathing room," he said.

She opened her eyes. He was hanging his coat over the back of a chair. This was a man who'd had practice in doing without servants, she thought.

This man. She knew so little about him. Five days. And yet . . .

He unbuttoned his waistcoat. "Nymphs and satyrs frolicking on the walls. Candles and incense. It's your own little temple, isn't it? The Temple of Francesca, Goddess of the Canal."

"It's the Temple of the Vestal Virgins," she said. "I've never had a man in here before."

He paused in the act of pulling off his waistcoat. "I'm the first?"

"You've no idea how privileged you are," she said.

He got the waistcoat off and draped it neatly over the chair seat. "I have an excellent idea," he said. "Especially now that I've seen you naked."

"You don't need to flatter me," she said. "I don't need honeyed words."

"When have I flattered you?" he said. He undid the button at the neck of the shirt sticking wetly to his torso. It sagged open, revealing a V of his powerful chest, gleaming bronze in the candlelight. "I believe I called you an idiot more than once this morning alone." He sat on the chair, on top of his wet waistcoat, and tugged off his stockings. "And to think I nearly wore boots today. We might have both drowned. Or you would have done so, by the time I got them off."

"I don't know what to do," she said.

He stood up and pulled his shirt over his head. "Give me one more minute," he said. "I'll think of something." He began unbuttoning his trousers.

She ducked down, under the water, and came up again, looking like one of the nymphs in the frescoes. Only more beautiful.

She was right: James had seen countless women naked. Perhaps she wasn't perfect. Her high, round breasts could have been a bit fuller, her waist a bit narrower . . .

No. He couldn't be objective. All he could see was womanly perfection, a goddess.

He peeled off his waterlogged trousers, kicked them aside, and climbed into the tub.

She drew in her legs, making room for him.

For a moment he simply let himself sink into the warmth and the delicious scents swirling in the atmosphere of the intimate room. He slid down as she had done, bringing his head under water, and came up again. He let the back of his head rest on the thick towels draped upon the tub's rim and looked up at the ceiling, where nymphs and satyrs were cavorting among bunches of grapes and flagons of wine and Pan playing his pipes.

"I'd always thought these rooms were used as offices, like the ones below, on the *andron*," she said. "But I was told that in the last generation or so, the family used them as sitting rooms and parlors. I made this one my private bathing room because it's closer to the water supply and the kitchen. Less work for the servants, heating and carrying the water. And I liked the frescoes."

He sat up and reached beside him for a square of soap from the basket on the table. He reached under water and found her ankle. "You need a bath, my water nymph," he said. "And I'm going to give you one."

"Do you promise not to pull me under?" she said.

"No," he said. He lifted her foot above the water and began to soap it, taking his time. He worked his way up her ankles and up and round and over the shapely calves and onward, over her knees. As he washed her, he inched closer. But when he reached the juncture of her thighs, he simply let his hand drift over the bottom of her belly. He heard her inhale sharply, but he continued to the other thigh, and worked his way down that leg.

"You're not very . . . thorough," she said softly.

"Give me time," he said.

"No, you give *me* time," she said. "My turn now." She took a sponge from the basket, wet it, then took the soap from him, and rubbed it over the sponge until she'd made a lather. She draped her long legs over his thighs, and slid closer, until she was entwined with him in the middle of the tub. She drew the soapy sponge over his neck and shoulders, down over his chest, and down, where his cock strained to meet her hand—to meet any female part it could.

But it would have to wait.

He put out his hand. "My turn."

He did as she had done, moving the soapy sponge over her neck and shoulders and down over her arms and hands and between her fingers and over her palms and up again and down again, slowly, lovingly, over her perfectly rounded breasts. And while he did this the words came out, so easily, as though they'd been waiting for this moment. He told her, softly, in Dante's language, that she set him on fire, that he'd wanted her from the first moment he'd met her . . .

She reached up and tangled her fingers in his hair and she smiled the smile of a girl, a playful, naughty girl.

He was mesmerized. The sponge slid from his hands and they moved over her, skin to skin this time, over her neck and the sweet slope of her shoulders and her arms and down to her long, slim fingers, then up again and down again, over the smooth arcs of her breasts. And all the while he watched her unearthly face as she played with his hair. And all the while he was murmuring love words in his mother's language, like the romantic he wasn't.

Her green gaze slid down and met his.

They remained so for a long moment, their gazes locked.

Then she brought her mouth to his, but only lightly touching.

"*Per quanto ancora mi farai aspettare?*" he said against her lips. How long will you make me wait? "*Baciami.*" Kiss me.

She smiled.

He drew his lips along that long curve. "*Baciami,*" he said.

The smile his lips had traced was her harlot's smile, and he expected the harlot's kiss, though that wasn't what he wanted and he couldn't say what it was he wanted.

"*Baciami,*" he said.

And she kissed him.

Shyly. Sweetly. Tenderly, so tenderly that he trembled, and told himself it was the bath water cooling.

Not shy. Not sweet. Not tender. Not she.

Yet she was. She made his cold, hard heart ache. His arms went round her and he dragged her up against him. Her legs wrapped about his waist. He held her so, as the kiss went on, deepening and deepening, a drowning of a kiss. He held her tightly, as though she'd be pulled away, dragged out to sea, and be lost forever otherwise.

Perhaps it was then he understood what had happened to him when she fell from the balcony. Or perhaps he only felt something he did not understand until later.

Her hands slid down, from his hair and along his jaw and down over his chest. He broke the kiss to take her hand and kiss her knuckles, her fingertips, and then to press his mouth to the soft palm.

She kissed the back of the hand holding hers, and slipped her hand free, and down it went, reaching through the water until it closed around his cock. He groaned. She covered his mouth with hers, and stole his soul with another wrenching kiss. He reached down, and pushed her hand away, and quickly, more quickly than he'd ever meant, he was inside her. He still held her tightly, as though the world would end if he loosened his grasp.

*Slow*, he told himself. *Make this last forever.*

He tried to make it slow, but she was kissing his face, his neck, and her hands were so soft, and nothing was real. The water pulsed around them as they pulsed against each other.

He gave up trying to control any of it, and let the tide take him. They rose and fell together, higher and higher each time until there was nowhere left to go. Then she shuddered against him, and the world flew apart. Release came, and down he went, a drowning man, happily drowning.

# Chapter 12

They blush, and we believe them; at least I
  Have always done so; 'tis of no great use,
In any case, attempting a reply,
  For then their eloquence grows
    quite profuse;
And when at length they're out of breath,
    they sigh,
  And cast their languid eyes down,
    and let loose
A tear or two, and then we make it up;
And then—and then—and then—sit down
    and sup.

Lord Byron
*Don Juan, Canto the First*

He was kissing her so sweetly: scores of tender kisses on her nose, her cheeks, her forehead, her ears, her neck, her shoulders. Francesca kissed him back in the same way, like a girl in love for the first time. And when he stopped and drew away a bit and looked at her, she knew she was looking back at him with stars in her eyes, but she couldn't help it.

She'd been numb for so long, dead to feeling without realizing it. Until now. It was as though the long, sensual bathing ritual had washed away—not her sins, for she was deeply attached to those—but a coating or shell of some kind that had stopped her from feeling too deeply, too fully.

She felt now, deeply and fully.

Joy was coursing through her. It was not the simple physical pleasure of coupling but a bright happiness that lightened her heart.

He drew her upright, and she rose out of the water like one mesmerized. She couldn't make her eyes turn anywhere but up to him, to look up into his handsome face.

Later she'd ask herself why but for now she could only gaze at him in a kind of stupid wonder.

"Don't look at me like that," he said.

"Like what?" She said, as though she didn't know she wore the expression of a girl hopelessly in love.

He turned away to reach for a dry towel. "You'll put ideas in my head," he said. He wrapped the towel around her and helped her out of the tub. "I shouldn't have kept you here for so long. If you take cold, Thérèse will kill me."

"But it was great fun," she said.

"Fun," he said. Frowning, he picked up another towel and as smoothly and efficiently as Thérèse could have done it, wrapped her hair into it and twisted the towel about her head like a turban.

"Oh, you've done this before," she said.

"Never," he said. "You're the first."

She almost wished that were true. She almost wished he'd been the first for her and she could persuade herself he felt as she did.

She knew better.

Still, she told herself, if it had been the first time, she couldn't have properly appreciated what had happened. She wouldn't know enough to savor it, to store it in her memory.

"Go sit by the fire," he said.

She walked to the couch and sat.

She watched him take up a towel and vigorously rub his hair. When he was done, the shiny black curls bounced about his head. She ached to tangle her fingers in his hair again. She longed to touch everything. She let her gaze travel wistfully over his long body. Then she made herself turn away. She lay down on the couch and stared into the fire.

She wasn't aware of falling asleep.

She never heard him leave.


James had wrapped a towel about his waist and gone out to look for a servant to fetch them something to eat and to send for his clothes.

He found one too soon.

Sedgewick was sitting on the stairs nearby, waiting for him.

Arnaldo had already sent across the canal for a change of clothes. Sedgewick had brought the clothes. He'd also brought a message.

"It's from San Lazzaro," Sedgewick said. "You're wanted there. *Without further loss of time*, I was to tell you, sir."

* * *

"Monsieur left a note, madame," Thérèse said, handing it to her.

*Amor mio,*

*Those accursed monks! I had appointed to meet with them at San Lazzaro this morning. Something made me forget. A troublesome girl, I believe. Forgive me. Dine with me to-night in my bachelor lodgings and I will make it up to you.*

*Caramente,*
*C*

Francesca knew she was deeply, unforgivably foolish. Before melancholy and disappointment could settle upon her, one hastily scrawled note drove them away. She tried but she couldn't stifle the surge of relief and happiness. She laughed softly.

And when Thérèse scolded and said madame needed something to eat and a proper sleep, Francesca smilingly agreed.

She'd need her strength for tonight.

*Meanwhile, in less elegant quarters in Venice*

A ceramic Madonna flew across the sitting room of Marta Fazi's lodgings and shattered against a door frame.

The two young men waiting to collect their pay only watched Marta's hand, to see if she would throw anything else. But she was too puzzled to be truly enraged, and her temper cooled quickly, as it often did. She returned to her chair at the small table.

"These are not the letters," she said.

The two young men looked at each other then at her.

"I showed them to you," said the smaller one. "You said, 'Yes, let's go.' You made us hurry away. You gave us no time even to pick up some of the jewelry."

"I told you it wasn't real!" she lied. "You want to make the English whore laugh at how stupid you are? You think she keeps her fine jewelry in her house, in a drawer where anyone can get it?"

Even Marta, who'd been told of the jewelry, hadn't believed her eyes at first. But the English-woman was a rich whore with many servants. Those arrogant ladies never dreamed anyone would steal from them. They were always so shocked and outraged when it happened.

Though the messenger had hinted that she could help herself, Marta knew better. When one stole from the rich, the laziest authorities became brutally efficient—and the Austrians were not lazy. They'd caught Piero in no time. Of course, he was an idiot. Even so, it was clear that the great English whore was no mere *puttana* in the eyes of the Venetian governor. Had Marta and this pair made off with all the jewelry they'd found, they'd be swiftly hunted down . . . and if they were captured, the precious letters would fall into the wrong hands.

She'd taken a risk, she knew, to steal the emeralds. But that was only one set, among so many riches . . . and it was fine, as the messenger had promised. Fit for a queen.

All this was far too complicated to explain to this pair of fools. They didn't know she'd taken any jewelry. At the moment, however, she was not worried about being hunted down for one measly set of emeralds.

She was far more disturbed about the letters.

"These are in his hand," she said, half to herself. "But the dates are only this year and last year. The ones they want are old. And where are the names they told me to look for? Nowhere do I see them. But why does he write to her, still, the woman he hates?"

She might as well have asked the two to explain the Pythagorean theorem. They were little more than boys, because a person sporting half a day's growth of black beard does not make a believable nun. They only lifted their shoulders in the universal gesture of "I dunno."

Marta folded the letters, tied them with a piece of string, and set them down on the table. "He will explain this," she said. "And it will be a good explanation or he will be very sorry." She looked at the boys. "These are not the letters we want. I am finished playing games with the fine lady, the English whore. Enough."

"It's done then?" said the smaller one.

"Done? Did the Sicilian sun cook your brain? How can it be done when I have the wrong letters?"

"But you said 'enough.'"

"Enough with creeping about," she said. "Enough with looking here, there, everywhere. The next time we do it properly." The way Bruno and Piero were supposed to do it, the imbeciles. "The next time we *make* her tell us."

She took out her knife and held it up to the light. She smiled.

The monastery of San Lazzaro degli Armeni stood amid groves of cypress and fine gardens on a small island off the Lido. Early in the previous century, the former hospital island for lepers was given to an Armenian monk from Morea who'd been forced to flee invading Turks. Here, a few years ago, Byron had struggled to learn Armenian. He'd never succeeded, most likely because of all the women distracting him.

James had only one distraction in female form. The trouble was, she was more disruptive to his reason than the scores in Byron's harem.

Putting her out of his thoughts was out of the question, since she was the subject of the present conversation.

James was strolling—or giving the appearance of strolling while inwardly roiling with impatience—through the cloisters with Lord Quentin. This was the man who, half a lifetime ago, had saved him from a life of unsanctioned crime and lured him into a life of sanctioned crime.

Ten years older than James, his lordship had embarked on the life of secrets and conspiracies at an early age as well. In fact, in many ways he was better suited to the trade, being of average height and

unexceptional looks and having a way, as Sedgewick did, of calling no attention to himself. Men
like Sedgewick and Quentin rarely needed a disguise. People took little notice of them.

"If Mrs. Bonnard hears that you're here and I've
been talking to you, I might as well go home,"
James said.

"I know the risk," Quentin said. "But I needed
to speak to you directly. I heard about the attack
the other night."

"That came as a surprise," James said. "No one
told me she was in danger."

"We'd no idea Elphick would act so quickly."

"He was bound to hear of your visiting her,"
James said. "He has agents here. Not that he needs
any. She probably wrote to him about it." If Elphick was writing to her, she must be writing to
him.

"They correspond, yes, but unless they've a secret code, it's utterly trivial: who was at which
party and what they said. There's far juicier stuff
in the scandal sheets." Quentin shook his head.
"It's more likely he got the wind up as soon as he
learned I'd come to Italy. But I'd expected to be
here and back by the time he got word. Who could
have guessed she'd be so irrational about the letters
we wanted, given what he did to her? I was certain
she'd jump at the chance to ruin him. If I hadn't
been certain, I should never have approached her
directly."

That completely settled one question, then: The
not-love letters from Elphick that Thérèse had reported missing weren't important—to the mission,

at any rate. Bonnard hadn't been feigning indifference about their whereabouts. She truly hadn't cared.

"In any event," Quentin went on, "you don't seem to be making great progress. What the devil have you been doing for this last week—besides nearly killing a potential informant?"

"Piero is still alive, so far as I know," James began.

"I referred to the other one," Quentin said. "We found him yesterday, and we had the devil's own time getting him away without attracting attention."

"Bruno? He's alive?"

"Small thanks to you. What were you thinking?"

"I was thinking to stop him from killing Mrs. Bonnard," James said.

"And you nearly stopped him permanently from answering questions," Quentin said. "Has that troublesome woman got her hooks into you, too?"

*Yes,* James thought. *Yes, indeed, she has.*

He said, "I was on the brink of getting the information we're looking for when you summoned me here. Was it only to complain about how long it's taking me?"

Quentin glanced casually about him. The cloisters surrounded a large garden. Two monks walked slowly through the shaded passage on the other side of the garden, well out of earshot. "Our friend Bruno's too sick to be of much use," he said. "Pneumonia, damaged windpipe, dislocated shoulder, among other things. The only bit of luck we had was his fever. He had a bout of delirium. Along with the other ravings, he babbled something about letters and mentioned Marta Fazi several times."

James's last, very feeble hope—that he'd got it completely wrong—died a quick death. He'd got it right, and the situation, as he'd deduced, was very bad, very tangled, and about to become a great deal worse.

What else was new?

"Oh, there's a bit of luck, indeed," he said. "Dear Marta. I remember her well. The darling lass who promised to cut off my balls in little bits, slowly, first chance she got. The one who, last I heard, was locked away in the deepest, darkest dungeon in Rome. The one who apparently wasn't locked up anywhere, since *she was in Venice last night,* ransacking the Palazzo Neroni."

He didn't want to imagine what Marta would have done had Francesca Bonnard been home at the time. His mind imagined anyway, and he felt sick.

"That's not good." Quentin paused and shook his head. He moved to a stone bench and sat down, looking weary.

James sat down beside him, weary, too. He was angry, yes, but then he was often angry. Plans fell apart. Villains slipped through their nets. Documents ended up in the wrong hands. And comrades were killed, too often in appalling ways. Such was the nature of the work. He'd learned that early on. One dealt with human beings. All were fallible. Not all were trustworthy.

"You're sure it was Fazi?" Quentin said.

"They were dressed as bloody nuns! They got

into the house and drugged the food. It was exactly the same method she used in the other thefts. They took a lot of letters—the wrong ones—and emeralds. No other jewels. Only emeralds. Who else could it be?"

"So Elphick's set her on his former missus," Quentin said. "Bastard."

"How the devil did he come to hire Fazi?"

"Who's to say?" Quentin looked about him. "We've only started watching him closely in the last eighteen months—since you worked out that code. He might have met her years ago, back in the time when no one paid any attention to him. Or one of his agents in Italy might have hand-picked her to do the job. They must have paid a fortune to get her out of prison."

"That tells me Elphick knows her well, either personally or by reputation," James said. "In his place, she's what I'd choose for a job like this. She's no giant intellect, but she's cunning, daring, and very, very dogged."

Her cunning and daring had resulted in several remarkable jewelry thefts in the last year or so. Still, James and his associates had deemed her the local government's problem, until the affair of the emeralds. In that case, British agents had become involved as a favor to an important ally. The ally had repaid the favor by signing his name to a crucial treaty.

"Every instinct told me the first attack on Mrs. Bonnard was not simple robbery." James went on. "But it certainly didn't look like Fazi's work."

"You incapacitated her best men in Rome,"

Quentin said. "She's making do with what's available. I'll wager anything that pair the other night weren't following orders. There was a cock-up of some kind."

James considered. "Mrs. Bonnard was wearing a magnificent set of sapphires. They made my hands itch. Apparently Bruno lacked my superhuman powers of self-restraint. He got distracted by the sparkly gems and the beautiful woman. What are the chances, do you reckon, of a brute like that ever getting his hands on a beautiful, highborn woman? Too much temptation for his tiny brain. Then I interrupted before his partner could remind him what he was supposed to be about."

"I should like to know what exactly they were supposed to be about," Quentin said. "Our friend Bruno hasn't been terribly enlightening."

"They were supposed to terrify her," James said. Now that he had no remaining doubt about Marta Fazi's involvement, he had no difficulty working out the plan. "They were bully boys, sent to scare Mrs. Bonnard into telling where the letters were. If that didn't work, they'd take her away and torture her until she cooperated."

His stomach knotted and his head pounded. He stood up. "The moment I stepped into the gondola last week, I knew I was stepping into *un mare di merda*. I'd better get back to Venice."

Quentin rose, too. "I'd better make sure Goetz learns there's a dangerous fugitive on the loose in Venice. At this point, it doesn't matter who finds Fazi, so long as she's found and locked up. The last thing we want is for Mrs. Bonnard to come to harm. Her death would be—"

"Deuced inconvenient," James said. "Yes, I know."

It seemed to take forever to get back to Venice. The whole while James fretted, even though common sense told him Marta Fazi was unlikely to risk an attack in broad day, and even though he'd taken precautions. Before leaving for San Lazzaro, he'd sent a message to Lurenze, suggesting he play guard dog again. And to make sure Lurenze did nothing else but guard, James had sent a message to Giulietta as well.

Both would have heard about the burglar nuns soon enough. They probably would have hastened to the Palazzo Neroni in any event. But James wanted to make sure they stayed with Bonnard until he could take over. Fazi would never attack while the lady had important guests, especially royalty. Even the most lax and corrupt government would marshal all its forces and hunt down anyone who troubled important visitors.

Even so, he was angry and impatient all the way back, and short with Zeggio and Sedgewick, who only irritated him further by exchanging that look, again and again.

Not until they came up the canal, and he saw the two gondolas moored outside the Palazzo Neroni, did James begin to relax a very little.

Yet he remained uneasy while he dressed, and gave too many unintelligible orders regarding dinner. When the servants told him that Mrs. Bonnard's gondola was coming across the canal, he raced down the stairs to the *andron*. Her feet had scarcely touched the *terrazzo* floor when he pulled her into his arms and kissed her, fiercely and long, until they were both breathless.

He broke the kiss reluctantly, to let her draw breath. "Gad, I thought those accursed monks would never let me leave," he said.

She looked up at him in that way she'd done before, with the ghost full in her exotic green eyes, so that all he saw was a girl, a beautiful girl, gazing at him adoringly.

It was what he'd always wanted—for one girl to look at him so, with all her heart in her eyes—but he'd imagined it so differently. He'd pictured an innocent girl with an honest, caring heart, who knew nothing of life's darker side, who'd saved herself for him and who'd be true, who'd never deceive him.

"Wicked monks," she said. "Did they make you study Armenian against your will? Byron finally admitted it was beyond him."

"The curst fellow was there at last—the monk who had the key to the library," he lied. He saw the irony at once: He, who did little but deceive, insisting upon purity and truth in a woman. "But there were other visitors today, and what must he do but take the lot of us on a tour, and show us every last volume in the place. Then the visitors must ask idiotish questions, which he answered soberly, too patiently, and at interminable length."

She reached up and brought her soft palm to his cheek. "Poor man. Such an ordeal you've endured."

He turned his head to kiss the palm of her hand. He inhaled the scent of her skin, mingled with the teasing hint of jasmine.

"And all for naught," he said. "I heard not one word in fifty. My mind was in Venice, at the Palazzo Neroni, where a troublesome girl was probably sleeping—and I spent far too much time wondering if I was in her dreams."

Her hand slid away, and she looked away. "Have a care, sir. You are beginning to sound romantic."

"Lack of sleep, probably," he said. "I'll be better in the morning."

"Won't that depend on how you spend the night?" she said. The ghost vanished from her green eyes, and mischief twinkled in its place.

"I have a plan for that," he said.


It was meant to be a Roman orgy, he'd explained.

The trouble was, he hadn't any proper Roman furnishings. And so he'd had the servants take out most of the furniture, pile carpets and cushions on the floor of one of the canal-side rooms off the *portego*, and strew flower petals everywhere. It must be a Turkish seraglio instead, he told her. He would be the sultan and she would be all the women of the harem.

The way he looked at her when he said it made Francesca feel as though she were all the women in the world—or at least all the women he could ever want.

She supposed other men looked at her in that way.

But she remembered the way he'd pulled her into his arms as she disembarked from her gondola, and his kiss, so wild and hot that for a moment she'd believed there was desperation in it.

She'd felt desperate, too. Lurenze and Giulietta had heard about the burglarious nuns, and they'd been waiting for her when she finally woke in the afternoon. She'd had the devil's own time, first trying to quiet their anxieties and later, trying to carry on a rational conversation. All the while, all she'd wanted was to be on the other side of the canal. In this man's arms.

Only pride had kept her from flying from the house in her dressing gown. Pride demanded she wear a gown to make his mouth water. It was crimson, a perfect color for a harlot, and cut low, front and back. A corner of her tattoo, her mark of sin, was just visible above the back of the gown.

She knew that he, being a man, couldn't feel as desperate as she, being a fool, did. The wild heat she felt was merely lust, which she'd done her utmost to arouse. What he expressed was the intense passion usual at the start of an affair.

While they dined, she tried not to let herself build castles in the air. It was hard not to, when he treated her so tenderly and kindly.

Reclining as his Roman ancestors must have done, he fed her tidbits of this and that, olives and bread and delicately prepared shellfish, fruits, and cheeses.

After they'd eaten, she lay with her head upon some cushions while he lay on his side, leaning on his elbow, the two of them facing each other, in a strange sort of intimacy, like . . . friends, while they . . . talked.

He described the monastery and told her how the monks had made a shrine of the room in which Byron had studied.

"Shall you study there, too?" she said.

He blinked. "I?"

"Did you not come to study Armenian with the monks?"

"It seemed like a good idea at the time," he said. "But Armenian is impossible. No wonder Byron gave it up. I'd rather study you."

"Not too closely," she said. "And never in bright sunlight. No woman can withstand that kind of scrutiny."

"What, do you think the noonday sun will shatter my illusions? Do you think I have any, foolish girl?"

She was so foolish. When he smiled at her in that way, as though he were truly fond of her, and she looked into his deeply blue eyes, she forgot everything she'd learned in the last five years. All her illusions and delusions came back.

"The sun in England is kinder to women," she said. "There we needn't try to stand up bravely to its glare, since it so rarely glares."

" 'That sort of farthing candlelight which glimmers/Where reeking London's smoky caldron simmers,' " he quoted Byron.

"I miss it sometimes, though, the farthing candlelight," she said.

"Enough to wish to go back?"

She felt a stab, sudden and surprising, of loss. She had not felt it in a long time.

Perhaps that was what loosened her tongue. Or maybe it was the way he watched her, the way he listened so intently, truly paying attention, as men so rarely did. Even with her, their attention was not, really, on what she said but how she said it and how she looked saying it.

She knew this about men. She used the knowledge to manipulate them. She was finding it impossible to manipulate him.

She said, "I do wish, sometimes, to go . . . home. I know it's silly. Upon the Continent, I'm merely a divorcée. In many places that's respectable enough. I'm invited nearly everywhere, except where English society gathers. I ought to be happy, not needing to abide by their tedious and endless rules or to bear their special brand of hypocrisy."

"All the same, you're a foreigner here," he said. "It's natural, from time to time, to miss the world in which you grew up."

Of course he understood, and it had nothing to do with their being soulmates, she told herself. There was no such thing between men and women. She'd learned that the hard way. He understood her feelings because he was a wanderer, too. Early on he'd told her he'd spent little time in England.

"I miss the voices," she said. "I miss the sound of my own language in all its accents, high and low. And I do miss London Society, the Season. I was good at that, you know. I was a good hostess. I did everything I ought to do. I was a good wife, truly. I loved my husband. I wanted to be the best wife in the world. I thought it was part of the bargain, that we would be as good to each other as we could. I thought, if one loved somebody, and married that somebody, it was forever, exactly as the vows say."

Her chest heaved and the tears started. She brushed them away and said, "Curse you, Cordier. What is it about you that makes me weepy? How could you let me drone on about my misbegotten marriage? What wine was that, to make me so maudlin?"

He reached out and lightly stroked her cheek with his long fingers. "Maudlin or angry?" he said. "Women weep oftentimes because they're angry. Unlike men, they're discouraged from expressing strong feeling physically. Throwing someone in a canal, for instance, is a good way of dealing with a lot of annoying emotion churning inside."

She laughed, and the shocking pain subsided, as though it had never been. He drew his hand away, though, and she wished he hadn't.

"It's true," she said. "Women are trained to smile and be brave—or to relieve our feelings with words."

"You could write a novel, a thinly disguised *roman à clef,* like Caroline Lamb's *Glenarvon,*" he said. "Only think how wonderfully she savaged her beloved Byron."

Francesca shook her head. She raised herself up, took up her wine glass, and sipped. She looked into it as though it would tell her what to do, what to say, how far to trust.

"I have my own way," she said after a moment. "More direct. I write to Elphick, at least once a week."

Cordier's dark eyebrows rose. "So often?"

"Oh, yes. I'm quite faithful—in my correspondence."

"You write to rail at him, after all this time?"

She laughed at his baffled expression. "Certainly not. Then he'd believe I was unhappy and suffering. Instead, I let him know how delightful my life is. I tell him who calls on me, and what we talk about, and who invites me where, and who has commissioned a portrait of me from which famous artist, and who has bought me this and that and what it's worth. My letters are filled with great names—painters and poets and playwrights and such. But most important, they're filled with the names of Continental royalty and nobility—precisely the kinds of people he likes to hobnob with. I know he grinds his teeth when he reads such things, and it is a pleasant revenge."

Silence.

She drank more, bolstering her courage. "I think it serves him well. He'd turned every friend I had against me. My father had bolted. I had no one to take care of me. Naturally Elphick expected me to sink quickly into the gutter."

"Instead you're a queen."

"A queen of whores, but upon the Continent that is almost as good as being a real queen," she said. "Did you know that in some courts, there was an official position, the King's Mistress? It was so in France, and is still so in Gilenia, I'm told."

His expression changed, turning stony in an instant. He sat up, his face hard. "Were you aiming for that position with Lurenze? Have I thrown your careful plans into disarray?"

"I do not aim to belong to any man," she said,

"king or not." She made herself laugh. "Compose yourself, sir, or I shall imagine you're jealous."

"I am," he said. "Will you write to your former husband about that, as well?"

"Heavens, no," she said. "You're merely a younger son. He won't give a damn about you."

"It's stupid, you know," he said tightly. "A stupid, dangerous game. Your marriage was over five years ago."

"*He* won't leave it alone," she said. "Why should I? He taunts me with the social events he attends. He tells me who was there and what was said. He knows I miss it. He knows I miss my so-called friends. And so he makes sure to rub salt in the wound. I know he wants me to be scorned by everybody and left miserable and penniless—and so I torment him with my successes. What would you do in such a case?"

He took the wine glass from her hand and set it down. "I should never have let you get away in the first place." He moved quickly, then, gathering her into his arms. He kissed her, angrily, fiercely, and in a moment so deeply that she lost her moorings. Her head fell back and she let him take her where he would, do what he would. In no time at all she was flat on her back, laughing, while he pulled up her skirts.

# Chapter 13

The heart is like the sky, a part of heaven,
   But changes night and day, too, like the sky;
Now o'er it clouds and thunder must be driven,
   And darkness and destruction as on high:
But when it hath been scorch'd, and pierced,
     and riven,
   Its storms expire in water-drops; the eye
Pours forth at last the heart's blood turn'd
     to tears,
Which make the English climate of our years.

                          Lord Byron
                *Don Juan, Canto the Second*

James was angry for a hundred reasons: She played a dangerous game with a dangerous man; she was being hunted by some of the worst villains in Italy—and that was saying something; he had been false and she'd hate him when she learned the truth; and she must learn the truth—soon—for her own protection.

There was more, a great deal more, but he was

in no mood to contemplate all the nuances of his state of mind. He dealt with it as men usually deal with strong feeling, in physical action. He claimed her in a deep, impatient kiss. His impatience amused her and she laughed against his mouth. She laughed as he pushed her onto her back and pulled up her skirts, and he was aware, through the tumult of feelings, of the quality that had intrigued him from the first: the rare exuberance of her nature. He understood it better now: She felt deeply, experienced deeply, loved deeply . . . and she would hate him with the same ferocity.

He didn't trouble to undress her or himself. He unbuttoned his trousers and pushed them down, as he'd done in the Campanile. He was as mindlessly impatient as any schoolboy. He didn't care about his lack of finesse, and neither did she.

She tangled her fingers in his hair and whispered wicked words, in English and then, more arousing, in her English-accented Italian. He laughed, too. He couldn't help it. It was heated laughter—at his impatience, his mad lust, and at the sheer joy of her, the joy of touching her, and finding her heated and ready, too, in the soft, sweet place between her legs. Her fingers touched his as he guided himself inside. The touch melted thought and quieted anger, and he was lost again, inside her. He didn't even try for control this time. Theirs was a quick, fierce joining, a pulsing race to climax and completion.

He rolled off her, taking her with him. He held her tightly, her backside against his groin. He concentrated on the feel of her in his arms, where she fit so perfectly. He tried not to think of what the near future held. He refused to ask himself what he'd do, afterward, when she hated him.

She didn't hate him now, though.

She'd need to know the truth . . . soon, too soon. He couldn't go on playing games with her. They hadn't time. She was in too much danger.

But she didn't need to know the truth yet.

They had this night.

The moon had risen during their frantic coupling. Its light streamed faintly through the long window. In its glow, her skin shimmered like pearls.

He kissed the place behind her ear where she liked to be kissed, and she trembled, as she always did when he kissed her there. He kissed the nape of her neck, then drew back and began to undo the fastenings of her dress. The back slid down, revealing the shocking tattoo. He kissed the serpent.

He eased her out of the garments: the gown, petticoats, stays, and shift. She let him play lady's maid, smiling as he turned her this way and that until she was naked. He took off his own garments, not hurrying this time.

She turned fully onto her back, her hands behind her head, and watched. That was all she had to do—let her green gaze trail over his body—to stir his cock to life.

This time, though, it must wait.

This time he went slowly, exploring and memorizing her.

This time he drank in every inch of skin he exposed and touched. This time he savored the scent of her and let it burn into his memory. This time he learned by heart every curve his fingers traced: the sweet arc of her neck, the slope of her shoulders, the soft fullness of her breasts and the way they fit his hands. He traced the perfect contours of her waist and hips, the luscious swell of her bottom. He followed the gentle turns of her long legs, sliding down to trace the shape of her feet.

He kissed her toes, her ankles, her knees. On upward he went, to the soft, sweet place. While he pleasured her with his mouth and his hands, he memorized the scent of her and the taste of her and the sound of her: sighing with pleasure . . . laughing a little, too . . . then crying out softly when she came.

He slid up, kissing her as he went, imprinting her in his mind as he went, while he made it last as long as he could. Finally, when the last thread of his control began to slip, he entered her, and they rocked together, slowly, sweetly. She kissed him, her fingers moving gently over his face and neck. Her mouth followed where her hands went; and these kisses and her touch, so loving, stabbed him to the heart a hundred times.

He kissed her in the same way. His were traitor's kisses, but tender for all that, most unfortunately for him.

And when at last their bodies pulsed together, he surrendered with more regret than he ought to feel or wanted to feel. He let himself be swept away, on the silvery tide, for the last time.

For the second time in less than a day, Francesca slept like the dead. She might have gone on sleeping, if she hadn't felt him stirring beside her. Then she became aware of the noise outside.

While she was still half-asleep, he was up, pulling on his trousers and moving to the window. "That bitch," he said. "Is she mad? Or . . . Ah, I see."

Francesca came fully awake. After some fumbling about, she found her shift. Pulling it over her head, she hurried to the window.

Across the canal, flames were leaping from the ground floor of the Palazzo Neroni.

"Good God!" She stared in horrified disbelief for a moment. Then she turned away and began hunting for her clothes.

"Stop it," he said. He grasped her upper arm and drew her upright. "I was fooled, too, at first. But your house is not going to burn down. They daren't risk that. It's a diversion." He led her back to the window. "Look. They've used some sort of incendiary device. Fireworks, perhaps. It's meant to make a lot of show and noise. Wakes people up in the dead of night and throws them into a panic. Your servants will all be running this way and that, leaving the place unguarded, and—"

"What are you saying?" she said. "We can't stay here. Someone could be hurt."

"It's a *diversion*," he repeated carefully, as though to a child.

Francesca thought he meant to say something else but he paused, his gaze upon her but seeing through her or past her. Then he nodded. "It's a trap, very possibly. The last thing you want to do is hurry over there. Someone may be waiting for exactly that."

"For me," she said.

"Yes."

Simple panic about her servants and house gave way to a darker, more insidious feeling. She felt as though the ground beneath her was shifting, and she wasn't sure where to step, where it was safe to step. "What do you mean?" she said. "Why me? What do you know of this?"

"I'm going to tell you," he said, "and you're going to hate me." He released her arm.

"Cordier." She felt sick. She'd *trusted* him. She wanted to trust him still. And yet she couldn't shake off the feeling that she stood on uncertain ground. What had he to tell her? She remembered the first night, the night he'd killed a man too easily.

"But before I tell you," he said, "I need to steal your clothes."

"You *what?*"

He didn't answer and she could only stare, trying to make sense of what made no sense. Of all the answers she'd awaited, some good, some intolerable, this was the last, the very last she could have imagined.

She stood, mouth agape, while he hurriedly gathered up her clothing from the floor. He straightened, clutching the garments to his chest. "I have to be you," he said.

The sick dread washed away. She wasn't sure whether she ought to laugh or cry. She knew of men who liked to dress in women's clothes. Some were extremely virile. Even so, she was not happy.

"They won't fit," she said.

He hugged the garments to him. "We'll make them fit."

"Cordier, you're nearly twice my size, and that's my second favorite gown!"

He looked down at the clothing he held in the way a child might jealously guard a favorite toy. "I wasn't worth your favorite gown?"

"My favorite gown is ruined! You threw it—with me in it—into the canal!"

"I didn't throw you," he said. "You threw yourself."

"You *looked* as though you were going to throw me," she said.

One side of his mouth quirked up and he looked like a boy, the wickedest boy who ever lived. He crossed to her, still clutching her garments. "God, I'll miss you," he said. He kissed her hard. Her body melted, and most of her mind with it. But something wasn't right. He'd distracted her, about the dress. A diversion?

He drew away. "I'll be back soon," he said.

"Tell me where you're going," she said. "Tell me what you mean to do."

"It will take far too much time to explain."

"No, it won't. I'm not an idiot, Cordier."

But he was already through the door. She went to the threshold, and watched him stride down the *portego*.

"Cordier," she said.

"Later," he said.

She swallowed an oath but she refused to run

after him in her shift, and let all his servants gawk at her . . . for free. Not that running after him would stop him doing whatever he meant to do.

"Don't you dare spoil it," she called after him.

James had donned women's garments before. But those had been carefully selected, cut to fit large women and adapted to his height and broad shoulders.

Bonnard's gown was far too small, smaller than he'd realized until he was down in a musty office off the *andron*, trying to get into it.

"We'll have to cut it, sir," said Sedgewick.

"You can't cut it," James said. "She'll kill me. This is her second favorite gown, and I've already ruined her favorite one."

Sedgewick gave Zeggio that aggravating look. "Sir, we haven't time to unstitch it," the valet said too patiently.

"No, no," said Zeggio. "To remove the sewing is unnecessary. Here is what we do, signore. Very easy. We leave undone the part where she keep her breasts."

"The bodice," said James.

"So. Everything there we leave it open. Then I think it is possible to bring it up, so, from the floor." He made a gesture descriptive of pulling a garment up over the hips. "Here"—he indicated his hips—"you are not so big as here." He gestured at his chest and shoulders. "Recall, it is not needed to see all of the gown. From here is enough." He indicated the area from his waist down. "Enough to show the color and to cover your legs, to hide the *pantaloni*. You put the shawl over your head, over the top of you, and no one can see that the neck of the dress is around your middle. It is night time. Even with the moon, how much can they see of you, when you are inside the *felze*?"

"Good point," James said. He should have thought of it. He should have seen instantly what to do about the gown. He was used to thinking on his feet.

"You'll be able to move easier, sir," Sedgewick said. "Want your arms free, for when they try to kill you."

Of course James needed his arms free. He knew that. The whole point was to trick the villains into attacking him—and the gown was bound to be spoiled anyway.

What difference would it make? She was going to hate him no matter what he did.

Ah well. For king and country. One more time.

They'd locked her in.

After she'd reentered the room, a servant brought Francesca a tray of food and drink. When he left, he closed the door behind him. She assumed he was shielding her scantily clad body from the household's curious eyes.

Eating would give her something to do while she waited but she had no appetite. After staring at the food for a time, she went back to the door. Perhaps someone in the household knew what the master was up to. She was a seductress, she reminded herself. She could seduce the information out of somebody.

The door wouldn't open.

She tried the other two doors. They wouldn't open, either.

Locked up for her own good or for his convenience? He probably assumed the two were the same. Who wanted a pesky female underfoot?

She considered screaming, and quickly realized it was pointless. He'd given orders and his servants would obey him. Hell, *her* servants obeyed him.

She paced for a time, and realized she was rubbing her arms. He'd left her nothing to wear but the shift she'd donned. Though the night wasn't very cold, a fire burned in the grate. All the same, she couldn't seem to get warm. She pulled up one of the rugs and wrapped it about her. But the chill came from within, from doubt and its favorite companion . . . dread.

She made herself think, calmly.

He had told her that the fire and noise was a diversion and a trap. Someone was at or near the Palazzo Neroni, waiting for *her*, he said. She knew they weren't after her jewelry. They wanted the letters. They'd given up trying to search for them and meant to *make* her reveal where she'd hidden them.

Elphick must be in a panic.

Finally, after five years.

But he'd no reason to worry previously. He'd ruined her so thoroughly that no one would believe anything she said about him. At the time, even she hadn't been sure the letters signified what she thought they did. Yet she knew they must be important. Otherwise, why should he keep them in a locked drawer?

Quentin's visit during the summer had erased

any remaining doubts. If those letters weren't important, he wouldn't have asked for them, and come back, repeatedly, trying to persuade her to give them up. He'd said he and his associates had gathered other clues, parts of a puzzle they'd been trying to assemble for years.

The trouble was, knowing how devious and ruthless her former husband was, she found it all too easy to believe he'd sent Quentin.

Naturally Elphick would want to tie up loose ends, now that he'd grown so popular. He had hopes, she knew, of replacing Lord Liverpool as prime minister. Meanwhile, thanks to her letters, Elphick was aware that she traveled in high circles, among influential men. Foreigners, yes—but some foreigners had influence at Whitehall. An important foreign nobleman or royal would be heeded, where a discarded wife would not.

She remembered what Magny had told her about Cordier's parents. They'd risked their lives to save French nobles and others from Madame Guillotine. There were many foreigners with similar sympathies, who'd be happy to bring down a traitor.

Elphick had reason to be afraid now, and thus reason to act—as Magny had warned her more than once recently.

But Magny didn't trust Quentin any more than she did.

Magny trusted nobody.

She would be wise to do the same, probably.

Restless, she moved to the window. The moon, past its full but still three-quarters visible, bathed the canal in its glow. The excitement across the way seemed to be dying down, as was the fire. Few onlookers remained on the nearby balconies.

Cordier was right, then. It hadn't been a real fire. In these ancient houses, fires were rarely doused so quickly and easily. It was ironic, wasn't it? to be in the middle of the sea, in a structure built on wooden poles in water, and watch a house burn to the ground. But she'd seen that happen during her first year here. The Doge's Palace had burned to the ground several times over the centuries, she'd been told.

Still, those had been real fires and this was a diversion, according to Cordier. And he . . .

*I have to be you.*

She saw her gondola start across the canal. A woman sat inside . . . wearing her red gown. The color stood out against the black, even at night, as Francesca had wanted it to do. She loved the drama of a vivid color against the black of the gondola. And what could be more dramatic than red?

She pressed her nose to the window.

*I have to be you.*

It was he.

He had to be her because he was the *bait*.

Her heart thumped once, hard, then beat so violently that she couldn't draw her breath.

She watched the gondola make its away across the canal. It had but a short distance to travel. As it came to a stop, the water gates flew open. Several dark figures burst through and leapt onto the gondola, pushing the gondoliers into the water.

In an upraised hand, a blade gleamed in the

moonlight. The one holding it lunged toward the *felze*.

It was an ambush, and they'd taken no chances this time, James saw.

This time there were not merely two villains but half a dozen at least. They must have secreted themselves somewhere on the ground floor during the uproar. Now they spilled out through the gates into the gondola.

Uliva and Zeggio were expecting an attack, but not in these numbers. As he was drawing his knife, James saw the two gondoliers thrown overboard. The man coming at him, knife in hand, hesitated when James burst from the cabin and went straight at him. But James's foot caught in the hem of the gown, and down he went, sprawling face first. He felt rather than saw the man move, and rolled aside before the knife could plunge into his back. He kicked out at the ruffian's ankles, and the fellow crashed to the deck. James rolled up onto his knees and raised his own knife.

"Look out!" a female voice screamed.

He dodged, reacting instinctively, and the club *whooshed* past his head and slammed onto the deck.

"*Aiuto! Aiuto!* Help! Help! Murderers!"

The feminine screams pierced the nighttime quiet. In the distance, dogs barked and howled. The men in the boat froze briefly, eyeing their surroundings. People rushed out onto their balconies, everyone shouting.

While his assailants were looking wildly about

them, James attacked. He got the club from the one who'd tried to break his skull. Meanwhile Zeggio clambered back into the gondola and subdued the one with the knife.

The others were trying to get away, but Bonnard's servants had rushed down to the water gates. Leaving the villains to them, James turned his attention to the direction from which the screams had come. He saw her, then, clinging to a gondola mooring.

She could swim to the house, Francesca told him indignantly as he pulled her into the gondola. It was only a few feet, she pointed out. She was only catching her breath after screaming.

She found herself swiftly transported from the gondola to the *andron*.

All of her servants were there, some with villains in tow, all of them brandishing improvised weapons: candlesticks, kitchen knives, pots, trays, and bottles. They lowered the weapons as Cordier pulled her inside.

He gave her a shake. "Don't ever." Another shake. "Do that." Shake. "Again."

"I was creating a diversion," she said.

"You're creating a diversion, all right," he said. "You're wearing a shift that's soaked through. You might as well be wearing nothing. And everybody's looking."

"That will never do," she said. "I'm a harlot. They must pay to look."

"I'm going to kill you," he said. He turned away. "Zeggio, stop gawking, and fetch the lady's shawl before she catches her death."

Francesca wasn't thinking about being cold. She was taking him in. He had on his shirt and waistcoat as well as her gown, which he wore backward, the bodice hanging over his bottom.

He noticed her studying it. "It didn't fit," he said. "I told you that."

Zeggio approached with the shawl. Cordier snatched it from him and wrapped it about her. Then he marched her to the stairs.

Thérèse pushed her way past a pair of kitchen maids. "Oh, madame," she said.

"I know," Francesca said. "He's ruined my second favorite gown."

"It isn't ruined," Cordier said. "I took pains not to get blood on it. Did you notice that I did not jump into the canal to rescue you this time? Look." He whirled about, so gracefully, as though he'd been wearing skirts all his life.

She giggled. She couldn't help it. He was an excellent mimic. She hadn't realized . . .

A mimic.

A host of images crowded into her mind: The comical Spaniard who moments later turned into someone more disturbing—the long-legged man lounging at the door of her gondola . . . later, the same man sweeping off his hat in the Caffè Florian and making a flourish of a bow . . . his black hair glued down with pomade. Countess Benzoni looking not at his hair but at his tall, strong body. *This* tall, strong body.

Another tall, strong body appeared in her mind's eye. She saw again the long, muscled legs in servant's breeches: the servant at La Fenice who spilled wine onto Lurenze's trousers . . . the servant with the mouth-watering physique.

*This* physique.

She remembered what he'd said a short while ago, before he'd taken her gown: *I'm going to tell you, and you're going to hate me.*

"You," she said. "That was you."

He stilled, his playful expression fading, his eyes wary. "What was me?"

"You," she said, searching for words, unable to find them among the images churning in her mind: the Campanile, the lovemaking, the seraglio, the lovemaking. "The servant. The Spaniard. *You*. Whoever you are."

His expression hardened. "Thérèse, you'd better take madame upstairs," he said.

She turned to Thérèse, snatched the tray from her, and threw it at him. He dodged and it struck the floor with a crash. "You weasel!" she cried. "*Donnola!*" She went on in Italian, the Italian of the streets, "You lying sack of excrement. I should have let them kill you. I hope they do, and you rot in hell. Come near me again and I'll cut off your balls."

She stormed up the stairs. Thérèse hurried after her.

James watched her go. He cleared his throat. "That went well, I thought."

"Yes, sir," said Sedgewick.

"Signore, it is nothing," said Zeggio. "Women, they always say they will cut off the balls. It is like when the man say, 'Tomorrow, I will respect you still.' It means nothing."

"It doesn't signify," James said. He looked toward the servants, all of whom regarded him with the same disappointed expression. Even the villains wore that look. They all expected him to run after her and make a great scene. A lot of screaming at each other, then a lot of lovemaking.

*Italians,* he thought.

Then he remembered: He was Italian, too. "*Per tutti i diavoli dell'inferno!*" By all the devils in hell!

He ran up the stairs after her.

"*Vai al diavolo!*" she shouted back. "*Vai all'inferno!*"

Go to the devil. Go to hell.

Ah, yes, the usual intelligent exchange.

"You ungrateful, impossible woman!" he shouted.

She'd reached the archway leading to the *piano nobile*. She paused and turned to him. Her exotic eyes were molten green fury. "You black-hearted, fraudulent swine!" she cried. "You are nothing but trouble, and you've done nothing but cause trouble from the day you came. I had a good life, a beautiful, peaceful life—until *you* came to Venice!" She swung round and marched damply down the *portego,* leaving wet footprints behind her.

"Your life was *merda* and you know it!" he shouted. "None of this would have happened if you'd owned a grain of sense. You started this!"

"My life was *perfect!*"

He'd caught up with her. She quickened her pace but he stayed with her. "A perfect lie," he said.

"You're a fine one to talk. I don't go about pretending to be—"

"That's all you do!" he snapped. "Pretend and

play games and lie! Shall I call you an actress? It's a gentler word—and you'd say that acting is what your profession requires. It's the same for me."

She turned into a doorway. Thérèse tried to close the door but he pushed through. "It's the same for me," he said more quietly. "And can we *not* talk about this in front of the servants?"

"Why don't I stab you in front of the servants instead?" she said.

James looked at Thérèse. "*Allez-vous en*," he said very quietly.

"Don't you dare," her mistress said.

Thérèse darted one look at her employer and one at him, then she hurried past him, out of the room.

"Thérèse!" Bonnard started after her.

James blocked the doorway.

"I hate you," she said.

Of course she did. He'd lied to her from the start. He'd betrayed the trust of the innocent girl-ghost in her eyes.

He looked down at himself, at the gown he'd taken without explanation, because he was afraid of what would happen after he explained. He stared at the gown he'd taken when he left her in that cowardly way . . . after they'd given themselves to each other in the way that lovers, true lovers, did.

He pushed the gown down over his hips, and it fell to the floor. He stepped out of it and picked it up. He held it out to her.

She snatched it from him and pressed it to her bosom, heedless of the damp shawl and the sopping shift clinging to her body, and the stains the wet would leave in the silk.

"I know you hate me," he said. "I know you can't bear the sight of me. Just tell me where the letters are, Francesca, and I'll go."

# Chapter 14

Alas! the love of women! it is known
　　To be a lovely and a fearful thing;
For all of theirs upon that die is thrown,
　　And if 't is lost, life hath no more to bring
To them but mockeries of the past alone,
　　And their revenge is as the tiger's spring,
Deadly, and quick, and crushing; yet as real
Torture is theirs, what they inflict they feel.

Lord Byron
*Don Juan, Canto the Second*

"*I* hate you," Francesca said. She was wet and ought to be cold but she was hot with rage and humiliation. She could not believe she'd been such an utter fool. This was worse, far worse even than her stupidity about John Bonnard. Then at least she'd had the excuse of youth and innocence. What excuse had she now, at seven and twenty years old, after her brutally rude awakening five years ago—not to mention the months she'd spent learning from Fanchon Noirot how *not* to be a fool?

She'd met this man not a week ago—not counting the times she'd met him without knowing who he was—not that she knew who he was. Less than a week with him and she'd let herself . . . fall . . . in love.

She wished she might call it something else but what else was she to call it, when she'd leapt into the canal to save him? She burned with shame, recalling. For a time, for those few precious minutes before she'd realized why he was here, it had all seemed so . . . romantic.

"I hate you," she said. "I hate myself more, if that's possible."

He closed the door. "I'm sorry," he said. "But you must tell me where the letters are. For your own safety."

"What letters?" she said, as she had said, repeatedly, to Lord Quentin.

"Francesca."

She looked about her. She had not been paying attention to where she was going, simply turned blindly into a doorway. Of all the doorways she might have entered, she had to pick the one opening into the Putti Inferno. Now the children were looking down and pointing their pudgy fingers and bums at, not the Great Whore, but the Great Fool.

She looked up at the ceiling. How many of those pestilential children were there? Had they multiplied since last she looked, like her troubles? "I hate them, too."

"Francesca, we haven't time to play games," he said.

"I'm not playing," she said.

"The letters," he said.

"What letters?" she said. *Whose side are you on?* she wanted to ask. But what was the point? Why should he tell her the truth? The truth didn't matter. Only the letters mattered, plague take them. Plague take *him*.

"I'm going to explain," he said.

"I don't want your explanations," she said. "I wish I could explain to myself why I risked my life—no, worse, my dignity—on your account."

"I know you won't believe me but I'm going to explain anyway," he said. "Then I'll choke the information out of you if I have to—because what's at stake is more important than you or me or whose *feelings* get hurt."

"You bastard," she said.

"That's how I stay alive," he said. "That's how I do my job. By being a bastard. If it weren't for you, I shouldn't have to do my job. If it weren't for you, I might be in England now, learning how to be a human being again. I might be wooing gently bred maidens and luring some naïve fool into marriage and making babies. I might be spending my days at my club, reading the newspapers or gazing out of the window and making jokes or bets about the people passing by. I might show off my fine horse and my superior horsemanship in Hyde Park in between ogling the eligible girls and deluding their chaperons. I might be dancing at Almack's with girls in white dresses. I might be getting drunk and telling dirty jokes with the other gentlemen after the women leave the dining room. I might be among normal people living a normal life. But no.

You had to refuse to help Quentin. A handful of letters. That was all he wanted. But you refused to help a group of loyal Britons bring down a man who sold himself to our enemies. Because of you, I couldn't go back to England. I had to come here—*and hurt your bloody damned feelings!*"

Her conscience stabbed, sharply enough to make her wince. She recognized the images he conjured and she understood exactly what he was missing, what he longed for. It was the world she missed, too, sometimes, despite the happiness and freedom she'd found after leaving it. The world that she'd left—the one that had cast her out—was not the best world, but it was familiar, and it had its joys. She'd liked her life there, before everything went wrong. At any rate, she knew too well what it felt like, to be locked out of what had once been home.

"How was I to know Quentin could be trusted?" she said. "Have you any inkling how many men have lied to me? Have you any idea how many of the people I trusted turned on me? Have you any notion what it's like, to have everyone you ever knew, *every single one*, turn against you—on one man's word? How was I to know Quentin wasn't another one of the ones on Elphick's side? They all were. Every last damned one of them. Even my lawyers despised me."

"Quentin and I are not on Elphick's side," he said. "Ten years ago, your former husband betrayed me and five comrades to agents of Napoleon. We ended up in the Abbaye. We were tortured. For weeks."

She shut her eyes briefly. She'd heard about the prisons in Paris. The Abbaye was infamous. Fanchon Noirot had told her of friends who'd gone there. The few who emerged went on to Madame Guillotine. She opened her eyes and found his blue gaze boring into her.

" 'And they are dead,' " he quoted from the Book of Job, " 'and I only am escaped alone to tell thee.' But why should you believe me?"

Why, indeed? All the same, she was finding it hard not to believe. His taut expression told her he'd watched or heard his comrades die—ugly deaths, she was sure. Too, she knew what Elphick was capable of—or thought she knew. Until this moment she hadn't fully grasped the implications.

She should have realized: Elphick had no conscience, no loyalty, no feeling at all. He was a monster. What he'd done to her was nothing to what he'd done to others.

She'd focused on herself and the misery she'd endured. She'd been so young, so naïve. His collusion with England's enemies—its consequences and the people who'd suffered—those were abstractions to her. Cordier had made them real. Human beings. Young men. His comrades. Himself. Tortured.

Perhaps it was all lies, but she felt sick.

She turned away and walked to the window. Across the way, the windows of the Ca' Munetti were lit. Elsewhere all was dark. The moon must have gone behind clouds or set. How fitting, the darkness. She'd thought she'd understood but she'd been stumbling in the dark.

"You're going to have to trust someone," he said. "It must be me or them."

"Must it?" she said. "How am I to know you're not part of it? How am I to know this isn't a great show, to make you seem a hero, so that I'll trust you?"

"What am I to say?" he said. "How do I make you believe me? Why don't I simply choke it out of you and have done with it?"

He paused, apparently to grapple with his temper, because he went on in a level voice, "Those two men who attacked you last week? The nuns from Cyprus who searched your house? The fellows who attacked your gondola tonight, thinking you were in it? Their chief is a woman named Marta Fazi. She's about your age, but I don't think you'll find her *simpatica*. When she was eight years old, she cut off the ear of a girl who insulted her. If those charming fellows tonight had captured you, they would have taken you to Marta. She would have persuaded you to tell her where the letters were. She would persuade you by cutting up your face. She likes to do that to beautiful women. If she's in a kind mood. In her less kind moods, the method of persuasion would be more unpleasant."

Francesca's ears were ringing. She felt herself swaying. He moved toward her, his hand outstretched. She pushed him away, staggered to a chair, and sat down hard.

"We're trying to find her," he said. "Quentin's even asked Goetz to help—though the governor doesn't know the half of it and is not to know.

Until she's caught—or until you give us the letters—you're not safe."

She laughed. Not a pretty sound, this one, but bitter, edged with hysteria. "All that time, no one believed me," she said. "When Elphick discovered I'd taken the letters from his desk, he wasn't concerned. He'd already ruined me. In putting me beyond the pale, he made it impossible for me to hurt him. And for all the time I couldn't hurt him, I was safe. He let me run away abroad the way duelists and debtors and other undesirables and minor criminals do. He didn't pursue me here. I would have stayed safe, would I not? had I only sunk into the gutter as he hoped. But no, I had to have nobles and royals at my feet. Now I matter. Now I have important friends. Now I'm worth killing."

And now she was cold. She shivered. She heard Cordier move. She was aware, through her misery and the ringing in her ears, of the clink of glass. He pushed something into her hand. A glass of brandy. "I wonder if it's poisoned," she said, and drank it down, all of it. It was liquid fire in her throat but it made the noise in her head subside.

"It's not poisoned," he said. "This is not an opera, and I am not the villain of the piece. Would you please be sensible, Francesca, and tell me where the letters are?"

She looked up into his handsome face, into those midnight blue eyes. She supposed, fool that she was, that if she had it to do over again, she'd jump into the canal again, for him. To save him. Her gaze rose past him up the walls and on up to the ceiling. Those provoking children. "It's complicated," she said.

"No, it isn't," he said. "It's very simple. You tell me where . . ."

She waited for him to finish. It took her a moment to realize what had made him break off. His hearing was so sharp, far sharper than hers. Only now did she recognize the sounds coming from the *portego*. Footsteps—booted footsteps. Official-sounding footsteps. Several pairs of them.

The door opened. No knock. No waiting for her *"Avanti."*

But it was Arnaldo who, as usual, had found her unerringly. He must be part bloodhound. He always knew exactly what room she was in. "His excellency the governor Count Goetz," he announced.

The Austrian governor followed close behind. After the first startled glance, he took care not to look at her.

"I beg your pardon, madame, for this sudden arrival, but you can guess the cause."

"Our little disturbance," she said.

"Not so little as one could wish," he said. "I must speak to Mr. Cordier."

"I thought you might," Cordier said, all at ease again, his usual self—whoever that was. "I'm sure Mrs. Bonnard will excuse us. She will want to—er—dress, at any rate."

"Madame has had a great shock," said Goetz. "As we have all had a great shock. We will not inconvenience her. You and I shall talk, sir, at the Ducal Palace. In the meantime, as soon as madame can be made ready, I must insist upon her vacating this house."

"Certainly not," said Francesca.

"I must insist," said the count. "The house must be thoroughly searched. It is possible that men or deadly devices have been hidden here. You will be safer elsewhere, with a friend. I shall send an armed escort with you."

He was the governor of Venice. When the governor insisted, one obeyed. The Austro-Hungarian regime exercised a degree of tolerance for Venice's peculiarities and foibles but they'd no tolerance whatsoever for anything hinting at disregard of authority. To the Austrians, disrespect for authority was the first sign of insurrection—and that would be firmly—brutally, if necessary—nipped in the bud.

It was the wisest course, perhaps, after all, Francesca told herself. She did not feel safe in this house at present. She did not know whom to trust. She wasn't sure what to expect or what to do. In any case, whatever else Goetz's men found when they searched, she was confident they wouldn't find the letters.

Not that the Austrians would have any idea what to make of them if they did find them.

"As you wish, Count Goetz," she said.

He nodded stiffly, still careful not to look at her. "You will wish to go to your friend, I believe."

"No," she said. "She'll be . . . occupied." She couldn't help smiling, thinking of Giulietta and her prince. If only Francesca could have taken a fancy to Lurenze instead. How uncomplicated her life would be.

"I shall go to Magny," she said. "I know I'll be welcome there, no matter what time I arrive."

She left the room, aware of Cordier scowling after her.

James did not feel nearly as cooperative as he pretended to be. He was greatly disinclined to go quietly to the Ducal Palace. For one thing, he was not at all sure he wouldn't end up in the *pozzi*. This would be exceedingly inconvenient, since it might take hours—perhaps as much as a day or more—for Quentin to arrange to have him released.

Prison, James knew from experience, was not necessarily bad. Except for the time in the Abbaye, he'd found it . . . peaceful. While uncomfortable, depending on the surroundings, it did offer a time to gather one's wits and think, without distractions. He had a great deal of thinking to do.

At present, however, he hadn't time to indulge himself in the cool, dark, damp, solitude of a dungeon.

Goetz certainly had reason to lock him up. The governor was not a fool, and James could guess what was going through his mind.

*I had a good life, a beautiful, peaceful life—until you came to Venice*, Bonnard had told him.

Goetz would be thinking along the same lines: Venice had been quite peaceful until James Cordier arrived.

There was going to be an interrogation, beyond question, and that would be tiresome. Another great waste of valuable time.

Perhaps, after all, James thought, he should have followed his first instinct and bolted as soon as he heard the footsteps: military footsteps, a sound he'd recognize anywhere.

But he hadn't known what they—whoever they were—wanted, and it was unchivalrous to leave Francesca in the lion's den—though he would have abandoned her, he assured himself, if only she'd told him where the damned letters were.

That was all he wanted. The rest—jealousy and hurt feelings and betrayed trust—didn't signify. This was work, and he knew better than to let feelings get tangled with work. Let her go to Magny if she wanted. She might go to the devil, for all James cared.

Meanwhile, the sooner he smoothed Goetz's ruffled feathers, the sooner he could get back to work.

"I'm fairly familiar with this house," James said. "Perhaps the search will go more quickly if I help you."

Since Marta Fazi wasn't in the middle of the melee at the Palazzo Neroni but watching from a small rowboat at a safe distance, it took her far less time than it did her hired ruffians to realize that Plan C wasn't going well.

She did not wait about, hoping it would come out right. She might not be able to read as easily as some people but she had no trouble recognizing a fiasco when she saw one.

It was a good thing she had her hands occupied rowing, else some innocent bystander might have found out—in an acutely painful manner—exactly how disappointed she was.

However, this was Venice, and it was hard to do

bodily injury to others while rowing a boat, trying to find one's way in the middle of the night while keeping clear of the accursed gondolas that cluttered the waterways.

The best Marta could do was relieve her feelings aloud, in her own language, incomprehensible to those who might overhear her as she passed.

"This is what happens when you must work with incompetents," she raged to the world at large. "It's all well for him, in London, with all his lackeys, to say 'Oh, Marta, my dear, will you get me some letters, if you please.' Why did he let the great whore take those letters in the first place? Why did he not beat her and make her give them back? Why does he write to her still? Why does he care anything about her? She is too tall. Why does he not buy me a red dress? When was the last time he sent me jewelry? If I want it, I must steal it for myself. Not her. The stupid men give it to her, only because she goes on her back and gives them what most women would give them for free. I hate her and her stupid letters. She thinks she is so clever and every man will do her bidding, the fine lady. Only let me get my hands on her, once, and we'll see. We'll see who is beautiful and who is clever. Oh, yes, let me get my hands on her, only once. Then I will know what to do."

Yes, indeed, Marta knew what to do with the so-clever English whore. The only question was, how to get her hands on her.

Goetz was thorough. His men began on the roof and worked their way down. Though James helped, he'd not much hope of finding the letters. Francesca would not have appeared so unconcerned at the prospect of a search had she hidden them in the *palazzo*. Whatever else had troubled her each time she or her house had been attacked, she'd not seemed in any anxiety about the letters.

What in blazes had she done with them?

And *blazes* was not the cheeriest turn of speech. Was it possible she'd burned them?

But no, she couldn't be so stupid. Whatever else she was, Francesca Bonnard was not stupid.

Difficult, temperamental, cynical, obstinate, reckless, and very, very naughty, yes. If she had not been all these things and more—intelligent and witty and so fiercely, passionately, alive . . . and expensive, mustn't forget that—deuced expensive—if she had not been all these things, James would have solved the problem in three days at most.

But she was all those things, and the letters were nowhere in the Palazzo Neroni. He'd stake his life on that. He'd even climbed a ladder and searched the numerous chinks and crooks and crevices of the plaster children and draperies. He'd checked the frames of paintings as well, for hollow places. He told Goetz he was looking for wires or springs for traps.

Late in the day, having found neither insurrectionists nor murderous devices, James went on with the governor to the Ducal Palace and a lengthy interrogation.

He managed to pacify Goetz by claiming to have heard rumors that one Marta Fazi, a criminal known in the south and in the Papal States, was at large in Venice. Very likely she'd made Mrs. Bonnard her target, James said, because the English lady was (a) a woman and thus vulnerable and (b) the owner of a fine collection of jewelry.

"Fazi is a thief," James told the governor. "A violent one, like so many in the lawless parts of Italy. No finesse. They make a lot of noise and kill people needlessly. They're vengeful. It would seem this Fazi woman has tried and failed several times. The angrier she gets, the more determined, violent, and reckless."

"The Papal States are a disgrace," Goetz said. "Two hundred murders in the last year alone. But here we have the rule of law. We will find this woman, and the rest of the criminals will learn to stay in their own disorderly countries."

*Good luck*, James thought.


Having returned to the Ca' Munetti shortly before midnight, James slept well into the following day.

Sleeping—no matter what the circumstances—was a skill he'd learned long ago. In the Abbaye prison, their tormentors had, among other amusements, kept him and his fellows awake for days on end, until they were hallucinating. James had taught himself to sleep with his eyes open. He could make himself sleep anywhere, any time, and wake up quickly.

He was deeply angry, deeply unhappy—and that was about as far as he cared to examine the turmoil within—yet he slept.

When he woke, matters did not appear much brighter.

He was having a late breakfast when the message arrived.

It was not from Francesca.

It was on expensively masculine paper, written in the clear, formal hand of a secretary, and worded in the formal style of, say, a royal proclamation.

In sum, he was invited to tea with the comte de Magny.

James sent an equally formal acceptance, then summoned Sedgewick and spent the intervening hours fretting about what to wear.

Francesca had had to send back to the Palazzo Neroni for clothes. Resisting the temptation to fuss, she simply told Thérèse who was coming to tea, and let the maid decide.

The result? Ruffles, wave upon wave of them. White ruffles, no less.

They began at the base of her throat, fluttering about a modestly high neckline. They quivered in a line down the front of her gown and shivered along the hem. Her arms were encased in a series of puffs, trimmed in silk ribbons and ending in, yes, ruffles. The first time she'd looked in the glass, she'd put herself in mind of those great cakes she'd once served at parties in London.

At one moment, she believed she looked equally delicious—and Cordier must eat his heart out. At another, she feared she looked ridiculous, too girlish—and he'd die laughing.

So long as he died, she could have no complaints.

This is what she tried to tell herself as Cordier entered the room, and her imbecile heart fluttered like the ruffles.

He was impeccably dressed in a tailcoat of the finest wool, in a shade that most unfairly emphasized the deep blue of his eyes and contrasted splendidly with the pale yellow waistcoat. His trousers fit like another skin over his muscled thighs. His snow-white neckcloth was simply, perfectly tied, every crease exactly where it ought to be. An onyx gleamed darkly in its folds.

But her mind turned cruel and offered an image of him naked, and of the pair of them entwined among the rugs and exotic trappings of his pretend seraglio, making love, impatiently and passionately at first, and later, so tenderly.

But it had not been lovemaking to him, she reminded herself, merely copulation and a means to an end.

The reminder helped her arrange a cool expression upon her face and a frigid little smile. It helped her pretend she felt no more about this meeting than Magny did: It was a business negotiation, he told her, and she, after all, was a businesswoman.

Thus the greetings were polite, the gentlemen's bows and her curtsy precisely what was required. Cordier and Magny were resolved to behave as men of the world and she, a woman of the world, could act with the best of them.

*That's all you do*, Cordier had said. *Pretend and play games and lie . . . you'd say acting is what your profession requires. It's the same for me.*

She felt a twinge. Well, perhaps he wasn't entirely wrong about that. Even so . . .

Oh, what was the use? What stuck in her mind was herself, in nothing but a shift, jumping into the canal to save him, like the greatest romantic ninny who ever lived.

*Don't be childish*, Magny had told her yesterday, when they'd argued about what to do. *Stop thinking with your emotions and your pride and use your reason.*

She was not a child. She'd borne worse betrayals: her father's abandonment precisely when she most needed him, her husband's cruelty, unchecked by anybody, unsoftened by any friend's intervention.

She could easily bear this small emotional setback—and carry her head high.

She held her head high and acted the gracious hostess, the role she'd always played so well and enjoyed so much at home and in the course of her travels. She poured the tea, urged the gentlemen to sample the delicate pastries Magny's cook had prepared, and all the while she kept up her share of entertaining if inconsequential talk: of books and poetry and plays and operas, all interspersed with that most interesting subject, gossip about one's acquaintances.

Then at last, when all the usual topics had been covered, Magny said, "Monsieur Cordier, you know my purpose in inviting you today was not purely social."

"I am sure that if Mrs. Bonnard has a purpose," said Cordier, "it is to cut out my heart—perhaps with that alarming-looking cake knife near her hand—and feed it to the pigeons in the Piazza San Marco."

Francesca smiled sweetly. "Now there's an idea."

"Later, perhaps," Magny said, "but at this moment Francesca agrees that you are more useful alive than dead. It took a great deal of persuading, I promise you, to bring her to this amiable state of mind. But she and I are now in accord, are we not, *ma cherie?*"

"*Mais oui, monsieur,*" she said demurely.

Cordier's black brows knit and his eyes glittered dangerously.

"It has become clear," Magny went on, "that so long as Francesca has the articles in question, she is not safe. To be safe is more important than revenge for old injuries. She has no affection for her countrymen, none of whom defended her in her time of trouble. She cares not what becomes of her *ci-devant* husband. Who tells the truth and who lies? What does it matter? But since you have not openly tried to kill her, I have advised her to give the articles to you. Then you may give them to the good people or the bad people, as you please. All we require in return is that you take these tiresome articles and get out of Venice and out of our lives."

After all the difficulties, complications, trials, and tribulations, how simple it was, James thought.

They would give him the letters and all he had to do was exactly what he'd wanted to do all along: go back to England.

He had a job to do and it would be done and he would be done with her.

"I quite understand," he said. "I'm relieved that you've been able to persuade Mrs. Bonnard to . . ."

He paused and looked at her, at those mad ruffles that made him think of petticoats and tumbled bedclothes. In his mind's eye he saw her tumbling over the balcony rail and into the canal. He saw her clinging to the mooring post . . . creating a diversion.

She was a diversion, from everything he'd planned, from his duty, from his reason.

"The terms," he began, and paused.

*Don't be an idiot, Jemmy.*

"The terms," he said. "I cannot agree to the terms."

"What terms?" said Magny. "How much simpler can we make it? We do not ask for money, even knowing there is nothing to stop you from selling these letters to this Fazi woman—or to Elphick directly."

"I'm not going out of your lives," James said. "I'll do what I must because it's my duty. But after that's done, I'm coming back, Francesca."

She went utterly still. If it were not for the ruffles fluttering at her bosom, one would not know she was breathing.

James looked at Magny. "All's fair, you know, in love and war, but I'll give you fair warning, monsieur. I will not let this woman use and abandon me. You might have her now, but I'll get her back, whatever it—"

"Please." Magny held up his hand. "No more. I shall be sick."

"I don't care," James said. "I'm not French and practical. I'm English *and* Italian and—"

"And you must be blind," said monsieur. "I shall always have her, can't you see?"

"Not always," James said.

"*Always,*" said Magny. "*Toujours.*"

"Always," said Francesca and she smiled the slow, wicked smile.

"She's my daughter," said Magny.

# Chapter 15

Perfect she was, but as perfection is
   Insipid in this naughty world of ours,
Where our first parents never learn'd to kiss
   Till they were exiled from their
      earlier bowers,
Where all was peace, and innocence, and bliss
(I wonder how they got through the
      twelve hours).

Lord Byron
*Don Juan, Canto the First*

$\mathcal{J}$ ames was sure the look on his face was price-less.

Hers was, certainly. She was as shocked as he was. But while he was gaping like an idiot, his head swiveling from her to Magny while he tried to discern the resemblance, her face turned a deep pink. She jumped up from her chair.

Still looking from one to the other, James rose as well, naturally. Whatever else he was, he was born and bred a gentleman.

The green eyes flashed at Magny. "Have you taken leave of your senses? I told you when you came here—"

"You do not set conditions for me," said monsieur—or Sir Michael—or whoever he was.

She threw her hands up. "I can't believe this! It will be all over Venice—and then—and then—"

"*Aspetti.*" James held up his hand. "Wait. Please. You did say, 'daughter'?"

"He is impossible!" she raged. "He's gone when I need him, and then, when I don't need him, he turns up and tries to arrange my life."

"Your life is *merde*," said Magny.

James winced, recalling that he'd said the same to her, but using the Italian noun.

"No, it isn't!" The green eyes flashed from one man to the other. "Why don't you understand, either of you? I chose this life. I have had lovers, yes, and with one exception"—she scowled at James—"they've paid handsomely for the privilege. But always—*always*—I choose. I!" She pressed her fist to her bosom. "I have never, once, done anything for any man against my wishes—except when I was married. I have done no more—no, a great deal less—in the way of carnality than either of you."

"Well, I should hope so," Magny said. "After all—"

"But because I've chosen not to live like a nun," she cut in, "you say my life is excrement? It isn't. I've been happy. And free. And the only flies in the ointment are you—the pair of you. And you can go to hell, the pair of you."

She swept to the door.

"*Un momento,*" James said. "A moment, if you please."

She swung round, and shot him a volcanic look. "*What?*"

"Um . . . the letters?"

Her eyes narrowed.

"Sorry," he said.

"That was a magnificent exit," she said.

"I know," he said. "I am so sorry to spoil it."

She stomped away from the door but not to the tea table. She crossed the room and flung herself onto the sofa near the fire.

"Her mother was a little temperamental, too," Magny said apologetically. No, not Magny but Saunders. Yet James could not stop thinking of the man as French, and a count. Perhaps this was because he continued to speak English with the correct French accent.

"My mother, indeed," she said. "You are always throwing temper fits about every little thing."

"My daughter is a courtesan," said Saunders-Magny. "That is not precisely a little thing."

"Mr. Cordier is not interested in our domestic squabbles," she said.

"Oh, yes, I am," James said. "Very interested."

"I'm not," she said. "I'm sick of them. It's very boring, being treated like a child."

Her parent sighed. "If fathers could have their way, our daughters would remain virgins all their lives. We would shut them all up in convents if we could. But we cannot, else the world will come to an end. Or perhaps not, since rogues get into convents all the time."

"And I reckon the nuns thank God most heartily for that," she said. And she laughed the irresistibly wicked laugh.

James was aware of the melting sensation within and had no doubt his countenance must be softening into an expression of pure besottedness, but it couldn't be helped. "Oh, you are naughty," he said.

"Yes," she said.

"No wonder I've come to such a pass," he said.

"You're infatuated," she said. "I've told you again and again."

"I think you're right."

She waved her hand dismissively. "I don't care. It's your problem. My problem is how to end this skullduggery and stop people trying to kill me."

James bowed. "Of course. But I am a trifle curious about your—er—about monsieur?" He turned his gaze to the beleaguered parent. "The title. No one questioned your assuming it? Wasn't there a difficulty with passports?"

James never had difficulties with his false identities, but his superiors saw to that. This man, however, was supposed to be dead. When he was alive, he was wanted for fraud, an astounding fraud.

"If only there were, he would not be here plaguing me," the loving daughter said.

Saunders-Magny gave her an incinerating look. She returned it. It was then James finally discerned the resemblance. It was not so much in physical appearance but in manner: the way they carried themselves and their facial expressions.

The so-called count moved to the window. He

stood with his back to the late afternoon light, his hands clasped behind his back. "My mother's family was French," he said. "The title belongs to my cousin. There is a resemblance. When we were boys, sometimes we tried to fool people. Sometimes we succeeded. We were good friends, you see. And so, when my financial troubles occurred, I went to my cousin in France. This happened at the time Napoleon escaped from Elba."

James well remembered those times, especially the slaughter at Waterloo that ended Bonaparte's attempt to reclaim his empire.

"I helped my cousin in his efforts against the Corsican," Saunders-Magny went on. "I was merely a courier, you know, nothing as sophisticated as what you do. My cousin, on the other hand—" He broke off, shaking his head. "Best to be discreet. Enough to say that it became most convenient for him to lend me his identity for a time while he had business elsewhere."

"You can imagine how impatiently I've been waiting for his cousin's business elsewhere to be finished." Francesca threw an odd glance at her father. It happened too quickly for James to be certain, but it seemed to mingle affection with exasperation. It vanished, though, as she turned her gaze to James. "But to return to our business, Mr. Cordier. You wish to know what I've done with the letters."

"Yes, actually. I know they're not in your house."

She smiled.

This was not the serpent smile, luring a man to his doom. This was amusement, with a dose of triumph in it.

"*Che io sia dannato,*" he said. "I'll be damned. It *is* there. You clever little devil."

"When I tell you," she said, "you'll slap your head and say, 'How could I be so stupid?'"

"It won't be the first time," he said. He thought of all the stupid things he'd done since he met her, all the mistakes he'd made. He'd made a mistake yesterday, in failing to trust her. He should have taken his chances, like a man, instead of acting like a coward, putting off the inevitable.

*I have had lovers, yes, and with one exception, they've paid handsomely for the privilege,* she'd said.

It was a privilege, truly, to be her lover. And he'd been the most privileged of all, because she'd let him into her heart.

And now, he realized, if he wanted to win her back, he would have to pay for the privilege.

"It won't be the first time I've been stupid where you're concerned," he said.

"I won't disagree," she said. "I am so tempted to make you guess, and drive yourself wild. But then we should be at it forever, and I should like to get on with my life."

*Without you,* she meant.

*Not without me,* he thought. *Not if I can help it.*

"Yes, the sooner this is over with, the better," said Saunders-Magny.

*Think,* James told himself. *Think fast.*

"It's complicated, as I said," she said. "I am not going to shout it across the room." She crooked her finger at James. "Come, you stupid man, and I'll whisper it in your ear."

He started toward her.

Then he paused, frowning. He thought. He thought some more.

"Cordier, it's a little late to play hard to get," she said.

"I'm thinking," he said.

"Don't hurt your head," she said. "I've already done all the thinking, *mio caro*. All you have to do—"

"Don't tell me," he said. "Please don't tell me."

Francesca wanted to strangle him. She'd been looking forward so much to luring him to the sofa and torturing him, whispering in his ear and making him want her. She'd looked forward so much to punishing him for making her love him.

"This is the last straw," she said. She rose and walked out.

She heard his footsteps behind her.

"*Va via!*" she said without looking back. "Go away. *Vai all'inferno!*"

"That is where my mama tells me I will go," came the voice of Don Carlo from behind her. "But in time, most beautiful one. Not too soon, I hope. I beg you will not make me hurry to the place of punishment and the imps with the sharp forks to prick my bottom. Because first, you see, I have things most important to do." He reached her side. "I have the plan most cunning."

"I don't care," she said.

"Do be sensible," he said, reverting to Cordier, the provoking, patronizing Englishman.

"The sensible thing to do, I've decided," she said, "is to keep far away from you."

"You want to be safe. Your—" He broke off, glancing about the *portego* for eavesdropping servants. "Magny said the important thing was for you to be safe," he went on in a lower tone. "You will not be safe while that woman is on the loose."

Her heart began to race. "Don't try to alarm me. I'll be safe when you give her the . . . articles."

"I'm not giving them to her. I'm not on that side. And don't say you don't care whose side I'm on or that it doesn't matter."

"I won't say it," she said. "But I'll think it."

"It does matter," he said. "Listen to me, please, Francesca."

She didn't want to listen. He was too persuasive and she wanted him too much. Time and again he'd caused her to act against good sense, to break the rules she'd spent so much time and suffering learning. She saw the great marble archway at the head of the stairs, only a few feet away. She could run down to the *andron*, and out to the courtyard and quickly disappear in the maze of narrow Venetian streets and alleys . . . where she was sure to get lost and, with her luck, fall straight into the hands of one pack of villains or other.

The other direction, toward the canal, was probably safer, but then she must wait while a gondola was readied for her. So much for dramatic exits. So much for running away.

She stopped at the archway and looked at him, into his handsome, deceitful face.

"You think I don't understand but I do," he said. "You're angry with England. It's Parliament that grants divorces, and all those men—the country's lawmakers—treated you like the Whore of Babylon. They destroyed your name and your life. Why should you wish to save such a government? Why stop Elphick? Why not let them have the leader they deserve?"

She looked up, at the sculpted figures adorning the top of the archway: Neptune in a stormy sea with strange creatures about him. She'd left the stormy sea behind when she left England, or so she'd thought. It had followed her and found her, eventually. "I could put it better," she said, "but you've got it in a nutshell."

"All the same, you know it matters," he said. "You've always known. That was why you kept the . . . articles. If it didn't matter, you'd have destroyed them long ago. But you kept them, even though you knew there was a chance they'd become a dangerous possession one day."

"I've decided they're too dangerous," she said. "I've decided it's not worth the risk, the unpleasantness. Why should I risk my neck for England, for that government and those monstrous men?"

"It was a bad time," he said. "As your—as Magny pointed out, Napoleon had escaped from Elba. The upper classes were full of fear and hate already. They were worried about his returning to power and his possibly overthrowing them, with the help of malcontents at home. The Terror was and is still vivid in many people's minds, recollect. Easy enough for the gentlemen in Parliament to picture their wives and children under the blade of the guillotine."

"But I was not fomenting revolution! I had an affair! One! My husband had scores. He had a mistress before we wed and kept her while we were wed and has her still—and no one thinks the less of him!"

"I am not saying that you were trying to overthrow the Crown," he said. "I am saying that these men were in a state of mind that made it easy for Elphick. A great scandal, a depraved woman—he redirected the general fear and hatred at you, a clear target. They could deal with you. Napoleon and political unrest constituted a more complicated proposition. You were simple. You were the diversion, don't you see? With everyone fixed on you, no one noticed what Elphick was doing behind the scenes. They behaved badly, I agree. It was neither the first nor the last time they've done so. But they were wrong, and I know that in your case they'll make amends if you'll give them a chance."

She didn't want to understand the men who'd degraded and humiliated her. But she hadn't considered the context. It didn't make them any the less hateful to her, but it made their behavior a degree more comprehensible.

"I'm not stopping them making amends," she said. "If you are who you claim to be, if you are one of the good ones—"

"Not *if*," he said. "I want you to *know*, without

the slightest doubt. Not in six months or twelve or whenever we get it all sorted out but *now*. I want to prove it to you." He paused. "And I have an idea how to do it."

Francesca looked up at Neptune, then further along the great hall to Minerva, Goddess of Wisdom, standing guard over another portal. Could a woman ever be truly wise, when it came to men? Probably not, else the species would not survive.

"You are so aggravating," she said. "After all this time, I'd finally decided to get rid of those dratted letters. Now I'm wild to get them off my hands, and you won't take them."

"I will, but not today," he said. "Until I get matters sorted out, they're safer where they are."

"And I am supposed to fold my hands and wait patiently for you to carry out your cunning plan? I am to wait about, not knowing how or when that Fazi creature will strike next?"

"She needs to regroup," he said. "She needs reinforcements. That gives us as much as a week. But I promise not to make you wait that long. A day or two, no more."

What choice did she have? "Very well. Sort matters out. In the meantime, I'm going home. I have had as much as I can bear of my—of Magny. And you, if you are wise, will keep out of my way until you've something worthwhile to bother me about."

The next day found James at the Ducal Palace, facing a still-suspicious Count Goetz.

"We have questioned the man Piero again and again," he told James. "Naturally, it occurred to me that he had lied, even to you, about his motives. He is from the south, it appears. That abominable dialect. This Fazi woman is from the south, I am informed. For the two of them to come to Venice at the same time is no coincidence. But he claims he has never heard of her. He holds to the same story, like a dog with a bone. I know he is lying. What shall I do? Hang him by his thumbs? Then someone will complain of our brutality and make inflammatory speeches in one of the squares. The next we know, they make an insurrection. They are very obstinate, these people, and of a quick temper."

"I don't think he's obstinate," James said, "so much as terrified."

Goetz stared at him for a moment. "What difference does it make? Either way, he tells us nothing."

And even if Piero did tell them, they wouldn't understand one word in twenty. If that.

"I wonder if you might let me have a go," James said.

"No," said Goetz.

Two hours later, James returned to the Ducal Palace, this time with Prince Lurenze.

Though he cast an unamiable eye upon James, Goetz was all gracious welcome this time, eager to know what he could do for his highness.

There were certain advantages to being royalty.

"Please to explain," said the Prince of Gilenia, "why Mr. Cordier is not permitted to try where you have failed, to obtain information which may prevent harm coming to Mrs. Bonnard."

Goetz began to recite certain rules about prisoners and foreign visitors.

Lurenze held up his hand. "Please to explain," he said, "where is the rule to endanger a lady instead of doing all that is possible to protect her and capture dangerous persons?"

Goetz gazed down at his immaculate desk. His jaw set.

It wasn't difficult to guess what he was thinking.

People spoke of the Austrians as rulers of northern Italy but of course it was Austro-Hungarian rule. Goetz knew as well as James did that a certain Hungarian lady of high birth had been proposed as Prince Lurenze's consort.

The governor of Venice would be most unwise to risk offending the crown prince of Gilenia, especially over such a small matter: merely giving one of the prince's English friends a few minutes alone with a prisoner.

The count, upon further consideration, decided he was not sure he'd interpreted the rule correctly. "You may try your luck with him, Mr. Cordier," he said. "But you will give me your word as a gentleman to tell me everything he tells you."

"Certainly," James said. Gentleman or not, he'd lied before and would do it again. Not that he necessarily needed to lie. After all, Goetz had not specified *when* he must be told.

James had been through the Ducal Palace before. On his previous tour, when the governor had felt more kindly toward him, he'd been given a tour. They had not gone as far as the prisons, however. On the last visit, Goetz had had Piero brought to them.

This time, James deemed it best to go to Piero.

Lurenze insisted on going with him, in case anyone made difficulties, he said.

"I am not happy with the behavior of the governor to you," he said after they left a deeply annoyed Goetz. "His look is unfriendly. If I am by, he will not make up some foolish rule to put you in prison, too."

Ah, well, at least someone trusted him, James thought. Ironic that it was a rival. Or perhaps not—or not so much of a rival as previously.

James had chased all over Venice looking for Lurenze, and finally run him to ground—or water, rather—en route to Magny's *palazzo*. In the gondola with his highness was Giulietta. They had seemed quite cozy, though Giulietta persisted in addressing his highness in the most ridiculous terms: "your celestiality," "your luminescence," "your magnificence," and the like, all of which Lurenze bore with a straight face.

His absurdly handsome face was solemn now, as they followed the guard assigned to take them to Piero.

The route from the Ducal Palace to the prisons was not calculated to lift the spirits. They traversed a narrow, uneven, and dark passage that led to the Bridge of Sighs. From the outside, the arched bridge was quite beautiful. Within, all was gloom, proving how it had earned its title. A pair of corridors ran its length. Two heavy grated windows dimly lit the way. The guard, bearing a lighted candle, led Lurenze and James through narrow passages and down the stairs to the nether regions, to the dungeons known as the *pozzi*, the wells.

The guard, clearly accustomed to the role of guide—and probably in the habit of conveying tourists through the place, was cheerfully talkative. He told them there were eighteen cells built in tiers. The cells were about ten or twelve feet long and six or seven feet wide, he said. They were arched at top, with a small opening in front. The lower group were level with the water in the canal.

He pointed to little niches in the stones on the wall. These, he informed them, were made to hold bars on which convicts were hanged or strangled to death. He called their attention to other niches, black with smoke. Here the executioners used to set their lamps, to allow them to see what they were doing. With relish, he explained certain holes in the pavement. When criminals were quartered, he explained, the blood drained off through the holes and into the canal. He indicated a door, from which the corpses were thrown into boats and taken away to be disposed of.

"I was told these were the modern prisons," said Lurenze. "Prigioni Nuove is the name. The New Prisons."

"They were modern two hundred years ago, when they were built," James said.

"This is barbaric," said Lurenze.

"I've seen worse," said James. He'd been confined in worse.

They arrived, finally, at the cell in which Piero had been left to ponder his sins and the advisability of telling his captors what they wanted to know. He had been left in the dark. When the door was unlocked, the stench wafting out into the passage was nigh overpowering.

It seemed to overpower Lurenze, who staggered back from the door.

"This is abominable," he said.

"You needn't come in," James said. "It's going to be very close in there."

"No, I come," said Lurenze. "A moment is all I need." He squared his shoulders. "There. I am ready."

A prince, perhaps, and pampered, but he had some solid stuff to him.

Still, this had better not take long, James thought. Brave or not, the lad wasn't used to it, and was all too likely to faint or cast up his accounts. That was no way to awaken fear and respect in the prisoner.

"Very well, your highness," James said. He lowered his voice and reverted to English. "First, I advise you to stay near the door. You'll get a bit of air—such as it is—from the passage through the little window. Second, you must give me your word you will not speak until spoken to, and then you will follow my lead. This is most important, excellency. A matter of life and death."

"Yes, of course," said Lurenze.

James told the guard they were ready. The man lit the lamp in the passage and gave James the candle. James entered the cell, Lurenze following.

The door clanged shut behind them.

Piero was sullen. His week in the cell had turned him into a lump. Even the sight of James could not rouse him to emotion beyond a grimace. He squatted in a corner, staring at his bare and unspeakably filthy feet.

Lurenze dutifully took up his position by the door. James wondered how long he'd remain upright. The stench was beyond anything.

*No time to waste*, James thought.

He came directly to the point. In slow, simple Italian, he said, "We are looking for Marta Fazi." Piero's dialect might be all but incomprehensible but he understood the language of the educated—or enough to get by, at any rate.

"Never heard of her," said Piero.

"That's a pity," said James, "because I have something the lady wants. Something the English lady had. Not jewels. Some papers."

Piero did not respond, but his posture stiffened.

"I know Marta Fazi wants these papers," James said. "I can sell them to her or I can sell them to the other side."

"It's nothing to me," said Piero.

"I think it is," James said. "If I can't find her, I will sell them to someone else. When she learns you had a chance to help her get these papers and you did nothing . . ."

Piero shifted uncomfortably.

"If she learns you failed her, she will not be pleased with you," James said.

Still no response.

"I'm not sure you'll be safe from her, even here."

No answer, but something changed. The man's fear was palpable. James pressed his point. "Ah, well. You say you know nothing. Perhaps you don't know her, as you say. In that case, it's unfair to keep you here. I had better arrange for your release."

He heard Lurenze's gasp and glanced that way, as Piero did. But the prince, to his credit, said nothing. Or maybe he dared not open his mouth for fear of vomiting.

Piero's gaze came back to James. The sullen expression was gone, and the fear was plain on his grimy face. "They won't let me out," he said.

"Of course they will," James said cheerfully. "Don't you fret about it. I'll simply tell them that, when I looked at you again, more closely, I realized I made a mistake, and you are not the man who attacked the English lady."

"I tell you nothing. I know nothing."

He was afraid of Marta, clearly. Still too afraid of her to tell what he knew.

"This is annoying," James said. "I am tired of this stinking hole and tired of you. I have tried to be reasonable but you won't be reasonable. So this is what I'll do. I shall spread a rumor that you've betrayed Marta Fazi, and as a reward for betraying her, you are to be released." He looked once more at Lurenze. It was hard to be sure in the dim light, but he seemed to be turning green.

"Your excellency," James said. "Would you be willing to use your influence to arrange this man's release?"

"Assuredly," the prince said, gagging on the syllables.

"I say nothing," Piero said doggedly. "I know nothing." But his voice was less sullen now, the pitch a degree higher.

"Rumors travel so quickly in Venice," James went on. "If Marta Fazi is here, she'll hear the news by this time tomorrow if not before then. I should be able to have you released in two or three days' time. Maybe you'll be able to get away before she finds you. Or maybe she'll be waiting for you when you come out of this place. Or maybe some friendly men will offer to take you for a drink. Or maybe they will not be friendly. Maybe they will take you somewhere, and not for a drink, eh, my friend?"

"You are the devil," Piero said. "But the name you say—she is a devil, too."

"I only want you to take a message to her."

A silence while Piero considered. "This, maybe I will do," he said. "But send that one away before he pukes on me."

# Chapter 16

But who, alas! can love, and then be wise?

Lord Byron
*Don Juan, Canto the First*

*I*n response to James's message—not long after his interview with Piero—Mrs. Bonnard agreed to meet with him the following morning, Friday, at ten o'clock.

The first thing he noticed as he entered the *putti*-infested drawing room was her pallor. She did not look as though she'd had enough sleep. Or perhaps it was the frock that made her seem so pale. It was high-necked and plain white, adorned with only a bit of pale green embroidery. She wore no jewelry. She had some sort of scarf arrangement wrapped about her head. Other women wore caps with morning dress but Francesca Bonnard in a cap—however lacy and beribboned—was out of the question.

Still, the frock seemed out of the question, too. It might have belonged to an innocent schoolgirl.

Certainly it offered a striking contrast to the woman wearing it: the exotic eyes, the mouth promising sin, and the sinfully voluptuous figure. The effect was startling . . . and enticing as well.

"I thought you didn't rise before noon," James said, not bothering with polite greetings.

"I don't," she said. "But I am frantic to get this over with."

"My dear girl." He crossed the room to her and took her hands in his. "I'm a beast. I should have sent word yesterday and at least let you know what I was about. But I'm not accustomed to—to—"

"To accounting to a woman for your where-abouts?" She smiled, and there seemed to be genu-ine amusement in it. Perhaps he was on his way to forgiveness?

"Not since mama demanded to know what I'd been up to," he said.

"When you were eight?"

"Eighteen," he said. "Twenty-eight. Whenever she sees me, she expects a complete accounting."

She cocked her head to one side, studying his face. "I daresay she gets it."

"I'm afraid of my mother," he said. "As a fellow ought to be."

"Horrid man," she said. "You are determined to charm me, even when I can scarcely keep my eyes open and I'm cross at having to keep them open. What an inhuman hour to be up and about!"

"We could go back to bed," he said.

"Dream on," she said. "You'll want a great deal more than charm to accomplish that." She slid her hands from his and moved away. It was only then, watching her walk away, that he finally noticed the oddity in the room.

It was not as though it was hard to miss: a tall ladder in one of the corners on the side opposite the windows. He'd missed it because he'd come in looking for her and all he'd seen was her.

Now he watched her take up a narrow object from the console table near the ladder. James joined her. And stared at the thing in her hand. "A paper knife?"

"You have correctly identified it," she said.

He looked at the knife, then at the ladder, then up, at the *putti*-encrusted ceiling. Then his gaze came back to her amused green one.

"I looked there," he said. "I thought the children were hiding them. And it was no small chore, looking. There are so many plaster figures, not only here, but throughout the house. I thought you might have put the letters between the legs of one of the buxom ladies holding up the plaster draperies in the corners. That would be your idea of a good joke. But I couldn't find them there or anywhere else."

"I know," she said. "I knew you'd look. And I knew you wouldn't find them. But you're not far wrong. Here, hold the ladder for me."

"Hold the ladder? Are you mad? You're not going up there."

She turned fully toward him and regarded him with the level look a woman tended to employ instead of punching a man in the head as he richly deserved.

"Once, only once," she said with exaggerated

patience, "I should like to do something without having to argue with you about it."

"You do exactly as you please all the time," he said. "You do it before anyone has a chance to argue with you. Jumping into canals, for instance."

"I am not going to jump off the ladder," she said. "The only way that would be fun would be if I fell on you and broke your thick head, and I suspect it's too thick to break. Are you going to hold the ladder for me or not?"

"Who held it for you originally?"

"Nobody. The last thing I wanted was witnesses. I did it one night while most of the servants were away at one of the festivals. I dragged a few of the heavier tables over here to support the ladder. I should have done that today but I thought you'd want to look up under my dress."

The ceilings were high, the ladder alarmingly tall. Still, she was stubborn and he was a man. "Well, if you put it that way . . ."

James manfully resisted the urge to lick her beautiful ankles as they passed his line of vision, and settled for looking. He admired as much of her calves as he could—not nearly enough, for the dress and petticoat clung to her legs in the most provoking manner.

But she was soon at her work, and then he became engrossed in watching her insert the knife into a seam of plaster. As she'd said, he had judged her well—her sense of humor, certainly. She hadn't hidden the parcel between the legs of the buxom lady in the corner but nearby, where a little boy's legs and bottom stuck out from under the plaster draperies.

As bits of plaster fell on his head, he wondered why he'd never thought of that: tuck the packet of letters into a convenient crevice and plaster the lot over. It wanted only a thin coat of plaster and a little skill to make it blend in. An artist—the one who'd done the work in the first place, would have noticed. But even a sharp eye like James's could easily miss it. The packet would appear to be another fold in the drapery—and he'd been looking for letters, paper.

"You needn't fear they're damaged," she said as she went on with her cautious work. "I took care. I wrapped them in oilcloth to protect them from the wet plaster, then I wrapped a rough cloth over that, so the plaster would stick properly. It worked out well. It made the packet more rounded, so it resembled a fold of the drapery."

"I had read that the great courtesans of Venice were extremely well educated and multitalented," he said. "But I never heard of their learning plasterwork."

"They were blondes; did you know that?" she said. "I think a reddish blond was the fashionable hair color. The ones who didn't come by it naturally used a rather ghastly bleaching process."

"I like your hair exactly as it is," he said. "But did these beauties work in plaster?"

"They might have done," she said. "Lots of ladies do in England, certainly. We learn in the schoolroom. Artistic pursuits. Sticking shells and such on the walls of playrooms, decorating man-made—or woman-made grottoes. Making plaster casts of our hands. Masks."

More chips fluttered down. She reached behind the boy's bottom and took out a rounded packet. Then she quickly climbed down. Her eyes sparkled and her face was flushed.

He moved out of the way back as she stepped off the last rung onto the floor.

She set down her knife. "There," she said. She held out the packet. Bits of plaster still stuck to the outside. He took it.

He stared at the thing in his hand. After all this time, after all the trouble, here it was. If he'd had to search again, he still wouldn't have found it.

He looked up at the ceiling, at the little bottom and legs, where only a few chips in the plaster offered any hint of something extra having been there. Even then, who'd know? The plasterwork was more than a century old, cracked here and there, patched here and there.

"The only thing that truly worried me was the house burning down," she said. "That was why I panicked the other night."

He nodded.

"What?" she said. "Are you dumbstruck at last?"

His gaze drifted down to meet hers. He saw the triumph in her eyes, and laughter, too . . . and the ghost.

"Only you would make a little boy's bum your hiding place," he said. "What fun you are."

"Yes," she said. "Yes, I am." She backed away and gave a little wave of her hand. "Well, run along now and do whatever it is you have to do."

He remained where he was, gazing at the packet in his hand, then at her, in her schoolgirl dress, which she contrived somehow to make exotic and seductive.

He thought of how clever she'd been, how she'd outwitted her devious spouse and England's best agents. He thought of how brave she was—stupidly brave, as one needed to be at times. He thought of the shame and misery she'd undergone and how she'd turned disgrace into triumph.

He thought of what he'd felt like when he first came to Venice: utterly weary, in body and soul, and utterly disgusted. He didn't even know who that man was anymore.

Because of her.

Because he'd fallen in love, stupidly, hopelessly, incurably in love.

But if he said so she wouldn't believe him and he couldn't blame her for not believing him.

And so, instead, he said, "This thing I have to do . . . I wonder if you'd like to do it with me?"

She studied his face for a moment. "Is that an innuendo? Forgive me if I didn't quite understand but it's wretchedly early in the morning."

"Not an innuendo," he said. "I told you I had a plan. I didn't tell you much about it. Would you like to be my accomplice?"

Her face came alight then, the way it had done the first time he'd spoken to her, when he'd been Don Carlo and she'd started to talk of Byron. "Cordier, that is the first sign of true intelligence you've shown this morning."

"I take it that's a yes?" he said.

She threw herself at him so hard that he dropped the packet. He didn't care. She pulled his head down and kissed him hard, too. He didn't mind that, either. He wrapped his arms about her and kissed her back with the same energy, and hoped he had not just offered to make the gravest mistake of his life.


*That night*

It was not hard to hide in Venice if one were clever, knew where to go, and made friends easily. This was not the case for Piero, unfortunately.

He would not have ended up in the *pozzi* had he not tried to steal a gondola. He had not realized how much skill it required to maneuver them. He had not realized how possessive gondoliers were about their ridiculous boats.

Marta Fazi should have told him. Unlike him, she'd traveled a great deal, especially during the war, and she'd been to Venice before. She had money, and a comfortable room in a house in the neighborhood of the Rialto Bridge.

When Piero appeared at her door, she welcomed him as one might a long-lost son.

While not the world's deepest thinker, he knew better than to believe she was so very happy to see him. Still, he knew, too, that she was desperately short of men, because all the ones who'd gone after the Englishwoman the other night had been captured. Unless Marta took one of her fits, he ought to be safe from her knife.

She sat at a small table in a comfortable little room. Two other chairs stood at the table. Under it lay a rug. A fire burned in the little fireplace. He knew she was used to grander surroundings these days. Yet once upon a time, she'd lived on the streets. She could make herself at home anywhere.

At present, she sipped wine from a pretty glass. He had known her to drink straight from the bottle. She offered him none. But she didn't take up the knife that lay on the table next to the bottle. She listened patiently while he explained why the governor had let him go.

"It's because of the English lady," he said. "She's afraid of you."

"Why? She doesn't know me. You wouldn't be such a fool as to tell her or anyone else about me."

He shook his head. "They said your name to me—one of the foreigners did, the first night. Then the governor said your name. But every time, I said I'd never heard of you. Only tonight, when they say what they want me to do, I tell them I will try to take a message to you."

She glanced at the knife, which gleamed in the lamplight. "Piero, I hope you haven't been an idiot again."

"One tried to follow me," he said. "I lost him in a crowd near a theater." He didn't add that he'd got lost several times before and after that.

"And the crowd didn't scatter when you came?" she said. "You stink like a fish ten days dead."

"I'm sorry for the smell," he said. "There was no time to wash. I came as fast as I could. When I tell you how it is, you can judge if I was wrong."

She waited.

"I know you want papers from this English lady," he said. "One of the foreigners knew about those papers, too."

She nodded. "If they didn't know, my friend in England would not have asked me to perform this little service for him."

"The two men who came to me tonight did not want to give the papers to you," Piero said. "But the English lady is afraid you will hunt her wherever she goes. She makes her friends do as she says. The prince—the one with the yellow curls—he's one of her friends."

"Oh, yes. I've seen him. Very pretty."

"He's the one who made them set me free," said Piero. "He argued with the other one—a bigger man, dark. That one's obnoxious. To make the time pass, I dream of ways to kill him."

"Poor Piero! The time goes slow in prison, I know."

She would have let him rot there or be hanged or have his head cut off on that devil's device, the guillotine. But Piero would have done the same if she had ended up in the *pozzi*. One had to look out for oneself.

"The prince doesn't care what anyone else wants. The lady is more important, he says. He wants no more trouble for her. He wants you to go away. He says you're a nuisance."

Marta gave a short laugh. "A nuisance? It's true. But I wouldn't be this great nuisance if my men did as I told them. We should have had those papers the first night we came here. But no, you and Bruno had to play with the whore." She lifted her glass and eyed him over the rim.

"That was Bruno's fault," Piero said. "He was the one who didn't follow orders."

"And you were stupid enough to get caught," she said. "Trying to escape in a stolen gondola. What kind of imbecile steals a gondola?"

Piero lifted his shoulders in the "I Dunno" gesture.

"This is what happens when one uses inferior tools," she said. "I come to Venice with incompetents, with idiots. Why? Because my best men are in prison or crippled and useless. All because of that scoundrel."

Piero waited patiently while she went into the rant he'd heard before, about the tall, handsome bastard who'd seduced her, stolen her emeralds, and maimed her best men a few months ago in Rome.

"Nothing goes right," she said. "This stupid little city with more rats than people, and crazy streets. To go anywhere, you must go in a boat, and listen to the Venetians talking their gibberish. The last time I came here, I told myself never again. Still . . ." She poured herself more wine and drank. "I've faced worse for smaller rewards. But this time . . ." She scowled at Piero. "What's she offering to make me go away? Does the bitch think a big bribe will be enough?"

"The papers," he said. "The papers your friend in England wants."

"That's all?"

"They say she'll give you the papers to make you go away."

"I don't believe it. I smell a trap—or is that smell only you?"

Piero lifted his shoulders again. "I don't know. This is what they tell me. They say the English lady knows you won't trust her. And so she asks you to pick the time and place. This is the way she can prove there's no trick or trap. Wherever you tell her to come, whatever time you choose, she will come. But since she's afraid of you, she will take a man with her for protection."

"Which man?"

"Who knows? One of her lovers. The prince, probably. He's like a puppy at her feet."

She waved the bottle at him. "Come, have a drink while I think about this."

Piero found a glass and poured himself a drink, then another.

After a time, she said, "I know what to do. There's a small risk. But there always is." She stared at him and he put his glass down on the little table. "Do you understand what those papers are worth, little man?"

"I hope they're worth a great deal, for all the trouble they cause."

"When my friend in England has these papers, nothing more stands in his way. He'll be like—like a king. And he'll reward me well, as he did before. But this time he can arrange to make me a noble lady. For—how does he say it?" She thought. "Ah, yes. For service to the Crown." She laughed. "And the women—like the English lady—they must all bow at my feet and call me 'your excellency.' Oh, I'll enjoy that very much, to see the English bitch,

his wife, bow at my feet." She refilled Piero's glass
and her own. "I think it's even worth letting her
live." She paused. "And yet I looked forward to
cutting her face a little." She took up her knife and
turned it, watching the deadly sharp blade catch
the candlelight.

Piero hastily downed his drink.

She stroked the flat side of the blade with her
finger. "We'll see," she said. "We'll see what happens, won't we?"

"We?" said Piero, looking about the small room.

"You and me, little one," she said. "She will
bring a man. I will bring a man: you. And if this is
a trap, and you have betrayed me . . ." She smiled.
"I'm quick. Quick on my feet and quick with my
knife. Pray hard, Piero, that you have not been stupid again."

*The following night*

Cordier's job, Francesca decided, was not one
she'd choose. For one thing, there was too much
waiting. She wasn't used to waiting. She wasn't
used to being at anyone's beck and call, let alone
the beck and call of thieves and murderers. She
didn't like it.

Giulietta and Lurenze had joined them for dinner but afterward the prince had a social gathering
he was obliged to attend. Though Giuletta had offered to stay behind, Cordier had encouraged her
to keep the prince company. "I doubt anything
will happen tonight," he'd said, "and I know the

dreary diplomatic business will pass more pleasantly for his highness if you are by."

Assured that they'd be sent for the instant the situation changed, Lurenze and Giulietta had left an hour ago.

At present, Francesca and Cordier were in the private parlor adjoining her boudoir. She was trying to write a letter to Lord Byron, but it was very difficult to concentrate with Cordier asking her questions and looking over her shoulder and breathing down her neck.

He had started out lounging on the sofa, and she'd assumed that he, accustomed to waiting, would take a nap. But the instant she commenced writing, he became deeply interested in that.

She set down her pen. "Perhaps you ought to wait at your house," she said. "If a message comes, I can let you know in minutes."

"As I told Lurenze, I doubt a message will come this soon. Fazi is more likely to make us wait another day or two while she makes arrangements to get away. And while she scouts Venice for the best site for a rendezvous."

Francesca turned around in her chair. "You are so sure she'll agree to this?" she said.

"Oh, yes. Do you write to him regularly?"

She turned the letter over and pushed it to one side of her cluttered writing desk. "Not as regularly as I would like." She recovered the inkwell.

"Sorry." He straightened. "But spying is what I do. Among other things."

He smiled a smile so full of wicked meaning that

she was strongly tempted to grab his neckcloth and kiss him until he fainted.

It would be a good way to pass the time. It would relieve the tension.

No, it probably wouldn't. She was, in fact, deeply uneasy about what was to come, though she was doing her best to appear as nonchalant as he.

"You're supposed to understand these matters better than I," she said. "But if I were Marta Fazi, I would be making myself scarce about now. I find it hard to believe she'll risk a noose on Elphick's account, no matter how much he's paying her. It's hard to believe she can be that desperate."

"She's a desperado, not desperate," he said. "They hired Fazi because they know what she's like. She doesn't give up. She's tried three times to get the letters from you and failed three times. That's not cause for surrender. Now winning is a point of pride. After all the trouble she's gone through, I don't see her letting an opportunity go, even if she suspects a trap."

"She'd have to be an idiot not to suspect one."

"She's daring and resourceful," he said. "She has to be. Men don't like taking orders from a woman. But she's always managed to get a lot of cutthroats to do her bidding."

"Not this time, though, you said."

"The chances are small," he said. "The men who tried to kidnap you are in custody. Piero's friend Bruno is incapacitated. That leaves Piero. Fazi needs more than a few hours to recruit new henchmen. She doesn't understand Venetian. Being short of help and frustrated might make her more dangerous. On the other hand, it does make her more willing to take a risk. The sooner she responds, the less likely it is that she'll have anyone but Piero with her."

His blue gaze became searching. "Are you getting cold feet? It's not too late to back out. I can get Zeggio to dress up as you—as I'd planned originally."

Oh, she was tempted. "And let the pair of you ruin another gown?" she said. "I think not." Yes, she was frightened. But he'd invited her to—to be his partner—and to her, that was almost as good as a gift of diamonds.

Well, perhaps it was better, if one wanted to be stupidly sentimental and romantic about going out to confront a desperate—or desperado—woman.

"Speaking of gowns," he said.

Though she'd understood she might spend this night waiting for word that didn't come, Francesca had not dressed for an evening at home. She'd dressed at her usual time in the usual way, for an evening out. She wore a blue crepe gown, set off with a suite of pearls. Her headdress was adorned with pearls, too.

His searching blue gaze traveled down over the gown to her slippered feet then up again to the pearls encircling her neck and dangling from her ears. "That's a little excessive, don't you think, for a rendezvous with a killer?"

"It's evening," she said. "In the event I'm obliged to go out, I want to be properly dressed."

"Improperly, you mean. If the neckline were any lower, I could see whether your navel went in or out."

"Don't you remember?" she said.

"In," he said.

She remembered, too, and heat washed through her in wave after dizzying wave. But she was not a naïve girl, to be disconcerted by mere words. With her index finger she traced the décolletage.

The blue gaze smoldered. "On the other hand," he said, "if that wicked neckline is all for my benefit . . ." He bent his head.

The door opened and Arnaldo walked in, silver tray in his hands. "A boy has brought this, signora," he said.

Cordier came to attention, every evidence of lust erased, his face hard and alert.

"A dirty little ruffian," the butler went on. "He gives it to me and runs away."

He carried the tray to Francesca. She took the note from it. He bowed and went out again.

She opened the note, her fingers trembling despite her best efforts. Cordier lightly touched her hand, and that was all it took to still the tremors.

"Eleven o'clock tonight," the painstakingly formed letters informed them amid numerous ink blots. "San Giacomo di Rialto. No masks."

It was a frantic few minutes. The message arrived shortly after ten o'clock, leaving little time to think, let alone prepare. However, Francesca had done her thinking on the day Cordier told her his plan for dealing with Marta Fazi.

She had only to step into her boudoir briefly and collect the parcel waiting there. Thérèse had her evening wrap ready. It was not five minutes before

Francesca was hurrying downstairs with Cordier, who was rattling off instructions to various servants as they went.

Not long thereafter, he and Francesca were in her gondola. As instructed, they were not wearing masks, though this would be nothing out of the way in Venice.

Once they were well on their way and there was no chance of Cordier sending her back, she withdrew from under her shawl the parcel and held it upon her lap. It was wrapped in pink silk and tied with blue ribbons.

"What is that?" he said.

"A gift."

"Pink silk? Not for me, then."

She swallowed. "It's for her."

He stared for a moment at the package clutched in her gloved and braceleted hands. Then, "Are you insane?" he burst out. "A gift? For *Fazi?*"

"A bribe, actually."

"A bribe? A *bribe?* Are you mad? Do you know who you're dealing with?"

He was very angry. His face had the marble-hard expression he'd worn the night he threw the big cutthroat in the water.

"I'm dealing with a woman who wants to kill me," she said. "A *woman.*"

"You don't know this kind of woman! She's not like you! She's not like Giulietta!" He paused and took a breath. When he spoke again, his voice was quieter. "I recognize the shape of that parcel. You are *not* going to do what I think you're going to do."

"She came to my house," Francesca said. "She saw my jewelry. She probably had it in her hands. But she left it behind. All she took were the emeralds."

"She's mad about emeralds. Literally. Mad. As in *non compos mentis*."

"She's a *woman*," Francesca said. "She left all the rest of the jewelry behind. What an effort of will that must have been."

"I'm going to tear my hair out," Cordier said. "What possessed me to involve you in this? I should have known you'd come up with a harebrained scheme—"

"You said it's a point of pride with her to get the letters," she said. "They're paying her to do it. But what if I pay her more? I can't believe Elphick would give her a fraction of what these are worth." She tapped the oblong parcel.

"He's not going to give her anything," he said. "That's the point. She's signed up on the losing side. That's all she needs to know. This is her one and only chance to get away. If I could have arranged matters so that she couldn't get away, I'd do it. But Zeggio wasn't able to follow Piero and we don't have the faintest idea where she is. This is the only way to get her into the open—and we can't count on the forces of law and order turning up on time. *Maledizione!*" He flung himself back in the seat. "I did think we'd have more time. But this is what I get for letting my feelings get in the way of my brain. This is what I get for listening to my heart instead of my instincts. This is what happens when a man lets a woman lead him around by the—"

"Lud, the way you carry on about a little jewelry," she said.

"I'm a thief! A jewel thief! Have you any idea what it does to me, to see you give away a fortune in gems?"

She looked at him. "I have an idea now," she said. "It's as good as an opera."

The look he flashed her must have been the kind his Italian ancestors had bestowed on inconvenient spouses, moments before issuing the orders for poisoning or strangling.

"You're beautiful when you're angry," she said.

He closed his eyes.

She thought, *He's going to throw me out of the gondola now.*

He shook his head. Then he laughed.

She let out the breath she'd been holding.

"You're impossible," he said.

"I told you that a long time ago," she said.

"You're also an idiot," he said. "But it can't be helped. I'm an idiot, too. I was so bedazzled tonight that I wasn't thinking clearly. Those curst pearls. I should have told you to leave them at home. You shouldn't be wearing any jewelry at all."

"Evening dress without jewelry?" she said. "What a quiz I should look! Besides, she'd think I was afraid."

"But you are not in the least afraid," he said.

"Are you mad?" she said. "Of course I'm afraid. What woman in her senses wouldn't be?"

"You put up an excellent front, then," he said.

"My back is highly regarded, too," she said.

He pried loose one of the hands clutching the

parcel and kissed it. Since she was wearing gloves, the kiss wasn't very satisfying. Still, the gesture comforted her.

"You do this sort of thing all the time," she said. "More alarming things, I'll wager. Are you never afraid?"

"I suppose," he said. "Sometimes I'm afraid. But other times I'm excited."

"And now?"

"I'd feel easier in my mind if we'd had a bit more time, if I could be sure Lurenze and his people were close at hand. But that was the whole point of making ourselves available at a moment's notice. She knew we wouldn't have time to summon our forces and we knew she wouldn't have time to assemble hers."

Or so they hoped.

Ah, well, it would be exciting, at any rate, Francesca thought. And he hadn't made her wait at home, worrying. She'd be in the thick of it, for good or ill. Her heart was racing, too, and perhaps it wasn't all fear. Perhaps there was excitement as well.

In any case, her hand was still warmly clasped in his, and he hadn't wrestled her for the parcel, and so she had hope that all would be well.

He turned his head away and she followed his gaze. He was looking at the Rialto Bridge. A moment later, they were passing under it, and coming up to the Riva del Vin, the broad stretch of pavement running alongside the Grand Canal, forming one of the busy market area's quaysides.

The boat glided to a stop.

"This is where we get out," he said.

# Chapter 17

'T is said that their last parting was pathetic,
  As partings often are, or ought to be,
And their presentiment was quite prophetic
  That they should never more each other see
(A sort of morbid feeling, half poetic,
  Which I have known occur in two or three)

Lord Byron, *Beppo*

San Giacomo di Rialto, an old but modest little church, stood a short distance from the Rialto Bridge. On one side of it ran the Ruga Degli Orefici, a street lined with silver and gold shops. The church overlooked the usual little square or *campo*, at one end of which stood a statue of somebody of historical importance. James couldn't recall at the moment who the somebody was.

The street and square were busy during the day with artists, tradespeople, and tourists coming and going from their hotels. At this hour, though, the working people were in bed and the upper classes were at the opera or other entertainments, leaving the place deserted.

Fazi had chosen her time well.

She'd chosen the right night, too. The sky was clear and half of the rising moon was brightly visible, shedding its silver glow upon the square. While shadows abounded, she would find it no easier to hide a gang of ruffians than James would to hide guards or soldiers.

As they entered the square, he glanced up at the beautiful clock in the church's tower . . . and frowned.

"No use looking there," Francesca said. "It hasn't told the correct time since the day it was installed, some two or three centuries ago."

"I hope she knows that," he said. While he talked, he was taking in their surroundings, as he'd done while they walked here. He'd perceived nothing out of the way. As he'd assured Francesca, the chances of an ambush—by either side—were very small. He had not had enough notice to organize an attack, and he strongly doubted Fazi had had time enough, either, or the inclination.

She would like this, he thought. She would like the simplicity. Like a duel. Two principals, two seconds. How easy she was to understand!

Most women were, for him. Where other men saw endless complications and confusions, James saw simple principles at work. In the past, he'd used those principles to manipulate Fazi as well as numerous other women. He'd thought he could use them to manipulate Francesca Bonnard.

That was his first miscalculation.

He had no time to count the other mistakes because he perceived a movement in the shadows under the church's portico.

A moment later, Marta Fazi emerged from the shadows, Piero at her side.

She walked out into the center of the square, her long black hair in a braid over her shoulder. No frills and ruffles and feathers for Marta.

She appeared taken with Francesca's pearl-adorned headdress, though. As she looked at it, a mocking smile formed on her lips. Her gaze went briefly to James, back to the hat, then back, the smile fading, to him.

She stopped dead. "You."

"You remember me," said James. "I'm flattered."

"I remember you, too," said Piero. "I remember what you did to me. You were a great fool to come. You should have sent the prince. I have no quarrel with him."

Fazi looked at her henchman.

"This is the devil who almost ripped my arm from my shoulder," Piero said. "This is the one who threatens to torture me, and tries to frighten me, telling me what you'll do to me."

Fazi's mocking smile returned, and she continued the last few paces toward them. "Ah, good," she said. "This is even better than I hoped." She looked at Francesca. "You have something for me, lady? A packet of letters? Or does your *cavalier servente* carry it for you, along with your handkerchief and fan?"

From the folds of her evening cloak, Francesca

produced the pretty parcel. "I would not let him carry it," she said. "He might be tempted to run away with it."

Fazi laughed. Her black gaze returned to him. "You did not win her trust as you did mine? Perhaps you disappointed her in the bed? Your prick was too tired, perhaps, after being so busy all over Italy."

"Oh, it never gets tired," he said. "Bored, sometimes, but never tired. The only difficulty is that the lady and I were not in agreement regarding the papers your friend in England wants so badly."

"Ah, yes. He wants these much more than he ever wanted his wife." Fazi looked Francesca up and down. "But her father had money and friends with influence. This is why he married her, you see. When he had all the money and friends, he could have killed her, but he took pity on her and made a divorce instead."

"Sweet of him," said Francesca. "A truly kind gesture, that."

"He was too kind, I tell him," said Marta. "And you—what do you do with the second chance he gives you, fine lady? You throw yourself away on this one?" She jerked her chin at James. "His heart is black and he's false, false. A thief and a whore."

This was not going well. Fazi was on her way to an eruption and he wasn't sure what Francesca's state was.

All things considered, perhaps he should have explained that mission in Rome to Francesca.

"*Vero*," he said, trying to inject an apologetic note in his voice. It's true.

Neither the admission nor the repentant note drew Fazi's attention back to him. She was raging about him but she wanted to provoke Francesca, in the hopes the English lady would say or do something reckless, and give Marta an excuse to wield her knife.

He knew better than to look at Francesca or try to warn her now, though. She seemed unmoved. He reminded himself what a fine actress she was.

Marta was no actress. She showed every feeling that moved her, and she was easily moved.

"A pretty liar and a cheat and a great whore," she taunted. "You give up a prince for this one? I would not give a blind beggar on the street for him—a blind, crippled beggar with black warts on his prick. Stupid cow, what men you choose!"

Cow, as Francesca no doubt knew, was a deadly insult.

"Yes, what a stupid cow I am," Francesca said with her coolest smile. She fingered the pearls at her throat. "Rich men shower me with jewels while you—"

"I had jewels!" Marta snapped. "Emeralds. Did this man tell you how he made love to me so sweet, only to steal my beautiful emeralds and run away?"

"So that's why you took mine, the other night, when you were playing at being a nun," Francesca said. "You wanted a replacement?"

"Mine were better!"

"Bigger," James said. "A great, vulgar lot of inferior stones."

"Vulgar?" Marta's eyes flashed dangerously.

But his success in drawing her off, to focus on him, was short lived. She wasn't interested in him. It was Francesca in her too-expensive clothes and magnificent jewels. Marta Fazi was far more jealous of those articles than of a mere male, a temporary lover. James came into it only as a way to taunt the expensively garbed lady.

"What does it matter?" Francesca said, dismissing the subject with a wave of her hand.

Oh, Marta would love that, the arrogant dismissal.

"We did not come here to quibble about who has better jewelry," Francesca went on, "or whether size matters or who lets an utterly faithless and ruthless man order her about."

"Your Gianni is faithful to *me*," Marta said, jabbing her thumb against her ample chest.

"Really? You know him personally?"

What the devil was Francesca doing? Was she deliberately trying to provoke her?

Or was she simply stalling, trying to give Lurenze and his men time to get here?

"I know him for a long time," Fazi said. "Years. Before he married you. After he married you. For me he keeps a beautiful house in London. When I go there to visit him, he gives me everything I ask for. Whatever I do for him, he rewards me, generously. When I am in trouble, he makes the trouble go away. But I have wasted too much time talking to you. Give me the letters."

"He does all that?" said Francesca. "Good heavens, how busy he must be. You are—what?

Mistress Number Fifty-two? Eighty-seven? No wonder he needed a rich wife."

"I am first, always," Marta said.

"Johanna Ide will be surprised to hear that," Francesca said. "But she's in London, with him all the time, and you're not."

Fazi was momentarily nonplussed. "I don't know this name."

"Of course you don't. Why would he tell you about his Lady Macbeth?"

"I don't care about their names," Fazi said, lifting her chin. "The rest are whores only, and men must have their whores, as you know. But I waste enough time. The letters, if you please, my fine lady."

"Oh, dear, I hope you haven't become too dependent on my former husband," Francesca said. "Because he's not going to be able to do any of that anymore—the house, the rewards, and making trouble go away."

Marta's eyes narrowed and the hand she'd stretched out for the parcel went to her waist, where she kept her knife.

James tensed, waiting for the attack.

"Sorry," Francesca said. "I never did walk the streets, as you did, and so I've always been uneasy about meeting people in the dead of night in deserted squares. I took a gondola ride yesterday to San Lazzaro and gave the letters to an English gentleman there. They're on their way to England now. But not to your dear Gianni. I should give up on him if I were you, and find another man. A beautiful woman like you, and still young—you can find someone better, a man who doesn't make you work so hard while he keeps a harem in England, and promises all his women the same things he promises you."

Marta had her head cocked to one side. She was listening, trying to puzzle it out. James had an idea how she felt. He should have realized Francesca wouldn't play by his rules.

"This is a joke," Fazi said at last. "I see the letters, in that little parcel in your hand."

"You mean this?" Francesca held out the parcel. "Well, yes, it's quite funny, actually. I felt sorry for you, for the wicked tricks men play on you. I felt sorry about all the trouble you went to."

Marta snatched the parcel away. But she was woman enough not to cut the ribbons. Her gaze darting about the square—putting James in mind of a bird of prey guarding its dinner—she untied them. She pulled away the silken wrapping, revealing a shallow box. She stuffed the pretty wrapping and ribbon into her bodice and opened the box.

Within sparkled a sapphire parure, the one Bonnard had worn the first night James saw her.

Fazi gave a little gasp.

James swallowed a groan. Any thief worth his salt would feel the same.

"They're yours," Francesca said. "For your trouble. Take them and go away. Before it's too late."

"There's nothing else here for you," James said. "You'll never get the letters and Elphick can't get you out of trouble anymore. If it were up to me, you'd get nothing but a noose. But it isn't up to me. This lady thinks you deserve something for your trouble. I don't, believe me. In any case, if I were you, I should get away while I could, before the soldiers come."

Marta took a step back. She turned away. And softly in his native tongue she told Piero, "Kill them."

Before she'd finished uttering the command, Piero had his knife out. "Gladly," he said, and lunged.

James pushed Francesca out of the way and flung out his hand, catching Piero's wrist. James turned his back on the smaller man, to add the force and size of his body to wrestle the knife from him. Pedro, small but tough and wiry, held on, and flung his free arm round James's throat.

James bent over, lifting the man off his feet, and threw himself backward. Piero hit the pavement first, James on top of him. He heard the crack of skull against stone, then the clatter as the knife fell out of Piero's outstretched hand.

James bounded up and looked around.

Marta was gone and good riddance . . .

But where was . . .

His gaze went wildly about the square. No signs of life. The square was empty.

There was only the man lying motionless on the stones.

James ran down the Ruga Degli Orefici. As he reached the bridge he heard a scream and a splash.

"*Francesca!*" he roared.

James ran down the Riva del Vin in the direction of the scream.

The first, shocked silence had given way to cries and shouts from the gondoliers. It was dark here, in the shadows of the buildings, and he had trouble making out figures. He slowed, his heart pounding. People were pointing to the water. Someone shouted, "There!" and another, "No, there."

"I see her!"

"No, over there!"

Then at last a woman's voice, sharp, English-accented. "There! Quick! That way! Can't you see?"

"No, signora. Nobody there. That is only a piece of wood."

James raced to her and pulled her into his arms. "You're safe. *Dio del cielo*, you gave me such a fright." He kissed the top of her head, where the headdress tipped drunkenly to one side. "You're safe, *cuore mio*." He crushed her to him.

She wriggled. "Cordier."

He held on tightly. The wriggling felt good. She felt so good in his arms. He'd never let her go again.

"Cordier." She struggled.

He held on.

She stomped on his toe.

He let go, and looked down at her in bewilderment.

"That woman," she said.

*That woman? What woman?*

Then he remembered what he'd forgotten in the blind terror as he raced here: Marta Fazi. She'd run away . . . and Francesca had run after her.

"You little fool!" he said. He grasped her shoulders

and shook her. "Don't ever." Shake. "Do that." Shake. "Again."

She broke away. "What? Did you want me to stay and help you fight one little man?"

"I wanted you to stay put, and not scare ten years off my life," he said. "She could have lured you into a dark corner and cut up your face. Have you any idea the delight she'd take in disfiguring you?"

"I have an excellent idea. Poor, ignorant creature—even *she* let Elphick play her like a fiddle. If she did go to the beautiful house in London, he must have had to evict the previous tenant. And she must have been eaten up with jealousy the whole time. Or maybe not. He would have told her, '*Ma amo solo te, dolcezza mia.*'"

But I love only you, my sweet.

James had uttered those words, teasingly, to her on the night she'd first been attacked, when she'd believed he was one of the villains.

"So easy for men to say," she said. "So impossible for them to mean, truly."

"*Ma amo solo te, dolcezza mia,*" he said. "I mean it."

She regarded him for a long time. He felt his face grow hot.

"If she had disfigured me," she said, "would you still feel the same way?"

The answer, the usual answer, was on the tip of his tongue: *Of course I'll feel the same way.* But was that true? And could he risk not being true, even if the answer he gave was the wrong one? "I don't know," he said.

Her eyes widened. "That's honest, by gad."

"But we'll never know, will we?" he said. He looked past her, at the canal, where the gondoliers and others in boats continued searching. "I think she can swim. But even so—with skirts and petticoats? I don't know. This is not an interior waterway but the Grand Canal, where the tide can be very strong. I am not sure a woman, fully dressed, could manage."

They were silent for a moment, listening to the gondoliers' voices and watching the search—as well as they could, for the night was growing darker. James looked up. Clouds had drifted in to dull the half-moon's bright glow.

"I don't know whether to be sorry or relieved," Francesca said. "What a cat she is! Those sapphires—a king's ransom."

James forbore saying, "I told you so."

"I can understand her being angry with us—but to be so impractical?" she said. "If she'd a grain of sense—never mind breeding—she'd have said 'Thank you,' and gone away. Instead she told her man to kill you. At least, I assume that's what she told him. I managed to follow most of what she said—but that last bit would have stymied me if he hadn't pulled out his knife and got that ugly gleam in his eye."

James hadn't the chance to ask how she'd contrived to understand Marta's far from literate Italian so well.

He saw Zeggio approaching, with another gondolier alongside.

"We have sent for more lanterns, signore," Zeggio

said. "But the clouds cover the moon and to find her is almost impossible now. She can hide many places. Or she can be on the bottom of the canal or carried away to sea. But this man, my cousin, he finds something."

Zeggio's cousin gave James a shallow box. "Zeggio says he believes this belongs to the lady. I hope it is not spoiled from the water."

James gave the dripping box to Francesca. "This is what you went after her for, I collect?"

She opened it. The sapphires were there, still pinned to the velvet lining. "Silly cow," she murmured. "She never even put them on."

"That's why you ran after her?" he pressed. "To get them back?"

Francesca closed the box. "I'm not sure. Perhaps. I was so furious. I wanted to tear her hair from her head."

"I hope you didn't risk your neck—again—on my worthless account," he said.

"Don't be absurd," she said. "I was furious because she cheated. I tried to play fair with her. I tried to be understanding, and she . . ." She frowned. "Actually, it's understandable, now I think of it. In her place, I should have wanted to kill you, too."

James became aware of sounds behind them. New voices.

He turned. Giulietta and Lurenze hurried toward them. Giulietta flung her arms round Francesca. "You are not hurt," she said. "I was so afraid, almost I was sick."

"I was afraid, too, believe me," Francesca said. "But I'm all right now."

"We come as quickly as we can," Lurenze said. "But all is over, I think?"

Bonnard looked about her, at the gondoliers, still searching, then down at the box of jewels she'd tried to give away to a woman who didn't understand generous gestures. Her gaze went up to James, briefly, then away. "Yes, it's over," she said. "Why is everything so bright?"

Then she sank to the ground.

# Chapter 18

For instance—gentlemen, whose ladies take
 Leave to o'erstep the written rights of woman,
And break the—Which commandment is 't
    they break?
(I have forgot the number, and think no man
    Should rashly quote, for fear of a mistake.)

Lord Byron
*Don Juan, Canto the First*

She'd fainted because she was not used to running, Francesca told them as they fussed over her in the gondola. It was Lurenze's gondola, fortunately, one of the large and ornate vessels normally used for ceremonial occasions. But princes were allowed to be ceremonial whenever they felt like it, and the four of them were a degree less cramped than they would have been in her gondola.

"Have you ever run in stays?" she said to James. "Oh, why do I ask you? Of course you have. But you're a man, and your lungs are larger."

He was chafing her wrists. "You should not have run."

"Don't scold," said Giulietta. "She takes great risks for you. Even to your former *amorosa* she tries to be gentle and kind."

"Fazi is not my former *amorosa*," Cordier said.

"What then?" said Francesca. "You made quite an impression on her. Something about 'sweet love-making,' as I recollect."

"He is a man," said Lurenze. "It is natural to wish to be sweet to the woman. What, is he a great boor—What is the word you told me, my sweet one? The word you say for these persons, ignorant and with no manners?"

"*Da cafone*," Giulietta said. "This is the term you seek, I believe, your celestiality."

"Yes, like that. The man of ignorance and low breeding is careless of the feelings of the woman. But the true gentleman is always gallant, even to the woman who is of a low position."

"Even when she is beneath him, you mean, your supremeness?" said Giulietta.

"You know what I mean, naughty girl," said Lurenze. But he chuckled and added, "It is a very pretty joke with words you make. Naughty but most amusing. I must remember it."

"Fazi was business," Cordier said, his voice oh-so-patient. "I made an impression because I stole her emeralds. Which, by the way, were not hers. They'd been stolen from their proper owner."

"Did you make sweet love to the proper owner as well?" Francesca asked.

"No," he said between his teeth. "I returned them to *him*. They happened to belong to a royal treasury, and the party who'd lost them was able to provide something of value to certain other parties with whom I was associated. And that is all I am going to say about it."

"It is politics," Lurenze said, nodding wisely. "I know of these things. Please do not be of too much curiosity, ladies. But Mr. Cordier, we must tell something to the governor. He will hear very soon of the disturbance at the Riva del Vin. You must advise me what to say. I do not wish to put in my mouth my feet."

"We'd better go to the Ducal Palace," Cordier said. "Someone will be waking Count Goetz with the news. It might as well be us. But *you*," he said, reverting to Francesca, whose hand he still held in his big, warm one. "You we're taking home first. And you must promise to go straight to bed."

"I promise," she said. "I haven't the wherewithal to argue. I haven't even the energy to make naughty innuendoes." She looked at Giulietta. "I must leave that to you, my dear."

"No, no." Giulietta took her other hand and kissed it and held it against her cheek. "This is no joke to me. I know you are tired and troubled. I will stay with you tonight. The men must go and do their manly things and have their plots and conspiracies and politics. It is too boring. Me, I would like a little something to eat, a little something to drink, and then to be lazy. We put our feet up, near the fire and maybe we look up and count all the little penises on the ceiling."

"That sounds delightful," said Francesca.

"And tomorrow night, when we are rested and ourselves again, we go to the opera."

"An excellent plan."

"And perhaps the men will join us there, if they promise not to speak of boring politics and the other women whose hearts they break."

Cordier attempted to speak. "I did not break any—"

"Say, 'yes, we promise,'" Lurenze advised. "To agree is more simple."

"Yes, I promise," Cordier said.

Francesca and Giulietta spent a pleasant night together. They did not sit in the Putti Inferno counting infant organs but adjourned to Francesca's boudoir, where they ate a little and drank a little and talked a great deal. And when at last they could no longer keep their eyes open, they climbed into Francesca's great bed, and murmuring drowsily of this and that, finally went to sleep.

There was nothing wrong with a man in bed, as Giulietta said. In fact, there was usually a good deal right about that. But sometimes, one wanted only to be alone. And sometimes one wanted only to be with a good friend.

Being with her friend quieted the turmoil in Francesca's mind. To Giulietta she could speak freely of Elphick and Marta Fazi and why she'd felt sorry for Marta and hated her at the same time. And she could believe Giulietta's reassurances that Francesca had done the proper thing in offering the sapphires. She'd acted decently and generously—and it was not Francesca's fault the other woman was too ignorant to appreciate it.

As to chasing Marta Fazi, Giulietta understood that, too.

"Me, I would like to shake her until her teeth rattle in her head," Giulietta said. " 'How can you be so greatly stupid?' I would say. 'Why take the chance to be hanged or have them cut off your head—for a *man*? What man is worth this? Where is your brain?' Me, if I could be in her place, do you know what I would do? I would make a pretty curtsy to you and I would say, 'Thank you, lady. This is a very beautiful gift. And this man who is with you? Now I look more closely, I do not remember that I have ever seen him before. Good-bye.' And then I would tell the man with me to put away his knife. 'Venice is too wet,' I would tell him. 'Let us go to another place, far away, where there is less water and they speak a language I understand.' This is what I would do."

"But you would never be in that situation," Francesca said, "because you have a brain and a good heart."

"All the same, we must remember: Without the grace of God, there is where we go."

And with such talk, and the philosophy of her friend, Francesca found herself more at peace than she'd been in a very long time. As she'd told Lurenze, it was over.

The long, demented game she'd played with Elphick was over at last. She was finished with that and she felt heart-whole, finally.

She hadn't realized one nasty little thorn had

remained in her heart for all this time. She only knew it now, because it was gone, and she breathed free, at last.

As to Cordier . . .

"I think this one is to keep," was Giulietta's considered opinion when Francesca turned to this subject. "You know—like Countess Benzoni and her devoted Rangone. This one, I think, is devoted to you."

"We'll see," Francesca said drowsily. "And Lurenze?"

Giulietta gave a sleepy smile. "Oh, he is delicious. I fear he will grow bored with me long before I am bored with him. But this is the gamble I take. And I take it with my eyes open." Then she closed her beautiful doe eyes and fell asleep.

The following afternoon found Francesca at Magny's *palazzo*. He'd sent a note, demanding to know what had happened: He'd heard the most ridiculous rumors.

He was not pleased with her account. She did not expect him to be pleased. He objected to her going into deserted squares in the middle of the night to meet villainous women. He objected to her offering her sapphires to a lunatic felon. He was speechless with rage when she told him how she'd chased Marta Fazi to the canal's edge.

"Are you quite, quite mad?" he demanded, when he found his voice again.

"I was angry," she said.

"That does it," he said. "From now on—"

He was unable to complete the sentence because

a servant entered to announce that Mr. Cordier had arrived and sought permission to see the count.

"Of course he has permission," Magny said irritably. When the servant went out, Magny said, "I don't understand all this ceremony. He sent a note this morning. He had a private matter to discuss, he said."

The so-called count rose and went to his writing desk. "There." He held up a thick piece of expensive writing paper.

Francesca, who'd followed him, took the letter from him. It bore only a few lines. She looked at her father, her eyebrows raised. "How formal he is."

"Something to do with my borrowed identity, I'll wager," he answered in a low voice. "I daresay Quentin asked awkward questions."

"Signor Cordier."

The servant stood aside and Mr. Cordier entered. He was even more elegant than usual, in a dark blue tailcoat over a spotted waistcoat with shawl collar. His pristine white trousers had stirrups to hold them in place over the gleaming boots.

Francesca casually dropped the letter onto the desk.

Cordier greeted her with excessive politeness. Amused, she followed his lead. After a brief exchange of banalities she said, "I know you wish to meet privately with monsieur. I'll see you later. At La Fenice?"

She moved past him, letting her skirts brush his

legs. As she passed she murmured, "Perhaps you could come in your servant disguise. That would be . . . exciting."

"I might," he said. More audibly he added, "There's no reason for you to leave, Mrs. Bonnard. You might as well hear what I have to say to Count Magny."

She was curious. The man pretending to be Magny expected her to tell him everything. He did not return the favor. Most blatantly, for example, he had failed to tell her he was not dead. He'd simply appeared one day in Paris, and frightened her out of her wits.

Cordier turned his attention to her provoking parent. "Sir, I won't sicken you with maudlin speeches. Plain and simple, then: I seek your permission to marry your—er—this lady."

Francesca felt her jaw drop.

Magny was, if anything, even more shocked. He put his hand to his heart. "You take my breath away," he said in a low, shaky voice. "Will you really? Marry her, I mean?"

"I see no alternative," said Cordier.

Francesca found her wits and her voice. "I do," she said. "Marry?"

"Yes, please," said Cordier. "I am fearfully in love with you."

"Yes, I know you are—but marry? Have you taken leave of your senses? Why would you wish to spoil a perfectly good liaison by marrying?"

"Because I want only you, my sweet."

"Of course you do, but I am not at all sure I want only you," she said.

"Francesca, really," said her father. "Here is a man, willing to make an honest woman of you, in spite of all you've done—"

"I don't want to be an honest woman! When will the pair of you get it through your thick heads?"

"I only want to see you happy and settled, child," said Magny. "And I should like not to be fretted to an early grave. And that is no way to talk to your—erm—elders."

"Then I shan't talk at all." She stormed out of the room.

To her dismay and displeasure, Cordier didn't follow her out.

She made herself walk quickly down the *portego* but she couldn't help listening for footsteps. None came.

She hurried down the stairs to the *andron* and out to her waiting gondola.

Magny looked at James. "Are you sure you want to marry her?"

"Yes."

"She's impossible."

"So am I. Who can blame her for being a trifle skittish?"

Magny looked at the door through which she'd dramatically exited. "Are you not going to chase her, fall to your knees, vow undying devotion and the rest of that revolting nonsense?"

"No."

"Well, then, would you like a drink?"

"Yes. Yes, thank you, I would."

*That evening*

Francesca gazed resentfully out of the gondola window at the Ca' Munetti, whence no devoted lover had come or even sent a note, the horrid tease.

She didn't care, she told herself as her gondola continued on, leaving the two houses to stare at each other across the canal. She would have a wonderful time tonight.

She'd had a new gown delivered, and that was a lucky thing, for she'd lost two or was it three of her best dresses—and she'd no one but herself to blame for getting entangled with a rogue, and an overbearing one at that.

Marry him, indeed.

She recalled the delicious bit Byron had sent her, from the Third Canto of *Don Juan*, which he was still working on.

There's doubtless something in domestic doings
   Which forms, in fact, true love's antithesis;
Romances paint at full length people's wooings,
   But only give a bust of marriages.

And rightly so, she thought. There was nothing like marriage to ruin a fine romance.

And nothing like a little rivalry and jealousy to bring a man to his senses.

The new gown was black crepe, trimmed in black satin with a subtle twining of silver threads. It was cut very low in front and back. Compared to other gowns, it was almost starkly plain. Which made it a perfect backdrop to set off her splendid diamond suite, whose focal point was a necklace of capped drops. The girandole earrings were among her favorites.

She saw herself against the blue backdrop of her opera box, flirting with every handsome gentleman who entered it. That would teach Cordier to take her for granted.

Of all things, to ask her impossible father for her hand in marriage—as though she were a chit from the schoolroom who couldn't be allowed to make up her own mind and hadn't learned all she needed to know about marriage . . .

A form appeared upon the *fondamenta* nearby, as the gondola was about to turn into the next canal. It was tall and—

And it leapt lightly onto the gondola. The vessel swayed.

Uliva swore. So did Dumini.

"What would you have me do?" came a familiar, deep voice, indisputably Italian. "When I try to speak to her in a proper place, in her father's house, she storms away in a temper. Here she cannot get away from me."

With that, Cordier ducked into the *felze*, closed the door, and sank into the seat beside her.

Francesca looked the other way, out of the window while her heart raced with anticipation.

"Very handsome diamonds," he said, incurably English now.

"The set was made by Nitot," she said, naming the jeweler who'd assembled gems for French royalty, from Bourbon to Bonaparte and back again.

"Some of the stones belonged to King Louis XIV. It was given to me by a very handsome, amusing, and devoted *marchese*."

"I know who you mean," he said. "But my mother's family is older and nobler than his. And my mama will give you a much warmer welcome than his would ever do. His mama is a great snob, because her family is bourgeois. My mama, on the other hand, will be delighted that I've found a wife with exquisite taste in jewelry. She will not fuss over trifles, such as how the jewelry was obtained. And you know I would never fuss, because I've obtained jewelry by more disreputable methods."

The trouble with him was, he was honest. An honest rogue. She turned to him. He was in elegant evening garb, all black, with a dash of white at the neck and cuffs. He'd taken off his hat, the great tease, and the black curls gleamed in the cabin's lamplight. He knew he had beautiful hair. He knew women liked to tangle their fingers in it. Oh, he was wicked.

"Cordier."

He took her gloved hand in his. That was not very satisfying. But if she took off her gloves, she must take off his, and then—and then . . .

"It's time to put the past behind us," he said. "We're done, both of us, with Elphick. I could never settle down while my comrades were unavenged. Now they will be. You will be avenged, too. And when matters are finally sorted out, your father will be avenged as well, absolved of the fraud Elphick committed."

She looked down at the gloved hand holding

hers and frowned. "Are you quite, quite sure it wasn't papa? Because, he is not altogether . . . reliable, you know."

"Whatever else your father may or may not have done, that great swindle was planned and executed by your former husband."

"Papa never let on," she said. "It was so very clever—and had such spectacular results—that I think he was a little envious and didn't like to admit he'd been a dupe, like everyone else."

"Never mind," he said. "That chapter is closed. I should like us to begin a new chapter."

"I should, too," she said. "I know you mean well, offering to marry me, but you don't understand. You're a man."

"I know. It can't be helped."

"You don't know what it's like for women, to be respectably married. I thought that was freedom—until I moved to the Continent and gave up being respectable. Women, married women, live in a prison of rules and don't even realize it. Respectable women can't do this and can't do that, and if they break the rules they must be very discreet. They must sneak about and be complete hypocrites."

"That's England," he said. "This is Italy. And your father and I have drawn up a proper Italian marriage contract—"

"Did the two of you lose your hearing simultaneously?" she said. "Did I not say no? This is so typical—the arrogance of males—"

"—which specifies a *cavalier servente*," he went on as though she hadn't spoken. He let go of her hand and began to strip off his gloves. "It is unthinkable for a lady of gentle birth and breeding not to have one. One must have a husband, which is a great bore. And so, to mitigate this oppressive state of affairs, there is the devoted friend, who goes where the lady goes and does her bidding and amuses her and who may or may not be her lover."

While he talked, his gloves came off.

She looked down at his naked hands, at the long, nimble fingers. She swallowed. "But you cannot be both my husband and my *cavalier servente*," she said.

"I thought that, if I could contrive not to be a great bore, perhaps you wouldn't require a serving cavalier—or any other supernumerary lovers to augment your happiness."

She watched the long fingers move to her arm and slide under her shawl. Then she felt those thief's hands drawing her glove down to her wrist. Carefully he drew the soft kid through her bracelets.

"You say that now," she said shakily. She believed him, though, in spite of good sense and bad experience. But a woman would believe anything with those clever hands stealing her reason away.

"*Amor mio,* if I cannot keep you amused and happy, I don't deserve fidelity." He leaned in closer and went to work on her other glove. "And if I cannot be content with one woman who is everything I could ever want—"

"Please don't forget that I am everything *every* man could ever want," she said.

"Believe me, I will never forget it," he said. "If I

cannot be supremely happy with you, if I cannot exert myself to make you happy, then I deserve to be cuckolded repeatedly." The second glove came off. She watched him toss it aside, on top of the others: hers, his.

"You have a point," she said.

"Then let me proceed to the next point," he said. His hand crept up to the diamonds at her ear. "As I have shown to your father's satisfaction, I may be a mere younger son but I have done well in my branch of the service." He toyed with the diamond. "I should be able to keep you in a style—well, not exactly what you are accustomed to, but very near." He kissed her ear.

"I am not greedy," she said, her voice hoarse. "Very near is near enough. But you must give me back the peridots."

He laughed against her neck, and his warm breath tickled her skin. "What, those paltry things?"

"They are the first jewels you almost gave me," she said. "I shall treasure them for sentimental reasons."

"Very well, you may have them back. Will you have me, then, *tesoro mio?*" He kissed her neck, in the special place, then lower.

Her mind was turning into warm honey. How could she not have him? she thought dizzily. She'd already risked her life, more than once, for him. Could she not risk her future?

She remembered what Giulietta had said last night, before they fell asleep.

*But this is the gamble I take. And I take it with my eyes open.*

It was always a gamble, love was.

"I'm thinking it over," she said.

"Now we're getting somewhere." He pulled her onto his lap. He bent his head and made a slow, hot trail of kisses over the skin along the edge of her neckline.

"Are you sure you won't be sorry later, that you didn't wed one of those maidens in white dresses?" she whispered.

He pushed down the neckline, and she gasped as his mouth slid over her breast.

"The maidens," she said weakly. "The clubs. The dining room and the men telling dirty jokes. Hyde Park."

"The hell with them," he growled. His tongue grazed the taut peak of her breast. She felt the tug down low, the same she'd felt the first time she saw him, when she didn't know who he was.

Mere lust, perhaps, for an attractive man.

Or perhaps it was the powerful pull to one's soulmate.

She didn't want to resist. Yet she was . . . afraid.

"And your family?" she said desperately. "Italian mothers. No woman is ever good enough for—"

"Trust me," he murmured. His hands moved down to her skirt. "She'll like you. She'll say I got the better bargain. How can you talk of mothers at a time like this?"

She didn't want to talk about such things. But she needed to, before she melted away completely. Her mother had died shortly after she was wed. She'd missed her very much. "I like . . . to be friends with women."

His hands had slid under her dress, under her petticoat. A part of her was lost, enslaved by his hands, by desire. How long had it been since they'd made love? Yet a part of her thought of friends, so many she'd lost during that ghastly time in her life.

"Giulietta," she murmured.

"I know," he said. He lifted his head and gazed into her eyes. "Trust me. We'll be happy. Close the shutters."

She closed them, squirming as his hands slid up over her garters. She cupped his face and brought it close to hers. "You are too hasty," she said. "*Baciami.*"

He laughed and kissed her and she tasted the laughter. He was a sinner, too, like her, and unrepentant, like her. He would never be quite respectable. He would never be stuffy. He didn't care if she was a harlot and he wouldn't care if her best friend was one, too. With this man she could be happy.

With this man she could be drunk in an instant on one hot, laughing kiss.

She reached down and unfastened his trouser front. She grasped him and he gasped at her touch. "Who's hasty now?" he said thickly.

"We're nearly at the theater," she said. She let her hand stroke over the hot length of his cock but she hadn't the patience to toy with him now. He pulled up her skirts and she moved to draw her legs up against his waist. His big, wicked hand stroked over her and "Yes," she said. "Yes, now." She wrapped her arms about his neck and kissed him, fiercely, as he pushed into her.

Warmth exploded through her, the warmth of pleasure and happiness and possession. She let go, gave up thinking, gave up her precious control, and let feeling take her where it would.

This one—this man—was to keep, and so she held on, as their bodies pulsed together, as their hearts beat harder and harder, together. She held on, kissing him and laughing through the mad rush to joy. She came to the peak, and then another, and one last time, as he surrendered, too. Together they crested the last wave, and together they gently floated into the quiet of pure happiness.

Outside, meanwhile, Uliva and Dumini had taken note of the fact that the shutters were closed though it was an unseasonably warm night and the few clouds passing overhead did not threaten rain.

The two Venetians merely glanced at each other, and patiently took the gondola on an extended detour.

# Epilogue

All tragedies are finish'd by a death,
    All comedies are ended by a marriage.

Lord Byron
*Don Juan, Canto the Third*

$\mathcal{T}$he scandal surrounding Lord Elphick's trial proved even more spectacular than the one that had attended his divorce. Newspapers devoted column after column to details of the trial. Mr. Cruikshank and his fellow artists created a feast of images for the print-buying public: Lord Elphick kissing Napoleon's bum, Lord Elphick in a drunken orgy with a group of poxy damsels, Lord Elphick's head as a toadstool growing on a dunghill, Lord Elphick defecating on a fallen Brittania, Lord Elphick stealing food from starving soldiers. These were some of the milder ones.

Each day, when his lordship was taken to Westminster for his trial, the mob pelted the carriage with dead animals and excrement, rotten fruits and vegetables being deemed insufficient to express loyal Britons' feelings.

The trial was very long—longer than that of Queen Caroline and a good deal more sordid. In the end, to nobody's surprise, he was found guilty.

Still he contrived to cheat justice. On the night before the execution, he was found writhing on the floor of his cell. He'd not been allowed a razor, knife, rope, or even braces, as a precaution against his doing away with himself. Excellent precautions but insufficient. He contrived somehow to get hold of poison. They found him still alive but it was too late. Nothing could be done. He died some hours later, in great agony.

Given the symptoms described in a newspaper clipping one of James's sisters had sent, he decided it must have been arsenic. He also decided it was not suicide. "If he could contrive to get poison," he told Francesca, "he could contrive to get a pistol or a razor. And of all poisons, to choose arsenic. So hard to get the dose right. I'll wager anything it was a woman. It isn't that hard to poison a prisoner."

"Even one under vigilant guard?" said his wife. "How would you go about it?"

"I'm not telling," he said. "If you decide to poison me, you must work it out for yourself, in the time-honored tradition of my ancestors."

"Well, I shan't try to guess who poisoned him," she said. "It might have been one of any of the hundreds he used."

"The ones who didn't run away the instant the scandal broke," he said.

"His dear Johanna didn't wait that long," she said. "She was gone before Quentin arrived in London."

Not long after this conversation, the letters began to arrive. Lord Byron had already written gleefully to Francesca, "At least one of us is vindicated." He'd enclosed a short poem he'd composed for the occasion, which included several naughty innuendoes about her second husband.

Lord Quentin had written, too, keeping them abreast of proceedings in London and thanking her for helping them complete the case they'd been assembling for many months.

But then, to Francesca's great shock, came letters from old acquaintances and friends. There were letters of thanks and letters of apology.

Most shocking of all was a letter to them both from the King. Having traveled by special courier, it arrived late one day in February, long after the servants had collected the post. James and Francesca were awaiting company: Lurenze and Giulietta were to join them for dinner before they all set out for the opera.

James was lounging on the sofa, studying the *putti*. When they were discussing where to live as a married couple, he'd suggested they remain here at the Palazzo Neroni because the plasterwork had sentimental meaning for him.

Letter in hand, she came to sit beside him. He slid up on the cushions in order to read over her shoulder. Among other things, his majesty thanked her for putting herself in bodily danger on behalf of her country.

"Didn't know that, did you?" James murmured, after they'd read for a moment in stunned silence. "When you were risking your life, trying to save me, you didn't know you were performing a public service."

"It was very good of Quentin to make me out to be a hero," she said. "But really, I was only being stupidly in love."

"It was very good of you to be stupid," he said. "Stupid, but very good."

She turned to the next page and read on. "Good heavens!" she said.

"*Santo Cielo!*" he said.

"The silly things," she said. "What can they be thinking?"

"Lord and Lady Delcaire." James looked at her. "How do you like the sound of that? We are to be ennobled—for state service, no less."

"*You* are to be ennobled," she said. "I merely go along as necessary baggage."

"So you do, you baggage."

"Oh, and I was just getting used to being Mrs. Cordier."

"There are several Mrs. Cordiers, *mia cara*," he said. "And more to come, undoubtedly. And only think: As my lady, you will get to wear a pretty coronet with silver balls and a coronation robe with ermine."

"But I missed the coronation!"

"You can wear your coronet and robe to bed."

She considered. "And nothing underneath."

"An excellent idea. One of the many things I love about you is your fashion sense."

"But we must go to London," she said.

"It would be the polite thing to do," he said. "Shall you mind? We needn't stay permanently. But perhaps for a few months? The height of the Season?"

"How can I mind now?" she said. "My friends have asked me to forgive them. My husband has been granted a title. The height of the Season will do very well. We'll have parties."

The letter slid from her fingers as she became lost in happy plans. "A dinner party to start, I think. Oh, what fun it will be! I wonder if we can persuade Giulietta and Lurenze to come to London. I am sure we can manage it. If he would make her a countess or some such, no one will mind. And he is a foreign prince. Everyone lets royalty do as they please—especially foreigners. They're not held to the same standards." She nodded. "Yes, we can manage it."

For a moment he only watched her, drinking in her exotically beautiful face, alight with pleasure. He could not count all the ways in which he loved her but this was, perhaps, the heart of it: her exuberance, the sheer fun of her.

"Come here," he said. He moved closer to the back of the sofa, to make more room for her, and patted the place beside him. "I've never kissed Lady Delcaire before."

"None of that," she said primly while devilment danced in her extraordinary eyes. "You'll wrinkle my dress."

"That was my intention."

"We have company coming."

"How shocked they will be! Come, you baggage. All I want is a kiss . . . and perhaps a little husbandly fondling."

She laughed and did as he bid, easing her beautiful body down alongside his. He turned her face to his and cupping her chin, kissed her, long and sweetly. She tangled her fingers in his hair and returned the sweetness.

And when at last they drew away, he looked into green eyes so soft, and thought, yes, he'd drown there, happily.

"When shall we set out?" she asked. "For London?"

"Whenever you like." His hands strayed over the bodice of her dress. "A fortnight? How long does it take a woman to pack for a long trip?"

"I can manage in a fortnight, I think," she said.

"We'll come back, of course," he said. "I'm not sure how long I can bear to be away from the children."

She looked up at the ceiling and smiled. "They're so ridiculous. And yet one does grow attached to them."

"Or one attaches things to them—to their innocent bottoms, for instance." He paused as his hand slid over the soft swell above the neckline of her gown. "That reminds me: When we do get to London, you are not to tell anyone where you'd hidden those letters."

Her eyes, which had been fluttering closed, opened. "You never told Quentin? He never asked?"

She had stayed in the gondola that day. Quentin had come out to the landing place at San Lazzaro.

Only James had left the vessel. "We don't usually hold long discussions in such cases," he said. "I gave him the packet and he said, 'It's about bloody time,' and away he went."

"If that was all the thanks he gave you, he doesn't deserve to know," she said.

"I wouldn't have told him if he'd asked," he said. "Who knows? Someday I might need the hiding place." He returned his attention to his wife's soft bosom.

"I thought you'd retired," she said.

"I certainly did," he said. "Despite how exciting it became with you as a partner in crime. Or anti-crime, rather."

"You said it was exciting, though. Your work."

"By the time I came here, I'd had a bellyful of skullduggery," he said. "But it stopped being boring when I met you. And that encounter with Marta Fazi was possibly the most hair-raising experience of my life."

She sank back more deeply into the cushions. She lifted her hand and brushed it against his jaw. "That was exciting."

He turned his head to kiss the palm of the hand caressing his face. "The unpredictability of you—that's what did it. It added a thrill I'd not experienced in a long time: the thrill of sheer terror." He frowned. "No, come to think of it, being married to you ought to be excitement enough. All the same, let's keep the secret of the *putti* to ourselves, shall we?"

She traced his lips with her finger. "*Sì, eccellenza*," she said.

He laughed, and she drew her hand away. "What?" she said. "Isn't every nobleman addressed as 'eccellenza'?"

"It's your accent," he said. "So English."

"The *marchese* said my accent was charming."

"It's delicious," he said. "You're delicious. Forget the *marchese*."

The devils were dancing again, there among the gold flecks in her eyes. "I'm not sure I can. I may need . . . a diversion."

He slid his hand down the length of her magnificently curved body. "Very well, Lady Delcaire. Let's see how diverting I can be."

# Dangerous Liaisons . . .

*W*ho doesn't love a little romance tinged with a sense of danger? In the coming months, meet four heroines who like to live on the edge with their deliciously wicked heroes . . .

Turn the page for a sneak preview of these exciting new romances from bestselling authors Jeaniene Frost, Loretta Chase, and a back-to-back appearance from Suzanne Enoch!

# One Foot in the Grave

A Night Huntress Novel
by *New York Times* bestselling author
Jeaniene Frost

It's been four years and Cat is sure she's moved on: there's a new man in her life and her vampire-slaying is now government sanctioned. But it becomes clear that a hit has been taken out on Cat and she must team up again with volatile and sexy Bones as they track down the mole inside Cat's organization, prevent her father from killing everyone, and try to resist their white-hot passion for each other.

*L*iam Flannery's house was as quiet as a tomb, apropos as that may be, and it had been a long time since I'd battled with a Master vampire.

"I believe the police told you that the bodies of Thomas Stillwell and Jerome Hawthorn were found with most of their blood missing. And not any visible wounds on them to account for it." I said, jumping right in.

Liam shrugged. "Does the Bureau have a theory?"

Oh, we had more than a theory. I knew Liam would have just closed the telltale holes on Thomas and Jerome's necks with a drop of his own blood before they died. Boom, two bodies drained, no vampire calling card to rally the villagers—unless you knew what tricks to look for.

Flatly I shot back, "*You* do, though, don't you?"

"You know what I have a theory on, Catrina? That you taste as sweet as you look. In fact, I haven't thought about anything else since you walked in."

I didn't resist when Liam closed the distance between us and lifted my chin. After all, this would distract him better than anything I came up with.

His lips were cool on mine and vibrating with energy, giving my mouth pleasant tingles. He was a very good kisser, sensing when to deepen it and when to *really* deepen it. For a minute, I actually allowed myself to enjoy it—God, four years of celibacy must be taking its toll!—and then I got down to business.

My arms went around him, concealing me pulling a dagger from my sleeve. At the same time, he slid his hands down to my hips and felt the hard outlines under my pants.

"What the hell—?" he muttered, pulling back.

I smiled. "Surprise!" And then I struck.

It would have been a killing blow, but Liam was faster than I anticipated. He swept my feet out from under me just as I jabbed, so my silver missed his heart by inches. Instead of attempting to regain my stability, I let myself drop, rolling away from the kick he aimed at my head. Liam moved in a streak to try it again, but then jerked back when three of my throwing knives landed in his chest. Damn it, I'd missed his heart *again*.

"Sweet bleedin' Christ!" Liam exclaimed. He quit pretending to be human and let his eyes turn glowing emerald while fangs popped out in his upper teeth. "*You* must be the fabled Red Reaper. What brings the vampire bogeyman to my home?"

He sounded intrigued, but not afraid. He was more wary, however, and circled around me as I sprang to my feet, throwing off my jacket to better access my weapons.

"The usual," I said. "You murdered humans. I'm here to settle the score."

Liam actually rolled his eyes. "Believe me, poppet, Jerome and Thomas had it coming. Those thieving bastards stole from me. It's so hard to find good help these days."

"Keep talking, pretty boy. I don't care."

I rolled my head around on my shoulders and palmed more knives. Neither of us blinked as we waited for the other to make a move.

# _Your Scandalous Ways_

An eagerly anticipated new novel
by _USA Today_ bestselling author Loretta Chase

James Cordier has done a lot of things for his country, and when he's called for one last dangerous mission, saying no is impossible—especially when he sees his target. Francesca Bonnard, a beautiful and powerful courtesan, has many secrets, and how much she knows about a plot against the English government is just one of them. She has always been able to bend any man to her will, but the enigmatic stranger who moves in next door may be more than her match.

*J*ames's attention shifted from the golden-haired boy to the harlot beside him. They sat at the front of the box in the theater, Lurenze in the seat of honor at her right. He'd turned in his seat to gaze worshipfully at her. Francesca Bonnard, facing the stage, pretended not to notice the adoration.

From where he stood, James had only the rear view, of a smoothly curving neck and shoulders. Her hair, piled with artful carelessness, was a deep chestnut with fiery glints where the light caught it. A few loose tendrils made her seem the slightest degree tousled. The effect created was not of one who'd recently risen from bed, but one who had a moment ago slipped out of a lover's embrace.

Subtle.

And most effective. Even James, jaded as he was, was aware of a stirring-up below the belly, a narrowing of focus, and a softening of brain.

But then she ought to be good at stirring up men, he thought, considering her price.

His gaze drifted lower.

A sapphire and diamond necklace adorned her long, velvety neck. Matching drops hung at her shell-like ears. While Lurenze murmured something in her ear, she let her shawl slip down.

James's jaw dropped.

The dress had almost no back at all! She must have had her corset specially made to accommodate it.

Her shoulder blades were plainly visible. An oddly-shaped birthmark dotted the right one.

He pulled his eyes back into his head and his tongue back into his mouth.

Well, then, she was a fine piece as well as a bold one, no question about that. Someone thought she was worth those sapphires, certainly, and that was saying something. James wasn't sure he'd ever seen their like, and he'd seen—and stolen—heaps of fine jewelry. They surpassed the emeralds he'd reclaimed from Marta Fazi not many months ago.

Bottle in hand, he advanced to fill their glasses.

Lurenze, who'd leaned in so close that his yellow curls were in danger of becoming entangled with her earrings, paused, leaned back a little, and frowned. Then he took out his quizzing glass and studied her half-naked back. "But this is a serpent," he said.

*It is?*

James, surprised, leaned toward her, too. The prince was right. It wasn't a birthmark but a *tattoo*.

"You, how dare you to stare so obscene at the lady?" Lurenze said. "Impudent person! Put your eyes back in your face. And watch before you spill—"

"Oops," James said under his breath as he let the bottle in his hand tilt downward, splashing wine on the front of his highness's trousers.

Lurenze gazed down in dismay at the dark stain spreading over his crotch.

"*Perdono, perdono,*" James said, all false contrition. "*Sono mortificato, eccellenza.*" He took the towel from his arm and dabbed awkwardly and not gently at the wet spot.

Bonnard's attention remained upon the stage, but her shoulders shook slightly. James heard a suppressed giggle to his left from the only other female in the box. He didn't look that way, but went on vigorously dabbing with the towel.

The red-faced prince pushed his hand away. "Stop! Enough! Go away! Ottar! Where is my servant? *Ottar!*"

Simultaneously, a few hundred heads swiveled their way and a few hundred voices said in angry unison, "*Shh!*"

Ninetta's aria was about to begin.

"*Perdonatemi, perdonatemi,*" James whispered. "*Mi dispiace, mi dispiace.*" Continuing to apologize, he backed away, the picture of servile shame and fear.

La Bonnard turned round then, and looked James full in the face.

He should have been prepared. He should have acted reflexively, but for some reason he didn't. He was half a heartbeat too slow. The look caught him, and the unearthly countenance stopped him dead.

*Isis,* Lord Byron had dubbed her, after the Egyptian goddess. Now James saw why: the strange, elongated green eyes . . . the wide mouth . . . the exotic lines of nose and cheek and jaw.

James felt it, too, the power of her remarkable face and form, the impact as powerful as a blow. Heat raced through him, top to bottom, bottom to top, at a speed that left him stunned.

It lasted but a heartbeat in time—he was an old hand, after all—and he averted his gaze. Yet he was aware, angrily aware, that he'd been slow.

He was aware, angrily aware, of being thrown off balance.

By a look, a mere look.

And it wasn't over yet.

She looked him up. She looked him down. Then she looked away, her gaze reverting to the stage.

But in the last instant before she turned away, James saw her mouth curve into a long, wicked smile.

🌿 *Coming July 2008*

# *After the Kiss*

First in The Notorious Gentlemen trilogy
by *New York Times* bestselling author
Suzanne Enoch

The illegitimate son of the Marquis of Dunston, Sullivan Waring has made himself into a respectable gentleman, allowed into the fringes of Society, but never all the way in. If he resented his legitimate half siblings, he never let it show—until they stole what was rightfully his. Now he is determined to exact a little bit of revenge on the ton . . . except Lady Isabel Chalsey was never in his plans.

A woman stood between Sullivan and the morning room. At first he thought he'd fallen asleep outside the house and was dreaming—her long blonde hair, blue-tipped by moonlight, fell around her shoulders like water. Her slender, still figure was silhouetted in the dim light from the front window, her white night rail shimmering and nearly transparent. She might as well have been nude.

If he'd been dreaming, though, she *would* have been naked. Half expecting her to melt away into the moonlight, Sullivan remained motionless. In the thick shadows beneath the stairs he had to be nearly invisible. If she hadn't seen him, then—

"What are you doing in my house?" she asked. Her voice shook; she was mortal, after all.

If he said the wrong thing or moved too abruptly, she would scream. And then he would have a fight on his hands. While he didn't mind that, it might prevent him from leaving with the painting—and that was his major goal. Except that she still looked . . . ethereal in the darkness, and he couldn't shake the sensation that he was caught in a luminous waking dream. "I'm here for a kiss," he said.

She looked from his masked face to the bundle beneath his arm. "Then you have very bad eyesight, because that is not a kiss."

Grudgingly, though occupied with figuring a way to leave with both his skin and the painting, he had to admit that she had her wits about her. Even in the dark, alone, and faced with a masked stranger. "Perhaps I'll have both, then."

"You'll have neither. Put that back and leave, and I shan't call for assistance."

He took a slow step toward her. "You shouldn't warn me of your intentions," he returned, keeping his voice low and not certain why he bothered to banter with her when he could have been past her and back outside by now. "I could be on you before you draw another breath."

Her step backward matched his second one forward. "Now who's warning whom?" she asked. "Get out."

"Very well." He gestured for her to move aside, quelling the baser part of him that wanted her to remove that flimsy, useless night rail from her body and run his hands across her soft skin.

"Without the paintings."

"No."

"They aren't yours. Put them back."

One of them *was* his, but Sullivan wasn't about to say that aloud. "No. Be glad I'm willing to leave without the kiss and step aside."

Actually, the idea of kissing her was beginning to seem less mad than it had at first. Perhaps it was the moonlight, or the late hour, or the buried excitement he always felt at being somewhere in secret, of doing something that a year ago he would never even have contemplated, or the fact that he'd never seen a mouth as tempting as hers.

"Then I'm sorry. I gave you a chance." She drew a breath.

Moving fast, Sullivan closed the distance between them. Grabbing her shoulder with his free hand, he yanked her up against him, then leaned down and covered her mouth with his.

She tasted like surprise and warm chocolate. He'd expected the surprise, counted on it to stop her from yelling. But the shiver running down his spine at the touch of her soft lips to his stunned him. So did the way her hands rose to touch his face in return. Sullivan broke away, offering her a jaunty grin and trying to hide the way he was abruptly out of breath. "I seem to have gotten everything I came for, after all," he murmured, and brushed past her to unlatch and open the front door.

Outside, he collected his hammer and then hurried down the street to where his horse waited. Closing the paintings into the flat leather pouch he'd brought for the purpose, he swung into the saddle. "Let's go, Achilles," he said, and the big black stallion broke into a trot.

After ten thefts, he'd become an expert in anticipating just about anything. That was the first time, though, that he'd stolen a kiss. Belatedly, he reached up to remove his mask. It was gone.

His blood froze. That kiss—that blasted kiss—had distracted him more than he'd realized. And now someone had seen his face. "Damnation."

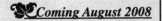 *Coming August 2008*

# *Before the Scandal*

Second in The Notorious Gentlemen trilogy
by *New York Times* bestselling author
Suzanne Enoch

When Phineas Bromley suddenly becomes Viscount Hamilton, his world is thrown into a tailspin. More used to battlefields than ballrooms, the adjustment to town life is not easy. But there's nothing like a little mystery to liven up what seems like a mundane life. Aware that someone is stealing from the family coffers, Phineas must come up with a way to expose the culprits. His plan is risky—but not as dangerous as his unexpected attraction to Alyse Donnelly, the young lady next door.

Phin Bromley. Alyse Donnelly had never thought to set eyes on him again. He was undeniably taller, but he also seemed . . . larger. Not fat, by any means, because he'd always been lean, but . . . more commanding. Yes, that's what it was. And—

Richard jabbed her in the shoulder. "Who is he?" her cousin hissed.

Alyse shook herself. "Their brother," she answered in the same low tone he'd used. Either the footmen knew already or they would soon, but if Richard didn't want to be seen gossiping, she could understand that. "The middle sibling."

"You never mentioned another brother."

"He's been away for a very long time. Ten years or more." She smiled a little, remembering. "I haven't set eyes on him since I was thirteen."

"Well, this could be an opportunity for you then, cousin, couldn't it?" Richard murmured. "After all, if there are things you don't know about him, then there are bound to be things he doesn't know about you."

Her face heated; she couldn't help it. After four years she should have been used to the insults, direct or implied, but obviously they still had the power to cut her. "Thank you, Richard," she said softly, "but I prefer to make his acquaintance first."

"I suggest you speak to your cousin with less sarcasm, Alyse," her Aunt Ernesta cooed. "You are not who you once were."

And no one in her family ever let her forget that fact. "I remember, Aunt Ernesta."

"Then have someone fetch me a blanket. My legs are cold."

Carefully hiding her annoyance, Alyse motioned to the nearest of the footmen and passed on her aunt's request. Things in the Bromley household might have taken a turn for the unexpected, but her life progressed with the predictability of a clock. An endlessly ticking clock.

The dining room door opened again. Lord Quence entered first, being wheeled in on his chair with a somber look on his pale face. Beth followed a heartbeat later, her expression tense. The door closed again, but Alyse kept her gaze on it.

Phineas Bromley. Phin. The last person she ever would have imagined joining the army, though he obviously had. She didn't know what the insignia on his shoulder meant, but he was clearly an officer.

A moment later he walked into the room, his gaze touching on the rest of the occupants, then finding her. Alyse blushed again at those clear hazel eyes, wondering what she looked like to him. Other than his eyes, she wasn't certain she would have recognized him. His dark brown hair was a little long, as though he'd been too busy to seek a barber, and his face leaner than she remembered. And a narrow scar dissected his right eyebrow, giving his appearance the rakish bent he'd always seemed to have inside.

"Alyse," he said, and took the seat across from her. "Miss Donnelly. William told me that your parents passed away. I am truly sorry."

"Thank you. It was . . . unexpected."

Richard leaned over to cover her hand with his. "I'm only glad that we've been able to give Alyse a place in our household."

Phineas glanced at her cousin, then back to her again. "Do you still like to ride?" he asked.

It felt odd to have someone pay attention to her these days. "I haven't had much opportunity," she hedged. "My aunt is unwell, and I sit with her a great deal."

"If I stay long enough, we should go riding," he pursued.

Alyse smiled. "I would like that."

"How long *will* you be staying?" Richard cut in again.

This time Phin glanced at his brother. "As long as I'm needed. I have several months of leave coming, if I require it."

"Where are you serving?" Alyse asked, disliking when that gaze left her.

"The north of Spain at the moment. I'm with the First Royal Dragoons."

"A . . . lieutenant, is it?" Richard asked, eyeing the crimson and blue uniform.

"Lieutenant-Colonel," Elizabeth corrected, pride in her tone. "Phin's received five field promotions."

"That's extraordinary." Richard lifted a glass, not in Phin's direction, but in the viscount his brother's. "You must be very proud of him."

"Yes," Lord Quence said, returning to his meal. "Very proud."

Clearly all was not entirely well at Quence Park, though Alyse had known that before. But for Richard to poke a stick into the tension—it was so unlike him in public, though in private he did little else. "When we were all children together," she said into the air, "we had the most hair-raising adventures."

Phineas sent her a short smile. "I can face cannons fearlessly after surviving the infamous pond-jump dares."

Alyse snorted, then quickly covered her mouth with one hand and made the sound into a cough. "You were fearless well before then."